WARTIME SWEETHEARTS

LIZZIE LANE

Boldwood

First published in 2015. This edition first published in Great Britain in 2021 by Boldwood Books Ltd.

Copyright © Lizzie Lane, 2015

Cover Design by Colin Thomas

Cover Photography: Colin Thomas

Every effort has been made to obtain the necessary permissions with reference to copyright material, both illustrative and quoted. We apologise for any omissions in this respect and will be pleased to make the appropriate acknowledgements in any future edition.

A CIP catalogue record for this book is available from the British Library.

Paperback ISBN 978-1-80280-832-2

Ebook ISBN 978-1-80280-834-6

Kindle ISBN 978-1-80280-835-3

Boldwood Books Ltd
23 Bowerdean Street
London SW6 3TN
www.boldwoodbooks.com

1

It was warm those last few days of August 1939 before the world went to war. The sun shone and Ruby Sweet was certain she would remember this time for the rest of her life. She couldn't help smiling at the thought of what was about to happen, which had nothing to do with the worsening situation in Europe.

People in the village of Oldland Common, just a few miles from the City of Bristol, had been talking for weeks about the possibility of another war with Germany. The wireless broadcasts were going on and on too and Ruby had got to the stage where she could almost repeat what they were saying word for word.

...it must be remembered that we are an island nation and unlike the landmass that is Germany, are unable to feed ourselves. Therefore, should war occur, the enemy will do its utmost to sink our merchant ships. Rationing will come in earlier than in the last war. Every crust of bread, every potato grown...

Ruby grimaced. How to make a meal from crusts of bread!

Potatoes cooked in their skins! For goodness' sake!

Advice given in a plummy accent about making do with less expensive joints of meat had preceded the broadcast.

Consider using braising or even stewing steak instead of a more expensive cut.

'As if anybody round here can afford anything better than braising or stewing,' Ruby muttered. Judging by her twin sister Mary's expression, she was thinking the same thing.

The wireless broadcast droned on and on. Ruby was tired of hearing advice about food that didn't form a regular part of most people's diet.

Hopefully the war would never happen and then all this talk would be only so much hot air.

The Prime Minister, Mr Neville Chamberlain...

Even now her brother Charlie and her father, and even her sister, continued to give the radio broadcast their full attention, more specifically to what was happening in Europe, especially Poland.

Ruby wasn't interested in Poland. It was too far away and anyway, she had something else on her mind, something more important to her than a war that might never happen. Still, at least it kept them from noticing that she had dressed up prior to slipping out.

While they were engaged, she skipped up the stairs for one last look in her dressing table mirror. She applied a little more lipstick before patting her glossy brown hair, swinging it this way and that, loving the way it fell forward on to her left cheek. Strangers assumed her hairstyle merely aped some of the Hollywood vamps they'd seen at the movies, their silky hair half hiding their sexy smiles. Ruby let them think that. The truth was it hid a small mole on her left cheek. She hated that mole; she wanted it hidden.

'Ruby, you look a picture,' she murmured to her reflection, admiring the blue and rose-red dress she was wearing. This was her favourite dress and although it made sense to keep it for special occasions, she'd decided today was special, though only for her, not for anybody else – except for Gareth Stead. Last night she had helped out behind the bar of the Apple Tree pub as she always did when it was busy. They'd exchanged lots of smiles and adoring looks, Gareth sometimes winking at her when he thought nobody else was looking, his hands brushing her hips when he passed behind her, supposedly to change a barrel or fetch a crate of brown ale.

She hadn't minded him touching her so intimately because he was always whispering how lovely she was, how he couldn't do without her, how he hoped she would be here forever. His kisses between the time when he shut the pub and she was expected home had been frantic and stolen. So had the touch of his hands upon her breasts and her bottom, furtive at first but becoming bolder when she'd raised no objection.

Nobody else had seen. Nobody else knew. Or so she thought, but the night before last, Mary had popped in just before closing time. Charlie had been with her, not that he'd noticed much, straightaway taking his pint and joining his friends in a game of darts. Although Ruby helped out in her father's bakery, there weren't enough hours to give her a living wage. Serving behind the bar helped bridge the gap, though her father had insisted that her brother and sister accompany her home. That way there were no wagging tongues and no chance of Gareth Stead getting his wicked way – or so her father thought.

Mary had stayed by the bar sipping at a port and lemon. She had often offered to help Ruby clear up, but her sister had always declined citing that it was her job and she would do it. The moment they left the pub she had commented pointedly that Gareth Stead should learn to keep his hands to himself.

'I couldn't help noticing,' she said in that disapproving manner she sometimes had. 'I know you're sweet on him, but do you think you should be letting him take such liberties?'

'We're engaged,' Ruby had replied hotly.

'Says who? Him in there?'

Ruby bridled at her sister's tone. Mary had a cynical streak in her that was completely absent from Ruby's nature. As twins, they were alike in looks and some character traits, both were strong-willed and stood up for what they wanted, but in other ways they were as different as it was possible to be.

Ruby was convinced that Gareth Stead was in love with her and that meant marriage. He'd told her he never wanted her to leave. She felt obliged to convince her sister of his interest.

'Are you trying to tell me that he's in love with you?' Mary had demanded.

'I think so.'

Mary had persisted. 'You mean he's told you so?'

'Not in so many words, Mary—'

'Not in any words!' Mary snapped. 'Ruby, stop being such a goose. You know what he wants and it isn't marriage. Gareth Stead is the sort who wants his cream cake now and once eaten he'll be fancying a slice of bread pudding. When he's tired of you, he'll move on to pastures new.'

Ruby congratulated herself that she'd chosen to ignore her advice. She knew better. Gareth loved her, and last night before she'd left, he'd told her to come to the pub at eleven o'clock this morning. 'Not before. There's something boiling between us, Ruby my love. We can't ignore it any longer.'

Her blue eyes sparkled at the thought of this meeting. The 'something boiling' was their passion for each other. And he was right. They couldn't ignore it any longer.

All night she'd tossed and turned, pondering what he'd really meant by that, and then it came to her in a flash.

'He's going to ask me to marry him,' she exclaimed. After that she turned over and fell asleep.

This morning the thought had come to her anew.

'He's going to propose,' she whispered breathlessly to herself, resting a white-gloved hand over her fluttering stomach. 'That's what he's going to do.' He'd hinted as much at the harvest dance last Saturday evening after he'd apologised for asking her twin sister Mary to dance in the belief that he was asking her, Ruby.

'Once I was close up to her, I knew it wasn't you. We're made for each other, you and me.'

Mary would have none of it. 'He propositioned me, Ruby. He's that sort.'

'I don't know what you mean!'

Mary had given her that piercing look she sometimes had, as though she was years older than her twin sister and not just a few minutes.

'He's not a one-woman man. He likes to think he can have any girl he wants and plenty of them.'

'He wants me to stay with him forever! He told me he did.'

'Did he? Are you absolutely sure?'

'Yes. He did.'

Mary had shaken her head dolefully. 'Ruby, I just don't see what you see in him. He's been married once already...'

'His wife died.'

'That's what he says. I've heard—'

'She died!' Ruby had repeated, barely resisting the urge to cover her ears with her hands. Gareth Stead was thirty-five years old, sixteen years older than she was and far more interesting than the young men closer to her own age in the village. Gareth was almost as old as her father, but her father still treated her as a child. Despite comments from her sister and friends that the landlord of the Apple Tree was too smooth and too confident for his own good, she ignored it all. Gareth made her feel special and she was convinced he felt the same way about her. He'd once said that if she truly loved him she wouldn't protest when his fingers caressed the bare skin between the tops of her stockings and the legs of her knickers.

She didn't even protest when he made overtures to her sister or to other local women. They all said he was a saucy so and so, and he'd assured her there was nothing in any of the rumours she might have heard that he was a Jack the Lad, a man who'd had more women than hot dinners.

'Sweetheart, it's jealousy. That's all it is. Just jealousy.'

So she ignored the fact that some of those women blushed and lowered their eyes, as though afraid their sparkle might betray the absolute truth. She also ignored the warnings from her sister and her brother, Charlie.

Charlie was three years older than the twins and worked alongside his father in the family bakery.

'Be warned. He's a man that won't be tamed,' Charlie had said to her.

Ruby's smile and the gleam in her eyes had lit up her face. 'Nonsense, our Charlie. It's just a case of him finding the right woman.'

Like her twin, Charlie had shook his head and only smiled. He had a passionate nature just like his sisters, though he couldn't get serious about village girls. He flirted and got to know one or two on an intimate level, but he wasn't serious about anyone and certainly not Miriam Powell who ran the grocery shop with her mother and blushed profusely whenever Charlie was in range.

Ruby was adamant. The village lads were dull and stupid in comparison with Gareth. She much preferred his worldliness, the way he treated her as a woman, not a child. Ruby believed him utterly and totally; he had stolen her heart. And now her belief in him was about to be rewarded: he was going to ask her to marry him. That's what this secret assignation was about; she was certain of it.

When she got to the Apple Tree, the swing of her hips and her bouncing step was brought to a sudden halt. Someone had left a handcart close to the back door leaving only the smallest of gaps to squeeze through. Whether she was meeting him or reporting for work, it was always via the back door. Even the fact of having to enter through the front door rather than the back failed to dent her buoyant mood. What did it matter which door she entered by? The outcome would be the same. Gareth would drop to one knee like the brave hero on some old-fashioned painting. He would be her faithful knight forever and she would be his wife.

Gareth came running in response to her gloved fist pounding on the front door.

'Ruby,' he said in that honey-brown voice of his, a sound that made her stomach flutter and her flesh tingle. No hello or how are you. There was no need; the way he said her name was more than welcoming, as if she were a chocolate pudding and he relished the thought of tasting her.

He had the most remarkable green eyes flecked like the inside of a glass marble with splashes of amber. She dreamed of those eyes at night; that, and his corn-coloured hair. Mary had told her that she was colour-blind and that his hair was silver in places.

'He's an old ram that thinks he's a spring lamb. Watch out for him,' she'd warned, yet again, the previous evening.

They'd had a row after that, Ruby accusing her sister of being jealous. Their young cousin Frances had been listening, twirling her braid around her fingers, her big blue eyes full of childish curiosity.

'Do rams put their hands up girls' skirts?'

The sudden question had brought the arguing to an instant halt. They'd looked open-mouthed at eleven-year-old Frances then burst out laughing.

Embarrassed by their laughter, Frances's heart-shaped face had turned red before she turned and ran upstairs. They'd heard their bedroom door slam shut and the sound of springs as she threw herself on to her bed.

Neither her sister's serious warning nor her cousin's funny comment could hope to deter her from meeting with Gareth. Just wait and see when she asked them to be bridesmaids. My, but were they going to be surprised!

Gareth was dressed in tune with the warm day. His shirt sleeves were rolled up to his elbows revealing strong arms covered with a fine layer of golden hair. A few swirls of chest hair poked up over the open neck of his shirt.

'Come along in, me love. Come along in.'

He made a sweeping movement with his arm.

Her heart raced when he stepped to one side, leaving only just enough room so her upper arm brushed against his chest. He smelled of sweat and shaving soap. His striped shirt was spotlessly clean but collarless. She wondered how a man alone could get his shirts so clean, so fresh-smelling. Mrs Burns, she thought. I expect Mrs Burns does his laundry. Mrs Burns, a woman in her forties with few teeth and a headscarf, cleaned the bar area and the draughty outside toilets. She arrived early and was always gone by ten in the morning, her metal curlers rattling as she swept and polished, a cigarette hanging from the corner of her mouth. Ruby, who only helped out in the bar of an evening, rarely bumped into her unless Gareth had asked her to work extra hours and her father didn't need her in the bakery. It was on such an occasion that Gareth had first kissed her – once Mrs Burns was out of the way, that is.

Oblivious to the smell of cigarette ash and stale beer ingrained into the walls and ceiling, she felt herself blushing, stupidly wondering whether the old grey flagstone floor was clean enough for him to kneel on when he proposed to her; not that she minded if he didn't kneel down. All that mattered was that he was about to ask her. Even though her father's permission had to be sought, she would not refuse. After all, twenty-one wasn't that far off, and then she could please herself.

She looked over her shoulder at him, saw him leaning back against the door, his eyes travelling slowly over her as though savouring every inch.

Ruby blinked in an effort to adjust her eyes to the inner gloom. The old pub had walls of burnt sepia, a bar of rough oak and an odd assortment of beer-stained tables and rickety chairs. Once, she'd laughingly asked Gareth if everyone in the village had donated an odd chair, the rest of the set burned years ago on a bonfire.

He'd laughed at that and called her cheeky. That was when he'd first arrived in the village just seven years ago. Even back then when she'd seen him at church or around the village he'd never really treated her as a child, smiling as he told her what a beauty she was. And he'd never tickled her. Some of the village boys had tickled her wanting to make her laugh until she was in danger of wetting her knickers.

But that was back then, when Gareth and his wife had only just moved to the village. His wife hadn't lasted long. The story was she'd died of TB just after she was taken to a sanatorium. Ruby only vaguely remembered her. Even back then, Ruby had surmised that Gareth was very aware of her, paying her the same attention as he might an older woman. And that was when I was just a kid, she told herself. Fatherly affection. And now....

'I wasn't sure you'd come,' he said, his voice low and hushed, his fingers tangling in her hair.

To her ears it sounded as though he couldn't quite believe she was here.

'I had to come. You said it was about something special.'

She couldn't stop her voice from trembling. Her legs were doing pretty much the same thing and her face felt as though it was about to burst into flames.

His smile took her breath away, his gaze holding hers as the gap between them closed until she could feel the whole length of his body pressing against hers. Her heart seemed to pound in her ears, so much that she could almost believe it was the freight train down on the adjacent railway line heading up to the Midlands.

But it wasn't a train. This was her moment. It was all about her.

When he began unbuttoning the bodice of her dress, it felt as though a small bird was trapped close to her heart, its wings fluttering against her ribs.

She held her breath relishing the feel of his fingers burrowing inside her brassiere. It felt good and she wanted him badly, but there could be consequences. She would not, could not, bring shame to her family.

'Gareth! No!' She attempted to force his hands away. 'What if Mrs Burns comes in?'

'She isn't coming in today,' he said, his fingers groping her breast. 'I wanted for us to be alone. This place and the world to ourselves. Don't you want it too?' he asked, his breath hot and moist against her ear, following the line of her jaw, falling over her face until their lips finally met.

She so wanted to give in, and yet she still held on to a strand of resistance.

He hadn't asked her to marry him yet, but she still believed he would. Besides, it wasn't the first time he'd caressed her bare breasts. He'd also tried shoving his hand up her skirt – just as Frances had mentioned. The little brat must have been watching, though kids picked up all sorts of naughty ideas in the school playground.

So far she'd just about kept the burly Gareth Stead at bay, insisting she was keeping herself for the man she married. Now he was telling her that the time had come, whispering into her ear that he wanted her and her alone, now and for evermore.

She tried to ignore the fact that the word marriage had not been mentioned. To her mind the words he was whispering into her ear meant the same thing. If she hadn't been aroused, if she'd seen it happening to somebody else, she would have told them they were making a fool of themselves. But it was happening to her and she wanted to believe.

He took hold of her hand, holding it tightly, guiding it down to the front of his trousers. 'Touch me,' he said, his moist breath gasping on to her face. 'This is what you are doing to me. I can't help it.'

'No... Gareth... I don't...'

She clenched her hand into a tight fist while trying with all her might to pull away. He held on to her firmly, fingers clamped around her wrist.

'Here!' he exclaimed. 'Touch me here.'

She let out a little gasp as he pressed her palm flat against his buttoned flies where the hard contours of his erection pulsated against her touch. The size of it was bad enough, but that hardness! It wasn't what she'd expected. She wasn't sure what she'd expected, but it scared her.

In her youthful naivety, she'd expected something similar to the sight of her brother and the village boys when they had stripped naked as youngsters, hurling themselves into the brook at the bottom of Court Road.

Gareth didn't seem to notice her reluctance and she in turn didn't realise just how determined he was to have her there and then.

'This is for you,' he whispered, his voice thick and breath hot against her face. He planted a warm moist kiss on her lips then said, 'Unbutton me while I explore your secret parts.'

She felt a draught of cold air as he lifted the hem of her dress, her favourite dress that she'd taken care to wash and press before responding to his invitation. It occurred to her that he hadn't passed comment on her dress; in fact, he had paid no compliment to her at all.

His hand caressed that part of her leg just above the knee before climbing further and further up her leg. Finally his strong fingers and calloused palms were caressing the bare flesh between her stocking top and her knickers.

It wasn't the first time he'd ventured there, but this time he seemed more determined.

Her heart was pounding, her blood racing. She wanted him. He wanted her, but a warning voice began to seep through and as it gained strength pointed out the reality of what was happening at this moment.

She'd come here expecting Gareth to ask her to marry him, to share his bed for the rest of their lives. But he hadn't mentioned marriage, so it was up to her to bring up the subject before things went any further.

'No!'

She struggled to free herself and because he was engrossed in dipping his fingers between her legs, the hand that held hers against his groin loosened.

She managed to hold him at arm's length. He looked stunned that she'd refused him.

'Ruby, my darling girl. You don't mean that. You want it. You want it badly.' He shook his head mournfully though there was laughter in his eyes.

Suddenly she could see that he was mocking her. 'I'm saving myself for marriage!'

'No, Ruby my sweet. You've been asking for it for years, ever since you were a gangly girl with ribbons in your hair. I thought about giving it to you then, but held back. Decided I would be a gentleman and let you come of age – ripen, so to speak.'

Still clinging to her hands, fingers interlaced with his, he tried to kiss her. She acted swiftly, turning her head so he ended up kissing the side of her nose.

Ruby uncoupled her fingers from his, pushing him away at the same time as desperately trying to push down her dress.

'Nobody says no to me,' growled Gareth, his face growing red with anger.

He attempted to grab her wrists, cursing that she should feel grateful, a little no-account village girl like her, without grace, without manners, without the elegance or experience of the city women he'd known, including the one he'd been married to.

Somehow he managed to gain a hold on both her wrists. Ruby twisted and wriggled. When that failed she began to kick and then suddenly she screamed.

Gareth's face turned white.

'Shh!' he said, putting a finger to his mouth, his eyes more furtive now, wary of her scream being heard. His frustration turned to anger. 'If you didn't want it, why the bloody hell did you come here?' he said, glowering at her with chilly hard eyes, the mouth she'd loved to kiss no longer seductive but cruel and petulant.

'I thought... I thought...' Ruby stammered.

'That's the exit,' he said to her, pointing at the rear door that he'd momentarily forgotten was blocked by a handcart.

Ruby realised he sounded impatient for her to be gone. Ruby tried again. 'I thought...'

Hands on hips, Gareth threw back his head and gave his exasperation, and his contempt full rein. 'Go on. I might as well hear it. What the hell did you think I wanted?'

Ruby felt a hot flush coming to her cheeks. Suddenly she was again a little girl, not the sophisticated woman she so wanted to be. She felt such a fool.

At first she thought about just leaving him there without mentioning her belief he had asked her here to propose. But then if it was left unsaid he might presume that she had indeed come here for what he'd wanted but had chickened out. She had to say it.

'I thought you were going to ask me to marry you,' she said in a small voice, eyes lowered as she rapidly buttoned up her dress.

For a moment his expression was implacable, as though his face was carved from stone. He stared at her, a withering stare that made her feel as though she were just a stupid little girl who wanted to play at being a bride; not for real. Just pretend.

He shook his head.

Ruby wanted to believe that, despite him trying to force himself on her, there might still be hope. She'd imagined herself in a white dress walking down the aisle on her father's arm, Gareth standing at the altar, turning his head and smiling, the light of love in his eyes.

The truth of the matter was that even her father had voiced his disquiet that she seemed too close to the man.

'Running down there to help behind the bar, cleaning the place when old Mrs Burns has a day off. The man's taking advantage of you,' her father had grumbled just the other day.

* * *

Gareth Stead, a man with a passion for fresh virgin flesh, prided himself on being able to read female minds, to ingratiate himself with innocent young women until they trusted him.

Once they trusted him, they were his to do with as he pleased and no matter what anyone said, including their family, he was the one they turned to.

He had believed that Ruby had fallen under his spell, that she was ready and willing to let him have his way with her. Even though it might have seemed otherwise, Ruby's belief that he would ask her to marry him had come as no surprise. If there was one thing Gareth Stead could do it was to sow the right seeds in a young mind, entice them with words and actions to make them believe one thing, when in fact he was feeding them lies. That these simple little girls misinterpreted his intentions amused him. The fact that he'd left broken hearts, broken lives and the odd bastard scattered around, didn't worry him. Men ruled this world; women were the weaker sex. They were there to be enjoyed and kept in their place.

He decided to give it one last shot.

'We could be good together,' he shrugged. 'I tried marriage. Don't rate it much. You could move in if you like, but I ain't marrying you. And no babies either. Get pregnant, you get rid of it. There are ways and women who can do it.'

Shocked by this pronouncement, Ruby raised her eyes. Those amber-flecked green eyes seemed positively devilish now; how often had she dreamed of those eyes. In her dreams he had been warm and charming, making her feel as though she were a princess. In this last half hour or so he had made her feel like something far sleazier.

'Don't you ever want children?'

'No. I want sex. That's all I want.'

There was an air of finality to the way he answered. Gareth, Ruby realised, was not a man to be persuaded. He'd made up his mind as to what he wanted from women and from life. She wondered why she hadn't seen that before? The old saying jumped into her mind. Love is blind. Had she been blind? Was she still blind? She wasn't quite sure. Nobody got over things that quickly.

She sucked in her lips, a childish action that would take off her lipstick, but was something she did when she felt chastised, and she certainly felt that now.

'Do you need me behind the bar today?'

'No.'

The single word response was like a slap in the face. 'Then I'd better be going.'

'Yes,' he said, turning his back. 'You'd better be going.'

She paused, seeing him toss a glass cloth over his shoulder as he sauntered to the bar. It was terribly tempting to rush at his back, slide both her arms around him and ask his forgiveness. To say, yes, have me. Have me now. Whatever you want. But a warning voice that came from inside her but wasn't quite hers advised caution.

Ruby avoided Gareth's eyes as she listened to the voice inside her head that she knew belonged to her sister.

It was a well-known fact that twin sisters were closer than ordinary sisters. Sometimes they thought the same thoughts; sometimes they did the same things, though miles apart. They were like two sides of the same coin, though not even heads and tails. They were a double-headed coin, something rare and very special.

Even though Mary wasn't in the Apple Tree with her, Ruby could feel her presence, that warning voice telling her not to be stupid. They looked out for each other. They knew when one of them was worried or frightened.

'Yes. I think I should go now and I won't be coming back.' She said it abruptly so he would be in no doubt that she wouldn't change her mind. It seemed that he wouldn't be changing his.

'Well, it was fun while it lasted. If you change your mind, I might consider having you back.'

In between sips of a half pint of beer he'd poured himself, he smiled the old smile that had seduced her in the first place. She turned her back swiftly and headed for the back door, forgetting that she'd come in the front one.

The back door was at the end of a passage connecting the bar to the outside and the draughty old toilets, one for men, one for women. The plain plank doors had a gap at the top and bottom. A zinc bath hung on a nail between the two of them, grating against the uneven brickwork when the wind blew.

In the winter the toilets were freezing. A small lamp was left burning in the corner of the wooden, rectangular seat; it was meant to help stop the pipes from freezing but it didn't always work. In the summer the flies buzzed in and out of the gaps at the top and bottom of the doors. The waste pipes led to a cess pit at the far end of the untidy garden at the rear. When it rained heavily, the cess pit overflowed and stank. The toilets stank most of the time, despite Mrs Burns and her trusty bottle of chlorus.

The handcart was still there but it was now empty.

A sudden bang came from the direction of the pair of wooden doors through which barrels were rolled down into the cellar. Whatever had been delivered on the cart had gone down there. Someone was down there.

She managed to squeeze out through the gap. Just as she'd guessed, Gareth had followed her out, thinking perhaps that she might have to come back in and go out the front door. Nothing would make her do that!

'See you on Saturday. Hope you win. If you do I'll help you celebrate.'

Gareth was referring to the village fete and sounded as though he was back to his old self, perhaps even thinking it wouldn't be long before he could wear down her resistance. There wasn't much chance of avoiding him at the village fete, but at least it would be crowded. Whether she won or not was a different matter. Competition was fierce and her greatest rival would be her sister.

A dry stone wall separated the pub from the orchard next door. Nobody knew who owned the orchard, so everyone harvested the apples that hung low on the ancient trees. Some of its branches scraped against the side wall of the pub itself. The local kids built dens in there and played cowboys and Indians in the long grass.

Everything that was so familiar today seemed tired and ugly. Gareth had made it feel that way. Suddenly she wanted to leave this place that had been home all her life. She wanted something new and different far away from the village where gossip was rife and old wounds took a long time to heal.

As she passed close to the wall just before it joined the main road, she heard somebody calling her name.

'Ruby?'

She came to a halt as leaves and ripe apples bounced around her feet. The deluge was followed by her cousin Frances who was extremely good at climbing trees.

Ruby had hoped to get home without seeing anyone, and that included her cousin.

'Have you been scrumping?' she asked though there was little doubt what her cousin had been up to. Still flustered and red-faced from her ordeal with Gareth, Ruby feigned annoyance. 'Look at your knees! They're filthy. And you've ripped your dress.'

'I know.'

Ruby watched Frances scooping up what rolling apples she could catch, darting around then tossing them into the sack she was carrying with the others she'd scrumped. 'It'll mend easy though.'

'Easily. You mean easily,' said Ruby impatiently.

Frances, the daughter of Sefton Sweet, her father's brother, had lived with them since she was four years old when her mother had left her and a note with the local vicar. Sefton's wife had been determined, so she said, to start a new life. A child, she'd declared, would only slow her down and she had no intention of fading into a frump in a village where the high spot of the year was the village fete.

And so Frances had come to live with them.

Like her three cousins, Frances had glossy dark hair. Unlike them she had velvet-brown eyes fringed with dark lashes. Mary, Ruby and Charlie, their brother, had inherited their father's blue eyes.

'I thought you'd be pleased,' she piped up. 'I've got enough for you to make apple turnovers, apple pies, even baked apples with custard for our Sunday tea,' she declared. 'Our Mary will be happy.'

'I dare say,' Ruby said grimly.

She resumed walking, her stride quickening in the vague hope of leaving Frances behind. She was still smarting from her ordeal with Gareth and could not quite believe that all her hopes and dreams of marriage were now over so quickly. Should she have given in to him? No. She should not.

Heaving the sack over her shoulder, Frances kept pace with her.

'Have you done the cleaning already?' she asked innocently.

'I haven't been doing any cleaning. I've been to the post office,' snapped Ruby, her jaw firmly set, her cheeks still rosier than any of the apples Frances had in her sack.

'So why did you go into the pub?'

'I didn't.'

'Yes, you did. I was up in the tree. I saw you. That was after the man with the big sack went into the cellar. I think it was Mr Herbert. What did he have in his sack?'

Ruby stopped so abruptly that the two of them collided.

'I don't know what he had in his bloody sack. Were you spying on me?'

'Not really. I told you. I was up the tree. I saw you.'

Ruby gripped her cousin's shoulders and gave her a shake. 'You were spying on me!'

'I couldn't help seeing you. Or Mr Herbert.'

Ruby felt herself growing even redder, alarmed that Frances

might have been able to peer through the pub windows from her perch up in the apple tree.

She glanced back at the pub. Its four brick chimneys stabbed at the sky. Its windows were small and square and set into stone mullions. Those in shadow looked black, nothing of the inside to be seen. Those in sunlight reflected the old wall, the trees, herself and her cousin.

All the same, Frances might have seen something. 'You're not to tell anyone I was in there this morning. Do you hear me? You didn't see me. Do you understand?'

'But...'

Ruby eyed the puzzled expression. The child's black eyebrows were arched, her rosebud lips slightly parted. The brown eyes that looked up at her were as glossy as melted chocolate.

'No buts. I don't want to hear you speak of this.'

'Did Mr Stead do something bad?'

Ruby frowned. 'What do you mean?'

'Did he put his hand up your skirt?'

Ruby felt a huge rush of embarrassment. 'Frances, you really have to stop going around with that gang of yours. They're filling your head with naughty things.'

Frances frowned. 'They didn't fill my head.'

Ruby totally disregarded the child's accusation – certainly with relation to Gareth Stead. 'Did one of those Cooper boys try to put his hand up your dress?'

'No,' said Frances, shaking her head and turning away, something she did when she was deciding whether to tell the truth or not. 'Not them. He did. Mr Stead. He climbed over the wall into the orchard with a big sack. He dug a hole and buried it. Then he tried to put his hand up my skirt, but I kicked him and ran away. He told me not to tell.'

'Liar!'

The sound of the slap she gave Frances brought her to her senses. The child was talking about the man she loved – or had thought she loved. She held out her hand, the one that had left a vivid red mark on her cousin's face.

'I'm sorry, Frances. I'm so sorry. I didn't mean to...'

Frances backed away, her eyes filling with tears, one hand rubbing at the red mark on her cheek. However, Frances was very capable of standing up for herself. Her little jaw firmed up as the hurt expression was replaced by one of anger.

'I am not a liar,' she shouted. 'Gareth Stead stinks of beer and he buried something in the orchard. I'm not a liar!'

Ruby felt mortified. She had never ever slapped her cousin before. Inwardly she groaned. This is all your doing, Gareth Stead, and somehow I have to mend what I've broken.

She began to run after Frances, but her court shoes had quite high heels and were not made for running. She called out instead. 'Frances! Come back. I'm sorry.'

Her voice was taken by a sudden breeze which sent leaves flying and the sound of windblown apples landing on the ground on the other side of the orchard wall.

Frances kept going, the sack of apples bouncing against her back, her long legs kicking out behind her.

Ruby clenched the hand that had slapped her cousin's face. She deeply regretted it, though still could not bring herself to believe that Gareth, the man she'd thought to marry, had done such a thing. Frances was just a child, she thought as she headed for home. Children fantasise and liked to shock their elders. That was it. That had to be it.

2

Sweet's Bakery occupied a large corner site at the top of Cowhorn Hill on the opposite corner to the Three Horseshoes public house, which was run by a widow who was in the envious position of owning both the freehold and brewing her own beer in a shed to the rear of the property. Even so, the Three Horseshoes was in competition with the Apple Tree and a number of other hostelries in the village.

There was only one bakery and Stan Sweet often commented that he preferred to own a bakery rather than a pub.

'At least I've got no competition,' he declared while slamming down a pile of dough and kneading it this way and that with big meaty hands.

Good wholesome loaves were displayed on glass shelves in the shop window at the front of the property. Above the door, the sun glinted on a sign saying S. Sweet & Sons, picked out in gold lettering on a green background. The S in the name referred to Sefton, Stan Sweet's grandfather. There had indeed been two sons, but Stan's brother Sefton, named after his grandfather and father, had died some time back as a result of bad health caused by injuries sustained during the Great War.

Behind the shop was the bakery itself which was dominated by a big black oven with two arched doors, the higher one, used to bake every loaf of bread they made, closer to the main furnace than the lower one which was mostly used to make pies, pasties and cakes.

Built in Victorian times from locally quarried stones Sweet's Bakery had been established by Stan Sweet's grandfather back in 1877. The bread had originally been baked in wood-fired ovens, but Stan's father had had the foresight to install a gas-fired oven just after the war.

'No more wood piled roof-high out in the yard,' he'd announced to Stan and his brother. Stan had given thanks to God that he no longer had to feed the old oven. Turning the tap that let in the gas and putting a match to it was far easier. He didn't even mind the harrumph the gas made when he lit it. Anything was better than going outside on a cold dark wintry morning, hours before the rest of the village was awake, trundling in and out with fuel and trying to diligently set light to a pile of kindling. Even though the embers from the day before were kept in overnight, if the kindling and the wood was damp, it could take an age to get the oven up and running. Mary glanced up at her sister when she came in. 'You look very nice in that dress. You've had it on all day. Special occasion was it?'

'I went for a walk.'

Mary shook her head and eyed her knowingly. 'I don't think so.'

For a moment Ruby wished they were not twins. It was sometimes quite frustrating to have somebody knowing what was in your head or shrewdly guessing what you'd been up to. Ruby bit her lip, folded her arms and leaned against the kitchen sink, looking through the kitchen window though seeing nothing.

Behind her Mary continued to sort out the apples Frances had brought home.

The two girls said nothing, each waiting for the other to break the silence. There was an air of anticipation, as though they were playing tennis and Mary had batted the ball in her sister's direction. Now it was Ruby's turn to bat it back. She had to say something.

'I won't be working behind the bar in future,' she finally said.

Mary nodded and continued sorting the apples before commenting. 'So he finally showed his true colours.'

Ruby adopted an air of denial. 'I don't know what you mean. I just said, I won't be working behind the bar in future.' Mary was not fooled, but hearing pain in Ruby's voice, put the apples and her paring knife down on the scrubbed pine table, stood behind her sister and rested her chin on her shoulder.

She looked sideways up into her face, their cheeks touching. 'I'm sorry but I'm glad it's over. You're too good for him.'

'That's nice to know.'

Mary's chin dug into Ruby's shoulder.

'What's the matter with Frances?' Mary asked.

Ruby moved away from the window. 'Is something the matter?' Ruby replied trying not to sound defensive. Despite the fact that she was still wearing her best dress, she began setting up the electric mixer that helped to turn flour, water and yeast into bread dough.

Ruby made a big show of shovelling flour into the aluminium bowl of the huge mixer. She had no wish to look at the face that was identical to her own; china blue eyes, dark lashes, finely arched eyebrows. She had no wish to be reminded that her sister's face was blemish-free. 'I think you know there is.' Ruby was aware that Mary was eyeing her intently, but would not meet her gaze. She had already decided on the walk back that she would not repeat what Frances had said. It couldn't be true. She refused to believe it.

'I hadn't noticed there was anything wrong. Where is she?' She hoped she only sounded mildly concerned.

'Upstairs. In her bedroom. I heard her door slam. Do you want to help me with these apples? There's half a sack. I thought I would make apple rings. They should keep well in the outhouse. I've got a sulphur candle and plenty of twigs and string.'

'And apple chutney?'

Mary nodded. 'I think so. I'm also considering making apple bread for the baking competition, a nice country loaf – almost a cake. Do you think the judges will like it?'

'Not pies?'

'I don't think so. Every woman in this village can bake an apple pie. But apple bread, nice moist dough flavoured with a little cinnamon – well, that's something else. Lucky for us we've got the bread ovens. What are you going to make?'

Ruby shrugged. It had occurred to her to bake an apple pie, but wasn't sure now following Mary's comment. 'I don't know. I'm still thinking about it.'

The fact was that she wasn't thinking about it at all. Still smarting from her treatment at the hands of the man she thought had loved her, it would do no good to say she couldn't possibly concentrate on baking, all because of Gareth Stead. If she said that her sister would want to know exactly what had gone on. She had already commented about Gareth showing his true colours. There were rarely secrets between them. Mary had guessed or somebody – Frances, perhaps – had told her.

Ruby's father spoke to her quietly when she was washing up after a slap-up tea of Victoria sponge, a cream-topped trifle and apple tart generously sprinkled with sugar. He'd come in to help himself to another cuppa, certain his daughter would be alone. It was the first chance he'd had to speak to her about her losing her job at the Apple Tree, which evidently he'd heard about from her sister.

'So no more bar work. Can't say I'm sorry. You're worth better things than that.'

She nodded. 'I'm glad you think so, Dad.'

She felt his eyes on her and knew it wasn't really the job he was referring to. What he was really saying was that she was worthy of a better man than Gareth Stead.

'I know so,' he said, patting her shoulder, his voice kind and gentle. 'You're a diamond, Ruby Sweet. Better than that, you're a ruby,' he added with a chuckle.

Ruby stopped scrubbing at a sponge tin but didn't meet her father's gaze. Much as she loved him, she didn't want his opinion just now. She didn't want anyone's opinion.

'Dad. I know what you're saying. I know you don't like Gareth.'

She glanced at him. He wasn't quick enough to hide an expression of outright distaste.

In Stan's opinion, there was no point in beating about the bush, so he didn't. 'He's second hand, Ruby. He's too old for you and he's been married before.'

'He's a widower. Not all widowers are unworthy.'

She fancied her father winced. He himself was a widower. 'That may be,' he said slowly. 'All the same, I think you can do better.'

*　*　*

Monday morning, and the smell of freshly made bread was warm and inviting.

Each time the door opened, the smell seeped out into the street. It rose with the steam from the chimney serving the bread oven. Anyone passing had no real need to read the sign above the door of the shop. All they had to do was follow the delicious aroma that enveloped the bakery like a scented veil.

Seeing as Ruby no longer had her few hours' work at the pub, there was nothing for it but to do some housework, get the laundry on the go and help Mary in the shop, though only if needed. For the moment she wanted to be alone, to lick her wounds and not have anybody feel sorry for her.

Frances had gone to school and their father was putting in bread and setting timers for each batch of loaves.

Ruby took Mary a cup of tea and brought one for herself, placing everything on a tray, including some coconut biscuits she'd made the day before.

Mary thanked her. Ruby pretended she didn't hear, but Mary called to her before she could retreat into the family's living accommodation at the rear of the shop and to the side of the baking room.

'Ruby, I've something I need to talk to you about.'

'I expect you do,' snapped Ruby assuming that Mary would challenge her about Gareth.

Mary had no intention of doing so. There wasn't really enough work in the bakery for the two of them, and Mary had intended voicing the subject when the door leading to the shop suddenly burst open.

Their brother Charlie bolted in, looking as though the hounds of hell were after him. 'Hide me!'

The twins exchanged wry glances. Despite herself Ruby had to smile.

Mary barred his way to the back of the shop. 'Miriam?'

Their agitated brother nodded. He looked pink-cheeked and it wasn't from tending the ovens. Miriam was after him.

'Can one of you go serve her and tell her that I've been requisitioned by the army or navy, or even kidnapped by Hitler?' he pleaded.

'I've got apples to peel.' Ruby looked tellingly at her sister and giggled. 'Your turn.'

Mary pulled a face and sighed. 'I'll deal with her,' she said grimly.

Miriam Powell had a freckled face and reddish hair. Twenty-eight years old, she was a spinster who, up until fairly recently, had spent her time caring for her elderly parents. While her father had been alive, she was not allowed to even be alone with a man. 'For fear the closeness of a masculine thigh heats her blood to the point of no return,' her father had sermonised. Her father, Godfrey Powell, had been a lay preacher who used to run the grocery shop, a place of piled-up tins, a bacon slicer, and a truckle of Cheddar cheese, ripe, pungent and bright yellow.

Poor Miriam. During her father's lifetime he had resolutely kept his daughter indoors, never allowing her out unaccompanied. Following his death, she now had more freedom than she used to have. Her mother was not nearly so demanding, mainly because it was not in her nature to order anyone around; all her life she'd been ordered around by others, including her husband. Her one sticking point was insisting that Miriam accompany her to church three times during the week and twice on Sundays. They made a meagre living in their shop, Miriam's father having died owing money that they were still trying to repay. There wasn't any extra money for clothes and they were known to live mostly on the vegetables left on the dusty shelves at the end of the week.

Despite the church-going Miriam was beginning to enjoy herself. She'd also discovered she very much liked the opposite sex, especially Charlie Sweet.

Judging by the way she looked into Charlie's eyes while buying a split tin and a cottage loaf, she was his for the taking – except that Charlie did not reciprocate her affection. He had tried telling her this, pushing her away when she came at him with her lips pursed and her big coat undone. Even at the village dance, where she was only allowed to stay until eight o'clock, she still wore her big coat.

Undaunted, or perhaps unaware of Charlie's rejection, she came in three days a week, her order always the same: one large split tin loaf and a cottage loaf.

'I think she must be feeding every sparrow in Oldland Common,' Mary had commented.

Ruby grinned. Her sister could be funny as well as deadly serious. She also knew how to dress, the shades she chose always suiting her colouring. Today she was wearing a bright blue dress under her apron, the colours accentuating her eyes.

'Perhaps it's all her and her mother live on.'

Mary made a disbelieving sound. 'Sandwiches every day? I don't believe it. You can't tell me that just her and her mother are eating all that bread. I don't believe it.'

Miriam came dashing in just moments after their brother, bringing a breeze and the first of the autumn leaves with her. She was wearing her usual checked coat that despite the breeze looked far too warm for the weather they were currently having. It was the one she always wore, winter, summer, spring or autumn.

Her face was pink, not because she was hot, but because it was the normal colour of her complexion. The sprinkling of freckles helped tone down the colour, but all in all it could be said that Miriam had a 'busy' face.

'Is Charlie not working in the shop today?' Her expression was one of enduring hopefulness, her voice lilting up and down in a sing-song way. Not surprisingly, she was a member of several church choirs and was known to sing a very good solo rendering of 'Abide with Me'.

Mary took on an apologetic look and primed her voice to match. 'I'm afraid not, Miss Powell. Our father had to visit the yeast merchant which means that Charlie has to tend the oven. Then get the dough ready for the morning.'

Miriam's face sagged. 'My word, but it's hard work running a bakery. You and your family are on the go all the time. I don't think I could do it. I never was very good at getting up in the morning. You should be up with the lark, my father used to tell me. I was always up by seven, but never with the lark.'

Mary smiled sweetly. 'It wouldn't do for you to marry a baker then, would it, Miss Powell.'

Miriam's face fell even further. 'Oh. I've never thought of that.' Her look of dejection was short-lived. 'I suppose marrying a baker would be the opportunity I need to change my ways,' she said, her face alight with hope. 'And of course if one has a family. Families all help each other, don't they.'

Mary agreed with her and although she smiled, she stopped it from spreading too wide or she might burst out laughing. She had no wish to hurt Miriam, but she just couldn't see her brother Charlie and Miriam together, not to mention the red-headed children the two of them might produce.

Mary wrapped up Miriam's order in brown paper and took the money. Once she'd gone, she locked the door, turned over the sign saying open to closed, and pulled down the biscuit-coloured blinds.

Charlie came through the door between the shop and the place where the bread oven hummed with heat. He was swigging back a cup of tea. 'That woman gives me the willies. I wish she'd stop pestering me.'

'That woman is in love with you,' said Ruby, flipping at her brother's head with the corner of a tea towel.

'Not my type. I don't go for redheads. Never have.'

Ruby sliced the last apple into the saucepan and added the sugar. 'So what is your sort?' she asked, an amused smile flickering around her lips.

Charlie threw back his dark head and closed eyes that were identical to those of his sisters.

'Now let me see.' His brow was deeply furrowed. 'I know what I'd like. I'd like one of them South Sea Island girls: dark hair, dark eyes and wearing a grass skirt and flowers in her hair.'

'Ha!' said Mary. 'I have it on good authority that she'll be at the fete tomorrow. You won't be able to avoid her.'

'A hula girl?' he asked hopefully.

'No,' Ruby added with a grimace. 'Miriam. She'll be there.' The look of hopefulness fled his face.

'In that case I'll hide myself in the beer tent. Even though her old dad is dead, she still won't go in there, the demon drink and all that.'

'Charlie Sweet, are you telling me that you're only going to the village fete for the beer?' Ruby couldn't help chuckling.

'It's my day off. A holiday. Of sorts.'

'You're not entering anything?' Mary asked him, eyeing her beloved brother sidelong, noting the impish grin and the way he ran his finger over his top lip.

He grinned. 'How about a rich pudding soaked in ale, loads of sultanas and candy peel?'

'Are you serious?' Mary said to him.

'No,' said Ruby. 'He's just being stupid.'

The girls had entered the village fete baking competition every year since the first time they'd mixed their own bread dough. But for Charlie baking was work not pleasure. Baking for the village fete he would leave to his sisters. Besides, it took up valuable drinking time.

Still their father had encouraged all of the children to have a go as early as they could sprinkle flour through their fingers. He'd laughed those first few times they'd baked their own bread, made pies or pasties and cakes. Not at their efforts which he praised to the roof telling all three of them – Charlie included – that they were chips off the old block and he was proud of them. 'Thing is you're wearing as much flour as you're putting in the bowl.'

His laughter and obvious pleasure was accompanied by him dabbing more flour on all their noses – not that it made much difference, seeing as their faces were already covered in it.

Frances came home from school at lunchtime, darting through the back kitchen and up the stairs.

'What's up with her?' asked Charlie as a cloud of flour floated down from the ceiling when Frances banged their bedroom door. No matter how careful they were, flour got everywhere.

'She's of an age,' said Mary.

Charlie looked puzzled. 'An age? What age?'

Mary shook her head and reached for the rolling pin. 'Never mind, Charlie. Let's just say it's women's trouble.'

'Women's?' He said incredulously. To him Frances was just a nipper.

Suddenly he realised she meant the monthly business and turned beetroot red.

'I'll just pop up to see if she's all right,' said Ruby, taking off her white apron and hanging it on the hook at the back of the door.

She headed for the stairs, closing the door tightly behind her.

'What's up with Ruby?' asked Charlie once they could hear her footsteps overhead. 'Same thing?'

'Not quite. I'm surprised you noticed.'

He shoved his hands in his pockets, swaying backwards and forwards, mainly because he wished the subject of *women's trouble* hadn't come up. The women outnumbered the men in this house, which sometimes made him feel something of an outsider. He might find women fascinating, but they were also a little frightening.

'Of course I noticed. Why shouldn't I notice? So, what's up with her?'

The contents of the saucepan containing apples chose that moment to reach boiling point. Mary turned it off.

'Well,' she said, her attention focused on the apple slices. 'You may have noticed that she went out on Sunday morning all dressed up and looking as though the world belonged to her and her alone. She returned looking as though she'd lost it somewhere.'

'Where'd she been?'

'For a walk. So she said.'

'You don't think so?'

Mary set the saucepan on the window ledge to cool. 'She went to the Apple Tree. I knew by the look in her eyes that she hadn't been for a walk. She looked desperately unhappy and I didn't need her to tell me the reason why. I could guess. She thought Gareth loved her.'

'I see.' Charlie nodded into his teacup. 'So that's why she's dumped her job pulling pints. I take it he let her down?'

'Of course he let her down.'

'I hoped it would wear off, otherwise...' Charlie pulled a face. 'I was going to say that I would have had a word with the bloke, but then, what good would that have done? She had to find out for herself.'

Mary agreed with him. 'Thank goodness she has. Now perhaps she'll forget the man.'

Charlie set down his tea cup and clenched his fists. 'I suppose I could still go along and have a word with him – keep away or else?'

'I don't think you need to, unless he starts pestering her. But I don't think he will. He'll move on to easier girls.'

She knew he was suggesting that he warn Gareth Stead to keep away from his sister. It was the 'or else' that worried her.

'If you're sure...'

Mary set a pan of milk on to the gas ring, let it heat up then added custard powder and sugar. 'Leave it Charlie. Let sleeping dogs lie. In time she'll forget him and find someone else.'

Charlie took another sip of his tea as he considered the rumours he'd heard regarding Gareth Stead. The man was a lecher, preferring younger women to those his own age. One girl in the village, Cathy Page, was only sixteen when her family sent her away to live in the city. Rumour had it that her staying away was necessary until the baby she was expecting had been born and instantly put up for adoption. Even then Cathy didn't come back. A ruined reputation was easier to hide in a big city with a large population than it was in a village where everyone knew everyone else's business. Ruby was lucky, even though she didn't know it yet.

3

Frances was lying face down on the bed, one arm thrown over her head, the other beside her cheek.

'I want a word with you,' Ruby said, closing the door firmly behind her.

Frances said nothing and didn't move. Her hair was loose from its usual braids and hid her face. It looked as though she were sucking her thumb.

'Have you been spying on me, telling Mary everything that's been going on?'

Although her tone was confrontational, she was careful to keep her voice down. The last thing she wanted was for her sister and brother to hear, but it was hard not to shout when she was feeling so angry.

Frances raised herself on one arm and looked over her shoulder.

'I didn't tell Mary anything. She just seemed to know that you and Mr Stead weren't friends any more. She said it was for the best. So did Charlie. What's a lecher?'

Ruby's jaw dropped. 'What? Who told you that word?'

'Charlie. He said that Mr Stead is a lecher and that he wouldn't leave a bitch in his company for long. I know what a bitch is. It's a female dog.'

'That's disgusting!'

Frances frowned. Growing up, she decided, wasn't easy. There was so much to learn, so many things she could do when she was younger that she couldn't do now, like Mary telling her that she was too old to tuck her dress into her knickers so she could climb trees more easily especially since that bleeding had started. She wished she didn't have that bleeding. It got in the way of everything, gave her stomach ache and the ugly towel she had to wear would probably show through her knickers if she ignored Mary and went scrumping. She decided to mention it to Ruby.

'Mary told me not to tuck my dress into my knickers. Is that disgusting too, especially when I've got my – you know – when I've got to wear that towel thingy?'

Frances looked so confused and sounded so innocent, Ruby felt her anger melting. Anyway, she realised it had been misplaced. She smoothed her cousin's hair back from her eyes, noting that the childish face was beginning to thin as she approached adolescence.

'Well, you are getting a bit old to be doing that. Boys look at you different as you get older.'

'Differently. Mary said it's differently not different.'

Ruby laughed. 'She's probably right. She usually is though sometimes I can't help pulling her leg about it. Here. I called in to Powells' on the way home from the post office.'

Frances's eyes opened wide at the strip of liquorice she gave her. 'Thank you.'

'Just don't give me away. And don't ever tell lies about Mr Stead. It could cause a lot of trouble – for everyone.'

Frances pulled a face and pouted her lips when she promised not to tell. After Ruby had gone, she sat herself up straight on the bed, the strip of liquorice lengthening as her teeth tore into it. If Ruby hadn't given her the liquorice, she would have protested that she hadn't been lying, that Mr Stead had helped her down from the wall after yet another foray into the orchard next door. That was when it had happened. That was when he'd sworn her to secrecy and told her it was just a game that adults played. Unconvinced, she'd kicked him on the leg and run away.

* * *

Stanley Sweet was up at four o'clock every week day morning to knead the rested dough and flash up the bread oven. As the oven whooshed into life, he listened for the sound of movement upstairs. Mary was down first, a white kerchief covering her head turban style, her face pink from the wash flannel and her eyes bright with excitement.

'Is that enough dough for you, Mary?'

She prodded the plump mound he'd indicated with her finger. It felt springy beneath her fingertip. 'That dough has the makings of a good loaf of bread,' she said, looking up at him, and laughed.

It was a frequent saying of her father and made him laugh too. 'Your apples are ready. Better get on with mixing them in with the dough before they go brown.'

Mary barely acknowledged him, her attention fixed on the job in hand.

Her father watched, breathing deeply as she folded the apples into the bread mixture. He'd never tired of the fragrance of a freshly baked loaf. Even the scent of the dough before it was cooked was a pleasure. Mixing the yeasty smell with that of sautéed apple slices and cinnamon only doubled his pleasure.

'It smells really good, my girl. Can't wait to taste it.'

He'd taught all his children to bake, and they were all good at it but Mary *loved* doing it and because of that, she went that extra mile, always aiming for perfection, a genius at making bread, but also cakes, pasties and all the other things they made for sale in the shop.

At Christmas it was Mary who decorated the cakes, even the great big one they baked especially for the folk up at the big hall, a splendid cake full of nuts, cherries and spices, moist with the flavours of ingredients sourced from all over the world.

Today was special. Today Mary was making her apple loaf to enter in the Oldland Common Best of Baking Award, Speciality Bread Baking Class.

The baking competition at the village fete had been a topic of conversation for some weeks. All three of his children were looking forward to it, as was Sefton's girl, Frances, though not all for the same reasons.

Mary and Ruby were both entering the baking competition, Mary with her apple bread and Ruby with a straightforward apple pie despite her sister's comments about any woman in the village being able to bake one. Hers would be better than any of them.

He frowned at the thought of that apple pie. Ruby was capable of so much more than that, something more elaborate. Not that he could say that Ruby had thrown it together, though he had to admit she'd seemed more slapdash than she usually was. She's best serving in the shop, he thought to himself, best dealing with customers. He dismissed her oft-spoken comments about leaving the village and seeking her fortune in the big city – and that was before this fall out with Gareth Stead. She'd always had her head in the clouds.

'Perhaps I could get a job baking at a posh hotel,' she'd said only the other day.

Stan refused to believe she would really go. He couldn't face any of his children leaving home. But if one of his girls should get the opportunity, he wouldn't step in their way.

He went into the garden, got his spade and fork from the shed and proceeded to stab the latter into the compacted earth.

It was due for a good turning over and slamming the fork in helped alleviate the angst he was feeling.

'Damn the competition,' he exclaimed as the prongs of the fork stabbed deep into the soil. If one of his daughters won they might be tempted by the bright lights of the city and want to leave home. He drew it out and was about to have a second go along with an exclamation damning the village fete when he thought better of it.

The village fete had been going for years and the whole village enjoyed it. So did his family. When the prongs went in this time, he damned Adolf Hitler instead then leaned on the handle, lit his pipe and mused on the pleasure the village fete gave to them all.

Frances would head straight for the fairground running alongside the fete, a place where old gypsy women told fortunes if you crossed their palms with silver, and half-naked children ran around dragging scrawny dogs or ponies on long lead reins or leashes. Swarthy-faced men stood around smoking something that smelled like weeds while they inveigled passers-by to buy their painted tin cans, freshly killed rabbits, and baskets woven from long fronds of cut willow.

There would be a helter skelter, a tombola and this year a carousel. If they were lucky there might even be a big wheel.

Charlie would make his way to the beer tent along with his mates. It wasn't often any of them had a day off, and this day was the most special of the year.

Stan would be content to see his children enjoying themselves, and he'd be more than happy if one of his daughters should win one of the baking categories.

The baking competition was taking place in the main marquee

situated at the heart of the fete. This year was the most special, the only year in which the winners of the four categories would go forward to a 'Best of Baking' regional final in nearby Bristol, and then on to London if they won that round. A prize of ten pounds for the best British baker was at stake.

'Right,' Mary said once the apple loaf was ready for the oven and she was slapping the flour from her palms. 'I think it looks good.'

Her father agreed with her. Understanding the pride a baker takes in their work, he held back while she stood beaming at the risen dough, oddly greyish-green thanks to the apple mixture.

'Ready?'

She nodded, biting her lip nervously as she watched her father scoop it on to the big wooden paddle and slide it into the oven.

When the iron door clanged open, the heat of the oven filled the room. The bread entered the oven, an amorphous shape of doughy whiteness. Father and daughter waited until the sweet moment the smell of yeast and apples fell over them like a blanket.

This was the moment Mary liked best when the very air in the room became imbued with the essence of bread, its smell and its moistness. When she took a breath she could taste it.

'It already smells good,' said her father.

The aroma began to swell in much the same way as the loaf itself until it felt as though they were breathing in its taste.

Her father beamed at her.

'Now you'd better go and wash that flour from off your nose!' He dotted her nose with his finger just as he had when she was a child.

Mary laughed. All these years of baking and she was still getting flour on her face.

She was still smiling to herself when she encountered her sister coming out of the bathroom. Ruby looked pale and there were dark circles under her eyes.

Mary's smug contentment disappeared. If her sister wasn't feeling happy then she wasn't either.

'Are you in trouble?'

Ruby's lips were slightly parted, her eyes heavy with contemplation. 'No. I'm just not feeling very well.'

Mary felt a nervous churning in her stomach. At the same time she prayed that her sister was not pregnant.

'It's not what you're thinking,' said Ruby on noticing her sister's alarm. 'I wouldn't let him.'

Mary heaved a sigh of relief. 'Thank goodness for that.'

'The trouble is...' Ruby began. It was difficult to put her thoughts into words or even to admit the possibility of what she was thinking. Still, it had to be done.

'I'm afraid I might reconsider – well – not reconsider exactly, I mean I might not be able to help myself if he should come after me. I still feel drawn to him – ever so slightly,' she added.

'Perhaps Charlie should have a word with him.'

Ruby shook her head. 'No. Anyway, there's no point in doing anything unless Gareth does come after me.' Ruby sighed. 'It's so hard to switch off my feelings. Have you ever felt like that?'

Mary wanted to give her sister a big hug, but held back. Ruby was in no mood to be patronised. 'I haven't had those sorts of feelings for anyone yet, so I'm hardly the right person to ask,' Mary said, a touch more feebly than usual. 'You know he's no good.'

Ruby's wry smile only added sadness to her eyes. 'I read somewhere that you can love somebody despite them being no good.'

'So I hear. But do you really want to end up like Mrs King?'

Mrs King was married to a slaughterer who worked at the abattoir. Her husband Ned King was a big drinker who put the meat on the table – mainly offal he got free with his job – but frequently beat his wife and kids, until the eldest grew taller than he was and hit him back. It hadn't stopped him from still slapping his wife around, so the village gossips said.

Ruby considered saying that Gareth had never hit her and she didn't believe he ever would, but stopped herself. Gareth drank heavily. She wasn't aware of it at first, but over the six months she'd worked for him she'd noticed it more and more and who knew how things might progress as he got older?

Ruby stood with her back against the wall, head bowed as she considered her options. Gareth Stead could be a thorn in her side if she stayed in the village. She voiced this to Mary.

'Then you have to ignore him—'

'No,' Ruby said abruptly. 'I'm not sure I'm strong enough.'

Mary shrugged her shoulders. 'What then?' There was a furtive look in Ruby's eyes. Mary guessed there was something on her mind.

Ruby took a deep breath because she was about to ask her sister to do something dishonest. She'd been thinking it over all night.

'Mary, I want to win this baking competition. I want to go to Bristol and then London. I need to win that prize. I need you to let me put my name to the apple loaf. I want to win. I want to leave Oldland Common.'

Mary stared at her in disbelief. She, too, wanted to win this prize. She'd won in other years, but this year was special. The prize money would certainly help them out as a family, but more than that, this year it wouldn't be just the judgement of the local area, it would be nationwide – if she won this round. 'What about your apple pie? You stand a good chance. Your pastry is always better than mine.'

There was an intense look in Ruby's eyes. 'I want more than one chance to win. I want to get away, Mary, and besides – like you said – plenty of women in the village make apple pies, but they don't bake bread to the Sweets' standard.'

It was true. Some of the village women did bake their own bread, but Mary and Ruby had the advantage of tried and tested family recipes and a very hot bread oven.

Mary sat down on the bed and slid her feet out of her shoes. The apple bread had come out of the oven perfectly baked. The smell was heavenly, the crust golden brown, the underside firm but not tough. She'd tapped it with her fist and been pleased with the sound it made. The loaf of apple bread had a good chance of winning the speciality category.

'I had plans for that prize money,' she said while kneading the ache out of her toes.

The prize money this year was a definite plus. It had come as a great surprise to everyone when they were told that the local competition would be part of a nationwide search for the Best of British Baking. The winner of this round would win the right to go through to the next which would be held at the Victoria Rooms in Bristol. The winner of that round would then go on to the finals in London. Travel and hotel accommodation was included, plus two pounds for the winner of the regional event in Bristol and twenty pounds for the ultimate prize in London.

Ruby knew she was asking a lot, but this might be her only way to get away from here and she desperately wanted to put Gareth and the village behind her. Perhaps her present mood would pass in time, but for now there was nothing more important.

'I want to go to Bristol. I think I might also like to go to London, but I don't want to come back.'

Mary stared at the bedroom window. Her sister was asking her to forgo her chances of winning and take her place, entering the apple loaf as her own. Her first inclination was to turn her down flat. She wanted to win and have the chance to go to Bristol and London herself – or did she?

She looked at her sister, a mirror image of herself except for the mole on her cheek which was roughly the size of a sixpence. Not that it could usually be easily seen; her hairstyle saw to that.

'You're asking me to give up quite a lot. You do realise that?'

Ruby nodded.

Mary considered what her sister was asking her. Would she really be giving up so very much? On the one hand, Ruby asking to enter the bread as her own made her angry. Her sister was being selfish. Or was she? Gareth was not a nice man. Why hadn't Ruby been able to see that when Mary had seen it so clearly? Perhaps because there wasn't much choice in the village?

Thinking that Ruby might not have been telling her the truth about a possible pregnancy, she repeated the question. 'Are you sure you're not in trouble?'

Ruby's expression turned angry. 'Mary, I've already told you! I am not pregnant! Honestly, Mary, I'm not. I just need to get away.'

Mary thought about what this would mean. The recipe and loaf she'd given such thought and time to would not be entered in her name. But she wanted it confirmed, she wanted her sister to voice exactly what she did want.

'You think my apple loaf will win and you want to enter it in your name. Is that right?'

'Yes,' said Ruby, her arms folded beneath her generous breasts, her chin nodding avidly. 'You're as good as Dad; he says so himself.'

'And you really want to leave?'

'That's what I'm telling you. I want to go. I'll make no bones about it, Mary, I was tempted by Gareth and I do want a sweetheart, but I'm not a tart.' Ruby pulled a face. 'I'm still a virgin.'

Mary raised her eyebrows. 'Is that so bad?'

Ruby pouted and tossed her head. 'I want to live a bit before I settle down.'

Mary was even more surprised. 'You mean...?'

'Why not? At least if I get a bit of experience, I won't be taken in so easily the next time I get involved with a bloke. So? What's it to be?'

'I'll have to think about it.'

'Please,' Ruby implored.

Silently Mary shook her head and backed away, suddenly desperate to breathe the fresh air outside the bakery, to see a patch of sky as she thought things through. 'I don't know. Let me think about it.'

Even after coming in from her short sojourn in the garden, she still hadn't made her mind up. It was her apple loaf. Could she bear to let her sister take the glory – if it won, that is?

She thought further about it as she took two mugs of tea to her father and her brother who were engaged in placing the second batch of bread into the oven. Her apple loaf was out cooling with the first batch of bread.

'It's a winner. I'm certain it is,' said her father, his face red with the heat from the oven.

'And our dad is always right,' Charlie added cheerfully, his cheeks just as red as those of his father.

Mary set down their tea on the table in front of them together with a plate of almond-and-coconut-flavoured biscuits. 'Well, that's three of you think so, but it's the judges' opinion that matters.'

'Let's hope they know something about bread,' grunted Stan Sweet. 'None of them women who know how to throw a pie or a Victoria sponge together know anything about bread. I hope they've got proper bakers doing the judging.'

Stan Sweet was right to be concerned. In past years the baking had been restricted to fruit cakes, Victoria sponges and iced fancy cakes. Bakers were coming from miles around to enter their best and most imaginative breads. This year there were three classes in the bread alone: best batch-baked bread, best plaited and the third category was for a speciality loaf that is made from an unusual combination of ingredients.

Mary felt her father's eyes on her. 'I hope you gets what you deserves, me girl,' he said softly, wiping his floury hands in his apron and laying them on her shoulders. There was affection in his face, gentleness in the touch of his hands.

'Dad,' she said, shaking her head and smiling up at him. 'What are you on about?'

'About winning,' added Charlie, leaning back as he opened the oven door to check the loaves.

Stan Sweet frowned. He loved his children to the extent that he'd made sacrifices with his own life on their behalf. He'd never remarried after his wife died and said he never would.

'I wish you well, love, but I can't say I'm keen on you going down to Bristol, winning that, and running away to London. When you've tasted the big city, you might not want to come back.'

Mary beamed her biggest smile at him. 'Of course I will,' she said. She loved the village, loved her family and could never envisage ever leaving, not forever anyway. 'I love baking bread. I love cooking and I've never wanted to do anything else. Besides, I can't possibly leave my old dad to himself can I?'

She realised she was speaking the absolute truth. Being away from the bakery for any length of time made her feel anxious.

Stan gave a big boisterous laugh that made his shoulders shake. As he did so he saw Mary's resemblance to his wife. Both twins were very alike and very much like their mother.

'That's not the point,' he said, the light of knowledge and ultimate abandonment alternating in his heart and in his eyes. 'It's not the city itself; it's what you might find there. Your mother found me here, and even though she was brought up in Bristol, she left city life behind and came here to be with me. That's what I'm thinking about you. You might find somebody that really bowls you over.

When it comes to you like that, you're left with no choice. That's the way it is. Shame, because you're a natural baker. Better even than your brother here and soon...'

His brow became more creased with frown lines as he contemplated Charlie's future. Unlike the girls Charlie would not have a choice. He was bound to be called up sooner or later and there was little his father could do about it.

Deep in thought, Charlie was drawing lines through a film of flour with the toe of his boot, both hands tucked behind the bib of his white apron.

'I want to go, Dad. If war comes, I want a bit of adventure before I die.' His manner was subdued, his voice calm and serious.

Stan Sweet sighed. He knew it would happen. All he prayed for was that if war did come Charlie wouldn't be called away too soon. He knew about war. He'd fought at the Somme. It had been a mind-numbing experience, the sort of thing nightmares are made of. He still had those nightmares.

'I have to say that I wish there were a way to avoid it, but have to admit it isn't likely. They'll force the issue and take you, especially as I've got two daughters to help me. But I have to say, son, here and now, that the army is no picnic.'

'I'm not going into the army. I'm going to join the navy. The merchant navy, I think. There's plenty of merchant ships coming and going in and out of Bristol. Now that's not too far, is it?'

Mary saw fear enter her father's eyes before he blinked it away. 'I suppose not. I'll be worried about you, but you're a man now, and if this war does happen, well, a young man wants to do his bit. At least you won't be stuck in a muddy trench taking pot shots across no-man's-land.'

4

The sky over the village fete was a patchwork of blue sky and fluffy white clouds. A slight breeze stirred ladies' skirts and cooled the sweat of the men, some with their shirt sleeves rolled up as they swung a hammer in order to ring a bell at the top of a mast and win a prize.

There was a tombola, a coconut shy and a dog show for Jack Russell rat catchers, hare-coursing lurchers and sheepdogs; the latters' owners were required to bring their own sheep in order to demonstrate their dog's superior skills.

Slap bang in the middle of the fete stood a couple of marquees. In one the produce of Oldland Common Horticultural Society was being judged. The keen gardeners were competing for no less than ten silver cups, everything from flower arranging, the biggest marrow and best Harvest Festival basket. The marquee where the regional heat of the best bread-baking competition was being held was next door to that of the horticultural society. It was fuller than in past years, the air heady with excitement and the warm, yeasty smell of freshly made bread.

A long table had been placed at one end of the baking tent on a raised platform. There were three chairs placed behind it and the loaves entered for the competition arranged so they could be judged in their respective groups.

A big man with a booming voice announced that the judging would now commence.

'Ladies and gentlemen! It is my pleasure, indeed my very great privilege...'

Anyone who had dared to carry on talking was pointed at with a finger as thick as a sausage, the knuckles almost as hairy as the thick dark eyebrows that frowned in their direction.

'Madam! Please!'

It was mostly the women who continued to talk but after one look from the man nicknamed Bullhorn, real name Jeremy Wilkes, they dropped the hands they had been talking behind and faced forward.

Like a ringmaster in the circus, 'Bullhorn' made a big show of being in charge and of introducing the judges – as if they were lions or performing seals, thought Mary, who was standing with her sister and father about three rows back from the front of the crowd.

The judges were all from London, two master bakers with round bodies and plump facial features, plus a top chef with black oily hair and a drooping moustache. A nerve flickered beneath his right eye so it seemed as though he were continually winking and his face was almost as greasy as his hair.

Bullhorn went into action.

'And now!' Just in case he didn't have their attention... 'First, the split tin loaves will be judged.'

Most of the entries for the bread section were not from the village. Mary spotted a number of strangers in the crowd. One in particular caught her eye. He saw her looking, turned his head and met her gaze. He winked.

Blushing profusely, she turned to face the front. She told herself that she wasn't interested in handsome young men who winked at her. She was interested in the baking competition, and that was all. All the same, she glanced that way again. This time he was facing the front and not looking at her. She was only slightly disappointed. He was not the reason she was here. She was here to see what was going on.

Each loaf was looked at, then smelt, then upended and tapped on the bottom by all three distinguished personages. Once that was done, they put their heads together, backs and bums to the crowds. The crowd began to murmur.

Bullhorn ran his beady eyes over them, but made no move to hush them up. The judges were in conference. The crowd had free rein until they'd finished conferring.

The whole village plus the supporters of the other competitors, some of whom had come from quite a distance, were gathered as tightly as sardines in a can. Necks craned for a better view. Children were perched on parents' shoulders and some young men had purloined a few wooden crates from the beer tents to stand on.

Following the initial inspections, a slice was cut from each loaf and then cut in three so each judge could savour a piece. None of them added butter. Their jaws moved; their eyes glazed over.

Mary and Ruby were standing side by side watching the event. Charlie had been spotted by Miriam Powell and had promptly headed for the beer tent, wishing Mary good luck before leaving. Mary had said nothing to anyone about the favour Ruby had asked her. After all, both the apple loaf and the pie had been entered by a Miss Sweet. Either of them could claim the prize with impunity.

The judges still had their heads together.

Stan Sweet, having cast a beady eye over the entries for each category, didn't exactly trust people from the big city to know what a good country loaf should taste like.

'All done with machines that don't need a master baker to knock it into shape,' he grunted.

The honest truth was that he too had mechanical help in his bakery, but he didn't approve of making big batches. 'Too many to keep an eye on,' he sniffed before turning his attention to the number of entrants for the speciality loaf.

'Only six entered,' he whispered to his daughter, his face shining with excitement. 'You're definitely in with a chance, my girl.'

Mary exchanged a furtive look with her sister, one that said, 'Perhaps we should have told him.'

Ruby gave a slight shake of her head.

'All we have to do is win,' Mary whispered.

The apple loaf was a favourite of hers; something moist and fruity, good to have at tea time with butter and jam, or even by itself.

'I'll always be grateful for this, Mary. Always,' said Ruby.

'You'd better be,' growled her sister. 'But let's not count our chickens yet. The competition looks pretty good.'

Ruby had to admit she was right. The three of them had taken a look at the other loaves they were up against. One of the loaves was entitled Sunlight Blush, the dough stated to have been mixed with tomatoes that had been dried in the sun plus a hint of garlic. 'Not very British,' their father had grumbled. 'The British don't like garlic. It'll never catch on.'

Two of the loaves favoured sultanas and nuts. The other two were as dark as fruit cakes and when cut had the distinct smell of alcohol, probably brandy but just as likely to be whisky.

Mary couldn't help being pragmatic about their chances. 'Oh well. Either you're going to Bristol and perhaps then to London or we don't win at all; then we both stay at home.'

'I can't stay at home. It would be just too unbearable,' Ruby said, once their father was out of earshot. 'You know how people gossip.'

Mary gave her sister's hand a tight squeeze. 'I know.' Then, after a pause. 'I will miss you.'

'I'll miss you too.'

After a good deal of deliberation, the judges made their decision, which was given in writing to the man with the foghorn voice.

Bullhorn stepped up on to the rostrum, his voice ringing out loud and clear.

'Ladies and gentlemen, the first winner has been decided and will be announced once the other categories have been judged and decisions made,' he bellowed.

There was a humming of outraged conversation, a shaking of heads by people impatient to know the results.

'Oh, lord,' whispered Ruby, her breasts rising tightly against the bodice of her favourite blue and rose-pink dress. It was the same dress she'd worn on her last meeting with Gareth Stead. 'One more category before the apple loaf gets judged.'

The same procedure for the split tin was used for the plaited bread, although because of its nature – beautifully twisted seams plaited like golden hair – inspecting the plaits took longer than smelling and tasting. Bullhorn explained the judges were looking for ingenuous presentation as well as smell and texture. 'A presentation of plaits and twists likely to bring a sparkle to the eyes of John Barleycorn himself!'

There were a few titters, though some of the professional bakers thought the master of ceremonies should take his job more seriously. A bit of grumbling resumed.

'Shhh!' he hissed, putting a fat finger to his mouth. 'Shhh! Quiet please.'

The crowd's grumbles quietened but didn't go away. Their craned necks were leading to dry throats and the beer tent was selling out.

'Get on with it,' somebody shouted. Ruby recognised the voice.

Gareth Stead was here, likely taking a break from running the beer tent. Her heartbeat increased, the blood flowing faster to her face.

'How he's got the nerve to show his face,' Mary growled.

She might have said more, but the proceedings were now moving swiftly along.

'Here it is! We have the results for plaited breads.'

Bullhorn held up another piece of paper on which each judge had declared their findings.

Mary sucked in her breath. Her heart refused to stop hammering against her ribs.

Ruby let out a deep breath like a balloon slowly deflating. 'I think I'm going to faint,' she whispered.

'Don't you dare,' Mary whispered back. 'If we win, it wouldn't look good if you can't even go up to collect your prize.'

Yet again she had referred to the apple loaf as though they'd both had a hand in baking it. She felt only a slight twinge of regret. Does it matter, she asked herself? The Sweets baked it. That's all that really counts.

Ruby smiled haltingly. Her sister was being outstandingly generous, but there was no guarantee that the apple loaf would win. The suspense was incredible. It was time for the judging of their class.

Unlike the other categories, small cards were propped up against each of the loaves in this section detailing the ingredients added. Just as Mary had guessed, sultanas, fruit, nuts and alcohol topped the list. As for the bread infused with sun-dried tomatoes and garlic – it might be interesting, but as her father had intimated, it might not appeal to the British palate.

The chef's face had brightened on smelling then tasting the savoury offering. The two bakers had been less impressed.

Their expressions were almost as impassive when sampling the breads mixed with fruits.

'Get on with it,' somebody shouted.

Ruby was in no doubt as to who that was. Gareth – again, and he sounded drunk.

His outburst was followed by impatient whispers. Obviously the crowd also wanted the judges to get a move on.

The judges huddled together, the two bakers nodding in agreement, the black-haired chef looking red faced and unhappy.

Bullhorn joined the huddle, the whispering somewhat intense, the odd word tumbling out like a tin can thrown over their shoulders.

'Superior...'

'Classical...'

'Traditional...'

'British taste...'

Then there was quiet. The judges came out of their huddle, the bakers looking pleased with themselves, the chef looking resigned, the corners of his mouth drooping beneath his moustache.

Bullhorn looked self-satisfied as though, just like a circus ring-master, he'd tamed professional egos. Before announcing the results, he had a quick word with a representative of the company sponsoring the competition.

'Ladies and gentlemen!' He began shuffling his papers, back to the first category, the split tin loaf. 'And the winner is...' A roll of drums was intimated, though none was heard. Bullhorn was standing with his arms above his head, like an auctioneer about to bring down his hammer on the last bid.

'Mrs D Leyton!'

A loud cheer went up in response to Bullhorn's resonant pronouncement as Diane Leyton, an active member of the local WI, went up to receive her prize and the chance of going forward to the next round.

As they beamed round at everyone, she waved the five pounds

she'd won. Her supporters, all of whom were in the WI too, cheered loudly.

The next winner of the plaited bread section was a baker from Quedgeley near Gloucester and turned out to be only sixteen years old. Her mother had come with her.

'Miss Joan Forester!'

The cheers weren't quite as enthusiastic, but young Joan didn't seem the sort to enjoy being the centre of attention as, after accepting her prize, she marched swiftly away, head down, as though winning was something to be ashamed of.

Now it was the turn of their category to be judged. Mary patted Ruby's shoulder. Smelling of best bitter and red in the face, their father and Charlie joined them.

'Lost Miriam?' Mary whispered.

Charlie grinned. 'Her mother sent a message she wanted her at home.'

Mary grinned. 'Lucky for you.'

He didn't answer, his gaze attracted to a dark-haired beauty who seemed to be standing slightly apart from anyone else.

'Who is that?' he asked his sister in an oddly awestruck voice.

The young woman was wearing a dark blue hat, a crisp veil skimming the bridge of her nose.

Mary shook her head. 'I'm not sure. She might be the woman staying with Mrs Hicks at Stratham House.' Eyeing her brother sidelong, she gave him a warning nudge in the ribs. 'And before you get entangled, I hear she has two children with her.'

Mary turned back to the main event. There was no sound from Gareth Stead. He wouldn't dare make a move now her brother and her father were with them. She smiled reassuringly at her sister. Ruby smiled nervously back.

Bullhorn cleared his throat. 'And now we come to the loaf that, in the judges' opinion, is an imaginative use of ingredients. This is the category for something creative as well as tasty.' He paused, cleared his throat again and nodded at the sponsor before proceeding.

'Ladies and gentlemen. The judges could not agree on an outright winner in this category...'

The crowd gasped. Mary and Ruby looked at each other in dismay. This couldn't be happening.

'Therefore, our honourable sponsor, Mr Leonard Neate of Spillers Flour Limited, has decided to award two prizes. The first to...' The crowd held its breath. 'Miss Ruby Sweet for her apple loaf.'

A vast cheer went up from the gathered locals. For a moment Ruby stood with her mouth open until her sister pushed her forward.

'Go on. Go on!'

Mary covered her mouth with her hands. Ruby looked like a little girl collecting her prize, half excited, half scared to death. It should have been me up there, she thought to herself and felt a pang of regret. Even if Ruby did leave home, it wasn't likely she would stay away forever.

A pink flush of pleasure was spreading over her sister's face. Even from this distance, Mary could see that her eyes were shining.

I can't bear for her to leave home, she thought to herself. Another thought occurred to her: she was the scared one, not her sister up there accepting the prize.

Bullhorn raised his meaty arms and spread his hands, fingers splayed as he ordered the crowd to be quiet.

'The joint prize winner is the loaf containing garlic and sun-dried tomatoes which our chef from London declared an Italian classic. The joint prize winner is Mr Michael Dangerfield.'

Heads turned this way and that, murmurs running through the crowd. There were plenty of master bakers there, but nobody seemed to know who this man was. Nobody seemed too keen on the ingredients either.

'Garlic! It's too foreign,' somebody said.

'The Johnnie Onions sell it,' a female voice added. 'I saw one of them at the market. I thought it was small onions and would 'ave bought some, but the Johnnie Onion said it were garlic. I had a smell of it. Didn't like it much though.'

The French onion sellers the woman was referring to came over from France on their bicycles selling onions to shopkeepers and door to door and at weekly markets. They were a familiar sight with their tanned faces and dark berets, and their heavily accented English.

'He's not local. I for one don't recognise the name,' declared Stan Sweet, his pipe clenched in the corner of his mouth. 'I know all the bakers around here, but definitely not this one. Not even from Warmley, is he, Charlie?'

Charlie wasn't paying attention. The dark-haired beauty standing at the back of the marquee was far more interesting, even if she did have a couple of kids. He'd never seen such an exotic woman before and he couldn't stop looking at her.

His father repeated what he'd said along with an elbow in his ribs. 'I said he's not from Warmley, is he?'

A bone in Charlie's neck made a cracking sound as he jerked his head round. 'No. I don't know the name.'

'Excuse me, ma'am. I need to get past.'

Such was the timbre of his voice and the unusual accent Mary felt an overwhelming compulsion to see from whom it came.

On turning her head she found herself looking up into a bronzed face. White streaks radiated from the corners of his eyes as though he had spent a lot of time squinting into strong sunlight.

For a moment it seemed as though the world stood still until he spoke again and broke the spell.

'You're twins, right? You worked this between you?'

She heard his voice but didn't like what he was saying. 'What do you mean?'

He glanced at Ruby up on the stage then back to her. 'Just that I thought I was seeing double. Her up there, you down here.'

'We're sisters,' Mary blurted. 'Twins.' There was no way she was going to admit to collusion. She only hoped her guilt didn't show on her face.

Bullhorn's voice bludgeoned its way between them. 'Mr Dangerfield. If you are here, will you please come up to the rostrum!'

His smile was memorable. 'Excuse me.'

Her gaze followed the back of his head as he made his way to the front of the crowd.

'So that's Michael Dangerfield,' she heard her father say. 'He's definitely not from around here.'

'No,' she said, unable to take her eyes off the man standing up front with her sister. 'No. He's not.'

Ruby smiled with her lips and glared with her eyes at the man joining her on the rostrum. He nodded and smiled back.

'Ma'am.'

Ruby nodded back.

'A pound each,' said the bald-headed Mr Neate, his smile exposing large yellow teeth. His hands shook as though he suffered from some nervous disorder when he handed them their prize money.

'Congratulations,' he said to both of them. 'And may the best man – or woman – win when you attend the next heat in Bristol.'

'It's an Italian classic,' stated Michael Dangerfield.

Ruby gritted her teeth. Surely this competition should be about British baking not foreign stuff.

A photographer from the Evening World asked if he could take a shot of them holding their respective entries outside the tent on a nice patch of green grass away from everyone else. He insisted they stood close together.

'Like a bride and groom,' he trilled in a sing-song Welsh accent.

'Hardly,' said Ruby, her teeth fixed in an insincere smile.

Once the photograph and names were taken, Ruby's co-winner turned and said, 'Something about you reminds me of a Hollywood film star. Jean Harlow perhaps?'

'She's blond. I'm not.'

'Must be that peek-a-boo style. That's what they call it, don't they?'

'Do they?' Ruby was purposely offhand.

He nodded. 'Yeah. As though she's trying to hide one half of her face.'

This was too much. Ruby spun away. As she did so she dropped the loaf. At the same time a runaway pig shot past behind them pursued by a gang of giggling, drunken men.

Michael Dangerfield stepped back as he turned to see what was going on. His foot landed on the apple loaf.

'I'm sorry,' he shouted once Ruby had picked it up and was stalking off back to the tent.

'Sorry? You just might be,' she muttered.

5

Stan Sweet frowned and growled noises that sounded like 'ger-rumph' and 'errrrmmm' when Ruby went up to collect the prize rather than her sister Mary.

'That was your bread,' he said a trifle testily. 'What the bloody 'ell's goin' on 'ere? Our Ruby's already won the apple pie bake off. What's she doing goin' up collecting your prize?'

Even if she hadn't been listening, Mary could have told by his beetled brow that her father was not amused.

'Well?'

Mary beamed at him. 'Whoever wins this goes through to the next round in Bristol, and whoever wins that gets to stay in London for a while.'

'So?'

'You said it yourself, Dad. I'm the baker. I'm needed here. It's Ruby that wants to leave for pastures new. She needed my help to make it happen. You need me here, and anyway, I don't want to go.'

'It got stepped on,' said Ruby when she finally caught up with them in the beer tent.

Her sister sighed. 'What happened?'

'I just told you. Someone stepped on it,' said Ruby in an irritated tone.

Her father shook his head. 'Now that's typical of you. Ruby, you should learn to be more careful.'

Ruby could have told him that it wasn't her that stepped on it, but his chastising comment riled her, made her feel as though she wasn't quite perfect – like the mole she had on her face. Mary was never accused of being careless. Mary didn't have a mole.

Even after a supper of thickly sliced home-cooked ham, farm fresh butter and bread still warm from the oven, Stan Sweet was still a bit miffed, though mellowed after a few beers over the road in the Three Horseshoes.

He stated his last words on the matter after eating another slice of ham, pickles and bread, one foot on the bottom stair. His bed was calling him.

'We'll speak tomorrow.'

He saw that Ruby was uncharacteristically quiet, but told himself she'd be fine in the morning.

* * *

The morning light of the first Sunday in September found its way through a gap in the curtains of the big front bedroom the twins shared with their cousin, Frances.

The bedroom had previously been occupied by their parents before their mother died a victim of the terrible influenza pandemic that had swept through Europe in 1919, as if the deaths in the Great War were not enough.

Their father slept in one of the small bedrooms at the back of the house, and their brother, Charlie, in the other.

The really good thing about the arrangement was that the resonant male snoring was kept at bay, thanks to the fact that there were two doors between them, their own and the ones to the rear bedrooms.

Sunday was the one day a week when no bread was baked and everyone could lie in, though the habit of getting up early was difficult to break.

Ruby was wide awake by about six-thirty. Even though she turned over, hugging the bedclothes around her head and willing herself to sleep, she was too excited. Her thoughts were occupied with the semi-finals and the prospect of going to Bristol and then possibly to London for the final. London was where she would seek new opportunities. Perhaps she might meet a handsome millionaire and be swept off her feet. Her plans, even though they might never reach fruition, came thick and fast.

Sleep wouldn't come. The clock struck eight. 'Are you awake, Mary?'

Mary sighed and rolled over on to her back. 'Of course I am. I can hear you wriggling. The springs on that bed play a tune every time you move.'

Ruby was already lying on her back, eyes wide open, one arm behind her head. One of the bedsprings made a twanging sound as she shifted again. She had to share what she was feeling.

'If I win, I won't come back from London. I might not even come back from Bristol – depending on circumstances.'

Mary sucked in her lips so she wouldn't voice what she really felt. Her sister could be both unrealistic and selfish in equal doses.

'Mary? Did you hear what I just said?'

Mary closed her eyes and sighed. 'I must have drifted off for a minute. But I did hear you.'

'You do see why I want to leave, don't you?'

For people who rose at four in the morning on every day but one, staying in bed on Sunday was almost compulsory. Even though Mary wasn't feeling that tired, she was determined to stay where she was, delaying the moment when she had to swing her legs out of bed as she did on every other day of the week.

'If that's really what you want to do.'

'It really is!'

'Then do it. I'll be here for Dad.'

Ruby rolled on to her side and raised herself on her elbow. Mary's comment had made her feel uncomfortable. 'You sound resentful.'

And you sound pretty displeased, thought Mary. 'I'm just stating the facts.'

'Well, so am I. I'll be glad to go. Glad to leave the village. Sad to leave everyone behind...with a few notable exceptions...'

'Especially old bastard Stead!'

Ruby gasped.

Mary's eyes flicked open.

'Frances Sweet! You are not to use that language in this house.' She'd thought their cousin was still asleep. Obviously she was not.

'It's what the boys call him,' Frances grumbled sulkily from beneath a mound of twisted bedding.

Frances was a restless sleeper, her bedding always bundled like a small mountain by morning.

'I don't care what the boys call him. You do not!' Mary ordered. 'Don't let me ever hear you using such a word again. Is that clear?'

Frances fell silent, her scowl hidden by the bedclothes as she thought about it.

'All right. I'll call him Stinker Stead instead.'

Ruby preferred not to hear the name Stead mentioned at all. 'For goodness' sake! What is it with you and Gareth Stead?'

Frances dragged herself up into a sitting position, bending her legs so she could rest her chin on her knees. 'I just don't like him. Just because you do. Kissing him and all that... like this...'

Frances smacked her lips imitating the sound of the kisses Ruby had exchanged with Gareth Stead.

Ruby was furious. 'Frances Sweet! Just you wait...'

Ruby threw back the bedding and rolled out of bed, but her cousin was too fast for her. In a trice she was out of bed and out of the door, her footsteps thudding down the stairs, her voice rippling with laughter.

'Sometimes I hate that child,' Ruby murmured.

Mary rolled over on to her back and stared thoughtfully up at the ceiling. All this talk of war and friction between members of the family tried even her patience.

She looked over at Ruby who was already brushing her hair so that a silky tress fell over the mole on her cheek. Her routine never varied. The first thing she always did when she got out of bed was to arrange her hair to hide the mole.

'You used to love her.'

'Well, today I hate her. Really,' said Ruby, shaking her head. 'I just cannot cope with her taking against Gareth like she does.'

'Perhaps she's jealous that you're fond of somebody else besides her.'

Ruby reached for her stockings, rolled up together on the bedroom chair. 'It's all over between me and him! Bright lights here I come!'

Having fastened her girdle and pulled up one stocking, Ruby sprang to her feet hoisting up her skirt so she could fasten her suspender, snapping it into place with an air of finality.

Mary was glad to hear it but refrained from saying so. Ruby was rarely receptive to criticism – one of the reasons why her baking wasn't as good as it should be.

'I will miss you,' Mary said softly.

Ruby finished brushing down her skirt and looked at her sister. 'I'm very grateful, you know. Really I am.'

Mary, hands folded behind her head, sighed. 'It was just a loaf of bread. Pies, bread, and such like, it's only food.'

Ruby disliked the pensive expression on Mary's face. She badly wanted to express exactly how she felt about Mary's generosity. She could have said that Mary had always been the better baker, but she held back.

'Shame about it getting stepped on,' Mary added. 'Clumsy oaf. I presume it was a man.'

Ruby was angry too and not just for his clumsiness. The way he'd declared his entry an Italian classic annoyed her, what with that and having to share a prize with him.

'That man who put tomatoes into his entry. He said he should have won outright. He said the British people had no taste and no imagination when it came to food and that the apple loaf was mundane and didn't deserve to be placed.'

Mary sat bolt upright. 'He said that to you?'

'Yes,' said Ruby. 'Didn't you notice he was a bit full of himself?'

Mary was hesitant. 'Not really. I was concentrating on the competition.'

The truth was she could still hear his voice in her head and could still see those expressive eyes. But what he said about British food was inexcusable.

'Well, he was downright rude when he was stood next to me up on the rostrum. Right arrogant sod he was. American, I think.'

'I don't care what he was. He's got a cheek. What does he know about British food?'

Ruby shrugged. 'If he's not British, it can't be a lot. But he definitely had a very sarcastic attitude. Mind you, he didn't say it too loud. He said it quietly so no one else could hear.'

Mary immediately raised herself on to her elbows. 'He said that and then stepped on my bread?'

'Like I said, he had a foreign accent. I hear he's staying with Mrs

Hicks at Stratham House. I think they're related.' Ruby frowned as a suspicious thought came to her. 'Do you think he might be one of them fifth columnists they were on about at the pub? Sent here by that bloke Hitler to find out our secrets and make us feel bad about ourselves?'

'I wouldn't have thought a spy would head for Oldland Common and enter a baking competition,' Mary replied while trying not to laugh.

'Well he did. He also said that women didn't make good bakers and that apple bread was a peasant bread. It was his fault I dropped it. And then he stepped on it.'

Mary sat up.

'He did it on purpose?'

'More or less,' Ruby grumbled.

She eyed her sister sidelong, waiting for Mary to get on her high horse about all things British.

'The cheeky sod! He stepped on my bread!'

The moment she was out of bed, Mary began grabbing clothes. Ruby instantly regretted expanding on the truth. The judge had said his entry was an Italian classic and Michael Dangerfield had merely confirmed it. He certainly hadn't meant to step on the loaf she'd dropped. But once a lie was out it was hard to take it back.

'What are you going to do?' she asked not daring to admit she'd lied.

'I'm off to have a word with our foreign friend. You said he was staying at Stratham House?'

'Well, yes...'

Ruby chewed at her bottom lip, wondering whether she should admit the truth. Mary was normally a very calm person, but unstoppable when she was roused.

'Then that's where I'm going.'

'Breakfast! What about breakfast?' Ruby shouted after her, regretting that she'd embroidered the truth a little.

Mary waved over her shoulder. 'I'm having him for breakfast,' she shouted.

'Wait.'

Mary didn't wait and Ruby couldn't find her shoes.

* * *

True to her word, Mary marched off down along the High Street to Court Road and up the side road to Stratham House.

The house was stone built and although quite grand-looking, wasn't much larger than most of the cottages in the area. The main house looked imposingly detached but was in fact still linked to the shop at the front and the row of cottages running along one side and on a high terrace and approached up a flight of worn stone steps.

The grocery shop at the front was run by Miriam Powell and her mother. It sold everything from bacon to buckets and bulls-eyes. The blinds were down today and the door looked dusty. On weekdays Miriam would be out there cleaning everything, but today was Sunday and Gertrude, Miriam's mother, forbade any form of work on the Lord's Day. Every Sunday without fail they attended the morning service at the Methodist church, the Sunday School at the Baptist mission where they read from the Bible, and in the evening they attended the service at St Anne's, the parish church.

Mrs Powell, a rat-faced woman with jet black eyes and matching hair, favoured all denominations with her presence. Mary presumed it was some kind of insurance policy just in case when she got to heaven she found one church was more favoured than another.

A pair of high wrought-iron double gates protected the entrance to Stratham House itself. The garden was surrounded by an equally high wall.

The iron catch rattled and the rusty hinges squeaked as she pushed the gate open.

Beyond the wall and mass of trees and bushes, the garden was a haven, an apron of green fronting the house and edged by flower beds.

She paused for a moment while she considered whether it was worth proceeding. Perhaps she'd been too hasty. But, after a moment's reflection, she decided that she might have forgiven his comments about her *peasant* bread. However, to purposely knock her loaf to the ground and then step on it...

Stratham House hadn't changed much since the day it was built. This included the garden path, wide enough for two people, small flagstones laid on rough earth, though now tufts of grass and small wildflowers were growing in the cracks.

Mary was wearing court shoes, the heel just over two inches high, and she was looking straight ahead at the front door. Court shoes and a flagstone path did not mix. She tipped forward on to one foot, the other falling out of her trapped shoe, the heel stuck in a crack.

It was easy enough to pull the heel out, but just as she was about to slip her foot back into the shoe, she heard barking.

Suddenly, there he was: the biggest, blackest dog she had ever seen, bounding towards her, ears flying and barking for all it was worth.

Although the dog was wagging its tail, that didn't mean it was friendly. Both shoes now back on her feet, she ran for the gate, yanked it open and closed it swiftly behind her.

Craning her neck, she looked beyond the high hedges of lilac, birch, climbing roses and honeysuckle, all of which smothered the air in scent.

Although the dog continued to bark, nobody came out of the house to investigate, the door was firmly shut, the windows reflecting the sky and garden.

'Hello, doggy,' she said softly.

The dog continued to bark and wag his tail.

A well-mannered dog, Mary decided, not at all the sort to bite should I be brave enough to push this gate open and enter his territory.

Nobody came out in response to the monotonous barking so she presumed they were either deaf or the dog was a compulsive animal that barked for no reason and thus was ignored.

She applied pressure to the latch. 'Here goes,' she murmured before pushing it the rest of the way. The gate creaked open again, she took a deep breath and slid through.

The dog went crazy, the tail wagging stopped, the bark turned into a far from engaging snarl. It took a lunge forward, its jaws clamping on the hem of her dress.

Mary screamed as the dress ripped.

'Felix!'

She heard his voice and immediately felt a mix of anger and something else that made her stomach churn. It was him, Michael Dangerfield, the man she'd met at the baking competition.

'Felix. Less of that, boy.'

Strong fingers hooked into the dog's collar, yanking him back so the animal was almost standing on its back legs.

'Hi there! You! From yesterday. Are you all right?'

Mary was instantly disarmed. If he had made the comments Ruby had repeated or stepped on her bread there was no sign of guilt in his expression.

The dog had finally shut up and was only wagging its tail.

Flustered but more determined to speak her mind, Mary eyed

her torn hem with dismay and there and then decided somebody had to pay.

'Just look at my dress!'

The man chewed his lips as he eyed the torn hem. She blushed on realising that one of her stocking suspenders was showing. It seemed that her new friend had noticed it too, his gaze lingering just that bit too long.

'Hey. I'm sorry. He's never done this before. I suppose it's because he's not really used to women.'

Mary bristled with indignation. 'I don't care what he's used to and it doesn't mean he has to try and eat one on sight.'

Michael Dangerfield grinned. 'Can't say I blame him.'

Mary's blush deepened. 'It's not funny.'

She gathered up the torn material so her stocking top was hidden from view.

'Sorry. 'Course it's not. Never mind. I'll buy you a new one.'

'I don't want a new one,' she snapped, annoyed with how that look in his eyes made her feel. 'I want this one. It's my favourite dress.'

It wasn't quite true, but she wasn't going to let this man off the hook that easily.

'Very nice,' he said, eyeing the dress with more than a passing interest on what lay beneath it.

Mary felt hot all over. 'That dog is dangerous!'

Michael Dangerfield made a so-so kind of action with his hands. 'Let's just say he's just a bit overprotective.'

'Then you should train it better.'

'He's not mine. I'm looking after it for a friend. He's gone to Saundersfoot – that's in Wales – while he still can. He loves the thing. Found him when he was a puppy and he was at a loss. I think a girlfriend had given him the farewell and don't bother to collect the thing. The puppy was at a loss too, though I don't think it had anything to do with girlfriends. I think he just got abandoned. All the guys at Scampton are fond of it.'

She detected an accent. Ruby had been right. He sounded American. And he was good-looking. The eyes that had reflected his smile yesterday still smiled at her today and only his bold looks and the torn dress stopped her from smiling back.

He's arrogant, she told herself. He's not just smiling at me, he's laughing at me, and that blasted dog...

'Then he should be home looking after it not gallivanting off to that place in Wales you just mentioned.'

'Saundersfoot,' he said, his smile undiminished. 'He's gone on honeymoon. Not that he'll be that long coming back. Not now, the way things are going. He'll be back in Scampton before very long.'

'Where's Scampton?'

'It's an air base in Lincolnshire. RAF.'

'You're a pilot?'

He nodded. 'Sure am.' A more serious expression replaced the smile. 'Look, I'm sorry, but seeing as things are hotting up I do have to hurry away. You'll be glad to know I'll be taking Felix with me...' He began rummaging in his trouser pockets. 'Let me settle this. Guy will reimburse me wherever we end up.'

'Perhaps you might suggest keeping the dog chained up or—'

His mouth set in a grim line. 'I hardly think that's necessary. It's just a dress.'

'It could just as easily have been my leg.'

'I agree with you. That would have been awful. Here. Take this money. Will that be enough to buy you a new dress?'

She was inclined to snap back that she couldn't possibly let the matter rest there and perhaps it should be reported to the police, but somehow she couldn't bring herself to do that.

'Your name's Mary Sweet. Is that right?'

'Yes.'

'I'm sorry about your bread. If it hadn't been for the pig...'

'Pig?' What was he talking about?

'It was the pig's fault. Didn't your sister say? Funny how you and me get tied up with animals? Here we are with Felix and yesterday your sister's loaf got trodden on thanks to a pig.'

Mary's jaw dropped. 'My apple bread... my sister's apple bread got trodden on because of a pig?'

'Yep,' he said with a jerk of his chin. 'An escaped pig ran by pursued by what looked like a lynch mob. I turned, bumped into your sister, she dropped the bread and my size ten right foot stepped on it.' He paused. 'Or did she tell you a different story?'

A pig. Ruby hadn't said a word about a pig.

'I just happened to mention her hairstyle and she stalked off. Does she have a problem with compliments?'

Mary shook her head and promised herself to have more than a few strong words with her sister.

'She has a mole...' she said hesitantly while touching her left cheek.

She tried not to stare, but it was difficult. His looks appealed to her. Why is that, she asked herself? He's no Errol Flynn or Clark Gable. He has wrinkles at the corners of his eyes and his teeth are too perfect. And I don't like men with fair hair. I like dark hair.

'So how about I buy you a new dress?'

'I'll get it mended,' she heard herself say, shaking her head at the crisp one-pound note he was offering. 'I'll call back once I know how much it's likely to cost.'

'Sorry,' he said, refusing to take the money back and glancing at his watch. 'But I can't hang around. I've got a train to catch.'

His response was irritating because he sounded as though the matter was settled and too trivial to consider further. That in itself angered her.

'Oh, so you're going to scurry off home are you, safe in the knowledge that money can buy or settle anything? I think that's just a shade irresponsible.'

He winced though his eyes stayed fixed on her, as though he was looking into everything she was and ever had been and wanted to know more.

'I've already apologised. Keep the money. Buy a new dress, buy a bicycle or a tea cosy or anything else you might fancy, but the matter has to end here and now. I can't hang around. I've got more important matters to attend to.'

Mary bristled. So! Despite that winning smile, he really did consider the matter done and dusted.

'Well!' she said, her anger undiminished. 'You may not be the fifth columnist my sister thought you were, but you're certainly not a gentleman brushing off my problem like this.'

'Fifth columnist!' He laughed at that, his laugh deep and throaty and in an odd kind of way, highly addictive in that she wanted to hear it again – and again.

'She told me what you said about my... her apple bread.'

He turned his head to one side so he was almost in profile, a half-smile playing around his lips. 'Excuse me?'

'My sister told me that you said my... our... her... anyway, you said you should have won the competition out-right and that British people had no taste, that apple bread was mundane.'

His smile petered out as though she'd hit him rather than blasted him with accusation.

He shook his head. 'I didn't say that, but I haven't got the time to stand here and argue. I have to be going.'

'Back to whatever country you're from?'

He looked amused. 'I'm Canadian. My father was English, Aunt Bettina's brother in fact. My mother was Italian. That's where I got the recipe from. My family has a bakery in Winnipeg. Now look,' he said taking another glance at his watch. 'I do have to go to war. You do know that don't you? Your prime minister, Mr Chamberlain, broadcast fifteen minutes ago. He gave the Nazis two hours to get out of Poland, but they're not budging.' He shrugged. 'Looks like I might have a pretty serious job to do. A whole load of us have joined up. There were plenty of openings in the RAF for us colonials. And the pay's not too bad.'

Mary had intended saying that if she saw him at the bake off next week it would be too early for her, but that wasn't what came out.

'Where is it you have to be?'

'Scampton. It's a bomber base.'

She jerked her chin in silent acknowledgement.

'It's unlikely I'll be going forward to the next round, if that was what you came around to argue about. Might do if I thought I'd see you there, but hey, I've got a bomber to fly. Adolf Hitler's expecting me to pay him a visit. Look. I am sorry about the dog. My friend Guy will be mortified when he hears about Felix's bad behaviour. He'll also be put out that his honeymoon is going to be cut short. Adolf Hitler has no consideration.'

His smile was irresistible.

War! Had she heard right? Was England really at war? 'I didn't know...'

'Will a pound be okay?'

Too surprised to say anything, she nodded. Yes. Of course it was all right. A pound was his share of the winnings from the baking competition. The matter of the dress was now of no consequence. While she's been hounding this man – for more than one reason – a war had broken out.

He noticed her concerned expression. 'Are you okay?'

Mary shrugged as the realisation that what had been building up for months had finally begun. Britain was at war. What would that mean for her family, for Charlie especially?

'Look. I know we've got off on the wrong foot, but I hope I might see you again sometime. I'll spend some of my leave with my aunt, and saying that...'

He looked again at his watch. 'Hell. Time I was leaving. Can't stop. Have to say goodbye to my aunt before I take off. Felix will be going with me. Just to be on the safe side, I'll tie him up while I let you out.' She realised he was referring to the dog.

She watched him walk down the garden path dragging the dog with him. Stretching, he took down the clothes line, lashing it into the dog's collar and tying it to the post. She watched it all silently, her thoughts elsewhere although she did recall he'd suggested they meet again.

He smiled down at her. 'I wish I had time to at least walk you home, but things being the way they are...'

'It's finally happened,' she muttered, feeling as though somebody had tipped a bucket of cold water over her head. 'Everything now seems so... trivial in comparison. Though I still think my bread was worthy of winning,' she added quickly, not wanting him to feel he'd got the better of her.

'I didn't say it wasn't worthy, and anyway, I thought your sister baked it.'

Her eyes met his shoulder before lifting to study his face.

His expression and tone seemed sincere enough.

'My sister...' She stopped. 'Perhaps she misunderstood.'

'You can say that again, but hey. It's water under the bridge,' he said as he opened the gate to let her out.

'Yes. In more ways than one,' she said, her anger all but gone. The news of war had altered everything.

'I'll see you again?'

She nodded. 'I expect so.'

'I have to go.'

An odd wailing sound suddenly rent the air which set the dog

howling before he lay down flat on the ground, his paws over his
ears.

'Air-raid sirens,' said Michael, his eyes narrowed as he looked
up at the sky before smiling reassuringly at her. 'Don't worry. It's
only a test run. Hopefully that's all it will ever be.'

The dog continued to howl.

'He's got sensitive ears,' said Michael.

'It's a dreadful sound.'

'Until we meet again.'

'Yes. I have to go. My family will be wondering where I am.'

What she meant was that they too would have heard the wail of
the sirens and wondered if anything drastic was about to happen.

'Be my guest.' He opened the gate wide, his eyes watching her
with interested intensity.

She could feel that look, but couldn't bring herself to meet it. All
she wanted was to get home. Once through the gate, she began
to run.

'No need to run,' he called after her. 'Nothing happens that
quickly.'

'And how do you know,' she whispered, her legs kicking high
out behind her despite the height of her heels. How much do any of
us know? she thought. We didn't know this was going to happen
today, so how can we know what will happen tomorrow, in the next
hour, in the next minute?

Getting hot under the collar about a silly loaf of bread now
seemed excessively stupid; focusing on a baking competition, she'd
ignored the portents of bad things happening.

There'd been talk for days that the world was on the brink of
war. The German army had invaded Poland on the first of
September and all she could think about was winning a stupid
competition! Would there even be a semi-final in Bristol? And what
about the final in London? Worst of all, what about Ruby? She'd set

her heart on leaving home. Would it be easier or more difficult to leave now?

Then there was Charlie. He'd already stated his intention to join the merchant navy.

'I don't fight much, but I do eat,' he'd said to them laughingly. 'I'll bake bread and cook food for the blokes who guard the grub. That's the job for a baker!'

By the time she reached the end of Court Road, the air-raid siren sited on top of the village hall had ceased its ear-splitting wail.

She ran all the way back along the High Street to the bakery, surprised that the village was so quiet, that nobody was around, and that not even the bells of St Anne's were ringing to call people to prayer.

It was as though the world was holding its breath, people tuned into the BBC, waiting for the next step. Pray God no bombs fall here, she thought, as she ran straight to the open door of the bakery and into her father's arms.

'Mary! Thank God you're safe.' His worried expression lifted.

'I'm fine, Dad.'

Stan noticed the rip in her dress. 'What happened?'

'I caught it on a bramble bush.' She knew better than to mention the dog. Her father might report it and she didn't want him to. The lives of Michael and his friend Guy were about to be disrupted enough.

'You should be more careful.'

'Dad? Where's Scampton?'

'I'm not sure. Lincolnshire I think. Why do you ask?'

'Someone I know is going there. He's a pilot. Have you heard the news? We're at war!'

6

That Sunday was the first time ever the Sweet family ate their roast lunch in silence. The beef was succulent and marbled with enough fat to moisten and tenderise the meat, the roast potatoes crisp and neatly browned at the edges, the cabbage, peas and carrots freshly dug from the garden.

Mary had baked an apple and blackberry pie for dessert.

Ruby managed to burn the custard.

'Ruby! Whatever's the matter with you?'

'I lied about Michael Dangerfield purposely stepping on the bread.'

Mary stopped laying the table and looked at her. 'Why?'

Ruby took the saucepan and its contents outside to the pig bin. On her return she braced herself for telling the truth.

'He criticised British baking and British taste. I thought it was unpatriotic. Well, it is, but then when you told me he was with the RAF, over here to fight – well. I shouldn't have done it.'

'No. You shouldn't.' Mary took the apple pie out of the oven, setting it on top of the stove.

'Do you forgive me?'

'Of course I do,' Mary said brightly. 'We'll just have to make do with tinned cream instead!'

On being told it was to be tinned cream rather than custard, Stan Sweet raised his eyes in distaste but then resigned himself that he had to put up with it. Ruby seemed to be taking the news of this war worse than any of them. On the other hand nobody was quite themselves today and who could blame them?

At the end of the meal, Stan pushed his plate away and prepared to put his thoughts into words. His children read the signs and knew he had something to say.

'Leave the washing up for a minute,' he said when Mary moved to take the dirty dishes. 'Ruby. Get some glasses. Charlie, get that bottle of sherry we were saving for Christmas. And Ruby, get a glass for Frances. I know she's only a child, but we'll all be needing a bit of liquid courage before this lot's over.'

'Do you want to do the honours, Dad?' asked Charlie. He held the bottle with both hands as he passed it to his father, as though afraid he would drop it.

'Might as well.'

Stan Sweet poured a measure of sherry into each glass, a half measure for Frances.

The glasses were passed round, each family member refraining from drinking until their father gave the word, though if left to their own devices they'd knock back the lot: the situation called for it.

Pressing down on the table with both hands, Stan Sweet rose to his feet and reached for his glass. The rest of the family followed suit.

'To our family,' he said, raising his glass in a toast. 'Dark days are coming. May God protect us all.'

His son and daughters repeated the toast. 'May God protect us all.'

Frances, pleased at first to be given her first grown-up drink, had wondered why everyone had been so quiet when they were eating their meal. She hadn't heard the BBC broadcast because she'd been too busy hiding her snail farm under the bed while the twins were not around. Frances liked snails. She also found insects quite fascinating. She knew from the worried tones she'd been hearing over the last few weeks that war was bad. Very bad.

Her face turned white as she scrutinised her cousins and her uncle. Her uncle had asked God to protect them. But could he? He hadn't protected her father. He hadn't stopped her mother from leaving... What if?

There was a loud thud as she returned her glass to the table before bursting into tears and running from the room.

Mary made to go after her, but her father bid her stay. 'Leave her, Mary. It might be just as well she doesn't hear what I'm about to say. First things first. As you know, I fought in the last war, baking bread for the soldiers at the front and using a rifle and a bayonet when I had to. I fear this one is going to be worse than that and all of you, all of you,' he stressed a second time, 'will be involved in it one way or another. To what extent you'll be involved and in what field, we don't yet know, but I remember enough from the last lot to know that what they was saying on the wireless is right: this island is incapable of feeding itself. So let's pour another drink. Matter of fact, why don't we finish the bottle. It might be the last we'll see for a while.'

By the time the bottle was finished, they spoke less nervously, more intensely as though every word counted. The main subject was Charlie making plans to join the merchant navy before his call-up papers arrived, though not until he was sure his family could cope without him.

Even when the girls began to clear the table and wash up, the conversation continued against a background noise of clattering pans and crockery.

'Call up's likely to be men under forty,' said Charlie. He was looking and acting subdued yet both twins detected a sparkle in his eyes. So did his father but pretended nothing had changed. Inside he worried deeply. He'd seen that sparkle back in the days of the last war, a young man's yearning for excitement. For most of them it was also their first foray into a foreign country.

A lot of those young men had never come home. He hoped and prayed his son would survive or that the great powers even now might come to their senses before a terrible tragedy unfolded.

Despite everything, Stan Sweet felt obliged to keep their spirits up even though his heart was breaking. His country would want his children, especially his son. He didn't want to hand them over. He was the one who'd raised them. There had been no government official to give a hand when one of them woke crying in the middle of the night, sick with measles or some other childhood ailment. Where was his country when he needed it? And now his country would send his son to war.

He sipped more sherry to help him concentrate and say what he wanted to say.

'Yes, there'll certainly be a call up. There'll be rationing too. Bound to be. They brought rationing in too late at the end of the last war. My guess is it'll come in earlier this time – that's if they've learned their lesson from doing too little too late. We need to take stock of what we have, both for the bakery and for our own stomachs. It's a sin to hoard, but let's just say everything will count in this year's harvest festival. Nothing's to be wasted and everything that doesn't ruin must be stored. I fancy putting in some early broad beans. And if you can find me some old net curtains, I'll throw them over the sprouts. No sense in making a gift of greens to the snails and sparrows. Let 'em go plant their own!'

They all managed a subdued laugh.

Leaving Ruby to clear the last of the dishes, Mary excused herself. 'I'll just go and see how Frances is.'

While taking the dirty plates and crockery to the sink, Ruby cocked an ear to what was going on.

'They'll be calling you up, Charlie. We know that.'

'And the girls? I hear it's on the cards.'

Stan Sweet held his glass in both hands, gazing at the dark red liquid so he could concentrate his thoughts and control his expression. He didn't want them to know that he was worried the girls might be called up too.

''Course, women did a lot in the last war,' he said. 'Munitions, factory work, driving trams and even enrolling in the services, only office jobs and such like, but it did get them away from the kitchen sink, that's for sure. I reckon this time they'll end up doing even more in the services now, even go abroad to the front line I shouldn't wonder.'

'Getting away from the kitchen sink? Well, that's for me,' exclaimed Ruby, halfway between table and a sink brimming with dirty dishes immersed in hot water. In order to tackle the grease, she'd thrown in a handful of soda crystals.

Stan Sweet wished he hadn't said anything, not with Ruby within earshot. 'You'll be safer at the kitchen sink, my girl.'

'Perhaps I don't want to be safe,' she said somewhat crossly.

Her father threw her a warning look. 'You've no idea what it means to be in danger. Stay put, Ruby. That's my advice to you.'

'Isn't that up to the government?' Her face was turned away, her hands now in the hot water. The steam rose in a thick cloud, reddening her face and plastering her hair to her head.

Mention of women being called up had grabbed her attention. There was still a chance of getting away from the village and she sorely wanted to get away. News of her no longer pulling pints behind the bar of the Apple Tree had spread. Various conclusions had probably been made and Gareth himself would have added fuel to the fire. She could hear him now. *'Oh, she was a hussy that one. And me an innocent widower.'*

Then there were his other women, the ones who smiled at him, winked and hinted at things that might have gone on between them, things she'd refused to believe. She believed them now and the thought that people were lumping her in with them rankled.

She'd seen a few housewives tittering behind their fat hands, women with hands red from laundry and household tasks. She brought one of her hands out of the water. It was very pink. In time it would be like theirs, reddened through being immersed in hot water, the prerequisite of most household tasks.

She washed the dishes quickly while listening to her father and brother exchanging views on what would happen next and how the British forces, along with the French, would stack up against the Germans.

After wiping her hands on a tea towel, Ruby pulled her hair from behind one ear and over her face. Her mole safely hidden, she joined them at the table.

'What sort of things would they want women to do this time do you think?' She adopted a disinterested expression, as though getting involved in war work was the last thing on her mind.

Her father regarded her with a concerned frown. He'd been led to believe that twins were alike in every way. He knew from experience that this wasn't quite true. His girls looked alike, but differed in character. Mary was the strong, serious one while Ruby could be careless and defiant. It was that defiance he feared. He could see it in her eyes and wished it wasn't there. Soon, very soon, she would leave and there was nothing he could do about it. Still, now that she'd asked, he couldn't deny explaining what he thought women might end up doing.

'Nursing of course. There'll always be nursing to do and if

things do get going, we're going to need a lot of women to do it. Things on the home front, like driving a bus or tram like they did in the last war.' He refrained from mentioning that they'd also driven ambulances behind the front line. He was worried enough about his boy going to war. He couldn't bear the thought of his girls going too. He didn't want to lose any of his children. He'd fought too hard to keep them alive.

'I could join the women's services. Wrens, or the Women's Royal Air Force.'

'Hey! You're missing out the army,' said Charlie.

Ruby grinned and shook her head. 'I don't look good in khaki, but I do look good in blue.'

'It's not a fashion parade,' Charlie exclaimed.

'Girls will still be girls,' Ruby retorted.

Their laughter helped lift the sombre mood, though their father only smiled a little sadly. He was thinking of his wife, their mother.

When Sarah died of the 'flu back in 1919, he'd vowed over her grave that he'd move heaven and earth to bring his children up just as she would have wanted.

He'd sacrificed a lot to keep to that promise, including his own happiness. He'd remained a widower.

Although other women had expressed an interest in the broad-shouldered man with the same dark hair as his children, he'd abstained from getting involved. He'd made a promise to Sarah and he would damn well stick to it.

Charlie had been three years old when his mother had died.

The twins had only been babies.

People had expressed that a man on his own couldn't possibly bring up young babies, but he'd ignored their sorry shaking of heads. His parents had still been alive when they were babies. With their help the children had thrived, and even once they were gone, dead and buried in St Anne's churchyard, he'd had Sefton to help in the bakery, the two brothers doing a good job to keep things going despite Sefton's slovenly wife.

Ultimately Stan had proved them wrong and was proud of his children. Frances, too. Very proud indeed.

He would do anything and everything to protect them from harm. The armed forces would insist on taking Charlie, but the girls? He would do all in his power to keep them at home.

7

Mary knocked quietly before entering the bedroom she shared with her sister and cousin. The room had two dormer windows, floral wallpaper and gingham-checked curtains. The dressing table, wardrobe and chest of drawers had once belonged to their grandparents. There was something safe and solid about the rich mahogany, the solid lines, the heavy brass handles on the drawers and the wardrobe doors.

Frances was lying face down on the single bed positioned in the alcove at one end of the room which ran the full length of the house. It wasn't much in the way of privacy but served its purpose and each of them had plenty of space.

Her cousin's shoulders were shaking following a period of sobbing.

'Frances?' Mary sat down on the edge of the bed, then reached out and gently stroked the dark hair, so similar to her own and the rest of the family.

Frances's hair was usually fastened in two thick braids. Right now it was undone, two white ribbons thrown on to the floor, and each braid half undone.

'Is it the war?' Mary asked softly. Frances nodded into her pillow.

Mary smiled. 'You mustn't be frightened. Nothing bad will happen to you, and besides, our country hasn't fired a shot yet. They might still come to some agreement.'

In her heart Mary thought it unlikely. The German regime had swallowed up half of Europe. Unless they backtracked pretty quickly, the war would most definitely occur.

'I can't... help... it,' Frances snivelled into her pillow. 'What if we get bombed? What if you all die? You're the only family I've got left!'

Mary smiled ruefully. 'I don't think that's likely to happen. After all, Oldland Common is only a village and we're on the outskirts of Bristol.'

It occurred to Mary that they weren't far from the aircraft factories at Filton so might be in more danger than first imagined. Best not to say it, she decided. Frances was frightened enough.

'Will soldiers march in?'

'I take it you mean German soldiers.'

Frances nodded.

'They'll have to be very good swimmers. They have to cross the English Channel before they come marching in. Invading England isn't that easy. It never has been, in fact it's been nearly a thousand years since the last time it happened.'

Frances turned her big brown eyes on her. 'Really?' Grateful she'd paid attention in the history lesson about William the Conqueror in the year 1066, Mary said that it was indeed the case.

'I don't... want... to lose my family... I'm frightened.'

Mary raised her from the bed and wrapped her arms around her, the girl's head resting on her shoulder.

'You mustn't think that way. No matter what happens, I'll always be there for you.'

She closed her eyes as she said it. Poor little Frances. She'd never realised before that the cheeky grin and effervescent vitality hid such a sensitive little soul. She felt for her.

Uncle Sefton had died of injuries sustained during the Great War when Frances was only four years old. Apparently a piece of shrapnel had altered position, sawed through a blood vessel and caused internal bleeding. The bleeding had not been noticed until it was too late.

Her mother, Mildred, unable to face the responsibilities of raising a child on her own and with nothing but a war widow's pension, had taken off. Nothing had been heard of her since.

Stan had taken the child in, caring for her as he did his own. At times a little wild, they had all accepted Frances more as a baby sister than a cousin. The girl needed a mother figure, and if it had to be Mary, then so be it.

Mary stroked her cousin's hair away from her hot forehead. 'Anyway, there's still time. It may never happen. A pilot in the RAF told me that,' she said, hoping to reassure the girl. 'Did he?'

Mary thought about her ripped dress and the black dog. She also thought about Michael Dangerfield.

On reflection, there had been a lot to like about Michael Dangerfield. She now very much regretted running off like that, almost as though she'd expected the bakery to be surrounded by an invading army when she got home; he must have thought her a total fool.

The whole of today's episode now seemed a wasted opportunity. They could have been friends if she hadn't reacted so sharply to the criticism reported to her by Ruby.

Up until this moment, she'd shown little interest in men even though they'd shown interest in her. The local curate had tipped his cap at her, but she couldn't bring herself to see beyond the stiff white collar to the man beneath. And heaven forbid, but marriage to a clergyman did not appeal.

Mr Michael Dangerfield did appeal.

Closing her eyes helped her memorise the laughter lines around his deep blue eyes, the way his hair curled behind his ears, the shape of his jaw and the sound of his voice.

She sighed as she opened her eyes. The moment had passed. He was gone, off to fly aeroplanes, though he had said he'd be back to stay with his aunt when he next had leave. She hoped it wouldn't be too long, but in the meantime it did occur to her to get his address from Mrs Hicks and write to him. It might seem a bit forward, but these were drastic times. Seize the day! Whoever had said that must also have lived through a time of war. Yes, it seemed a good idea.

* * *

It was Monday evening and Ruby was scraping potato peelings into the scraps bin. The contents were destined for the half dozen or so pigs her father kept in partnership with Joe Long, a long-time friend who had no job as such but survived by his wits. He also had a shotgun with which he helped keep down the local rabbit population. Many a poor family survived on the generosity of Joe Long and his rabbits.

On straightening she regarded the two flower beds either side of the garden path. Another path divided the flower beds from the rest of the garden where kidney beans trailed from thick foliage like long green fingers and rows of other vegetables had been recently planted by her father in straight lines, a bit like soldiers going into battle. The beans were nearly over but other vegetables were beginning to flourish.

Dad is planning ahead, thought Ruby, and instinctively knew he was right to do so. The planting of leeks and cabbages was as important as guns, ships and soldiers in uniform.

Some people were saying that city folk would fare better than country folk. Others said that living in the country was a blessing. As least they had room to grow things. Everyone in the village grew their own vegetables already; if one gardener had too many of one crop, he or she would willingly swap it for something else: cabbage for cauliflower, kidney beans for carrots.

In the case of her father's friend Joe Long, he would willingly swap a couple of wood pigeons, rabbit or hare for a bucket of potatoes. He'd even been known to pay for his beer in the Apple Tree or the Three Horseshoes with a dead pheasant. Nobody asked where it had come from: game was plentiful and even private land was fair shooting territory to a man like Joe.

Ruby frowned at the memory of seeing Joe Long doing a deal with Gareth. Gareth had only been willing to let Joe have two pints in exchange for a rabbit. Her father had called Gareth a mean sod when he'd heard about it. Ruby had turned deaf to the comment, taking Gareth's side. She'd always refused to hear anything bad about him, but that was when she'd considered herself in love with him. But now?

Being foolish was bad enough, but there was also the hurt to cope with. She'd wanted things to be very different.

The sound of the fork screeching against the enamel saucepan made her grit her teeth as she scraped the last of the vegetable peelings into the bin.

'Ruby?'

Her father emerged from the kitchen, pausing to strike a match on the stout stone of which the house was built. The smell of pipe smoke, puffed from a brown briar she'd bought him for his last birthday, mingled with the crisp smells of evening and the sweetness of autumn fruit.

Ruby poured water from the butt into the bin, slopping it round before throwing it on to the garden, all the while aware of her father eyeing her thoughtfully.

Another lecture, she thought petulantly. He'd already lectured her on the foolishness of getting involved with older men. Now she was about to get another, a few words of wisdom that she wasn't sure she wanted to hear.

'You know,' he said after a few puffs on his pipe. 'I always thought you or your sister might have been married by now. Thought I might also have had a nipper – grandson or granddaughter – by now. How about you and Gareth Stead? Any hope is there?'

Ruby blushed. This was not at all what she'd expected! Her dad had changed his tune considerably!

'Dad! Me and Gareth are finished with and there's nobody else in view. Anyway, there's plenty of time. I'm only twenty.'

He lowered his eyes as he bit on the end of his pipe. 'Your mother was only seventeen when we were wed. Had to, of course, your brother being on the way.'

'I'm not exactly an old maid!' Ruby blurted, once she'd got over the shock of her father being so open with her, though on reflection she'd always known there was only six months between her parents' marriage and her brother's birth.

He shook his head. 'No. No. Of course you're not.'

Ruby put the bin down and wiped her hands down her apron. Talking about marriage and babies after what Gareth Stead had put her through was unsettling. The conversation was crying out to be changed, and it looked as if it was she who must do it.

She took out a cigarette from the packet of Woodbines in her pocket and lit up. The smoke curled upwards.

'Dad, you're not angry about me taking Mary's place at the baking competition are you? You know, entering it in my name and going up to claim the prize?'

When he looked at her, he lifted both dark eyebrows. He had the same colour eyes as she and Mary, the same enquiring set to his chin, and the same dark hair, though now a little thin on top. 'Did I say I was?'

She shook her head.

'I know what you were about; if either of you are going to leave home, you're the one. Though I'll worry about you, my girl in Bristol or London – baking or not. Frightening places, big cities. Still,' he said with a heave of his shoulders, 'might not happen now, not with a war being declared. There's more important things to do than enter competitions. Baking bread is going to be important and so's making the most of what we've got.'

Hit with a sudden pang of disappointment, Ruby realised he was right. 'I might still go away. Women are likely to get called up too. You said so yourself.'

Stan Sweet knocked the pipe against the wall of the house dislodging the tobacco even though there was plenty left for smoking.

Ruby was the child who caused him the most concern. She had such a strident way about her that for the moment there was no pleasure in smoking. The taste of fear was in his mouth and nothing could smother it, not even his favourite pipe tobacco.

'I would prefer you not to join up. You know that don't you.'

'But I might have to,' she said with a defiant lifting of her chin.

'Not if you were married. How about you and Stead making it up? Is there any chance?'

Ruby couldn't believe what she was hearing. He'd been dead set against her relationship with Gareth Stead and had disapproved of her working behind the bar.

'Dad! I'm not going to throw myself at him.'

'You mean he hasn't asked you. Still, in time...'

Suddenly she recognised what this was all about. He needed

hope, he didn't want her to go away as Charlie surely would. And in her father's eyes it was better her married to a man like Gareth Stead and close to home than far away, perhaps near to where a battle was raging.

But she couldn't lie. Now, more than ever, she wanted to get away.

'It wasn't marriage he wanted,' she said quietly, turned and went back into the kitchen.

She left him there tapping the stem of his pipe against his palm, his eyes seeking the last rays of the setting sun, streaming salmon pink through the old plum trees at the bottom of the garden.

Suddenly he felt very lonely and wished with all his heart that Sarah was still alive, but then, life, he'd decided long ago, was often unfair. All you could do was live it and accept the consequences. It didn't stop him from missing his wife every day.

His shoulders bathed in the dying warmth of the sun, he wandered the garden paths, eyeing the fruits of his labour without really seeing them. Concern for his children made him forgo his coat hanging on the back of the kitchen door. The evening wasn't that cold anyway, a lovely September, despite the declaration of war casting its shadow.

His footsteps took him out of the garden and along the High Street where he turned into Court Road and headed down into the valley. At the bottom of Court Road he crossed the bridge spanning the brook and walked up the steep incline on the other side of the narrow road to St Anne's church. Once within its grounds he made his way to Sarah's grave.

At the sound of fluttering wings, he glanced up to see a bat drop from the church tower, circling silently before returning to its roost. Something scurried through the long grass. Life existed even among the gravestones.

The air was cool, a slight breeze sending the first fallen leaves rustling through the cornstalks in the field next door and making them rattle like a peel of rusty bells.

Stan Sweet headed for the quiet spot shaded by a silver birch where his wife was buried. Even though she'd died twenty years before, he still came here to speak to her. In the early years he'd told her about the twins taking their first steps, Mary walking before Ruby. Not that Ruby had been outdone for long, struggling on to her feet, determined not to be left behind.

He'd also told her about Charlie's first day at school, how hard the lad had found it to leave his favourite toy at home. The funny thing was that following that first day of being a 'big boy', he'd never looked at that old teddy bear again.

'Our Mary is more forward than our Ruby, but all the same, they're like two peas in a pod,' he'd said to her. He'd also promised to do all in his power to keep them safe. Now there was going to be a war. What could he tell her now?

He frowned heavily before bending down on one knee. As he considered what to say, he tugged at a thread of bindweed attempting to climb her headstone. The moment could not be put off forever; he had to tell her the dreadful news.

'There's going to be another war, Sarah.'

A nightingale chose that moment to sing sweetly from the branches of a nearby tree.

Stan tilted his head, almost as though the bird was Sarah and was talking to him.

'I know,' he said to her imagined response. 'They told us it was the war to end all wars but it weren't, me girl. It weren't. I fear for them, Sarah. I fear for all of them and still hope it comes to nothing, but this German chancellor has taken over half of Europe. I can't see it being avoided. God knows when it will end. Funny thing is I've heard some folk say it'll be over by Christmas. Now where have we heard that before?'

He gave a little laugh. In his head he heard her voice expressing her fears and what could be done for the best.

The nightingale stopped singing, replaced by the harsher note of a nightjar.

'Ahh!' he said, which meant yes in the local idiom. 'Our boy favours the navy, not the Royal Navy mind, but the merchant navy seeing as Bristol is so close. He reckons he might get home more often if he joins a ship registered in Bristol. I only hope he's right. And being a boy, I can't stop him from doing that. Anyways, the government will insist he signs up for one of the services no doubt. He's keen to do his bit – just as we all were in the last lot. It's the girls I'm concerned about. I've heard talk that they're likely to get called up too.' He shook his head sadly. 'I'm not having that, Sarah. They might take my son off to war, but they're not having my daughters as well. I won't have it. Over my dead body.'

8

Just as everyone had expected, the next round of the baking competition was cancelled.

'...*it is felt best to cancel this, at least in the short term...*' it said in the letter that Ruby received.

'I hear the picture houses and theatres are closing too. Shame. I did like going to the pictures,' Mary said wistfully.

Ruby was very put out. 'Why? I don't understand. Why?'

'In case a bomb drops on one of them and the audience is killed.'

'I don't need an audience,' grumbled Ruby. 'Just the bloody prize.'

'No need to swear,' said Mary in a chastising tone her father reckoned she'd inherited from her mother. 'And anyway, just bear in mind who really baked that bread.'

Ruby fell silent. Being reminded that her sister had actually baked the bread also reminded her that she'd lied about what had happened to the loaf and been found out. The twins might have had an almighty row if it hadn't been for the outbreak of war. So far it had brought her luck and might yet work to her advantage. She might get called up to work in a munitions factory or even to join the army, the navy or the air force. The prospect excited her.

Now, though, Ruby was lumbered with the laundry which mainly consisted of bed linen and big white aprons they wore in the bakery.

Today it was Mary's turn to serve in the shop out front while her father and brother tended to the last batch of bread, though it wasn't only bread in the hot oven this morning. Mrs Martin, a farmer's wife, had brought in a huge leg of pork the night before. No normal oven could have taken such a large haunch of meat, and Stan didn't mind helping her out, especially at the mention of a bit of pork for himself.

'Old Spot had to go,' Mrs Martin explained. 'He was gettin' on and I've got a growing family to feed.'

In her late fifties, Mrs Martin's arms were almost as meaty as the pork she'd presented. Busy on the farm, she didn't get much chance to talk to other people, so when she was out she chatted nineteen to the dozen, never giving anyone else a chance to interrupt. She told them all about her son Ronnie being excused the call up because they needed him on the farm. 'We left it up to him. He's a big strong lad and no doubt would have served his country well, but somebody has to feed the troops don't they?'

Stan agreed that feeding the troops was important. He didn't add that Ronnie wasn't that bright, most definitely all brawn and little brain. It made sense for him to stay on the land where all he had to do was what his parents told him to do. Mrs Martin had other sons with a bit more brain and almost as much brawn. Two of them had been called up.

So it was at the time when they'd just fired up the ovens, Mrs Martin was telling them the saga of Old Spot interspersed with other details about her neighbours, the war and anything else that sprang to mind.

'The rest of him's been smoked and salted so it should last us a while. The smoke 'ouse is full enough, so I thought this leg is our feast for the week, what with roasting it, 'aving it cold on Monday, in a pie on Tuesday, stew on Wednesday, minced with onions on Thursday, and faggots on Friday. I kept a bit of liver and lights for doing that fer myself and you got some too. Makes sense to me to fatten ourselves up 'fore rationing comes in and old Masters calls the shots in the butchers. D'you know we're goin' to 'ave to register all our stock and tell 'em when we fattens and kills a pig? And how many suckers the old sow gives birth to? Everything's gotta be accounted for so they says. Now there's a thing!'

Stan agreed that indeed it was something to be reckoned with, but then things always got difficult in war and there were always people running around with pens and notebooks, taking stock of everything. He'd be doing the same himself with the pigs he kept with Joe Long.

Charlie kept his back turned, chortling to himself out of sight of the big woman and her prattling.

Later that morning once the pork had been cooked and collected, Mrs Martin came back in for a loaf of bread. She also came in with a sack which she passed over to Mary, winking and nodding in a secretive manner as she did so.

'A bit of something fer your dad's dinner,' she said, sliding the sack across the counter. 'Fer being so kind as to roast the meat.'

Mary encountered the dusty smell of potatoes from the sack. Hopefully Mrs Martin had wrapped whatever meat it was – she presumed it was meat – in newspaper before putting it in there.

'Make the most of it, me girl,' she said. 'And don't let on to that Rob Masters that I gave you it. He won't approve. Running round like a headless chicken he is, jumping the gun about people registering for rationing with 'im – as if he's likely to 'ave any more meat than any other butcher or farmer hereabouts. Tch!'

She spit into her handkerchief.

Mary tried not to wince, but determined to wash the contents of the sack before daring to cook it. Mrs Martin, who was also wearing another sack as an apron, didn't seem to care much about hygiene.

'I'll take some of them currant buns while I'm at it. Six, I think. Nice with a cup of tea. Did you make them?'

Mary nodded that she had. 'And Ruby made the pasties.'

'I makes me own pasties,' Mrs Martin sniffed while throwing a contemptuous look at Ruby's efforts. Ruby's pastry was golden and melt-in-the-mouth delicious. She paused before saying, 'I 'ear she don't work at the pub no longer. 'Ad a fall out 'ave they?'

'There's a war on, Mrs Martin, and more important jobs than working in pubs! Don't you think?'

'Reputations can be ruined working in pubs.'

'I'll bear that in mind. In the meantime let me give you one of our pasties to try – seeing as you're likely to get busier in this war, what with two of your boys off to fight. You might not have so much time in future.'

Mrs Martin recognised that the pasty was a kind of bribe in the hope that she'd stick up for Ruby when her name came up in gossip.

'I'll bring you in one of mine sometime,' Mrs Martin went on. 'Lovely they are.'

She wiped her nose with the corner of her sack apron. Mary hoped against hope that she would not fulfil her offer of a home-made pasty!

The bell above the shop door jangled when she left, the roasted pork wrapped in newspaper inside a flour sack tucked beneath her arm.

Mary sighed. Mrs Martin had left her drained with her unsolicited advice and unending gossip about what was going on in the village.

Ruby came out from the back room where the bread ovens were still emitting their comforting heat, the smell of yeast and a blanket of heat coming with her.

Their grandfather had built the baking room with a very high ceiling, logically concluding that the heat of the ovens would rise and stay up there. To a great extent he'd been right. Ruby slammed her hands palms down on the counter. 'Last night Dad suggested I marry Gareth Stead. He's repeated it again this morning. Not only that, but he's offered to speak to the man and ask him to reconsider his intentions. Can you believe that?'

'He said that?' Mary was astounded.

Ruby was almost throwing the bread on to the shelves, her features stiff with indignation. 'I didn't know what to say. I thought I made it clear last night when he mentioned it.'

'I suppose you can't blame him. He's about to lose Charlie to the war and is afraid of losing you. I take it he thinks that if you were married, it wouldn't be so likely.'

'I know.' She turned to face her sister. 'Mary, I know war is bad, but this could be such an opportunity for me to see a bit more of the world. I don't want to live and die here in this village. I don't want to marry Gareth Stead or a ruddy-faced, rough-handed farmer whose conversation centres on cows, chickens or the price of a pint of milk. I want more than that! And besides...' She slammed the last of the warm loaves from the wicker basket to the sloping shelves behind the counter. 'Gareth made it quite clear what he wanted and it wasn't bloody marriage. And don't tell me off for swearing,' she said before her sister could reprimand her. 'I felt humiliated, Mary. Downright humiliated!'

Mary patted her on the shoulder. 'He just wants to keep you safe. It's just his way.'

Ruby's expression was unchanged. 'Maybe I don't want to be safe. Maybe I want some adventure before I die!'

Mary tightened her lips. She was used to her sister's headstrong ways and wanting what she couldn't have. She also understood her father going overboard to keep them safe. It was hard to imagine what he was going through at present, wondering what the future held for his children.

'You must please yourself and then you've only got yourself to blame if things go wrong.'

'I can live with that!'

'Mrs Martin's been in.'

The sack was still on the counter. Ruby wrinkled her nose. 'That sack looks filthy.'

'I think it's meat. It usually is when she wants a joint cooked. It's probably offal, kidneys, liver and lights I bet.'

Ruby's nose stayed wrinkled. 'I hope it's wrapped up in newspaper.'

'Thankfully.'

'Liver and onions tonight, faggots tomorrow night,' Ruby said curtly.

She's right of course, thought Mary. It's always faggots or fried liver and onions when Mrs Martin pays for the privilege of getting a piece of meat cooked in the superior heat of a bread oven. The favour was usually asked around Christmas or for some other family celebration, also for the harvest festival, which was always combined with the village fete. The Martins always provided the meat for that, to be enjoyed by everybody, plus roasting for family occasions such as the recent wedding of their eldest daughter Bertha. Bertha had had a white wedding with all the trimmings. Mary reflected that her wedding dress had been too tight-fitting to cover the baby bump. The baby had been born three months later.

It had not escaped Mary's notice that village weddings regularly preceded the birth of offspring by no more than five months. She further concluded it had a lot to do with being born closer to nature than folks in the city; young people round here just did what came naturally.

A cloud of potato dust fell to the floor when she opened Mrs Martin's sack.

'There's two parcels in here,' she said, delving in with both hands. Both, she noticed, were wrapped in newspaper. Just as she'd surmised, the first package contained the necessary ingredients for making faggots, traditional West Country meatballs and loved by all the family. All she had to find were onions, stale bread and a few leaves of dried sage. Or she could discard the lights and caul and fry the liver with some onions.

'It'll definitely be faggots. They use fewer onions.'

Ruby made no comment and besides Mary was interested to see what the other parcel contained. Like the offal it was wrapped up in newspaper. She hoped it wasn't more of the same.

Her face lit up. 'Belly of pork! I'll roast it with apple sauce and a splash of cider for tomorrow night's dinner. What do you think?'

'Unless you want to save it for the weekend,' Ruby responded without any great enthusiasm.

Mary heard the off-handedness in her sister's voice and turned to look at her.

Ruby was stacking the wicker bread trays to one end of the shelves. There were about a dozen loaves left and being someone who abhorred waste, she thought about telling her father that he'd baked too much. On reflection she remembered that the boy, who worked in the kitchen of the big house in Willsbridge, hadn't arrived yet. He usually cycled over on his bicycle every morning to collect fresh bread for the family and servants who lived at Willsbridge House.

Reassured that every loaf would be sold, she returned her thoughts to when and how to cook the belly of pork. 'We could stuff it with apples and sultanas.'

'For the weekend?'

Recalling what Frances had said about the importance of belonging to a family, Mary thought about it only briefly. 'No,' she replied, her tone sombre. 'I think the sooner we have a family dinner together the better.'

On hearing the tone of her sister's voice, Ruby stopped what she was doing. Up until now she had been only half listening, immersed in the conversation she had just had with her father once Charlie had headed for the WC. Mention of having a family dinner together pulled her up short.

'Charlie says he won't go until he's got to.'

Mary grabbed the mix of offal, wrapping it in the newspaper before it slithered away. 'It won't be up to him. I wonder how long he's got before he's called up.'

The two girls fell silent, each with their own thoughts. Ruby was wondering how long it would be before she could join up. A quick glance at Mary and she decided her sister was worrying about Charlie. It certainly wasn't about a sweetheart. Mary had never had a sweetheart, nobody who had lasted more than one night.

In her mind Mary was seeing a rugged figure wearing the blue uniform of RAF Bomber Command, striding across to a waiting aircraft. His address was hidden inside her jewellery box along with some pearls that had once belonged to her mother and other trinkets.

Just after he'd left, she'd knocked on the door of Stratham House and explained her intentions. Mrs Hicks hadn't been surprised; in fact, she'd looked very pleased that Mary wanted to write to her nephew.

'He's got friends over here, but no sweethearts,' Mrs Hicks had confided.

Mary had been tempted to ask whether he had any sweethearts

in Canada, but hadn't had the nerve. And was that what she wanted to be, a potential sweetheart? It seemed Mrs Hicks thought so.

Ruby ran her hands over the tissue paper they used to wrap the bread, fiddling with those corners that refused to lie flat. She was thoughtful and regretful that her brother had to go away. Her father would be upset.

'Mrs Martin says that Ronnie is excused active service on account of the farm. She said that it's a reserved occupation,' said Mary.

'So's making bread,' Ruby replied tartly.

'Lucky that Dad's got us. We can both bake. He'll be depending on us, though I wish...' Mary's voice faded away.

'What?'

She met Ruby's look then quickly turned away. She hadn't told her about her decision to write to Michael Dangerfield.

Finally, she said, 'I just wish things were different. That's all.'

'So do I.'

Wisps of hair clung to the sweat glistening on Ruby's face. She looked tired and Mary knew she hadn't slept well; she'd heard her tossing and turning during the night, sighing as if the cares of the world rested on her shoulders.

'What is it, Rube?'

Ruby's eyelids flickered as though she'd been wakened from a deep sleep. Her wide pink lips, so like Mary's own, puckered in and out. Mary found her own lips mimicking the movements of her sister's lips. When her sister worried, she worried too.

Ruby came to stand next to her sister, folding her arms and resting her backside against the counter.

'I'm still surprised at what Dad said. He hates Gareth Stead.'

Mary grunted in agreement. Their father hated Gareth Stead almost as much as he did Melvyn Chance, the village postmaster, who used to be a member of Sir Oswald Mosley's black shirts. Rumour had it that he'd resigned only last week.

'Then it's just as well you won't be marrying him. Just imagine, father and husband at each other's throats all the time; a miniature war in your own home!'

Ruby grinned but it didn't last. 'The trouble was, Mary, that for a split second I really considered letting him go marching down to the Apple Tree, grab Gareth by the throat and drag him into the church where me and the vicar would be waiting, though I don't know how you get a man to say yes to getting married when he doesn't want to.'

Mary had to agree that the whole idea was quite preposterous. 'Perhaps he'd take Joe Long with him. A man with a shotgun can be very persuasive!'

Ruby's laughter lit up her face and Mary joined her, her laughing face mirroring that of her sister.

'I've been a fool, Mary, but there's still a tiny part of me that can't let go, but it is changing. I dreamed last night that I was behind the bar pulling a pint, but instead of serving it to the customer, I poured it over Gareth's head.'

'I'm glad to hear it. What happened next?'

Ruby frowned. 'I made a list of all the things I would like to do to him. None of them were very nice. I think rolling him in pig manure and attacking him with a pitchfork were on there.'

'I think that means you're well and truly over him.' Though what would I know? Mary thought to herself. I've never been in love. Michael Dangerfield came instantly to mind, but she pushed those thoughts away.

She opened the wooden drawer that served as a till and began counting the takings. Most of it was in coin: farthings, ha'pennies, threepenny bits, silver sixpences, shillings and pence. She piled the florins and half crowns in separate heaps. There was only one ten-shilling note.

Ruby pouted her bright red lips and tossed her head. 'I think I am over him. In fact I quite like the thought of doing all those things to him. Do you think that's normal?'

'Who's to say what's normal?'

A saying suddenly sprang into Mary's mind. Hell hath no fury as a woman scorned. Another familiar one was about there being a thin line between love and hate. She knew how aggrieved her sister had been by Gareth's behaviour. Now she wondered how far her sister's hate might take her.

A gang of men suddenly came barging into the shop setting the iron bell above the door jangling, their loud voices introducing themselves as the men responsible for the delivery of Anderson shelters.

Their arrival necessitated Mary putting the money back in the till. There was no knowing whether they would have the correct change for whatever they might purchase.

'Second phase,' said one of them, as if that might mean something.

The shelters were named after the government minister responsible for their distribution. They were little more than archways of galvanised steel, designed to sit in a pit in the ground and be covered by sandbags which in turn were covered in soil.

One of the men leaned on the counter, looked at Ruby and winked. 'I'm a man in need,' he said to her.

No stranger to dealing with cheeky men she tossed her head and asked him what he wanted.

'Something nice. You'll do for starters.'

'Less of your sauce! And get your dirty elbow off my counter.'

'You got one yet, love? An Anderson shelter. You got one 'ave ya?' The man who asked her appeared to be their leader.

Ruby said that she hadn't. 'Don't know that we want one, all that grubbing about in the dirt.'

'I expect you'll get one,' their leader said, his eyes twinkling, 'they're easy enough to put up, but if you ladies happen to be unattached and 'ave a bit of difficulty doing it, I'm sure one of us 'ere is willing to come along and show you 'ow it's done! We can all get dirty together!'

There was a lot of raucous laughter among the orders for Cornish pasties, bread pudding and apple pies, which were all swiftly disappearing, the shelves becoming bare.

Mary recommended pies once there were no pasties left and currant buns once the bread pudding had all disappeared.

It wasn't the first time they'd made bread pudding, though it was the first time they'd had it on sale. Made from stale bread, currants, candied peel, sugar and lard with a dash of cinnamon, its aroma alone, even cold, was enough to get the taste buds going.

Both girls watched the shelves empty with an air of satisfaction. Filled shelves looked good, but empty ones were a sign of success.

'Thank goodness for Anderson shelters,' Mary whispered to her sister.

'I'll have to make some more pastry,' Ruby whispered back. She much preferred making pastry than bread, but seeing as most women in the village made their own anyway, she could only make pies and pasties in small batches, selling to those who couldn't or wouldn't bake, people passing by or men having to fend for themselves.

'Lots more apple pies,' Mary murmured back. 'Thank goodness we had a mild spring.'

This spring the blossom hadn't been blown from the apple, plum and pear trees. Spring had been followed by a warm summer so by September the gnarled branches were heavy with fruit.

'Are all those shelters for Oldland Common?' Ruby asked them once she'd told them not to be so saucy and not to shout. The man who appeared to be their leader replied that they were not. He had a merry face and a pale blond beard verging on white. 'This is just our mustering area. The lists are being brought out by some chinless wonder from the county council. Once we 'ave them, we deliver to other places, like Warmley, Willsbridge and Frampton Cotterell.'

A ginger-haired man sighed with pleasure into the contents of his brown paper bag. 'Beats the cheese sandwiches my old woman gave me.'

'Tell the truth, Bert,' said one of his colleagues already biting into the golden crust of a Cornish pasty. 'We all ate our lunch by ten o'clock. Starving we was.'

By the time they had all been served and marched off, some already devouring their purchases at breakneck speed, it was midday and time to close. Not that there was much time to rest, the day being taken up with other things both in the bakery and in the general run of things.

Bread was baked every day except Sunday, but the shop only stayed open until midday. The afternoon was the time to clean up, cool the ovens to proving heat and make a fresh batch of dough. The dough would be left to prove until early evening when they would all give a hand in kneading it again, the dough becoming warm and spongy the more air was forced in.

There was a knack to dividing it up into even sections, a skilled baker portioning by hand without the aid of a scale. Cottage loaf, split tin, and crusty cobs, they were all measured out by hand, everyone kneading the dough until the very feel of it was like something living, something about to be born. Then it had to be laid by for a second overnight proving.

Once the dough was made, the afternoon was given over to housework, reading, sewing while listening to the wireless or whatever else anyone wanted to do.

Stan Sweet was spending more time planting, sowing and figuring out ways to get more from his garden.

'Being able to feed ourselves from what we grow is going to be more important than ever from now on,' he'd proclaimed.

He'd brought in some of the fruits of his labours, bunches of carrots swilled off under the tap, green beans and leeks.

Ruby was entrusted with the job of sterilising the jars and preparing the vegetables for bottling. Most of it would be boiled for three minutes before being blanched in cold water and then boiled for an hour. The runner beans he'd brought in would be stored in layers between salt.

'Once the shop's closed,' he added.

Hands on hips, Ruby sighed as she surveyed her father's harvest. 'That's a lot of vegetables,' she said to him. 'It'll take me all afternoon.'

He was in the act of taking his pipe out into the garden, liking a smoke after a good bit of gardening, but turned and frowned at her comment. 'Are you complaining?'

'No, Dad. I was just thinking how lucky it was that we had a decent summer.' Ruby winked at her sister.

'Do you need a hand?' asked Mary.

'No. I can manage. The afternoon will fly by.'

Mary noted the hint of sarcasm in her voice before the old bell on the shop door clanged loudly to tell them that a customer had entered.

It occurred to Mary that since the village fete, her sister was more willing to do jobs alone. It was as though she were trying to prove that she was quite capable without her sister being around.

At one time Mary would have insisted on helping in the bottling process, but she was burning with the need to run upstairs, retrieve Michael Dangerfield's address from her jewellery box and write to him. She had a writing pad and envelopes. She also had a stamp.

She was determined to write, not as a sweetheart because she was not. Just to be friendly. That was what she told herself. However, she didn't want anyone else to know. All she needed to keep her secret safe was for everybody else to be otherwise engaged.

Her chance came around mid-afternoon. Dough making finished, Charlie their brother was off that afternoon up to Perrotts' Farm with the Perrott boys, Martin and John, pressing this year's apple crop to produce cider while sampling last year's brew. 'Just in case it's gone off,' he'd said laughingly. He said the same every year.

Mary watched from the kitchen window as he strode off up the garden path, whistling something saucy. She didn't know all the words, but knew they were more than a little risqué. Her brother wouldn't be back until teatime.

Leaving her sister to the bottling, Mary crept upstairs, saying she had a bit of a headache and wanted a lie down. After glancing at the alarm clock at the side of the bed, she decided she had about an hour before Frances came home from school, flouncing into the bedroom, flinging her satchel on to the bed, then flouncing out again once she'd asked what was for tea.

Softly, so no sound would travel downstairs, Mary got out her writing pad, her envelopes, her pen and her ink. Heart racing, she then opened her jewellery box and retrieved Michael Dangerfield's address at Scampton.

The next thing she did was to write the address on the envelope. Her thinking was that the address, at present written only on a scrap of paper, might get lost. This way at least one letter would get through, but if she got no reply she would know he wasn't interested.

Writing the actual letter took some thinking about. She sat there at her bureau, pen poised in hand. Her gaze strayed through the bedroom window to the garden and the red, gold, though subdued sunshine of September. The colours reminded her of the dress she'd bought with the money Michael had given to her. She'd told nobody she'd bought it, although she would have to tell Ruby seeing as they shared a bedroom. But first she wanted to tell Michael and to do that she would have to write to him.

Dear Michael,

The view from my bedroom window is all golden and red and the sun is only just beginning to sink behind the wall at the end of the garden. The new dress I bought with the money you gave me has the same colours. I hope my description means you can visualise it better than me merely saying that I'd bought a red and gold dress and that it has a sweetheart neckline.

Your aunt is well and sends her regards. She is looking forward to your next visit. In the meantime she hopes you are safe and well. She also says that it might be best if we write to each other as her eyesight isn't as good as it once was and therefore writing is such a strain. She has asked me to pass on whatever is relevant in my letters with regard to your wellbeing.

We're having a rabbit stew tonight cooked with garden vegetables. Ruby has made a plum Charlotte for dessert. I hope this time she doesn't burn the custard. She did burn it on the last occasion, but her mind was elsewhere. I do hope you are well and that Felix the dog is not causing you too much trouble, though I suppose his owner is back from his honeymoon by now.

Wherever you are, take care. I look forward to hearing from you.

Kind regards.

Mary

Kind regards? She pulled a face. It did sound a little formal. On second thoughts *Love, Mary,* might have sounded too informal, after all they hardly knew each other, and yet...

She looked out of the bedroom window to where her father bent over his spade, turning over the rich dark earth, his unlit pipe clenched in the corner of his mouth.

The golden light of late afternoon was fading. The sound of the bell at the village school signalled that Frances would soon be home.

After folding the letter, she placed it inside the stamped and addressed envelope. She just had enough time to post it before Frances was home from school.

On her return, Frances headed for a freshly baked plate of jam tarts in the kitchen. Mary went upstairs where she found Ruby admiring her new dress.

'You didn't tell me you'd bought this. It's lovely.' Ruby eyed her enquiringly. 'You must have been saving hard.'

'Yes. I have been,' said Mary, and left it at that.

9

There was a loud crash. Ruby jerked her head up from preserving fresh eggs in silicate of soda, a method everyone thereabouts used when eggs were plentiful. As winter approached they would become scarcer, and who knew what the situation would be next year. Frances, who was scraping and eating the remains of cake mixture from a big china bowl, looked up and grinned.

'Charlie's home.'

Frances was right. The loud crash was down to Charlie falling through the back door. In the process the door slammed against the wall. Charlie fell forward, crashed into a chair, missed grabbing the edge of the table and slumped to the floor.

Ruby stood over him, hands on hips, eyebrows raised in disapproval. He stank of cider.

'Don't tell me. The boys decided to give you an early send off and there's still a gallon or two of last year's cider hanging around.'

Cap fallen off his head, legs splayed and eyes blurred, her brother looked up at her.

'I'm home.' He almost sounded surprised and definitely grateful.

He made another attempt to grab the corner of the table.

'Don't!' She grabbed hold of his arm. 'Your life won't be worth living if you crash into those jars.'

Vegetable bottling was over, but there were still peas and herbs to be dried and stored. Next was preserves.

The table top was almost obliterated by sterilised preserve jars waiting to be filled.

Ruby had gone out with Frances at the weekend picking the last of the blackberries from the hedgerows. The bushes had been heavy with fruit. Blackberries were her cousin's favourite and if Frances stopped eating them, there would be plenty to preserve with apples and ultimately to use in pies. Jars of gooseberries, rhubarb, raspberries and blackberries were already preserved in the same jars they always used. The cold shelf in the larder, a slab of marble that stayed cold all year, was almost full. Ruby was pleased with herself and determined her drunken brother wouldn't mess anything up.

His eyes were bleary when he looked up at her. 'Don't go on at me, sis. After all I'll be going soon. You wouldn't want us to part as bad friends would you?'

Ruby was in the mood to give him a piece of her tongue. 'Charlie Sweet, you've been having farewell parties with your mates two weekends on the trot.'

'Any chance of a cup of char?' he asked, clambering on to a chair.

Ruby tutted, picked up his cap and hung it on the hook behind the door.

Frances grinned at her cousin and offered him a blackberry. 'They're really sweet,' she said to him.

Charlie grinned. 'I can see that,' he slurred. 'You've got a purple tongue. And nose,' he added.

She giggled when he tapped the tip of her nose.

'Want one?' she asked, holding a plump berry between a purple finger and thumb.

Seeing as it was Frances, Charlie managed to smile and utter his thanks. He'd always felt sorry for the little girl who'd lost her doting father and whose mother hadn't wanted her. The kid hadn't had a good start in life, that's for sure.

Ruby made tea in one of the smaller of their teapots, presented to her parents as a wedding gift and used when only a few cups were required. The big brown pot was big enough for six cups or more. The less water was boiled the better.

Setting a cup down in front of him, she wondered at his expression, which had suddenly clouded over. He didn't usually come back from a session with the Perrott brothers looking so glum, not after pressing apples and drinking cider.

'What is it, Charlie? Last year's cider a bit sour?'

Charlie took a sip of tea, then another and another, not just because his throat was dry, but that it might help sober him up. He couldn't believe what he'd heard. Perhaps he'd been too drunk to understand or Martin and John Perrott might have been joking. He still couldn't believe what they'd told him.

Suddenly he became aware of his sister's face and her saying something to him.

What was that she was asking him? 'Charlie!'

Her voice was louder now, but he still looked at her with glazed eyes.

She repeated what she'd already said. 'Charlie, I asked if last year's cider had gone sour.'

His head was reeling, and when he shook it he almost fell off the chair.

'Worse than that. This year's cider will be the last up at Perrotts' place. Old Fred Perrott been told to dig up the apple trees, clear the ground and put the orchard to the plough. The Ministry of Agriculture have told him to plant an arable crop. Says we'll be needing wheat and oats if we're to survive a siege, not apples. Still, the old orchard next door to the pub will still be there; bet our Frances will be glad of that. So will we. Make cider from them we still got.'

After pouring herself a cup of tea, Ruby sank back on to her chair, staring over the top of it at her brother. There were so many things happening that were likely to change the countryside forever.

'There's never been much arable farming around here, has there?' she said to him.

'No, but there will be now. Most of our grain for making bread and such like comes from overseas; the wheat fields of Canada and America.' He shook his head. 'Don't take a genius to know that ships carrying supplies will be targeted by the enemy, and that's a fact.'

Ruby digested all that he'd said, then, noticing he'd drained his cup, poured him another.

'I won't let them tear up my orchard,' declared Frances who had listened avidly, her eyes growing round with alarm at the prospect of her orchard, the one all the kids played in, being ripped out and made into a smooth, flat field.

Ruby sighed and pointed out that the orchard did not belong to her and that just because Charlie said it would be safe didn't mean that it would. Charlie didn't know everything. 'It's up to the owners and the people from the ministry. And that's enough blackberries, my girl,' she said, snatching a bowl of them away from her cousin. 'They've got to last us a long time if what our Charlie is saying is true.'

'Ahh,' said Charlie, his arms crossed and his eyes closing as he began slowly to slide from his chair and under the table.

* * *

Just after tea but before bedtime, Frances made her way to the orchard, her very favourite place. The trees were twisted and gnarled with age, the grass long and the air held the heady aroma of rotting apples. When the wind blew, their rugged branches scraped against the side wall of the Apple Tree, the pub run by Gareth Stead. It sounded like razor-sharp fingernails scratching against glass.

Tonight they had had cottage pie for tea. On her return from school, Frances had turned the handle of the mincer which was clamped on the edge of the table while Mary fed the machine with minced meat and onions.

As far as Frances was concerned, it was the best part about minced beef, the way it went into the top of the mincer in chunks and came out like worms. But that was off-putting too: the taste was fine but it was hard to forget that it all came out of the mincer looking like worms before falling into the bowl and disintegrating.

The fact that she had not been allowed to leave the table before she'd eaten every scrap had caused her to sigh indignantly.

'Waste not, want not,' her uncle Stan had said to her, a saying she'd heard a hundred times. Only when he'd warned her that she'd get no pudding until she'd cleared her plate did she make the effort to down every morsel.

Ruby had made blackberry and apple pie that she'd sliced and covered with a thick yellow custard. Frances loved pies and custard, but feeling the weight of it in her belly as she ran, she wished she hadn't eaten so much.

She ran quickly because the sun was hiding behind a cloud and the air smelled of rain. Without faltering to judge its height, she bounded over the stile that separated the orchard from the narrow road. The road wound all the way from the side of the pub back to the toll house at the top of the hill.

The old orchard had been neglected for years and nobody was

exactly sure who owned it. The grass was long, its feathery tips tickling her knees. There were barely distinguishable paths made through the undergrowth by generations of village kids who came here to pick up the windfalls or climb the trees, make dens or play hide and seek in the long grass.

To Frances it was a magic kingdom where she made up stories about how one day her father (who had somehow been resurrected) would reclaim her. This was after he'd rescued his wife, her mother, from a wicked goblin who was holding her prisoner until she gave him the secret of how to weave straw into gold. His name was, of course, Rumpelstiltskin.

Golden rod, its yellow flowers beginning to turn to rust, nodded against the perimeter walls, hiding the ivy that wound in and out of the loose stones. Birds twittered in the trees and other living things scurried through the grass.

Breathless from her running, Frances came to a halt at the bottom of her favourite tree. While catching her breath she listened to the wind, the rustling leaves and grass and the frequent thudding of an apple as it dropped to the ground.

It was thanks to her that the family enjoyed so many apple pies, baked apples and jars of preserved apple rings to see them through the winter. She always collected the windfalls as well as climbing to pick fruit direct from the tree.

Uncle Stan had stated at teatime that from now on they would need every piece of food they could produce. Nothing must be wasted. Sometimes he said some really odd things such as the day would come when everyone would have refrigeration like the one in the Co-op store in Kingswood.

Frances had laughed and pointed out that if the cold room at the Co-op was anything to go by, they would never be able to get it in their kitchen, and besides, they had a larder with a cold slab of marble that kept things cool.

Charlie had joined the conversation, laughing as he told her that big ships had refrigeration so cold they could bring meat all the way from South America.

Charlie knew everything. Charlie was her Prince Charming, even though he was really her cousin. She'd fallen in love with him when she was only four years old and newly arrived to live with her uncle and cousins. Charlie had been kind to her, his smile an antidote to the forlorn sadness of a little girl with a dead father and abandoned by her mother.

She could barely remember the life she'd had before coming to Oldland Common except that her mother used to ignore her, preferring to daydream or sit for hours reading *Woman's Illustrated* magazine. Frances could remember her staring out of the window, not responding when her little girl spoke to her.

In the evenings while her father was in hospital as a result of his war wounds, her mother used to plaster on make-up and put on her best dress to go out. Frances had eyed her with dismay, knowing that she'd be locked in for the night and that her mother might not come back until the morning.

She'd been devastated when her father had finally died, but she hadn't really missed her mother. Because her uncle and cousins were so good to her, she'd swiftly settled into her new family, loving the wide fields, the brook at the bottom of Court Road where she fished for tadpoles in summer, the hedgerows where she picked blackberries in autumn. Most of all she loved the orchard, her place of refuge where she could be alone to dream her own dreams.

Making her way carefully through the long grass, she picked up every apple she could, placing it in the empty flour sack she'd remembered to bring with her.

She frowned because her sack was only half full despite scrupulously searching for every windfall that hadn't been nibbled by maggots or wasps. It occurred to her that word about the shortages owing to war would have got round and that every kid in the village would have been sent out to gather up whatever they could.

The apples would be like a treasure store from now on. Everyone would be picking them and pickling them or drying them on sticks with the help of a glass jar and a sulphur candle. She looked up into the branches of her favourite apple tree, the one whose branches fell like swooping arms over the dry stone wall. Her luck was in: bunches of ripe cooking apples hung from the branch just waiting to be picked. And she was the one going to pick them.

Agile as a monkey, she climbed the tree, the rough bark scraping the toes of her sandals. Once up high among the foliage, she reached out along her favourite branch of her favourite tree.

I'm going to pick them all, she decided, and reached out and picked the first four before realising that she'd left the flour sack on the ground.

Muttering under her breath, she looked down at it disdainfully, wishing she could will it to fly up and join her, like the magic carpet in her storybook story of Aladdin. Unfortunately nothing happened when she mouthed the magic word, abracadabra. The sack stayed where it was.

In the absence of anything else, she began sliding the apples into her knickers. The elastic around her waist and her knicker legs was strong and tight. She couldn't gather too many, before she had to climb down to put her harvest into the sack.

It was on her second sortie into the tree – this time with the sack in hand – that she heard voices coming from the other side of the wall.

Carefully she divided the leaves clustered thickly in front of her face.

Gareth Stead was standing in the space provided by his half-opened door. The man with him was dressed in work-worn clothes, a muffler around his neck, a cap pulled low over his eyes. She discerned a sack pass between them with large lettering on the side. It looked to be full up and stitched across the top. The lettering looked familiar.

As the sack passed to Gareth something passed from his fist into that of the man wearing the cap.

'Ten bob. As agreed.' He spoke quite clearly.

Ten bob was ten shillings. Money had changed hands, quite a lot of money as far as Frances was concerned. Ten shillings! Now what could be in that sack and worth ten shillings?

Frances leaned forward, careful to hold on tightly and not to lose hold of the apple sack. A sudden breeze caused leaves and apples to fall from the tree, the apples bouncing over the orchard wall towards the open back door.

Startled by the sound, both men looked in her direction.

Frances sank back among the foliage, her heart racing. In normal circumstances she would have shouted 'boo!' at the pair of them, pulled faces, then scurried off laughing and shouting along with the other scallywags in the village.

Today she was alone and didn't dare do that. Since the day Gareth Stead had tried to put his hand up her skirt, she'd kept out of his way. She'd told Ruby he'd done it, but her cousin had refused to listen. She hadn't liked that. It was as though she didn't really count as a member of the family and it had cut her deeply. She'd sworn never to tell her anything again.

On this occasion, she sensed that the meeting with the man in the muffler was also a bad thing. Gareth Stead was a bad man.

'What is it?' she heard the stranger say, his face turned towards her and the groaning tree branch.

Gareth Stead shook his head and passed his hand over his unshaven face. 'Nothing. Just the wind.'

Frances couldn't imagine why Ruby used to blush when he was

around. He certainly wasn't Frances's idea of Prince Charming and
certainly not like the one she'd read about in her story book. The
fairy-tale Prince Charming had shoulder-length fair hair, wore a
blue doublet and matching tights. The very thought of Gareth in
tights made her giggle.

'Right,' said the man in the muffler, his shoulders braced as he
faced the pub landlord. 'Then I'll be off. I'll be in touch if I gets me
'ands on anything else I think might be of interest to you.'

'You do that. Handy you working at the docks.'

'You're right there,' said the stranger and laughed. 'You'll make a
good profit on that little lot. Everyone says it's gonna be in short
supply. Food's gonna be like gold dust, mark my words. Sugar most
of all!'

'Well, you just keep your eyes open, and let me know whatever
it is you get hold of, Mr Green.'

The man in the muffler touched his cap. 'I will that. And call me
Ernie. The name's Ernie.'

Ernie Green. Frances stored the name to memory.

Gareth Stead stood with half his body hidden behind the open
back door until the man had gone, the sack now out of sight. He
stayed there a moment, looking directly at her hiding place, though
gave no sign that he'd seen her.

Frances froze herself into the branches, closed her eyes and told
herself she was a tree. Her logic was that if she thought she was a
tree, he might think she was too and not see her.

When she opened them again, he was gone, the pub door was
closed and the yard empty.

10

Two pieces of news came the next day. One was Charlie's call-up papers requesting him to attend the recruiting office in Kingswood two days hence where he would be assessed and his preferences considered.

Charlie was still sitting at the table having polished off a second breakfast of two rashers and two eggs after only having had toast earlier that morning. Getting the bread in the oven always came first.

'I'll get the bike out. Won't take me long to get there.' He sounded very casual when he said it, as though he were only going for a leisurely ride, not taking the first steps into danger, into war.

The old Douglas motorcycle was his pride and joy, locally built so strangely apt to be heading towards the factory up in Kingswood where it was made.

The legs of Stan Sweet's chair squeaked as he pushed it back and got to his feet. The news they'd all been expecting had arrived and he was having trouble coping with it. Head bowed, he squeezed his son's shoulder on his way through to take the bread from the ovens.

'Dad?' Sensing her father's concern, Ruby rose from her chair and made to follow him. Mary touched her shoulder, pulling her back. She shook her head. Ruby instantly understood that their father wanted to be alone.

Charlie was frowning at the second envelope they'd received that morning.

'This one's not for me.' His frown changed to a smile as he held it out to Ruby. 'It's for you. Got a sweetheart you ain't told us about?'

Ruby looked at the addressee and gasped.

Mary bubbled with laughter at the sight of Ruby's awestruck look.

'Well? Where was it posted?'

Ruby's hands were shaking as she screwed up her eyes and scrutinised the postmark.

'I can't tell... Yes, I can,' she cried on taking another look. 'London? It's London!'

The twins exchanged looks. Charlie rested his arms on the table, leaning forward as he urged his sister to get on and open it.

Frances just watched, munching sullenly until Charlie reached across and tousled her hair. 'Cheer up, mutt.'

She grinned. He always called her mutt on account of the way she'd always followed him around when she was small, like a puppy, he'd said. She didn't mind a bit.

Ruby's eyes were shining and so were Mary's, Ruby's because she had read the letter and Mary's because she guessed what it said.

Charlie was getting impatient. 'Come on. I've shared my news, now let's hear yours.'

Frances thickly plastered her toast with plum jam while she had the chance.

Charlie saw her and gave her a tickle in the ribs. 'Piggy!'

'No, I'm not!'

Ruby passed the letter to Mary who gasped on reading it.

'It's the baking competition. The next round is back on. In Bristol at the Victoria Rooms.'

By the time she'd finished reading it, Ruby could barely breathe and her cheeks were flushed. She began fanning her face with the letter.

'Let me read it again.' Mary snatched it off her. Charlie demanded she read it out loud.

Mary took a deep breath.

'We are delighted to inform you that the regional final of the Best of British Baking competition, which was to be held at the Victoria Rooms on the 27th of September at 2.30 in the afternoon will now take place on the 30th of November at 2.30 in the afternoon.

'However, in view of the present state of emergency and the likely effect of an enemy blockade on our food supplies, we have altered the criteria for baking to include pies and pastries plus a special section on recipes, the entries to be in the form of three recipes in writing that any housewife can create economically from the most basic ingredients, the emphasis being on the saying, Waste Not, Want Not.

'Entries are open to anyone and everyone, and not just to those who won the earlier round in the competition...'

Mary looked up, aware that her own eyes were now bright with excitement. 'I can enter some recipes in my own name.'

Ruby agreed. 'We both could do that stood on our heads,' she said to her sister. She frowned as something else came to her. 'Since when did they rename it the "Best of British Baking"?'

'Since we declared war on Germany,' said Charlie. 'Waving the flag and all that.'

Ruby took the letter back from her sister and sank back on to a kitchen chair. She sucked in her lips as she read it again devouring the words as quickly as she could.

'Recipes! It seems a funny thing to ask for in a baking competition. I mean, how do they know that a particular recipe works? How would they know you've tried it?'

Mary frowned and thought about it. Ruby had a point, but it was a wonderful challenge, something they could do together.

'There's a war on. It's an interesting concept and one we could do...'

'Together! We could do it together,' Ruby said, her comment echoing her sister's thoughts.

'I could help,' Frances piped up. 'Plum pudding! There's loads of plums on that tree in Mrs Tiley's garden. And the trees aren't very big. I could shin up them no trouble.'

'Plum pudding! I think we can do better than that,' Ruby stated ruefully. 'Something a bit more upmarket; recipes to impress.'

'They want recipes made from ordinary ingredients that are both nutritious and economical,' Mary reminded her.

Ruby was adamant. 'A little luxury wouldn't hurt.'

'Economical luxury – if there is such a thing,' said Mary.

Ruby sighed. 'I have a feeling that even if this war doesn't last that long, it's going to seem that way. Economy is all very well, but it's going to get a bit boring, don't you think?'

'I suppose so.'

Nobody noticed that Mary was disappointed, not because it was Ruby who was going forward to the next round of the competition, but because she'd been hoping that the second letter had come from Michael. Her hopes were dashed the moment Ruby said it was postmarked London. She'd so wanted her to say Scampton – and that it was for her, not Ruby.

It was hard, but she pushed the disappointment to the back of her mind. Mail was taking a long time to get through. The postman had told her so. All she hoped was that Michael was still safe and sound.

She stole a glance at her brother thinking how he was no longer a boy but a man and a young man who turned heads. Soon he'd be gone and here they were talking about baking competitions and plum pudding. She couldn't help voicing her thoughts.

'Never mind about plum puddings and competitions; our Charlie's going to have more than a competition to contend with.'

Charlie smiled. 'Don't worry, sis. I'll be fine and anyway, somebody's got to do it.'

It was the answer she'd expected.

'But why does it have to be you? You're going to be missed here.'

'Nonsense! You can bake bread just as well as I can, perhaps better.'

'I'm not talking about the bakery. I'll worry about you. We all will.'

His eyes shone with kindness. She was glad they were all close, glad of the way they all cared for each other.

Charlie masked any worries he had with a boyish grin. 'I'll worry about you too. You know it's going to be just as important stretching the rations as it is bringing the food across the ocean. I shall worry about you starving. That'll make me even more determined to get the cargo back home.'

'Yes,' said Mary softly, thinking how brave he was, and perhaps just a little naive. He showed no fear, but that didn't mean to say he wasn't frightened. Charlie was good at hiding his true feelings. 'Yes. You're right.'

Charlie got up, the legs of his chair making a screeching noise as he pulled it back from the table. He whistled on his way back to work, the smell of baking bread flooding into the kitchen before the door swung shut behind him.

Ruby was still studying the letter. Mary poured herself a cup of tea.

Frances picked up her satchel. 'I hope it will be the best in the world. Really scrumptious.'

Disturbed from their own personal revelries, the twins looked up at her.

'Of course it will be, and if it's the best in the world I can't help but win it.' Ruby sounded quite adamant.

'Not that silly old competition,' said Frances scornfully. 'I mean my school dinner. I hope it's nice, otherwise I won't stay in at all.'

Mary laughed. 'Frances, you'll eat the lot and ask for seconds, knowing you!'

Ruby shook her head. Young Frances was only concerned with the school dinners introduced by the government to ensure that children got at least one decent meal a day. Married and single women alike were being encouraged to take over men's jobs, working in factories and, in the case of those close to countryside, replacing farm labourers on the land, some of them in the Women's Land Army.

'I'm sure it will be,' said Mary. She attempted to give Frances a little peck on the cheek by way of goodbye.

'Don't kiss me. It's sissy,' said Frances swiping at her cheek.

Ruby grinned. 'At eleven and three quarters it might be, but just wait another five years. Let's see what you've got to say then.'

Frances didn't hear her, dashing out of the door just in case Ruby should kiss her too.

* * *

Two days later Charlie came home from the recruiting office with a spring in his step and the light of excitement in his eyes.

Strange, thought Mary, that young men got excited at the prospect of adventure without considering the danger they were likely to encounter.

She smiled at him and asked how he'd got on though she could already guess the answer. Enthusiasm was shining from his face.

Presumably he'd be serving where he wanted to serve, in the merchant navy. He confirmed that this was so.

'That's why I've been so long,' he said. 'First I went to the recruiting office for the three services – army, navy and air force. Then I got directed along to another bloke for "other services", whatever they might be. I told him I wanted to join the merchant fleet and he had me enrolled on a ship in no time. Meet Able Seaman Sweet. I'm to fill the gaps left by the Royal Navy pinching experienced blokes from the merchant fleet. I report for training in five days at King Alfred's, Winchester. There's quite a bit of training to be done first, but he said that basically I'd be joining a ship by the end of the month. Not much time,' he said, his expression saddening a little before brightening again. 'Still, never mind. Dad?'

Stan Sweet had remained silent while Charlie outlined what had gone on and how well he'd fared and was going exactly where he wanted to go.

His father was sitting in his favourite armchair beside the fireplace smoking his pipe and eyeing his son with a mixture of pride and fear.

'At least you won't be getting shot at,' he said. 'Let's hope you'll be safe out there miles from where the battles will be raging. Trenches are a terrible thing on land and battleships at sea. You're as safe as you're likely to be on a merchant ship.'

He got to his feet and shook his son's hand. In his heart of hearts he was mortally afraid: merchant ships were a prime target, but he couldn't bring himself to voice his fears. He forced himself to sound positive.

'I am proud of you, my boy, and your mother would have been proud of you too.'

* * *

During the five days before Charlie left home, a family conference was held. Mary had made tea, Ruby had made scones and Stan Sweet sat at the head of the table. Frances distributed the tea plates and butter knives and once that was done presumed she was free to leave. She'd spotted some rhubarb sprouting down by the railway track and also a big expanse of fallen hazelnuts and was going on about it. Her news was received enthusiastically by Mary and Ruby.

Uncle Stan spotted her heading for the door. 'You too, young lady.'

Frances pouted, but on seeing the stern look her uncle gave her, sat down without another peep of protest.

Once everyone was settled, he eyed each of them one by one.

'As I sees it, we have to plan things properly,' said Stan Sweet. 'Nothing can be done to dissuade either the government or our Charlie that his place is home here. That being the case, I wants him to have a bakery to come back to. This means we have to keep things going as best we can. People will still look to us for their daily bread and we mustn't fail them. You girls will take Charlie's place helping me run things. What with the house as well, that should give you both more than enough to do. I should think your work will be regarded as essential services and therefore you won't be called away to do anything else. Just as well you gave up that job at the pub, Ruby.'

'I'm glad too,' she declared defiantly. 'No future in working behind a bar anyway.'

She caught Mary looking at her. Like her she knew that if she did go back, Gareth would try it on again just as he had before.

He had sent a message asking her to return via Vera Crane, a flighty widow who frequented the pub far more than a decent woman should. Ruby had told her in no uncertain terms that she would never work for Gareth Stead again.

'Anyway, who needs a job as a barmaid when this war is likely to lead to lots of jobs for single women? I might join the Wrens or something.'

Vera had looked at her as though she was mad. 'That all right with you, Ruby?'

Her father's question jerked her back from her musings and into an instant response though she wasn't sure what he'd asked.

'Yes. Of course it is. Sorry, I was just thinking about the baking competition. One minute it was cancelled because of the war, and now it's on again and they're calling for recipes.'

'Simple recipes,' Mary added. She turned to her father. 'Ruby and I have been discussing what exactly it is they want. Judging by the letter, it seems they're not talking about careful measuring or buying in expensive ingredients. I think we're talking about making a leg of mutton last a week and stretch to feed a whole family.'

'That's one option,' said Ruby, her eyes darting between her sister and the rest of the family and glad to be on another subject rather than Gareth Stead and her job at the Apple Tree. 'We were also thinking about little luxuries to brighten people's lives at such a dire time. Like cakes and puddings, sweet things to eat after the main meal, something to cheer them up.'

The twins exchanged the kind of looks their father had seen many times before, the one that said they were in total agreement in thought and deed.

Mary took over. 'So we're each going to submit three recipes. One set of three will be for the main course and based on the Sunday joint. The other three will be puddings; delicious desserts that can be prepared and baked in a minute, and even eaten cold if need be in case they have to be taken out into the shelter.'

Their father looked impressed, puffing on his pipe, eyes half closed as he scrutinised them through a spiral of sweet-scented smoke.

If they'd been able to read his thoughts, they would have known just how relieved he was that his girls weren't joining up. They hadn't even expressed a desire to work in a factory or drive a tractor, though he supposed there would be plenty who would end up doing that. If anyone was going to, it would be Ruby who fancied herself wearing a uniform.

Ruby was the flighty one, the one who'd got involved with an older man. Mary was the home bird, the one never likely to leave the village. He only hoped that after this war there would be a local man worthy of having her as his wife. Unless she didn't marry, of course, but look after him in his dotage. He hoped not. It would be such a waste, though it would be nice to have her close at hand. In the meantime he had every intention of encouraging them to the limit with this baking nonsense – not that he would use the word nonsense in front of them. To him baking was a job but to the girls it was everything. They were enthusiastic and if it meant they'd be staying close to home, he'd encourage them.

'It sounds like a fine plan,' he said, his face beaming. 'I'll take you there in the van. There'll be room for all three of us on the front seat.'

'Seems I'll have to forgo that pleasure,' said Charlie, his wide grin almost splitting his face in half. 'Hope you win. You deserve to win.'

Up until now, Frances had been sitting on her hands, her bottom lip pouting. She didn't like sitting still for too long, didn't like being indoors, and didn't like being told what to do.

She also didn't like being left out of things. 'What about me? I want to go to Bristol too.'

'You? As if anyone can leave you behind,' said Charlie. He ruffled her hair vigorously so shorter strands stood upright on her head.

'You won't be here.'

Stan Sweet's comment took everyone by surprise, their attention on their father, waiting for him to explain.

'Frances, I've decided you should be evacuated, though not on the government scheme. There's an option to make private arrangements, and that's what I've done.' He looked at her fondly. 'I wouldn't want anything to happen to you. I'd never forgive myself if it did.'

'No!' She almost screeched the word, her face creased with dismay. 'No! I don't want to be evacuated. Only soft kids are sent away.'

Ruby declared what she'd said a silly statement. Mary wrapped one arm along her cousin's shoulders. 'You'll make new friends, Frances, wherever you are.'

The family looked to Stan for clarification. This was the first time any of them had known he was considering sending Frances away. But that was the way he was. He tended to plan what he thought was best and stick to it.

Stan Sweet frowned as he doused the flame in his pipe before tapping the contents of the bowl into the ash tray. Taking his time before speaking was a trait he was good at; the suspense kept everyone on the edge of their seats, ensuring they were fully attentive before he spoke. Finally, when he was satisfied the bowl was empty he reached for a pipe cleaner and began the process of cleaning his pipe.

'There may be fields all around one side of us out here, but the aircraft factories at Filton are a prime target and too close to us for comfort. I don't say we're sure to get bombed, but we can't rule it out. You girls have to stay and help me get the bread baked so the country won't starve and our Charlie will be out of it. I have to accept that.' He paused, his eyes downcast. 'The way I see it, there's no need to put Frances in danger too. As I've already mentioned she can be evacuated under the government scheme, or we can make our own arrangements. Voluntary arrangements they calls it. That's what I've done. Miriam Powell's grandmother has offered to give you a room,' he said, speaking directly to Frances. 'You'll only be the other side of the River Severn in the Forest of Dean, but it's away from built-up areas where the bombs are likely to fall. We can get the ferry from Aust to Bulwark; another grand trip for your uncle's old bread van, and there's the train once my petrol ration gets reduced some more. You'll be able to visit or we can visit you when we can. So what do you say, Frances?'

Frances scowled. 'I won't go.'

'Ada Perkins lives on the edge of the forest,' Stan went on as though she hadn't uttered a word. 'You'll see no bombs drop there, not unless that bloke Hitler has it in for flocks of Jacob sheep or wild deer. There's a lot of stories told about the forest, Frances, stories that might interest you. Knights and fair ladies, fairies and castles...'

As he went on outlining forest legends, Frances became less tense, her scowl replaced by a look of curiosity. Frances loved the outdoors but she also loved the *Fairy Tales of the Brothers Grimm* and *One Thousand and One Arabian Nights*.

Her uncle also pointed out that there were lots of trees, far more than in that old orchard she played in.

Her pout returned when she thought about school dinners and how much she was enjoying them. 'What about school dinners? We get custard for afters.'

'Every school has to provide school dinners,' Ruby told her, though she wasn't quite sure it was true. Frances had expressed her pleasure with what she'd received so far even though the biggest portion of the main meal had been cabbage. Frances did not like cabbage!

* * *

Mary was making brawn, a lovely meaty jelly that would be served with pickles and tomato chutney made from the last of the tomatoes from Uncle Stan's greenhouse. Frances watched silently, hands clasped in front of her mouth. She hadn't said anything more about being evacuated, but Mary knew her well. Just because she wasn't protesting about the matter didn't mean she had resigned herself to leaving.

Once an upturned plate had been placed on the brawn and weighted down with a flat iron, Mary turned to her cousin.

'Are you looking forward now to going to live in the forest?'

Frances shook her head. 'I might not have to go.'

Mary expressed her surprise with a raising of freshly plucked eyebrows. 'Now why would that be?'

'Well, Charlie said that everything in the world has changed now and people had changed. Perhaps my mother's changed too and might come along and take me with her. Then I wouldn't have to leave home. She might, mightn't she?'

The expression on her cousin's face clutched at Mary's heart. Mildred, her mother, was rarely mentioned, as though her name had been erased from family memory. Obviously Frances did think about her. Mary hadn't the heart to deny that her cousin's wish might come true.

She smiled. 'Who knows? Charlie might be right.'

11

Charlie was the first to leave, off to begin his training in Winchester.

Mary was left to run the shop, her father and Ruby going with him in the van to see him off at Temple Meads Station in the heart of Bristol. Frances wanted to go, but had to go to school. She was willing to forgo school for the day, but her uncle refused to countenance it.

'Never mind, mutt,' said Charlie giving her hair one last ruffle. He promised her he would write and, anyway, today was her last day at her old school. The day after tomorrow it would be her turn to leave. She was off to the Forest of Dean.

An air of apprehension travelled with Stan Sweet, Charlie and Ruby all the way through Kingswood and into the centre of Bristol. Their conversation was bright enough though brittle, a crisp aurora of light-hearted banter barely covering the fear beneath the surface.

The station was crowded with men in uniform, tearful women and children, each carrying a cardboard box containing their gas mask, a label giving their name tied to their coat lapels. It seemed to Ruby as though the whole world was off to war.

'There's a lot of people here, seeing as it's supposed to be a phoney war,' Ruby was moved to exclaim. 'It has to be real for all these people to be here.'

She looked around her to see if there was anyone she knew, but there wasn't. There were just a lot of people saying tearful good-byes, women with their arms thrown around husbands, lovers, sons and brothers, and the crocodile line of children to be evacuated and their bossy supervisors. And yet there was also cheerfulness, hope that it would be no time at all until the troops did their job thrashing Hitler's armies and came marching home.

Everyone was doing their best to look on the bright side, yet a ribbon of fear ran just beneath the surface, a tangible thing that affected Ruby just as much as everyone else.

'Charlie!' She flung her arms around her brother's neck, hugging him to her as though she might never see him again.

Charlie laughed. 'Come on, sis. I'm coming back. I promise.'

Slowly her arms left him and her father stepped forward. 'Son...'

Never one to be demonstrative with his children, Stan Sweet shook his son's hand. But suddenly, overcome by emotion, he threw his arms around his son's broad shoulders just as Ruby had done.

It was a sight Ruby would never forget, yet it was so right for the moment, a moment gone forever.

* * *

Back at the bakery, Mary took a lingering look at the cheese straws she'd made that morning from some leftover dough and a piece of cheese rind she'd been loath to throw away.

She'd grated what remained of the cheese until she was in danger of slicing her knuckles, determined to use every last morsel until she was left with nothing more than the linen gauze that had held the cheese together. To augment the taste, she'd sprinkled in a

little more salt than she would normally have done; basic ingredients indeed! Leftover dough and leftover cheese placed in the leftover heat from this morning's bread bake.

The smell alone was heavenly and they'd browned well in the
lingering warmth of the bread oven.

The idea had been to serve them at teatime on her father and
sister's return from seeing Charlie off, and Frances's return from
school. Teatime this evening would also be special because Frances
was being evacuated the day after tomorrow, her father having
saved enough petrol coupons to take his niece across the Severn on
the ferry that ran from Aust to Bulwark.

There were twenty-four cheese straws, lovely and crisp and big
enough to hold in a masculine fist without getting lost. The men
who delivered the Anderson shelters came to mind.

Thinking of them she divided the cheese straws in half,
reserving twelve for tea and twelve to sell in the shop. Most women
in the village did their own baking, but there were a few widowers
and even widows who didn't bother to cook much for themselves
and everyone liked a little treat now and again. There would only
be enough to sell in their shop, and certainly not enough to supply
the village stores and a few shops in Warmley, Hanham and
Kingswood High Streets as they did with their bread deliveries.
Charlie used to cycle to the closer ones and drive to those whose
orders were enough to make it worthwhile to deliver by van.

Mary eyed the cheese straws proudly already planning to
include free samples with next week's bread deliveries.

'But let's see how they go in the shop first,' she said out loud.

She was just setting them out on the counter when Mrs Darwin-
Kemp came in, a woman who lived in a big house with her retired
colonel husband and half a dozen servants.

Mary was surprised. Mrs Darwin-Kemp rarely did her own
shopping. She'd always had staff to do it for her.

Even though the weather wasn't even close to freezing, she was wearing a full-length fur coat and a black hat with a brim and stiff veil that covered the top half of her face. Her cheeks were rouged and her lips bright red. Her manner was furtive, glancing over her shoulder as though entering a shop was beneath her and best done in secret. She wasn't that big a woman, but still her presence seemed to fill the shop to bursting point what with her coat, her hat and her attitude.

'I'm having friends around for tea,' she said imperiously without responding to Mary's courteous welcome. 'What have you got?'

Her manner was rude. If Ruby had been serving she would have retaliated with some stinging remark.

Mary smiled politely. 'We have these. Fresh baked today.' She waved her hand over the display of currant buns, individual apple and blackberry tarts her sister had made, and the freshly baked cheese straws.

'The cheese straws are still warm. I've only just got them out of the oven,' she explained. 'They're a new line we're trying out.'

The woman's nostrils flared and then contracted as her eyes scrutinised Mary's suggestions. Mary guessed she'd smelled the savoury aroma and even fancied she'd heard Mrs Darwin-Kemp's stomach rumbling.

'How much are they?'

She asked the question sharply. Mary had the distinct impression she wanted to be out of here as soon as possible, that shopping for food was, in fact, beneath her.

Mary told her the price of the buns and tarts even though there was a price ticket standing rigid at the back of the display. With regard to the cheese straws she hadn't had a chance to put a ticket on them but she instantly doubled the price she'd had in mind: payment for bad manners, she decided, was justified. 'I'll take all of the cheese straws and six of each of the others, plus two loaves of bread. Can you slice them?'

It was unusual to be asked to slice people's loaves for them; after all, everybody knew how to use a bread knife, didn't they?

'Don't you have a bread knife?' Mary couldn't help but ask, puzzled.

The woman's thin face seemed to grow thinner, so much so that her curved nose seemed much larger. 'Don't be impertinent! It's my cook's day off.'

Mary relented. 'I suppose I could slice them for you, though not right away. You'll have to come back for them.'

'I cannot possibly do that,' said Mrs Darwin-Kemp with a wave of one gloved hand and a shake of her head. 'My husband has people coming for tea from London and this is all terribly inconvenient. As I have already told you, I have to get everything ready myself, which is quite a chore I can tell you. Perhaps you can send it round with your boy?'

'We don't have a boy, though I can get my cousin to deliver it. She'll be home from school by four o'clock. Will that be all right?'

A pair of hard eyes regarded her through the stiff black veil. The red lips were pursed so hard a sunburst of wrinkles radiated outwards. Mrs Darwin-Kemp heaved her shoulders inside the absurd fur coat. The imperious glare from behind the stiff veil remained. 'Well, I suppose it will have to do. Our visitors are expected at five o'clock. Please make sure everything arrives on time. I'm having to set tea up with just my maid. My cook's gone off and so has everyone else come to that; it is all very inconvenient. Now you won't let me down, will you. This meeting is very important; in fact, it's a matter of national importance. Oh,' she said as an afterthought. 'Don't repeat that. It's all very hush hush.'

Mary didn't believe her. 'On account?'

Mrs Darwin-Kemp shook her head. 'No. I'll pay for it now. I no longer have either the staff or the time to deal with such things. Servants joining the Women's Land Army and driving buses and whatever! Leaving me to do my own cooking.'

Mary felt like cheering the servants who had dared to leave Mrs Darwin-Kemp's employ. No doubt they were better paid and better treated even if they were working long hours.

She had heard rumours previously that Mrs Darwin-Kemp had trouble keeping servants. It must be even more difficult now, she concluded, that better wages were being offered for doing war work than domestic work.

Mrs Darwin-Kemp paused at the shop door before opening it, looking up and down the High Street before venturing out. Satisfied there was nobody she knew around, she pulled up the thick collar of her coat and tugged the stiff net of her hat down over her face. Suitably disguised, she stuck her nose out, again looking this way and that before finally dashing to her car which – horror of horrors – she was having to drive herself.

12

Frances was not best pleased about having to borrow Charlie's old bicycle and cycle over to the big house with Mrs Darwin-Kemp's order. For a start the bicycle was too big for her and even though Charlie had adjusted the saddle height before leaving, her toes only just about reached the pedals.

The big house where the Darwin-Kemps lived was called Swainswick, but nobody local called it that. It remained the 'big house', uttered in unflattering tones by the villagers as though it were another country, which to some extent to them it was. To them it was the place where 'the gentry' lived, people with lots of money who spoke with cut-glass accents. Besides having live-in servants, they employed people from the village but rarely mixed with them except to open the village fete or act as a judge in the annual horticultural show. Even then they relied on their head gardener, Archie Singer, for an opinion.

Tradesmen were directed by a sign at the main gate that they should make their way to the single gate at the rear of the property. Frances followed the instructions and eventually found herself faced with a smaller notice instructing her to press the bell and wait for admittance.

Frances stabbed at the white ivory bell which was embedded in a brass surround. She waited while standing on one leg, the bicycle leaning against one hip.

Nobody came.

Frances huffed and puffed impatiently and seeing as she hadn't as yet eaten the alluring high tea Mary had promised her, she was impatient to get going. She pressed again. In an effort to hear better, she cocked her head. No sound of footsteps. No response whatsoever.

Really impatient to get back to her tea and the cosy front room fire, she pressed for a third time, keeping her finger on the buzzer while she counted ten – very slowly!

Ten was always a good number and things usually happened if you really wanted them, simply by counting to ten. It was like the magic words from 'Ali Baba and the Forty Thieves'. Ali Baba had uttered 'Open Sesame', and hey presto, the door to rich treasures sprang open.

It had to be easy to open a garden gate if magic words could open the entrance to a treasure trove, or at least have somebody arrive that would open it.

She was just about to press for a fourth and final time, when an elderly barrel-chested man with rigid shoulders and an oiled hairstyle with a centre parting came ambling into view on bandy legs, his arms swinging at his sides.

'It's open,' he shouted at her.

So why didn't it open when I shoved it, thought Frances? 'Oh. I read the sign and thought it wasn't.'

Although she hadn't exactly met him socially, Frances knew she was face to face with Colonel Darwin-Kemp.

He was smartly dressed and looked very glad to see her. 'You've certainly helped us out of a fix, Rosie. Got the sliced bread with you?'

Frances said that, yes, she did have the sliced bread with her. 'But my name's not Rosie.'

The colonel had turned his back and didn't appear to have heard her. She presumed he was deaf. A lot of older people were deaf though sometimes it was only pretending because they just didn't want to hear what she was talking about. Too busy. Always too busy.

The kitchen was big and modern without a single crumb in sight. A pat of butter plus a plate of sliced cucumber was laid out on a large pine table, plus three serving platters with patterned edges.

'I expect you're tremendously capable of making cucumber sandwiches,' he said to her. 'I believe the bread you've brought us is already sliced. The memsahib, my wife, insisted that the baker should do so. I told my wife I didn't think the bakery usually sliced bread on demand, but she nearly bit my head off when I said that. It's been hard for her, you see, Rosie, what with servants charging off to war without a by your leave and us having to cook and clean and whatever for ourselves. You know, she's even serving the tea and everything herself this afternoon because our maid Lily, who we were counting on, has gone off to the station to say goodbye to her young man. I believe he's joined the Wiltshire Yeomanry. The memsahib's never done it before in her life. Brought up in India, you see. House full of servants. Not had to lift a finger, but there you are, every man – and woman – to the pumps, eh what?'

His gaze drifted around the kitchen giving her the impression that he'd forgotten she was there. He had a funny way about him and a funny way of speaking that was quite intriguing so she didn't get round to repeating that her name was not Rosie, and that she knew everything that went on at the bakery because she lived there.

'You can make cucumber sandwiches?' he asked suddenly.

'Of course I can,' Frances replied hotly. 'Anybody can make sandwiches. I mean, if they're used to it,' she added, unwilling to upset the memsahib, as the colonel had called Mrs Darwin-Kemp.

The colonel beamed at her. 'I should have known. You look very capable, Rosie, very capable indeed.'

'I'd better get on with it.'

Frances placed the bread on the table. Mary had placed the loaves in brown paper bags and tied the ends together with string to stop the slices falling out.

'Good start,' declared the colonel. 'Topping good start.' He leaned closer as though about to confide a very big secret. 'To tell you the truth, the memsahib nearly had a fit when I told her we were expecting very important guests. They have very particular tastes, so I hope the bread is very thinly sliced.'

Again Frances considered correcting the colonel's mistake about her name seeing as he continued to call her Rosie even when she'd informed him it was Frances. He just hadn't heard her.

So who was Rosie? The only Rosie she knew was Rose Syms, who was known to take casual jobs as cook or waitress, though only on a very basic level. Goodness knows where she'd got to, but things and people were very unpredictable at the moment.

She was about to own up and tell him her name again when the colonel informed her that she might very well be here washing up until seven o'clock, and he hoped her family wouldn't be worried. That was when it occurred to her that they deserved to be worried. They were sending her away, everything arranged without even bothering to ask her. This, she decided, was an opportunity to get back at them, though she felt a momentary pang for the tea she was missing.

Even though she was attracted to the Forest of Dean by Uncle Stan's forest folklore and having been reassured she would still receive school dinners, she couldn't help harbouring a deep resentment that everything had been arranged without asking her first. Uncle Stan had not considered how much she would miss everyone, so she would show them beyond doubt how much they would miss her. She wouldn't go home until late! Very late!

The time went quickly. As fast as she set things out, Mrs Darwin-Kemp whisked them off the table to serve to her guests, though not without Frances's assurance that they were of the very best quality, and also not without scrutinising the thickness of the cucumber slices and also of the bread.

'We have very important guests,' Mrs Darwin-Kemp declared imperiously for the third time that evening. 'They are used to eating the very best in the finest establishments.'

'Sweet's Bakery is the best for miles around. Everyone knows that Mary and Ruby are excellent bakers, and not just of bread,' Frances said defensively. 'They're very good at recipes too and have entered some for the Best of British Baking competition in Bristol. Ruby won a place there with an apple loaf.'

Mrs Darwin-Kemp looked suitably impressed. 'Really?'

Frances allowed herself a smug smile. Even though she was annoyed with her family she still loved them and would defend them against all comers.

After the food came the dishes. By the time she'd washed what was already in the sink Mrs Darwin-Kemp came out with the dishes from the tea tray in the drawing room. She also gave Frances a ten-shilling note.

'My guests were very impressed, so impressed in fact that they noted the name and address of the bakery. You did say Mary and Ruby, didn't you, and that they are also devising recipes for some competition?'

Frances said that she had, but wasn't really interested in

anything else that was said. She had earned ten shillings and intended not telling her family about it. Instead she would take it with her to the Forest of Dean – if she *really* had to go. Wisdom told her she might need it there, perhaps to escape and make a life of her own. Ten shillings should be enough.

13

It was gone seven o'clock and Mary was frantic. Tea was on the table, Ruby and her father were back, but there was no sign of Frances. She'd explained to her father that the woman up at the big house had demanded delivery and that she'd sent Frances along on Charlie's bicycle.

Stan Sweet had been in the process of taking off his coat and settling down for the evening, not that he'd be able to settle much. Seeing Charlie off had aged him, though he'd controlled his feelings, putting on a brave front so that Charlie would go off happy. He knew he wouldn't sleep tonight. There was just too much on his mind.

'I'll go and look for her,' he said, reaching for his hat.

Ruby had seen through his facade of joviality. She threw a look at her sister. 'I'll go. It's best you stay here, Dad. Our Mary wants to know all about the send-off. Be fair, she's run the shop all day by herself. It's a wonder she's sold a thing, worrying about our Charlie.'

Mary agreed with the suggestion. 'She's probably met up with the village boys and is in the orchard climbing trees, everything else totally forgotten.'

They all knew their cousin's love of the orchard – she'd been known to lose all sense of time in her favourite playground, and besides it wasn't that dark just yet.

It was now early October. The nights were beginning to close in and it would soon be time for the clocks to fall back. Ruby wondered if it would happen this year as usual. Probably. The farmers and growers would be clamouring for longer hours of light so they could get in the crops.

Out of sight of everyone Ruby opened a kitchen drawer and grabbed a rolling pin. What few street lamps there were in the village were blacked out. The countryside was blacker than ever with not even a sliver of light coming out from a window. The blackout had made her nervous, or at least cautious.

'I'll go. I won't be long,' she shouted as she reached for the door latch.

Once outside, Ruby took three deep breaths. It had been difficult not to cry in front of Charlie, though she had dabbed at her eyes with her handkerchief. She needed this time alone to think about her own future. Charlie was off to sea, off to defy a vicious enemy, to crew on a merchant ship carrying food to England, now a beleaguered country. If she could, she would do something more worthwhile too, certainly something more important than baking bread and serving in the shop.

Her eyes ached and so did her feet. It had been a long day and she had been looking forward to putting her feet up, listening to the wireless or reading a magazine. Frances had put paid to all that. By the time she got back all she'd want to do was flop into bed with a cup of hot cocoa.

'If that little madam is out larking about with her mates, she'll get the sharp edge of my tongue,' Ruby murmured as she marched off towards the steep hill that led down to Swainswick House.

* * *

Frances was thinking how pleased the twins would be to hear that Mrs Darwin-Kemp's guests had praised their baking when the front tyre of Charlie's bicycle hissed into flatness. She had a puncture.

Cursing naughty words that a grown-up might use, words she would never use in front of her family, she swung her leg off her bike. Curses and bad words were only for when she was out with the Martin boys and the village girls that didn't mind climbing trees and getting their dresses torn.

The hill leading up towards the old toll house and the village beyond was steep and pushing a bicycle with a puncture was never easy. By the time she got to the top of the hill she was breathless, tired and very hungry. She wanted to get home quickly so rather than continuing along the main road that passed the front of big houses and opposite the tiny little railway station, she opted to head down Pool Lane.

The lane ran alongside the orchard where she spent many happy hours. It was where the wall was the lowest and the old five-bar gate falling to bits. It was the gate she and her friends usually climbed over depending on the amount of nettles growing there, too many and they vaulted over the broken wall. Along a bit further was a stile, a more favoured entrance than either the gate or the wall. For some reason nettles didn't grow there.

The lane was narrow and wound away to her left, its hedges throwing dark shadows even in daylight. Dusk had come and gone and tonight the lane seemed to wind away like a long tunnel of blackness. No light shone from the windows of the few cottages bordering the narrow lane, their inner glow denied escape by the recent addition of hastily made blackout curtains.

Charlie had told her that an enemy bomber could detect the smallest glimmer of light from a great height.

'Even from the burning tobacco in the bowl of your uncle Stan's pipe,' he'd said to her.

Wide-eyed, she'd hung on to his every word, believing him as she always did until he'd burst into laughter and winked at her.

'Caught you there, mutt.'

Charlie wouldn't be there when she got home and it saddened her. She wondered where he was now and what he was doing. He was probably still on the train taking him to Winchester. Travelling anywhere was taking longer than usual, so her uncle had told her.

'The trains will be packed with lots of brave young men going off to war. Young men like our Charlie.'

Yes, she decided as she marched into the lane. Charlie was brave and if he could go off to fight nasty Nazis, then she shouldn't be afraid of darkness. The sun had gone to bed. That was all that had happened.

The familiar sights of day were totally immersed in darkness. The sounds of night were different too: the call of a fox, the hoot of an owl piercing and unseen.

The flat tyre made a wheezing sound as she pushed the bike along, reminding her of an old man in the village who made the same noise and coughed and spluttered before he could say a word.

Tree branches creaked with age as the wind began to rise, tugging at her skirt and sending black clouds racing across the sky.

In a moonlit moment, she spied the tall chimneys of the Apple Tree pub, black and solid against the rolling clouds.

The moment didn't last, clouds hiding the moon and returning the world to blackness. However, the end of the lane was in sight. A few more steps...

'Come to see me then, my darling?'

There was suddenly a voice and the glow of a burning cigarette, the smell of strong tobacco.

Gareth Stead! His figure was black against the turmoil of sky, just like the chimneys of the pub he ran.

Frances stopped. It was no longer so easy telling herself to be brave just as Charlie was being brave.

'No,' she said, making herself sound as much like Ruby as possible because Ruby always sounded defiant even when she wasn't.

'Where you been then?'

His words were slurred. The air around him smelled much like the empty barrels left for the draymen at the back of the pub. As her Uncle Stan had said, a pub landlord should not indulge too freely in his own spirits and beers. She knew he'd meant that Mr Stead drank too much.

She gathered up all her courage. 'It's none of your bloody business. And you've been indulging,' she retorted tartly, not caring about using a bad word when speaking to him. She didn't like him. She remembered that he'd tried to put his hand up her skirt, though nobody had believed her. Perhaps she should have mentioned it to Uncle Stan or Charlie rather than Ruby, but she hadn't because what he'd done had confused her. It was dirty and when she'd protested, Mr Stead had said she was just a tease and had egged him on. Ruby had made her swear not to repeat what she'd said. 'Little liars get their tongues pulled out with pliers.'

Terrified at the thought of having her tongue pulled out with pliers, Frances didn't insist that she was telling the truth. What if nobody believed you even though you were telling the truth? Would that still mean your tongue would be pulled out?

Gareth Stead did not like being sworn at. If she had seen his expression, she would have let the bike fall to the ground and run away. But it was now almost dark and she didn't see. Besides, she had to put on a brave front, just like Charlie, just like the country as a whole.

'You've got a sharp tongue and you're a tease. Do you know that?'

'And you're a drunk.'

Gareth Stead had been drinking since lunchtime, partly because he was celebrating buying knocked-off booze straight from the docks, stuff that hadn't so much fallen off a lorry as a ship. There was also the fact that the pub had been half empty and when there was nobody to serve, he served himself. No wonder the profits were down.

He was also commiserating with himself that Ruby had not come crawling to ask him for her job back. He'd fully expected her to, but she hadn't. The cow!

Still, not entirely her fault. The bloody war again! That stupid brother of hers had gone to war so she and her sister were left with the job of keeping the bakery afloat, them and that sanctimonious father of theirs. He was getting to hate the Sweet family, though he had to smile at the thought of old man Sweet coming along to ask him if he would consider marrying Ruby so she wouldn't go off and do something stupid like joining up. He'd actually told him he would think about it, figuring that way the old man might persuade Ruby to fill in with a little bar work now and again. It occurred to him that Ruby didn't know her father had come pleading for him to take her off his hands. Silly old bugger. Why keep a horse if you only needed a ride? Not a bloody lifelong partner. Never again. Once was enough, and anyway, with the men off to war, the women of the village would be starved of male company. He'd have the pick of the crop! He wouldn't be joining up, that's for sure. Catching rheumatic fever as a child had put paid to that. A dicky heart, so he'd been told. Unfit for duty.

He kept a grip on the post at the side of the stile; his knees buckled when he tried to stand upright. His head was throbbing, his eyes stinging. He wished he hadn't had so much to drink then he could see her better. It sounded like Ruby, though it was too dark to see her. Still, who needed to see the goose to stuff it? A grope in the dark was as good as anything. He'd know that body anywhere. It was just a case of getting close enough to feel her.

'Come on then,' he said enticingly, standing sideways so she could pass through the narrow gap. His head reeled every time he moved, but by leaning his back against the bushes and holding on to the post, he managed to stay upright.

Frances considered going back the way she'd come, but what if he came after her? There was a whole lane of darkness behind her whereas home wasn't that far in front.

She gulped and decided to go forward. Despite her cocky manner, the landlord of the Apple Tree frightened her. But she had to get home.

Tightly gripping the handlebars of the bike she gave it a big enough push to get it going despite the puncture. The entrance to the lane was only just wide enough for her and the bike to get through. Gareth Stead's thick-set body silhouetted against the light behind him narrowed it further.

As she came level she felt the heat of his body, the brush of his rough tweed coat against her hip. She smelt the tang of his breath and his sweat, heard the quickening of his breathing.

'Gotcha!'

She screamed as he grabbed her with one hand before his other hand pressed over her mouth. She hung on to the bike.

His palm was fleshy against her mouth. She bit him. 'Ouch! You bitch... I'll teach you...'

Her skirt was hitched up to her waist. She should have dropped the bike, but sensed it was an encumbrance to what he wanted to do. She clung to it, like a shield.

'Let me go!'

'Ruby! Ruby my love...' The moon suddenly shone clear.

Stead looked at her with bleary eyes. 'You!'

Frances kicked him.

'You bitch! I'll teach you...'

Gareth Stead didn't get the chance to teach her anything. Ruby came across the pair and gasped in horror at the sight before springing into action.

'Let my cousin go or you'll get this rolling pin around the back of your head!'

'Ooow!' Gareth warbled contempt as he attempted to focus on the figure wielding the rolling pin. 'Ruby, me darling. I've been waiting... I thought—'

'Frances? Come here.'

Frances did as she was told.

'Darling, I didn't realise it was the kid. I thought—'

'Don't you darling me!'

Ruby posed quite a picture, standing there with her arm raised, though shaking with anger so much that even the rolling pin was trembling.

'Ruby, I meant no harm—'

'Keep away from my family, Gareth Stead. Do you hear me? Keep away from my family or it'll be the worse for you.'

The moonlight lit up the sickly grin on his face. 'Certainly, but can you guarantee your family staying away from me? I mean, your father came and asked me if I would marry you. Did you know that?'

Despite the cold night air, Ruby felt her face getting hot.

He couldn't have goaded her better. Feeling only anger for the man she'd once cared for, she charged up to him and almost spat a warning into his face.

'Keep your filthy mouth shut, Gareth, or it'll be the worse for you.'

He laughed in her face. 'Hah! I could tell everyone—'

'I don't think so! Not if I spread a few rumours of my own. Do you know what happens to men who try it on with children in a village like this, Mr Stead? Do you? Well, let me tell you this, my father would chop off your most treasured assets if he ever heard of this, so I'm giving you a choice. Keep away from my family and keep your mouth shut about what my father asked you, and neither he nor the other men in the village will ever hear of this. Approach any of them ever again and he gets to be told. My father killed men in the last war, some of whom he thinks may not have needed killing but he did it because he had to. He's not easily riled to anger, but he would be for you, Gareth. He certainly would be for you!'

Ruby was silent and still trembling when she walked back to the bakery, angrily pushing the bicycle with the punctured tyre.

Frances knew when to keep quiet; she should have been home earlier. She shouldn't have been a bad girl and taken the short cut down Pool Lane. This was all her fault and she felt bad about it.

Far from feeling heroic, Ruby was considering what Gareth had told her about her father asking him to reconsider marrying her. However, her main concern was the possibility of her father finding out about Gareth's attack on Frances tonight. It struck her that Frances had been telling the truth from the start. Why hadn't she seen it? Surely love wasn't that blind? If it was then she resolved never to fall for another man again.

The main priority was to keep this incident from her father. If he should ever find out he would kill Stead. She knew he would.

One hundred yards from the bakery, Ruby, still pushing the

bicycle, a tired Frances at her side, came to a stop. 'Frances. I want to talk to you.'

'You believe me now?'

Although the darkness hid her features, Ruby heard the anguish in her cousin's voice. 'I believe you, but you must promise me this will remain a secret between us. You must not tell your uncle Stan. For Charlie's sake, you must not tell my father what that horrible man did to you. He's so worried about Charlie, about all of us, and anyway, I think my warning will be enough to keep Gareth away from us. Do you promise?'

'Yes,' said Frances. 'But can I ask something?'

'Yes.'

'Would you really have hit him with that rolling pin?'

Ruby laughed. 'I might very well have done, then instead of your uncle being in trouble it would have been me!'

14

Stan Sweet had been going to send Frances up to bed without supper for being late, but reconsidered on learning she'd been out on an errand for the bakery and the bike had had a puncture. 'I'll mend it in the morning. Good job you're not off until late morning. You look all in, you do. Now eat your supper and get yourself off to bed.'

Ruby shot Frances a warning look, reminding her of what they'd agreed as her cousin scoffed her supper in record time.

'Goodnight, Frances.'

Frances went to bed leaving Ruby relieved her father had not noticed anything unusual – or she thought so until he said, 'Hit anybody with that rolling pin, did you?'

'Rolling pin?'

'I saw you take it from the drawer.'

'Well. You never know, what with the blackout and everything...' she said as she folded up the tablecloth, turning her back on him as she placed it in a drawer.

'Ahh!' he said. 'The blackout.'

She waited until her father had gone outside to the privy at the bottom of the garden before speaking with Mary.

Mary, who was scrubbing down the table they used for mixing bread dough, listened in amazement as Ruby ran through the details.

'Did you hit him with the rolling pin?' To Ruby's ears it sounded as though Mary was hoping that she had.

Ruby shook her head. 'Not this time.'

'Shame,' said Mary and went on scrubbing the table.

'I still can't believe Dad asked Gareth to marry me. I'm mortified.'

Mary stopped scrubbing.

'Have you mentioned it to him? I mean, are you going to tell Dad that you know?'

Ruby shrugged and looked undecided. 'Should I?'

Mary gripped the scrubbing brush with both hands as she considered the likely outcome if her sister did mention it. 'I don't think so. We know why he did it. He was only doing what he thought was for the best. This war frightens him. He's afraid of losing us all.'

Ruby nodded and pulled a strained expression. 'I know. It's my fault. If I hadn't been such a fool with that man and if I'd believed Frances in the first place...'

'You're right, though – Dad must never find out. He'll kill him. You know how he gets if anybody dares upset this family. He sacrificed his own life for us. He'd lose his temper and get in serious trouble.'

'Gareth is drinking too much. More than he used to.'

'I had heard.'

'I still can't help feeling responsible.'

'You think he's upset that you don't work there any more?'

'Possibly.'

Mary looked down at the scrubbing brush as she thought things through. The problem was convoluted, affecting more than one person and in different ways. To start with there was Ruby and her hurt feelings. There was also Frances and her allegations. Although sworn to silence, she was a child. There were no guarantees that she wouldn't tell her uncle. Thank goodness she was being evacuated. Most important of all was preventing the pub landlord's behaviour towards the Sweet women from reaching the ears of her father. He was a calm man nowadays, but he hadn't always been that way. She'd heard the stories he told and recalled the ones related by her Uncle Sefton to Charlie.

'You can't say anything, Ruby. The thing is that Dad is under a lot of strain what with Charlie going to sea.'

Ruby nodded. 'That's what I thought. It still upsets me though. I feel so... cheap.'

'He'd be mortified if he knew how you felt, but you can't tell him.'

'I know.' Ruby poked a finger in a mound of dough. It sprang back immediately. And it won't happen again, she thought to herself. 'I've made up my mind about men. They're not worth bothering with.'

'Some are,' said Mary, her eyes downcast as she poured the water from the bowl into the sink. She was thinking of Michael Dangerfield. Why couldn't she get him out of her thoughts?

'You sound as though you have someone in mind, yet I've never known you—'

Ruby stopped in mid-sentence. There was something secretive with the way Mary kept her eyes averted, as though cleaning out the washing-up bowl and putting the scrubbing brush away beneath the sink were things that needed total concentration.

'Who is he?'

Mary looked at her open mouthed. 'Who is who?'

'You're blushing.'

'No I'm not. I was just thinking there's going to be a lot to do around here what with our Charlie gone to war.'

'I agree. There is. We have to keep this place going, plus dealing with these officials from the Ministry of Food. And the paperwork! Strikes me those officials know more about paperwork than they do about baking!'

She said it laughingly, though she knew it was far from a laughable situation. They'd already had officials visit the bakery to tell them that flour and sugar would be in short supply, fats and eggs would most definitely be on ration but that bread would not be, it being the staple element of most diets.

To the ears of the Sweet family it sounded as though the only things that wouldn't be on ration were vegetables and anything they could purloin from the countryside hereabouts. Thank goodness for Dad's pigs. Thank goodness for Joe Long and his shotgun. The gun was mainly used to shoot rabbits, but recently one of their pigs had gone missing. Should the thief attempt to take one of their pigs, Joe Long and Stan Sweet were ready to deal with them in their own way.

They'd also been notified about the introduction of a wartime loaf made from wholegrain flour rather than refined should the latter get scarce. Stan Sweet had been horrified. People preferred white bread.

'Only the very poor used to eat brown bread,' he'd remonstrated before going into a history of how only the rich ate white bread and the hard battles that had been fought so poor folk got white bread too.

The twins worked silently for a while, their hair held back from their faces by turbans made of twisted scarves wound tightly around their heads. Ruby had tugged the knot that should be at the front of her scarf to the side, letting the ends trail down so her mole was hidden.

Mary noticed but said nothing. She'd tried many times to convince Ruby that her mole did not detract from her beauty in any way. Ruby, being Ruby, had her own views and refused to be swayed.

* * *

The following day was the one when Frances was leaving to stay with Miriam Powell's mother in the Forest of Dean. The original plan had been for Stan to drive to the ferry at Aust, disembarking on the other side of the Severn at Bulwark. Unfortunately, he hadn't been able to get any petrol, certainly not enough to cover that particular journey. The priority had to be given to collecting flour and delivering bread.

It was therefore arranged for Mrs Powell's mother, Ada Perkins, to visit her daughter from the Thursday to the Saturday of the next week, mid-way through October. It had been suggested that she arrive in time for the weekend, but Mrs Powell had insisted otherwise.

'Too much church,' Stan Sweet had said with a grin.

When she arrived the next week, old Mrs Perkins, Miriam's grandmother, would have none of it. 'And I wants one of these new cremations and me ashes scattered in the forest when I'm stone cold,' she'd declared for all to hear. 'No coffin for me. The wood rots and the worms gets to eat you. Worms are only good for softening the earth. I don't want them softening me!' Mrs Perkins was tall. Piercing green eyes twinkled above high cheekbones in a wrinkled brown face that was splattered with dark brown freckles. Her hair was pure white and tied back in a bun with pink ribbon and her nose was curved like a bird's beak.

Neither the twins nor Frances had ever seen anyone dressed quite so flamboyantly: her hat was purple, her jacket a dark rust colour and her skirt green. She carried a cloth bag which hung on a multi-coloured string over her shoulder and she strode along purposefully, like a man about to chop down a tree. She also wore hob-nailed boots, just like the sort worn by road menders or miners. Apparently her father had been a miner, working the open shafts and shallow tunnels in the Forest of Dean.

Stan Sweet and his family watched as Ada Perkins, her daughter and granddaughter approached. The twins were full of curiosity; Frances had adopted a careless manner while unpicking the stitching of her skirt. As a consequence the stitching slowly unravelled and the hem drooped unevenly.

Ada Perkins approached like a drum major leading an army platoon. Her daughter and granddaughter trotted along behind her like two black crows. As usual they were dressed in black; in fact, they rarely wore any other colour and certainly weren't used to striding out at such a lick as the woman from the forest.

She came to such an abrupt stop in front of Frances that her daughter and granddaughter were caught unawares and bumped into the back of her.

Ada threw a reproachful look over her shoulder. 'Look where you're going, will you! So this is her then?' she said without giving the women with her time to respond. Closing one green eye, she looked Frances up and down, noticing the pulled stitching and lopsided hem of her skirt.

Without raising her eyes, Frances rubbed the front of one shoe against the back of her leg, a nervous reaction on meeting someone new. On doing so, she knocked over the brown case in which the twins had helped her pack everything she'd need. She'd prided herself on not crying even when the twins had hugged her and told her how much they'd miss her.

Uncle Stan assured her that he would miss her too. 'Be a brave girl,' he said. She'd grimaced at the roughness of his whiskers when he kissed her cheek.

'But you are going on quite an adventure,' Mary had assured her. She could feel the child's apprehension and couldn't help feeling sorry for her.

Hair brushed, her face shining as though it had been polished rather than washed in a tablet of Ruby's favourite soap, Frances stood defiantly, determined not to be cooperative. 'Right. Best be going,' said Ada after having shaken everybody's hand. 'Come along or we'll miss the train.'

The Sweets and the Powells accompanied her to the railway station which was situated on the other side of the hump-backed bridge. The line went up to the Midlands calling in at Gloucester on the way where they would change on to another train running down towards the Wye Valley and the Welsh hills.

'Be brave,' said Mary, bending down so she was level with Frances's pale face. She adjusted Frances's knitted scarf so it fitted more cosily around her neck.

Ruby gave her what remained of the scented soap she'd allowed her to use that morning. 'Be brave,' said Ruby.

'I won't forget,' Frances whispered into her ear as they hugged and kissed for the last time.

There were more waves from the carriage window, Frances unwinding the scarf from around her neck and waving that until the train vanished into a plume of white steam.

'Will she keep our secret?' Ruby whispered to Mary.

'Yes,' Mary murmured back. 'I think so.'

* * *

Things being so busy in the bakery, there was no time to brood on Frances's absence. The bakery competition had yet again been postponed and was now happening on the last Wednesday of November.

The twins had planned what to bake and what recipes relevant to a wartime diet should be considered.

In line with the letter they'd received notifying them that there was a new section in the baking competition, open to all, Mary had not actually come up with three distinct wartime recipes so much as three days' main meals based on a Sunday joint and using up easily available ingredients. Nothing must be wasted.

Ruby had gone in the opposite direction, devising three pudding recipes designed to disguise the fact that ingredients were likely to become scarce and their diet bland. Frugality still figured strongly, though, with Ruby's own take on what was possible if you really put your mind to it.

'Everyone likes a little treat,' she'd declared. Engrossed in being outstandingly creative, she forgot she'd left a tin of condensed milk on the hob. In fact she didn't discover it until the next morning.

She eyed the tin with dismay. 'I was going to make a rice pudding. I can't use it now. It never rains but it pours.'

Mary was mixing leftover vegetables in a bowl before turning it out on a floured board, forming the vegetable mix into roundels then placing each into a pan of hot bacon fat left over from breakfast that morning. The end result would be eaten for supper this evening, though she was saving two to take with her to Bristol. It didn't say anything about taking samples to the bake off, but she made up her mind she would do it anyway.

'Why is it pouring on you?' she asked her sister in response to her despondent tone.

'There's not going to be much sugar around in this war, and

flour is going to be on ration too. How do I make a dessert with the minimum of those particular ingredients?'

'Ingenuity, my dear Ruby, ingenuity!'

'And what is that supposed to mean?'

'Throw in what you can and see what happens!' Ruby laughed. Mary grinned.

The smell of frying rissoles filled the kitchen and didn't help Ruby's concentration. The rissoles were for lunch and made from some minced lamb left over from the Sunday roast, onions and potatoes mixed with freshly cut herbs from the garden.

While Ruby kept her eyes on the rissoles, Mary fetched the tin opener from the dresser drawer and picked up the tin of condensed milk.

'It's probably ruined,' Ruby remarked.

'The proof of the pudding...' said Mary and set to with the tin opener.

'Well,' she said once the contents were revealed. 'That's different.'

Ruby looked at her. 'What is?'

Mary was sucking her finger. 'It tastes like creamy toffee.'

'Let me look.'

Ruby left the rissoles for Mary to oversee. Mary half turned from the pan knowing very well that her sister was already creating a pudding in her head based on the contents of the heated-up tin.

'And?'

Ruby dipped her finger in again, sucking off the toffee-flavoured mixture until her finger was quite clean.

'Creamy toffee pudding on a light sponge base? Victoria sponge with creamy toffee pudding? Creamy toffee and hazelnut pudding – just a little gelatine added to make it set? Frances collected a load of hazelnuts. I used some hazelnuts in a cake, but with this added...?'

'Sounds good.'

'Frances brought me a sack full, there's loads left.' At the mention of Frances, they both fell silent.

'She'll be fine,' Mary said to her sister, though Ruby hadn't actually said anything. They were twins. They knew when the other was happy or sad. They both thought the same way, though one was more focused than the other. In the case of Frances they were of the same mind. They cared for her and hoped she was happy.

Ned Masters, the butcher's son, came into the shop to ask Ruby to go to the pictures.

'I don't think so,' Ruby replied.

Mary was quite surprised. Ned was a nice-looking young man, though perhaps a bit on the big side, but then he was a butcher's son and ate more beef than most people.

He looked disappointed, his cheeks reddening. Nobody liked rejection, thought Mary. She felt quite sorry for him.

'How about you then, Mary. Only I'm off shortly. I got my call-up papers.'

Mary was sympathetic. 'I didn't know that. When are you off, Ned?'

'Two days' time. I've joined the army. I'm off to Aldershot – wherever that is.'

Mary smiled at him. 'Aldershot is eastwards. That's about all I know. Good luck, Ned.'

'Do you fancy going to the pictures with me?'

It was foremost in Mary's mind to say no, but Ned was off to war, so she agreed to go with him.

'Anything good?'

Ned beamed with satisfaction. '*Wicked Lady*. Margaret Lockwood.'

Mary didn't tell him she'd already seen it. Neither did she tell Ruby the true reason she agreed to go with him.

'He's off to war. How could I refuse?'

In her heart she was thinking of somebody else who was also serving in the east of the country, at Scampton in Lincolnshire. She wondered if Michael Dangerfield was going to the pictures with somebody up in Scampton. In one way she hoped he was; it would be a pity for brave young men to be lonely. On the other hand she hoped he was not out with anyone else, but chided herself for being jealous of somebody she only knew vaguely.

15

END OF NOVEMBER, 1939

The village was agog with the news that the next regional heat in the Best of British Baking competition was on and one of their own was taking part. For a heady few days the baking of loaves and pastries displaced what was happening in the war.

The consensus of opinion was that the competition was more relevant to the village than a faraway war which didn't seem to have begun in earnest.

The war seemed to be something not quite real, leaflets rather than bombs being dropped on the enemy. Women had taken to using gas mask cases as handbags, half the time leaving the ugly, smelly rubber thing at home just so they could get their purse, cosmetics and hairbrush inside.

Ruby was like a firework, bursting with enthusiasm and excitement and keeping her vow not to get romantically involved with anyone.

Mary was more subdued, getting done all she had to get done while wondering if Michael Dangerfield would be able to make it to Bristol to take his place in the competition; after all, he was serving with the RAF.

Sometimes Ruby caught her smiling to herself, a faraway look in her eyes.

'Who is he?' she asked again as she had before.

'I was thinking about Charlie. I bet he's having a whale of a time. All those dishy Wrens in uniform.'

'Wish I was one,' grumbled Ruby.

Mary congratulated herself on having successfully eluded Ruby's question. The subject of being a Wren – or at least joining one of the women's services, was guaranteed to throw Ruby off the scent.

'I hope my co-winner is there,' crowed Ruby as she finished putting a glaze on her currant buns. 'Then I can beat him fair and square.'

Mary wasn't interested in beating him. She was only interested in seeing him and asking him why he hadn't responded to her letter. Perhaps because he hadn't received it? Or perhaps he hadn't wanted to respond. The third option was that he expected to see her at the bake off anyway. Her stomach filled with butterflies at the thought of it. She hoped he'd be there. She really did.

She'd gone to the pictures with Ned Masters and had even allowed him to hold her hand and give her a friendly goodnight kiss. He'd tried for a second kiss and asked her if she would be his girl. She'd said no to each question, explaining that she'd known him all her life and even though she valued his friendship, she was not inclined to become romantically involved.

He'd looked disappointed until Mary reminded him that he was off on a big adventure, perhaps abroad. He'd meet lots of girls in Aldershot, France, and perhaps even in Italy.

Much to Mary's relief, his expression brightened at the prospect. She guessed asking her to the pictures was merely because he was feeling a bit scared. She couldn't blame him. The few missives they'd had from Charlie told them it was no picnic and not just because of the enemy. Atlantic storms could last for weeks, the ship rolling from side to side and tossing up and down. He wrote that he was much looking forward to having some leave, though he didn't know when that was likely to be. The letters were being censored, though not too much. Charlie was a careful writer who could drop hints without the censor realising it.

Loved the socks you sent me. Mucho abrigado.

Nobody had sent him any socks, but the clue was in the way he'd said thank you. Mary checked it in a book at the library in Kingswood. He'd said thank you in Portuguese. He was either in Portugal or Brazil. South America was where shiploads of beef and grain were coming from and fruit, vegetables and bottles of port were coming in from Portugal. It could be either, though they hoped the latter country which was much closer to home.

With a mind on the category in the competition for recipes to suit a wartime housewife, Mary asked her customers for any particular hints regarding catering for a large family on meagre rations and a limited budget.

Some of them were derisive of the whole idea.

'Recipes for war? Living on meagre rations? What do they up in London think we bin doing all these years!'

'Then you're the right people to ask about making meals from leftovers and how to make a leg of mutton last a week,' Mary told them.

A little flattery went a long way. The village women and farmers' wives were good cooks, stretching cheap seasonal items as far as they could. This was especially true for those with a whole army of children.

Mrs Martin, whose children comprised of strapping lads and

near-grown men, suggested that the best way to add taste and flavour to leftovers and cheap cuts of meat was with onion.

'That's if you've got a home-grown supply, otherwise it's chives. Plant one chive and you've got dozens by the end of the year.'

Mary had received the advice amicably, but chuckled once Mrs Martin was gone after first begging a bag of stale breadcrumbs to feed to the chickens. 'Bread pudding, more like,' she said to herself.

That night, she told her father what Mrs Martin had said. 'Apparently the first thing we're going to go short of are onions.'

Her father didn't laugh, but nodded solemnly. 'She could be right, especially city folk with no room to grow their own. Most of this country's onions come in from France and Spain. I've planted some next to the leeks. Hopefully things won't get that bad, but you never know. Now how are you getting on with those recipes? Are you going to win outright? I am counting on it you know.'

Ruby stood at the table ironing, a big flannelette sheet folded several times spread at one end of the kitchen table. 'I hate ironing,' she muttered.

Mary reminded her that it was her turn. They took turns with most housework tasks.

Ruby pulled a face and took her favourite blue dress from the pile of clothes waiting to be laundered. 'I think I'll wear this. What do you think?'

Creased as it was, she held it against herself so Mary could better give her opinion.

'It's lovely. You'll be the belle of the bake!'

Ruby laughed. Another thought suddenly struck her. 'Are we going to be able to get there?'

There had been some concern about this. There would be no bus service that day from the village into Kingswood where they would have changed to a city route bus that would take them into

Bristol. Although the bread van was available, they didn't have enough petrol coupons for a special trip.

The answer came swiftly, the door to the room opening to reveal their father's big frame. The moment their father smiled in a boyish way he saved for landing snap surprises, the girls knew something wonderful had happened.

'Well, I have to say, the people of Oldland Common have done us proud. Enough people gave me a few petrol coupons to make the run into Bristol and back again. We've got good neighbours, you know. Very good neighbours. So no need to worry. You're going to Bristol courtesy of Sweet and Son, bakers of distinction!'

Their journey was further assured when a number of coupons came in the post from the Ministry of Food.

Stan Sweet was amazed. 'Now there's a thing. I wonder why they'd be sending me petrol coupons for a competition!'

* * *

The day of their travelling to Bristol was overcast and they'd had to battle through a fog most of the way from the village into the city. Despite the fact that Christmas was only a few weeks away, the city looked sombre and grey, no bright lights or gay window displays. The blackout was in full force.

Sandbags had been piled high between the Palladian pillars at the front of the Victoria Rooms, its imposing facade hidden for the duration of the war. So was the fountain in front of it. No longer were the reclining figures of half-naked mermaids drenched in water from fish-headed spouts, a fitting tribute to a city whose wealth had been derived from the sea and the ships that sailed on it. The fountain was hidden inside a plywood box and like everything else of beauty or importance, piled round with sandbags.

A policeman spotted the van slowing down in front of the cascade of fine steps leading up to the front of the Victoria Rooms.

'I suppose you're here for the competition, sir,' he said, both hands clasped behind his back as he bent to address their father.

'Can you read what it says on this vehicle, constable?'

The police constable gave the side of the van a brief glance. 'Yes, sir. I take it you're Stan Sweet? Baker of distinction?'

'You bet I am,' Stan Sweet responded proudly.

'Over there.' The policeman pointed to where he wanted them to park.

Mary stepped down from the van, glad to stretch her legs after the slow journey in. Despite the blackout and the sandbags, she felt the excitement in the air.

First she gazed in awe at the handsome frontage of the Victoria Rooms. Despite the sandbags, its steps and Palladian pillars reminded her of a Greek or Roman temple. Finally her gaze alighted on the crocodile of people queuing all the way down the steps and around the covered fountain.

'I didn't expect there to be so many people here.' Even to her own ears she sounded awestruck.

'Free admittance, I expect,' said her father who had now climbed out of his van and was standing beside her. 'A bit of light relief for nothing.'

He nodded to a sign stating, baking competition – open to the general public.

'Or the prospect of being gassed,' Ruby added, a cynical expression on her face as she nodded at another sign relating to the dispensing of gas masks for babies.

They made their way up the steps to where a sign said competitors only. Both girls were carrying large wicker baskets containing the items entered for the baking competition, plus the sealed envelopes containing their recipe ideas. The instructions about using sealed envelopes had been typed on the back of the letter they'd received.

'Conserving stationery,' their father had stated. 'It makes sense.'

Mary had baked a fruit loaf sweetened with blackberries picked from the hedgerows, the plumpest and sweetest Frances had managed to find before being evacuated. She'd added a tablespoon of honey for a little extra sweetness. 'It'll taste really sweet with a cup of sugarless tea,' she'd written on the entry form. 'If you go without sugar in your tea, this tea time loaf will taste even sweeter.'

Ruby was envious. Mary had always been better at baking bread than she had. She consoled herself with the fact that the loaf had been entered in her name, seeing as she was the one who'd won the regional heat for the Kingswood area.

Ruby had made a trench cake, a recipe she'd found in an old newspaper from the Great War. It seemed kind of apt seeing as they were presently in another war.

The third item was syrup loaf, made from simple ingredients and didn't take too long to bake.

They'd also brought the required recipes, three main meals and three desserts. The main meal recipes were entered in Mary's name, the desserts in Ruby's.

The addition of entering recipes for the competition had come as something of a surprise and it had specifically stated meals made from ordinary ingredients. On top of that it was open to all, which to Stan's mind had little to do with a competition, more as though somebody was gathering them in for a reason.

Remember that brave men in ships are risking their lives to bring us food. Not a scrap must be wasted. Be frugal and remember that every morsel wasted on the kitchen front means wasted space in ships, and wasted efforts on the part of our merchant fleet.

Ruby and Mary took that last line on board. Charlie was one of those brave merchant seaman. After Ruby had read it out, both girls looked at each other, determination shining in their eyes.

'This is personal,' said Ruby.

Mary agreed. 'We have to do our bit.'

They'd totally understood – or thought they did – that the organisers were actively requesting ideas for making something from next to nothing. The regional competition at the village fete had required exquisite innovation, a luxury now confined to a pre-war environment.

They'd talked about how to cut corners, how to avoid wastage and what recipes would better suit the likely rationing scheduled to come into being in the New Year.

Despite everything, the prospect of dreaming up ingenious dishes had excited them. They both put in the maximum effort, running their ideas past each other and also past their father. Stan Sweet became their guinea pig, sampling each recipe and giving his honest opinion. Like them he felt that doing their bit supported Charlie and others like him, crossing the oceans to bring them supplies.

The crowd queuing to view the competition, the 'free entertainment', Stan Sweet had suggested, turned out to be larger than those queuing for the latest gas masks made for infants. People jostled on all sides, but gradually the queue evened out and they were directed to where they had to go.

'Excuse me.' A well-dressed woman with an imperious manner brushed past them, the square shoulders of her impeccably designed suit hunched as though disinclined for her shoulders to brush against theirs.

The woman's eyes were fixed on the podium set at the far end of the room and she was flanked on either side by two officious-looking men wearing bowler hats and carrying rolled-up umbrellas and brief cases.

Ruby frowned. 'They're not the same judges as before.'

Stan Sweet felt uneasy. 'Don't look like bakers to me. Looks more like men from the ministry.'

Mary's feelings echoed theirs. She'd been feeling uneasy all morning and now even more so.

Ruby had confided she was feeling the same but had added, 'Today should be exciting, but somehow... Oh well,' she'd said, shrugging off her nervousness as normal. 'I'll keep my mind on what comes after.'

Mary suspected she was referring to leaving home.

The entries for the competition were laid out on a table to await judgement. Mary and Ruby were told where to place theirs.

For a moment they both stared at the entries, the gleaming steak and kidney pies, gorgeous-looking cakes decorated with chocolate, buns coated with icing and glacé cherries. Surely such ingredients would be in short supply before long?

Both harbouring feelings of misgiving, the twins exchanged worried looks. Their entries looked so mundane compared to the others.

Mary squeezed her sister's arm reassuringly. 'We've followed the instructions to the letter. Our recipes make sense. The judges have to see that.'

The envelopes containing suggested recipes for a wartime house-wife were handed to the snooty-looking woman with the shoulder pads. Without even looking at them, she pushed them across to the gentlemen their father had said looked like government officials. They were still wearing their bowler hats, umbrellas hung on the backs of their chairs, briefcases clenched between their ankles.

Without referral to the haughty-looking woman, the men began opening the envelopes, their heads coming closely together as they conferred with each other, the brims of their hats almost colliding in the process.

Suddenly the woman in the sharp suit with the sharp features sprang to her feet as though somebody had pricked her with a hat pin.

'Ladies and gentlemen,' she shouted in a shrill voice. 'May I have your attention. Please welcome Alderman Bentley, Lord Mayor of Bristol.'

Chin held high, she began clapping, nodding at the crowd as though urging them to follow her lead.

Those come to see what was happening turned respectful gazes on the august personage coming through the door. As though he were Moses parting the Red Sea, a path opened to enable him to gain the podium.

Mary and Ruby craned their necks. 'Can you see anything?' they each asked their father, the tallest of the three of them.

'Only his hat,' Stan Sweet replied.

The two girls stood on tiptoe and managed a glimpse of a silky black topper bobbing past between the heads in front of them.

The clapping got louder the closer he got to the podium, becoming more enthusiastic once he was up there, his golden chain shining, his black moustache as thick as a sweeping brush. He wasn't that tall, the top of his head barely reaching the square shoulders of the woman in the blue suit. Stretching himself to his full height, he began an opening address.

'Firstly my thanks to Lady Dorothy Huntspill, home economics and dietary advisor to His Majesty's government, who today has agreed to judge the delicious items entered for this culinary event. Secondly, I thank you all for coming here in these difficult times, though ultimately I am sure you agree, the British people will overcome their present difficulties. Hip hip hooray for the British Empire. Hip, hip hooray for our brave soldiers, sailors and airmen.'

A great cheer went up, the mayor waving his hat as though attempting to fan the flames of patriotism.

As the cheering died, the mayor turned to the woman in blue. 'Lady Huntspill? Can I ask you to commence judging?' The woman who he'd confirmed as the one and only judge, came down from the podium like a queen about to mingle with the peasants. She made her way to the table of delights where she moved slowly along, scrutinising some entries but hardly looking at others.

Mary and Ruby perceived a slight wrinkling of her nose and immediately surmised she was scrutinising their entries. Although her expression was unreadable, their hopes began to die.

Every so often she pointed at one of the entries, an indication she wished to taste a little. Only the smallest morsel passed her lips, each time using a fresh spoon or fork.

Ruby leaned towards her sister. 'Hardly a healthy appetite. No wonder she's thin.'

Mary agreed with her. 'I doubt she's ever going to work in a factory making bombs or drive a tractor. But then, looks can be deceptive...'

Ruby grumbled about upper-class women who only played at baking.

Mary grunted an agreement, her attention continually returning to the two men left on the stage. The judge had not had anything to do with the envelopes that she'd passed to these two officious types who were presently sifting through the contents of each one. Who were they? Why weren't they taking part in the judging? And what was their interest in the recipes?

'I can't stand this much longer,' moaned Ruby.

Stan Sweet reminded her that it was only a competition. It

would be all over by the end of the afternoon and tomorrow would be normal. 'And stop biting your lip.'

'I'm nervous,' Ruby said to her father. 'She wrinkled her nose at my bread. I'm sure she did. I don't think I can stand to watch much longer.'

She began playing with the strand of hair that covered her left cheek.

Her father put his arm around her shoulder. 'Tell you what. I saw a WVS van outside handing out tea and buns. How about we hang around there for a bit until we're called for?'

'If we're called for,' Ruby said glumly.

Mary refused the offer of tea and buns. No matter the result, she had to see this through to the bitter end. 'I'll stay and see what happens. I'll come out and fetch you if you're needed.'

Lady Huntspill moved around the exhibits like a feral cat about to leap on its prey. She did another pass of the table, revisiting the items she'd favoured on the first pass, pointing at certain items and totally ignoring others. To Mary's dismay she totally ignored her own and Ruby's entries, concentrating instead on some very florid items that would use up the envisaged rations and not be in the price bracket or experience of the everyday housewife.

Mary was vexed. She shook her head in dismay. What was going on here? Had she totally misread what was called for?

'Fancy meeting you here.'

Mary turned her head swiftly. She recognised that voice. At first the brim of her hat hid the speaker's face, but having tilted her head back, she saw him. Michael Dangerfield was here.

'You!'

'You,' Michael Dangerfield repeated.

'I wasn't sure you'd be here,' she said, trying hard not to stammer or sound breathless at the sight of him. She wanted to ask him whether he'd received her letter, but felt nervous asking him.

The tall young man who had stalked her dreams was really here, smiling down at her in such a way that she went weak at the knees.

'I knew you'd be here,' he said in that warm drawl of his. 'That's why I came. That and aiming to pick up the prize. Ten pounds. A useful sum. I can pay my bar bill back at Scampton with that and have plenty left over. Are you alone?'

'No. My father and sister couldn't stand the suspense. They went outside for a cup of tea. There's a WVS van outside.'

'Good for them. At least they know what's wanted at a time like this. Plenty of tea offered with a willing smile and a warm heart.'

So far he had not mentioned her letter, and she was loath to mention it first. She fancied he looked a little thinner, his face a little more careworn.

'So! How's the war?'

He shook his head. His look was grim and there was a strange haunted look in his eyes.

'Things are hotting up.'

'What does that mean?'

'Some of our guys are getting killed.'

Anything she could say would be a platitude, yet she wanted to keep him here, talking about anything and everything; just to hear the sound of his voice and see that boyish look on such a strong, masculine face.

'How about your friend, Guy? He hasn't been... I mean...'

Michael grinned. 'He's been decorated. A flyer's flyer.'

Mary heard herself laughing, a light, happy laugh of relief.

'And Felix?'

'Felix is still Felix. The guys spoil him rotten. He's cool with guys. I think skirts set him off – beg your pardon – until he gets to know them. And I don't mean that you're just a skirt... you're a bit more than that. And thanks for the letter. I would have written, but things are getting a little hectic. Anyway,' he added with a beaming smile, 'I was hoping I could thank you for writing face to face. Beats letter writing any day of the week.'

Mary felt a warm glow cover her from head to foot. She even felt herself blushing, which was not something she was used to. The silence between them persisted as they both gathered their thoughts and weighed up their options.

Michael couldn't stop looking at her, thinking how gorgeous she was and wishing he hadn't used the words 'skirts'. He'd dated plenty of 'skirts', fun relationships that hadn't lasted a month. Even at this early stage, he knew his feelings for Mary were different than the others. They had cooking in common and that had to be a good thing, though of course there were other things to be considered. He wanted to kiss her, hug her and yes, he wanted to go to bed with her. But, more than that, something was tickling at his heart.

For her part, Mary was trying not to appear too forward even though she hadn't stopped thinking about him.

'So you bought a new dress?' She said she had.

'A big improvement on the last one, I bet. Oh. Sorry. That came out all wrong.'

Whoops! He'd done it again. What was wrong with him, Mr Smoothie himself, known to have a glib line for every occasion?

'It wasn't that bad,' replied Mary tartly, smarting at the insinuation that her old dress wasn't up to much. It was enough to convince her not to appear too keen.

'I thought all girls liked new dresses.'

'I'm not all girls.'

There was a firm set to her chin and a proud look in her eyes. He wanted to say that he agreed with her. She certainly wasn't like all girls. She was special, but was now the right time to say that? He decided a rain check was in order.

'Sure you're not. All the girls I've ever met preferred powdering their noses with fancy stuff, not flour... what I mean to say is...'

It was too late. He could tell by the look on her face that he'd done it again, opened his mouth and shoved a foot in it. What was it about this girl? What was happening to him?

Mary tossed her head and looked away. 'So. First my dress isn't up to standard, and now I've got flour on my nose.'

'I didn't exactly mean you have, well not at this moment in time, but that morning...'

She rounded on him swiftly. 'Stop making fun of me, Mr Dangerfield. I fully admit that I'm not one of the sophisticated girls that pilots of aeroplanes are used to. Now perhaps we can concentrate on the judging? I dare say that's what you're really here for?'

The result of the competition was important and she knew Ruby would be very disappointed if she didn't win. So far the signs were not good. Lady Huntspill had looked totally disinterested in the more humble fare ordinary folk might make and consume. Mary was also possessed with an overwhelming desire to find a mirror and check whether she really did have flour on her nose. She settled for getting out her handkerchief and blowing into it, dabbing at the tip of her nose just in case.

'I think I could win this,' he murmured against her ear. 'For the wrong reasons...'

She frowned, not understanding what he meant until she saw her ladyship smile in his direction and she knew, she just knew that he was right.

'You know the judge?'

'Ahuh!'

He looked straight ahead, thinking girls weren't usually this difficult to get on with. Despite the lovely letter she'd sent him, he presumed it was out of pity – make the dude in the air feel good. He'd put his foot in it too many times already. She was bound to brush him off if he asked her out.

Mary too was having second thoughts. Men like him loved

receiving letters from naive girls like her. They thrived on it, naive young girls being putty in their hands. Well, she wasn't going to fall for him. That's what she told herself.

There was a reason they were here and she determined to stick to it. And now he was telling her that he knew the judge. She couldn't help but have a dig at him.

'Don't you think it was a good idea to challenge the competitors to create recipes to suit war rations? None of this foreign muck. Italian and suchlike. Just good British food.'

Michael Dangerfield eyed her sidelong. So that was the way it was going to be. He cleared his throat, shoved his hands in his pockets and put on the kind of voice a pal back in Canada used to use: Bragging Billy they called him.

'Nothing to do with the competition. Not really. It's all about the baking and her ladyship has very definite views on what makes a good meal. She has very cultured tastes. You can tell that by the way she dresses. Very elegant. She'll go for something very upmarket or foreign. One of my Italian breads perhaps, brioche, or that French lemon tart. Did you see that? Light as a feather and a very piquant taste. Very piquant!'

He'd heard a lot of French people use the word piquant.

Sharp as a lemon, he thought. Very apt.

Mary scowled at him. He was making fun of her again and smiling at her, then smirking, then smiling again as though he couldn't quite make up his mind how she would react. If she'd been able to read his mind she'd know just how clumsy he was feeling, undecided on how to get her to go out with him. But she didn't. Her tone was sharp – as *piquant* as the lemon tart he'd been praising.

'Surely not! If this war isn't over by Christmas, the ingredients will become scarce. Dishes calling for special ingredients – and lemons will be special seeing as they don't grow in this country – just won't be practical.'

'She wouldn't agree with you. Anyway, you might as well prepare yourself. I'm going to win.'

He didn't want to believe it, but Lady Huntspill knew his family. All the same he wanted to lose. He wanted to make it up with Mary. He wanted to do a lot of things with Mary.

Mary clenched her jaw while recalling how Ruby had felt over misinterpreting Gareth's intentions. It now looked as though she too had foolishly misinterpreted Michael Dangerfield's intentions towards her.

'I believe you're telling the truth,' she said solemnly.

'You mean that?'

He winced under the power of her beautiful eyes, detecting a hint of violet in the piercing blue. Perhaps it was her dark lashes aiding that impression, so black they looked as though they'd been dipped in soot.

Mary eyed him steadily, not caring to admit even to herself that she'd misread him so totally. She looked for some sign that she had not. Although the laughter lines at the corners of his eyes were still obvious, the eyes themselves held a cynical look.

'That would be so unfair.'

He shrugged. 'All's fair in love and war.'

He wanted to add 'and with us it could be love', but he did want to win that prize. He had plans for it and, besides, his mother would be so pleased.

This time when she looked at him he thought he saw contempt in her eyes, certainly not love.

Mary turned angry. 'You had no business entering if you know that woman. It's unscrupulous!'

Heads turned at her raised voice.

Michael shrugged helplessly, aware that he'd gone the whole hog and blown any chance of getting to know Mary better.

'I don't care about winning. It's not why I'm here. It just doesn't matter. I had a plan for the money—'

'Yes. Your bar bill. You said so.'

'And for my mom. She'd be so proud if I won. Things haven't been—'

Mary failed to pick up on everything he said, failed to ask him why he was really there. All that mattered was the competition and it being fair to everyone who'd entered.

Her eyes were blazing. 'My sister and I put a lot into those recipes and our entries. We used our brains to work things out based on what ingredients would be available. You upper-crust types just don't have a clue!'

'I'm sorry—' He laid his hand on her shoulder, but she shrugged it off.

'I'm sorry too. Forget I ever sent that letter.'

'I don't want to forget it.'

'Your aunt thought it would be a good idea. She asked me so I did it. She's a nice lady.' She hoped her words would hurt him, hoped he would take it that she had not written the letter on her own volition but at the request of his aunt.

Up until now Michael had believed she had fallen for him on the first occasion they'd met, just as he had fallen for her. That was why she'd written to him.

The disappointment stung. Baking competitions were fun and he prided himself on what he did. As it was, his duties with the RAF now took up most of his time, but he'd managed to wangle some time off – not really so much for the competition, but to see Mary again. He'd even held off replying to her letter because he much preferred to see her in the flesh. He had been going to tell her that. The situation had changed. It seemed things were not as he'd thought.

'You shouldn't have bothered,' he said disparagingly, his hands in his pockets, smiling as he shook his head. 'It isn't as though I'm starved of female company.'

She felt her face reddening and knew it wasn't just anger.

The Lord Mayor called for their attention. 'Ladies and gentlemen. Pray silence!'

All heads turned to face the front. In an attempt to calm herself Mary placed her hand over her racing heart. This was it. This was the moment they'd been waiting for, but instead of excitement she was already feeling dejected.

Lady Huntspill was once again introduced, this time by the Lord Mayor, returning the favour of her introducing him.

A picture of total confidence and upper-class poise, her ladyship rose to her feet and began to speak, her accent as plummy as a BBC announcer.

'It was with great pleasure that I accepted this opportunity to officiate at this glittering event. Let me begin by saying that just because there's a war on does not mean to say we can let standards drop. There is no excuse that nutritious, economic meals should become bland and unappetising. We should aim for the kind of standard we're likely to be served in some very good restaurants, and I am not talking about the Ritz: excellent food is readily available all over this country. Therefore, with that premise in mind, I hereby announce the results of each category in turn.'

At the sound of her ladyship's crisply pronounced vowels, Mary felt a chill emptiness in her stomach that had nothing to do with not eating any breakfast. The results were announced and none of them included anything she or Ruby had entered. Each announcement was followed by titters of approval from well-turned-out women in expensive hats; women who indulged in cooking as a hobby – and with help from professional cooks they just happened to employ.

She felt Michael Dangerfield stealing furtive glances at her, but could not bring herself to face him. The class system was alive and well. She found herself hoping that by the end of this war it was dead and buried.

In her opinion the ingredients of the winning entries were far beyond the purse of an ordinary housewife, but then it was unlikely that Lady Dorothy Hunstpill had ever met an ordinary housewife, certainly not a working-class one!

One prize after another was handed out to prim women whose husbands had well-paid jobs in banks and offices and who lived in spacious detached houses complete with a cook and a maid.

As at the regional contest in Oldland Common, the winner of the bread category was the last to be announced. Although she already guessed what was to come, she couldn't drag herself away and run outside to tell her father and sister their journey had been for nothing.

'I'd like to see you again.'

His voice was barely audible among that of the crowd.

Presuming she hadn't heard, he repeated what he'd said. 'I heard you,' she snapped back.

Still she couldn't look at him; not until this was over, and even then the anger would persist.

'I have the feeling I need to say something really dramatic to grab your attention. Or perhaps an apology?'

She remained focused on Lady Huntspill, a woman who had never in her life had to make a meal from scraps left over from earlier in the week. Who'd never made brawn from a pig's head or begged a ham bone or bacon bones from the butcher in order to make soup. She knew plenty of people who did have to do that.

Mrs Hicks's nephew repeated what he'd just said. 'It appears I was right,' he added.

'Does it?'

He assumed he had some of her attention. 'How dramatic shall I be?'

'What?' She glanced at him briefly, her attention swiftly going back to her ladyship. This was it. The winner of the bread section.

'How about I ask you to marry me?'

Mary looked at him and frowned. Surely she'd misheard. 'And finally the speciality bread. And the winner is... Mr Michael Ricardo Dangerfield...'

His name rang out louder than that of the previous winners. The applause was louder too, mainly because he was the only entrant wearing a uniform.

'Mary—'

Mary spun on her heels, her flight impeded by the press of the crowd. All she wanted was to get away. He'd lied to her. He'd said he was here because he knew she would be here too. But that wasn't the reason at all. He'd come to take the prize. He *knew* he would take the prize.

'Perhaps we could share...'

She didn't wait to hear the end of what he was saying and she certainly had no intention of sharing the prize with him.

Angrily, she pushed through the crowd. Her face was flushed, her heart racing. Michael Dangerfield had won outright.

Before passing through the double mahogany doors and leaving the building, she heard his name called again.

'Mr Michael Ricardo Dangerfield, please come forward to claim your prize.'

Michael Ricardo? The woman even knew his second name. Perhaps he'd entered under his full name. But then, he'd told her his family was known to her ladyship so she was likely to know his full name!

Pulling the brim of her hat more closely over her eyes, she went in search of her father and Ruby. She found them among a group of people gathered around the WVS van. Their expressions were stiff, as though already gearing themselves for disappointment. Mary concluded they'd guessed the result. 'I see you've heard the news. Oh well. It's not the end of the world,' she said as brightly as she could. 'I think we were too downmarket for her ladyship.'

To her surprise, the expressions of her father and sister were unchanged. Suddenly she saw the pain in their eyes. Her heart missed a beat. Something was wrong. Something was seriously wrong.

Her father pointed to a newspaper seller's billboard displaying the latest headline. 'Never mind the bloody baking competition. Look at that. Would you just bloody look at that.' Mary looked to where he indicated. The headline read:

Grain Ships Sunk in the South Atlantic.

Somebody passed her a newspaper. Her heart that had been racing during the baking competition now raced for a very different reason. She read the list of ships. One of them was very familiar. Its name was *Baltic Legend.*

'Oh my God!' She turned to her father. 'But we haven't heard anything. It doesn't mean that Charlie... he could have been rescued. That's right, isn't it? He could have been rescued.' She was fully aware that she was screeching, but she couldn't help it. She just couldn't help it.

Her father chewed thoughtfully on his unlit pipe and nodded. 'If you read on, it says that there were casualties but also survivors. The survivors were picked up by the battleship that sank her. They think it was the Graf Spee, a surface raider anyway.'

Mary took a deep breath, anger replaced by a cold heavy feeling in the pit of her stomach.

'So he could have been taken prisoner. It is possible, isn't it,' she asked in a small voice that didn't sound like her own.

Her father tapped the stem of his pipe against his chin. 'We don't know.' His voice was strong and his expression was unfaltering. 'We've received nothing official and until we do, we *can't* know.'

'Excuse me.'

A small man with thin grey hair and clasping a fistful of papers, came rushing up to them, colourless eyes peering at them through spectacles with very thick lenses.

He addressed the twins, his pale eyes blinking from one sister to the other. 'You are Miss Ruby Sweet and Miss Mary Sweet?'

Ruby glared at him, angry that he'd interrupted. 'That's us and we're not available at the moment.'

He looked taken aback. 'I'm sorry! But I have to inform you that you are wanted back inside. Both of you.' He looked at Mary then back at Ruby.

Ruby looked him up and down and decided he must be a doorman or someone who worked at the Vic Rooms.

'Unless we've won first prize, we're not bothering. We haven't won first prize have we?'

'Well, no, but—'

'Tell him to go to hell,' said Mary. She already knew they hadn't won. She assumed that Michael Dangerfield had sent him out to fetch them.

'But Miss Sweet. It's very important—'

'I'm sorry,' she snapped. 'We've just received some worrying news. We have to go.'

She looped her arm through that of her father's. 'Come on, Dad. Let's go home.'

It wasn't until they had left the city behind and were heading up past St George's Park, roughly halfway home, that it suddenly struck Mary that Michael Dangerfield, so full of himself in that air force uniform, had asked her to marry him. Something about it struck her as funny, funny and tragic.

She began to laugh, a high-pitched hysterical laugh. Both her sister and her father looked at her, both thinking this was hardly the time for laughter, until they saw tears streaming down her face.

* * *

Ruby pulled up the canvas shutter on the shop door. Normally the morning light flooding in made her feel happy. Today her sombre mood remained, mainly because of the news regarding her brother.

The weather wasn't helping. The sky was gun-metal grey and the wind and rain set the old door rattling in its frame.

How had the South Atlantic been, she wondered? She'd learned enough about geography in school to know that even though it was December, it was summer south of the equator.

News was slow in forthcoming. The postmaster, Melvyn Chance, had come around with a telegram from the merchant navy saying that Charlie was presently missing in action and that enquiries were ongoing. It was expected that more detailed news would be received shortly.

They waited desperately to hear of his whereabouts. Ruby preferred to see the positive side of this: at least her brother was only listed as missing. She couldn't – she wouldn't – believe Charlie was dead. Hopefully – and she knew it was strange to hope for this – he was a prisoner of war; even a long internment without seeing him was preferable to seeing his name listed among the dead.

Stan Sweet kept making enquiries, but nothing was yet clear. The people he'd managed to hunt down were disinclined to comment, except to say they were depending on the international Red Cross or a neutral embassy to acquire a list of casualties, fatalities and those interned.

Each morning, at the sound of the postman's footsteps, they all left the baking bread to congregate in the shop, opening the door before Melvyn Chance could post anything through the letterbox.

'Expect he's fine and dandy,' he'd say most mornings with a sickening grin. Instead of wearing his postman's cap, he'd taken to wearing a tin helmet with ARP written on the front of it as though that would somehow make up for his earlier association with the black shirts.

Stan Sweet asked when he was likely to be off serving his country.

'Reserved occupation,' Melvyn had stated falteringly. 'What with the post office and my new position as air-raid warden. One day this war will be over and I'd like my grandchildren – should I ever have grandchildren – to know that I did my bit. I wouldn't want to feel embarrassed.' His wide mouth expanded over yellow misshapen teeth.

'I think what you did before the war is likely to be more embarrassing,' Stan Sweet snarled, leaving Melvyn in no doubt that his dalliance with Sir Oswald Mosley's Nazi party would not be forgotten. At least not by him!

The weather worsened, the rain lashing against the windows. Branches of stout trees bowed and creaked in the wind, whipping backwards and forwards in the teeth of the gale. Broken branches and twigs littered the ground.

How had it been for Charlie, Ruby wondered again, all that stormy sea and then being sunk by an enemy battleship?

She bowed her head, tears filling her eyes. On looking up she found herself face to face through the glass with Miriam Powell.

Brushing the wetness from her eyes, she opened the door. 'Good morning, Miriam.'

'Is it true?' asked Miriam. She bustled in, her eyes wide and her face pale with fear.

Ruby nodded, saying that the news was indeed grave, but gave a tight smile in an effort to look brave even if she didn't feel it. 'We don't know whether he's been taken prisoner. We're waiting to hear.'

'I shall pray for him,' Miriam said softly, laying her hand on Ruby's arm, her eyes closed in prayer. 'Dear Lord, please hear our prayer. Fold thy wings around thy beloved servant, Charles Henry Sweet. Keep him safe from harm. Pluck him from the perils of the deep and the clutches of evil men. Amen.'

Ruby was taken by surprise. She'd presumed Miriam was referring to praying in church this coming Sunday. It had also surprised her that Miriam knew Charlie's middle name. Henry. Ruby found herself repeating 'amen'. She might not be as dedicated a churchgoer as Miriam was, but in the present circumstances, she would try anything if it meant Charlie's safe return.

'I've had a letter from my grandmother,' Miriam went on. 'She says that Frances has settled in very well and seems to like the forest very much.'

Mary joined them and couldn't help smiling. 'She would. She loves trees.'

'Have you had a letter from her?'

Both twins shook their heads. Mary laughed. 'Frances must be enjoying herself and wouldn't dream of writing to anyone unless they write to her first. I've been meaning to but...'

'I think I'll write to her today,' said Ruby, promising herself that she would.

Mary covered Miriam's hand with her own. 'Just one thing. Tell your mother not to mention about Charlie being missing, but if she does, tell your grandmother not to mention it to Frances. She'd be very upset.'

Miriam promised faithfully that her wishes would be adhered to and bought a loaf of bread.

'My mother will pray for him too and I'm sure Cecil Mayhew, the new Methodist minister, will be only too happy to oblige. He's very considerate.'

Mary noticed that Miriam's eyes glowed almost as much at the mention of the new minister as they did when she spoke of Charlie. Could it be that Miriam had transferred her affection from Charlie to the minister? Despite everything, she smiled at the thought.

The day continued to be wet and overcast, customers rushing in to buy bread during the infrequent lulls in rain and wind. Between serving customers, Ruby wrote her letter to Frances. She wouldn't mention Charlie: Frances adored Charlie and if she was to be told at all it was probably best if it came from their dad.

Mary went upstairs, toying with a piece of writing paper and a pen. She had it in mind to write to Michael Dangerfield and tell him that if he was the last man on earth, she wouldn't marry him. Surely it wouldn't seem out of the way to write and tell him about her brother Charlie – even though he'd never met him. She finally decided to leave things as they were until they had more accurate news.

Her father had announced a decision at teatime that Frances would come home for Christmas. He would tell her about Charlie then, face to face. Surely the enemy wouldn't bomb them at Christmas?

Before the news of the sinking of *Baltic Legend* they'd all hoped that Charlie might get leave at Christmas. Everyone agreed that if he wasn't home they would all go along to midnight mass at St Anne's. It was the least they could do.

Christmas, they all concluded, would be bleak this year. Nobody felt like celebrating until they knew Charlie was safe.

16

Frances had decided not to speak to Ada Perkins for the whole journey to the forest. Not that Ada seemed to notice. She herself hadn't spoken a word since they'd said their goodbyes at the station. She'd sat there, her head resting on the back of the seat, her eyes closed.

Frances contented herself with looking at the passing scenery, the silvery thread of the River Severn showing beyond the green fields on one side of the railway track, trees and scattered cottages on the other.

Only when she was certain the old woman was asleep did she dare look at her, the strong face in profile, mouth open, jaw sagging, nostrils dilating and expanding with the sound of resonant snoring.

Frances fidgeted, sighed and purposely sounded fed up and sorry for herself. In response Ada Perkins opened one eye surveying her like a snake who's just decided it's hungry.

'Let's get one thing straight,' she said at last. 'My daughter asked me to do this favour. So you'd better behave yourself. I have no time for girls who don't behave themselves. Have you ever read the story about Hansel and Gretel?'

Frances nodded.

'Then let it be a warning to you.'

Before being evacuated, Frances had made up her mind not to like either the place or the woman she was to be boarded with. Stan Sweet's powers of persuasion were exactly that – powerful – but once away from his influence, the seeds of rebellion sprouted into life.

Pouting and barely speaking was only part of her campaign. Another was adopting a hangdog expression and sloping shoulders, her hands held disconsolately at her side, fists clenched, like the orangutans she'd seen on a visit to Bristol Zoo.

Despite the intrigue of a forest and all its legends, she had made up her mind to miss her family, miss the village kids and Oldland Common in general. As for Ada Perkins, she was old and wore funny clothes. She also smoked a pipe, not that she was the only woman she'd seen do so. Some of the old women in Oldland Common did too, mostly the widows of coalminers and labourers, tough sorts who killed their own chickens and spat like men.

Ada was just as tough and uncompromising as those women.

'Stop looking as though you've only got a few minutes to live and get used to it. You'll settle in soon enough,' said Ada Perkins. 'I took you in out of the goodness of me heart. Like it or lump it! I don't care which.'

Once off the train and walking along a forest track to Ada's home, the old woman strode on ahead, leaving Frances to walk along behind, still lugging her battered brown suitcase.

Meaning to keep up her disconsolate manner, Frances kept her head down but found feeling sorry for herself wasn't easy to do especially considering she was surrounded by the most beautiful trees.

In some places no daylight penetrated the thick canopy of fir trees and pines. In other places oak trees grew. She couldn't resist slowing her footsteps and staring at them. It didn't escape her notice that they seemed to be planted in a circle.

'It's called a grove,' Ada Perkins shouted over her shoulder having noticed the girl's reason for slowing down. 'They're very old. It's where the priests of the old religion used to pray to their gods.' She turned, her bright eyes seeming to glow silver against a background of tangled branches and silver-grey tree trunks. 'Oak groves are sacred and should never be violated. Do you hear me, girl?'

Frances shuddered at the look in eyes that seemed to shine with different colours. She made a mental note never to do anything wicked within sight of those oak groves.

The track through the forest zig-zagged ever upwards through tall evergreens, big enough to make telegraph poles, which Ada informed her were probably what they would be used for once they were fully grown. She also explained that the track was mainly used by loggers, Free Miners – whatever they were – some of whom owned the straggly coated Jacob sheep that roamed the forest at will. Few other people ever came this way.

The house in which Ada Perkins lived was little more than a shack clinging to the hillside overlooking a wooded valley through which the River Wye meandered like a grey silk ribbon. Sheep grazed in green pastures and the sky curved over it all, like the inside of a silver lid.

Logs were piled to one side of the shack and a small shed on the other which Ada told her was a smoke house.

'So why do you smoke your pipe out here?' asked Frances having never come across the term before.

Ada Perkins closed one eye when she looked at her and lit her pipe. 'What d'ya mean?'

'The smoke house. Is that where you go to smoke?'

Ada threw back her head and laughed long and loud. 'No. No.

No. I smoke things in the smoke house. Fish, fowl, sides of Gloucestershire ham. I might even smoke you if you're not careful.'

During those first days, the local minister dropped by. Frances overheard him asking whether he might expect the young girl lodging with her at Sunday school.

'If she wants to, but don't expect me as well. You don't, do ya?'

'We...ll n...o,' he said slowly, sounding more than a little bit nervous.

'Then don't expect her if she don't want to go.'

'But the child might be used to going to Sunday school—'

'I was used to going to church until twenty-five years ago, my friend. I parted with God back then and have never regretted it, so if the girl wants to go, she can, but I'm not forcing her to.'

'You say that very loudly and eloquently,' he said in his hesitant, soft-mannered tone.

'You should try doing the same yourself, Mr Jones, then less of your congregation would be falling asleep during your sermons.'

Frances was relieved. It had crossed her mind that she might be expected to attend Sunday school at least, and possibly church too. Uncle Stan had told her that if it pleased Mrs Perkins for her to go to church, then she should do so.

'Be nice to her, Frances. She's lived alone for a long time and has given you shelter when she didn't need to. It's a kindness. So be nice. Be like a daughter to her, or a granddaughter.' Frances was glad that Ada Perkins had stood up to the minister and began to relax, her sullen manner slowly dissipating.

Ada began to open up, speaking in a strident tone about her daughter, her granddaughter and the fact that her daughter's husband had been a weak man with beady eyes that to her mind were too close together.

'Never trust a man whose eyes are too close together,' she said to Frances, her expression deadly serious.

Frances had said nothing but readily took in the information. She soon came to know that Mrs Perkins, or Ada as she insisted Frances call her, was full of such sayings.

'Never whistle indoors and never stare too long at a full moon. You'll go mad if you do.'

Frances began to hang on to her every word. She didn't have a living grandmother, but decided that if she should ever acquire one, she'd choose one just like Ada Perkins.

A few of her friends back in Oldland Common had grandmothers. Most of them knitted a lot, but none of them, not one single one, was as interesting or colourful as Ada. And none of them lived in a forest as beautiful as this – it was even better than the orchard back in Oldland Common.

Gradually Frances let go of her initial hostility. In time, Ada was talking about anything and everything about her life in the forest.

Frances listened, fascinated by Ada's stories and strange and interesting facts. Ada had a remarkable memory and spoke in vivid descriptions, so vivid that Frances saw pictures in her mind.

By the time she started school a few days later, Frances was quite content with her lot and had begun exploring the forest that surrounded Ada's shack.

The shack was made of wood. The front was painted green, the same green as the bus that ran three times a week through Oldland Common. The sides of the house were painted a dull burgundy and the rear bright orange.

The windows of the shack, which Ada called a bungalow, looked down from a gap in the trees at the glorious view. At night the crisp air of winter was punctuated with the hooting of owls, the high-pitched bark of a fox and other wild creatures. The moon seemed much brighter than back in Oldland Common, but she was careful to adhere to Ada's advice and not look at it for too long.

It had surprised her enormously on her walk to school to be confronted with a wild deer. For a moment their eyes had met, both dark brown and round with surprise. Then the deer was gone, bushes whipping behind it, dead leaves rustling where its feet had kicked.

A boy called Deacon was the first to speak to her. 'Bet you can't climb trees.'

'Bet you I can,' she responded hotly.

'You're a girl. My grancher can climb trees better'n you!'

'I can climb better than any grancher,' she further proclaimed. She presumed grancher was the name of his brother, but wasn't going to ask. A new girl in the class had to stand her ground. It didn't pay to appear ignorant or weak; making the right impression on the first day at school mattered.

His eyes narrowed. His grin widened. 'What's the bet then?'

Frances didn't hesitate. 'A catapult. I made it myself,' she said proudly. 'What you going to bet?'

The boy's hair was overlong, flopping like a carpet over his eyes as he thought about it. 'A rabbit skin. It's all cured. I done it myself. I'll bring it in tomorrow.'

Frances hadn't a clue what to do with a rabbit skin having never owned one before, but accepted the bet anyway.

She didn't fail to tell Ada when she got home.

'Hm,' said Ada. 'Should make you a nice pair of mittens. Not gloves, mind you. You'd need two skins for that I shouldn't wonder. P'raps even three. Now all you got to do is show 'im you can climb a tree.'

Frances dreamed of those rabbit skin mittens, all soft and furry and warm. The knitted ones she'd brought with her were warm enough, but got wet easily.

The contest happened on the way home from school the next

day. The tree was old, its branches curving upwards like the arms of the silver candelabra that sat on Stan Sweet's sideboard, a wedding present from a former employer given to his wife, Sarah, on their wedding day.

The kids stood in a semi-circle at the bottom of the tree, heads tipped back so that their eyes gazed skywards.

'That's the one,' proclaimed Deacon.

'That's a good one,' the rest of the kids agreed.

Frances pretended to be daunted. 'I think I can climb it. I'll do my best.'

'We know that. You're only a girl,' declared Ralph, the scruffiest kid in school.

Frances was overjoyed, though was careful not to show it. She'd show these foresters a thing or two about climbing.

First she searched out the best footholds and handholds, and then she spat on the palms of her hands. 'Here we go.'

With a bound she was on the tree, hand over hand into the holding spots she'd spied, her long legs striding swiftly up the trunk of the tree, fingers digging into crevices and cracks, and feet following behind.

She made the first branch, then the second, moving sideways where necessary and climbing ever upward, thrilling at the sight of the sky through the topmost branches.

For a moment she perched on that top branch surveying the carpet of treetops, some bare of leaves, their starkness pierced by dark green evergreens.

'Oi!'

The shout came from down below. Deacon was looking up at her, his hand shielding his eyes. 'Now you've climbed up, let's see you coming down!'

Agile as a cat, Frances began her descent, uncaring that the toes of her shoes were scuffing against the bark and that her socks lay in wrinkles around her ankles. Finally she landed feet first on the damp earth, her face alight with pleasure.

'There! So where's my rabbit skin?'

Once she'd climbed the tree designated by the rest of the class to be 'the one', there was no turning back. Deacon and the rest of the gang viewed her with goggle-eyed respect. She'd won their friendship and she in turn had impressed them so much she was instantly accepted, and not viewed as an outsider from a place where buses were more numerous than trees.

Although she still missed the only family she had ever known, her love for the forest crept up on her swiftly. The day following the tree climb, she walked back to Ada's with a smile on her face and a rabbit skin tucked under her arm.

Trees to climb and the same kind of kids she'd known at Oldland Common; Frances was in heaven. There was also the game, the plants, the fruits of the forest that outsiders were not privy to.

'Never mind them ration books. Nobody ever starves 'ere,' declared Ada. 'Though they might lose their way, though not all who wander and live alone are really lost; they're just looking for the right path.'

Frances presumed she meant that it was easy to get lost in the forest. She'd thought she was a few times, but ultimately managed to find her way home. Although not yet twelve years old, she had a sneaking suspicion that what Ada said had two meanings.

Ada Perkins was as strong as a horse. She chopped her own wood from logs brought to her by the foresters – the name the people thereabouts gave to themselves. Ada told her the foresters were descended from generations of people who held ancient rights bestowed on them by a grateful king. Frances asked her what it was the forest people had done for the king. 'Longbows. The

forest people made and fired longbows. I hear their bodkins penetrated the armour of the French knights they were fighting.'

Although situated in Gloucestershire and touching the borders
of Monmouthshire, the people of the forest regarded themselves as
something apart, neither English nor Welsh. From what young
Frances could gather, it had been like that for generations.

'This was the border, the Marches it used to be called,' Ada had
explained when she'd asked her why the people were so insistent
on being called foresters. 'The lords of the manor back then used to
march from here into Wales. The foresters were the best archers in
the world, so got paid well to serve their lord and also their king.
The French found that out at the battles of Agincourt and Plessey.'

Frances found Ada interesting and listened to her avidly. Ada
knew so much about everything and not just about history. She also
knew about herbs and medicines and how to birth babies. Those in
need of her services rarely paid her with money. Instead they
presented her with rabbits, hares, pheasants, wood pigeons and
sometimes a haunch of venison. Best of all was a wild salmon
poached from the river then poached in an entirely different way in
a pan of boiling hot water on top of Ada's black iron range. The
smell of good things cooking filled the shack. Nothing was wasted.

Frances was allowed to look in the smoke house where she saw
strips of salmon, pigeon and pheasant hung from hooks set into the
ceiling, the acrid smoke rising up from smouldering mounds of
woodchips.

'All that food,' said Frances in an awestruck manner.

'The forest is our larder. Nature provides,' Ada said to her. 'Nettles for greens, wild garlic, field mushrooms, nuts and berries, fish
and meat; it's all here.'

Ada kept a supply of apples and wild berries, both used for jams
and making pies.

Within no time at all, Frances was doing the same as the other kids on their way home from school, searching out sources of free food. Not all that they gathered was strictly legal, especially the trout they tickled in the private pond on the edge of the Rolls estate. To her great delight, Frances found she was good at tickling trout, her catch ending up hanging on hooks in the smoke shed.

'What we can't eat straightaway, we can barter or store for when the north wind blows,' Ada told her.

'What does the north wind do?' Frances asked her.

Ada puffed on her pipe while gutting a particularly large trout. 'The north wind blows strong in the winter, creaking and cracking the branches of trees until they can stand no more and snap off, falling on some poor unfortunate's head if they're not careful.'

Ada Perkins was full of stern advice; there was so much Frances was learning, and not only at school. So determined was she to learn all there was about forest lore – how to snare rabbits and capture pigeons – she began writing it down in the notepad Ruby had given her before leaving home. It was supposed to be for letter writing, but none had so far been received from her family, so she took the view she wouldn't write to them until they wrote to her.

Also before leaving, Uncle Stan had given her a photograph of her father. He was wearing a suit and had a flower in his lapel. 'To keep beside your bed.'

To be accurate, it was only half a photograph, three sides with the normal white border, the fourth obviously cut away.

Frances was bright enough to know that there had been two people in the photograph, her father wearing a flower in his jacket lapel, and a woman in a wedding dress, her mother.

Uncle Stan never referred to her mother and neither did anyone else; they'd receive short shrift and a dark frown if they did.

Frances had asked questions about her mother, but got no proper answers, her uncle's jaw stiffening as he declared her mother Mildred not worth mentioning.

Mary had given her a tortoiseshell comb as a leaving present with a warning to make sure she combed her hair thoroughly and washed it once a week. 'Be on the lookout for nits,' Mary had added.

Frances had nodded solemnly. She knew what nits were and didn't want them hatching into lice. Even so combing her glossy hair was not a favourite occupation, but something happened after the tree climbing. Frances began to take care of her appearance though didn't realise she was doing it. She also found herself blushing when Deacon was around.

Warmed by the old log burner that kept the shack warm, she noted down what she learned of forest lore and drew pictures of the forest and its people in her sketch pad. She also divided up the notebook and recorded what she'd eaten that day. Food was becoming the main topic of conversation at school, everyone comparing notes of what they'd already eaten and what they were likely to eat that night. They purposely left out what they had for school dinners which didn't seem to count in the way as meals at home counted. Displays on the shelves at the local Co-op were sparser than they had been. Things they'd taken for granted were getting scarce, and this before rationing had been introduced.

The weather turned colder as it got closer to Christmas.

People were sneaking out into the forest to cut down small fir trees to take home and decorate with tinsel, strings of nuts and painted fir cones. They also cut holly and Frances was called upon to climb up into an oak tree for mistletoe.

Deacon had glowed with pleasure when she'd presented him with a bushy sprig. People kissed under the mistletoe and that's what she thought he was going to do. Instead he told her he would sell it for a penny or even tuppence. 'I'll knock on a few doors,' he exclaimed.

Frances did her best not to look disappointed.

Ada complained that the price of salmon was going up, though in her case the salmon she cooked came by way of a little poaching. The forest people were rich in that they had the knowledge to make the most of the food around them.

It was a week before Christmas that the man from the post office in Coleford arrived on his bicycle at the village store to relay a message that had come over the telephone that morning. The telephone was situated in a bright red box outside the post office. Reg Grantley, the man who ran the post office, disliked mechanical and electrical things. He still rode a bicycle, didn't like motorcars and the post office was lit by strategically placed oil lamps on convenient shelves. Reg carefully avoided the telephone, insisting he was deaf to the ringing. Everyone took his excuses with a pinch of salt.

'He'd send messages by carrier pigeon if he had the chance,' somebody had remarked.

When Ruby Sweet phoned him from the red phone box in Oldland Common, he'd had to get involved. Mrs Sanderson, a local busybody, had answered the phone's vibrant ring. Before informing Reg Grantley, she elicited every bit of information she could before Mary realised she was nothing to do with the post office and insisted she fetch the person who was.

'There's a Miss Sweet on the phone out there who insisted you speak to her.'

Reg eyed her warily. 'Ask her to give you a message.'

'Tried that,' croaked Mrs Sanderson who seemed to have a permanent frog in her throat. 'Said it 'ad to be you. It's a message for Ada Perkins. I do know that much.'

Reg grumbled about being inconvenienced and why couldn't

Miss Sweet have sent a telegram via Coleford where they had a proper telegram boy with a motorbike.

'Well, she ain't done that,' remarked Mrs Sanderson who couldn't understand why he wasn't curious. 'I wonder what it's about?'

Reg grumbled right up to the point he pulled open the phone box door, hesitating before plunging inside.

Firstly Mary asked him if he knew Ada Perkins and where she lived. He'd replied that of course he did. Ada had given his wife some ointment for use on his haemorrhoids, a fact for which he would be eternally grateful. He was a martyr to haemorrhoids. Ada Perkins. Foxglove Cottage. Hardly a cottage, he muttered pulling himself up short when it occurred to him that Mary might have heard him.

Mary made him repeat the message word for word.

'Not too bloody far,' he'd grumbled on putting the phone down, mainly because he was thinking of his bicycle saddle and the bumpy forest tracks; terrible for his haemorrhoids. Tonight he'd need a double dose of that cream his missus had got from Ada Perkins.

'Bucketful at this bloody rate,' he mumbled to himself.

Frances was delighted to receive the message telling her that she was expected home for Christmas. Mary would be catching the train north to Gloucester where she would change to the line that would take her down into the Forest of Dean to collect her. She would be spending Christmas with the family that had brought her up – her family – the only one she had really known.

She made her way to the smoke house, drawn by its smell, its warmth and its darkness. The door creaked high and low notes as she pushed it open. The smell of smoke greeted her, coupled with that of the meats and fish, slowly tanning to a warm shade of brown. It was quite dark, but she liked that. Being in the dark helped you think and she needed to think.

With thinking in mind, she made for the very darkest corner where she crouched down to sort out her thoughts. She'd often wondered what it might be like to be a twin and wondered if it would be like the way she was feeling now, two different mind sets, one wanting to go home, the other wanting to stay.

In a very short space of time, she'd got used to her new surroundings and new friends.

On top of that there was Ada. She was an intriguing character with her potions and medical advice and her abstract points of view and total disregard to authority, church and state.

'Though I do like the royal family,' she insisted, a fact which seemed at odds with her less-than-conservative nature. Ada would countenance no criticism of the King and Queen or the Duke of Windsor, the man who had given up his throne for a woman.

'I blame her,' she told Frances. 'That woman who bewitched him. And don't you think there ain't no spells to capture a man's heart, cos there are; old Ada knows them all!'

Frances loved all the talk of spells and potions. If it hadn't been for the fact that Ada expressed contempt for Wallis Simpson, the woman who had snared a king, she could almost have believed that Ada had supplied the necessary love potion.

One of Frances's school friends had referred to Ada as the Foxglove Witch. Frances had repeated it to Ada who had merely chomped on her pipe, winked and said, 'P'raps I am.'

Frances was worried that she wouldn't be allowed to return, perhaps Ada had grown tired of her. After all, as she'd said at the beginning, she'd done the service out of the goodness of her heart. She hadn't had to. Like it or lump it, she'd said.

Ada noticed the mixed emotions flashing across the youngster's face when she came in from the smoke house.

'Cheer up. You're going home.'

'Can I come back here after Christmas?'

'Of course you can.'

Frances suddenly thought of Charlie and her mood instantly brightened. 'I expect Charlie will be there,' she said wistfully. Ada's daughter had written to her, but Ada decided that for now she would say nothing, her view being that if Stan Sweet hadn't told the child about Charlie being missing, then neither would she.

17

That first day back home, Frances ran all through the house, upstairs and downstairs, refusing to believe that Charlie wasn't hiding there, that this nonsense about him being missing was just that: nonsense.

She also refused to be consoled by Mary or her twin, running to her uncle to ask him to confirm that it just wasn't so.

'He's not dead. I prayed for him every night at Ada's to stay safe even though she said prayer had never worked for her.'

'And you were right to do so,' said Stan, rubbing the coldness from his knees as he struggled to his feet. 'And anyways, we've been told that he's unaccounted for, not dead. So just you wait. He'll be walking through that door before very long and he'll laugh at us all being so scared about him.'

'I shall pray again.'

'Good idea. Tell you what, how about if you and me pop round and 'ave a word with my Sarah. I've already told her that Charlie is missing and we haven't had a word, but nobody 'as said he's not coming back. Missing they said and missing it is: a prayer in the churchyard over where the earthly remains of his mother, my Sarah, lies might do the trick. How about it?'

Since living with Ada Perkins, Frances had begun to have her doubts about prayer, but she nodded anyway.

Although it was mid-afternoon by the time they got there, the sky was leaden and hung heavily above the stark branches of leafless trees. The frost from the night before was still crisp and white on the short-cropped grass between the graves.

Hand in hand, Stan and his niece walked across the white grass, the frost crunching beneath their feet. They were still hand in hand when they came to the headstone where Sarah Sweet's name was carved along with the date of her birth and her death. Below that it simply said, 'Sarah Sweet, beloved wife of Stan Sweet. Sweethearts forever.'

Stan let go of his niece's hand and took off his hat. He held it before him with both hands, his knuckles white with tension. He addressed the headstone. 'Nearly Christmas, Sarah. Thought I might attend the midnight mass this year – all things considered.'

He wasn't one for attending church that much, though he did enjoy the Christmas service, what with all the decorations and the welcoming interior exuding warmth in direct contrast to the cold outside. He intended keeping his vow to Sarah that this year he would attend. Despite his assurances to his niece, he wasn't sure it would do much good, but he'd do anything to have Charlie safe and sound.

'Sarah, I've got young Frances with me. She's as worried about our Charlie as I am. I suggested she come here and we can tell you all about it. Seeing as you're in heaven and closer to God at this moment than we are, perhaps you could pass on our deepest wish that our Charlie is all right. We don't mind too much that he's missing, but we do hope that he's still alive. That is our prayer and no doubt, if you were still here with us, it would be your prayer too.'

Frances looked at him wide eyed when he uttered amen. He'd been talking to his wife as though she were really there. It had been more of a conversation than a prayer.

She looked round half expecting a glowing figure in white standing behind a tree, a bush or somebody else's headstone. There was no one, just a sudden hush of wind in the treetops.

* * *

The next day the frost had hardened though by midday the sky had brightened with the promise of a thaw.

The last batch of bread was in the oven and Ruby was standing at the front window, the teapot clasped in both hands, her eyes staring out at the icy scene. She'd got over not winning the competition the moment she'd heard that Charlie's ship had gone down. What was winning a competition compared to her brother's life?

Just yesterday, she'd bumped into Gareth in the High Street and he'd asked her about Charlie.

'There's no news,' she told him while side-stepping to get past.

'I could take you to the pictures if you like. Might help you get over it.'

She stared at him, his facial features turning to fat, his neck beginning to bulge above his shirt collar and hair badly in need of a cut. She also noted the smell of alcohol on his breath. Everyone knew he was hitting the bottle; she wondered whether it was because of her. At one time she might have been flattered, but not now. Looking at him her eyes were finally open to his faults. She'd been an impressionable young girl. She wasn't that any longer.

'I'll never get over it, Gareth. Not until he's safe and sound, and a night at the pictures isn't going to help – especially a night at the pictures with you!'

She strode off, head held high and a new lightness in her step.

Gareth Stead was a part of her past but would never be a part of her future.

She thought about Charlie every day. Even now the scene before her eyes was blurred with tears. She wasn't seeing the weather, her head filled with imagined scenarios of where Charlie might be, perhaps cast away on some desert island like Robinson Crusoe.

Goodness, she thought, pulling herself up short. You're beginning to think like Frances.

* * *

Melvyn Chance, the postmaster, looked to be heading for their front door with a letter, maybe more than one letter, clutched in his right hand. He was striding quickly, head down almost as though he didn't want to be recognised. Before the outbreak of war he had whistled his way to every door in the village, his uniform as neat as a new pin and his eyes shining with the missionary zeal of a man of vision. Since the outbreak of war he had told everyone who would listen that he had terminated his membership of the British fascists after becoming disillusioned with Sir Oswald's close association with the chancellor of Nazi Germany.

Most people took his statement with a pinch of salt. Stan Sweet tended to spit blood just at the mention of the man's name and it had been observed that Melvyn crossed the road to the other side if he happened to see Stan coming his way.

'Dad. It looks like we've got post,' called Ruby.

Her father came into the shop rosy-faced from the heat of the oven. Hope was in his eyes, but despite his rosy cheeks his face was more lined and thinner than it used to be.

'Then let's 'ave a cup of tea out back,' said Stan. 'I'm parched.'

The living room to the rear of the shop and the side of the

baking room was always warm. Even in summer the heat of the bread oven kept it warm and a fire was only lit in the depths of winter.

'We've got post,' Ruby repeated to Mary who was sawing through a fresh loaf of bread still warm from the oven.

Mary left what she was doing and lit the gas beneath the kettle. Looking out for the postman and making a pot of tea on his arrival had become a ritual, hope overriding any antagonism they might feel towards him. So far they had hoped in vain so nobody dared to assume that today would be any different.

Mary heard the sound of letters being posted through the shop door.

'I'll get it.'

She was up and gone before Ruby had a chance to argue. Both envelopes were brown manila. The one that caught her eye and made her heart beat faster was the one marked War Office.

Mary stared at it, wanting to rip it open. Did it contain good news or bad? She swallowed the sickness she felt inside. Bad news didn't always come by telegram nowadays, she told herself. Sometimes it came through the normal post, especially if somebody had become a prisoner of war.

She licked away the dryness from her bottom lip before composing herself and went back into the kitchen.

Stan had made himself comfortable in his favourite chair at the head of the table. On seeing the look on her face, he put his teacup back into its saucer.

'Is it from Charlie?'

Mary shook her head as she handed him the two letters. 'One's from the War Office,' she said quietly. It was the only one that really mattered. Fearing what it might contain, she hadn't even bothered to check the other one, not even the addressee.

Her father's reaction was much the same, setting the second

envelope on the table, his attention fixed firmly on the first. He turned it round and round as though plucking up the courage to open it.

Mary sank into a chair beside her sister. They both looked at their father, their hearts in their mouths.

There was one empty chair at the table. Frances was up in bed still, pretending to be suffering from a cold. If the news was bad, then they would break it gently.

Please God don't let it be bad.

'Go on,' Mary said softly, touching her father's arm.

At the touch of her hand, Stan Sweet stopped staring at the envelope. He cleared his throat, a prelude to tearing it open, yet he didn't tear it. He did it carefully, sliding his butter knife along the top. Grasping the single sheet of paper between thumb and index finger, like tweezers, thought Mary, it was pulled out and opened up.

As he read it he let out a great gasp. There was no need to read the words. Joy lit up his face.

'He's alive! Our Charlie is alive!'

He passed the letter to the girls, got out his handkerchief and trumpeted into it. Tears squeezed out from the corners of his eyes.

After reading it, Mary slumped back into her chair, hiding her face, alternately laughing and crying with the sheer relief of it all.

Ruby read it at least four more times before her shoulders were shaking with sobs, great big tears running down her face and into her mouth.

The British embassy in Montevideo confirms...

More details followed. The merchant ship on which Charlie had been serving had been attacked and sunk by the German pocket battleship, the *Graf Spee*. In turn the aggressor had been attacked by three cruisers of the Royal Navy and forced to take refuge in Montevideo, Uruguay. Under international law, the captain had been left with no option but to release all prisoners. Charlie had been one of those prisoners and was on his way home. Christmas was already looking brighter.

Such was their relief, their joy and their laughter, that the other letter remained unopened on the table.

'He's coming home,' cried Frances, who, hearing the commotion, had joined them at the table.

Mary shook her head while dabbing at her wet eyes. 'For Christmas! I can't believe it.'

Stan Sweet buried his head in his hands. 'Thank God. Thank God.'

He kept saying it, face hidden and shaking his head. Yesterday he'd gone round to the churchyard and told Sarah he was going to Christmas mass. Today his prayers had been answered. He would go to midnight mass. He would keep his promise. He suggested in the meantime that they go to the Three Horseshoes that night. 'We can sneak our Frances in. Jack Holt wouldn't object I'm sure.'

'What's the other?' asked Ruby, jerking her chin at the unopened envelope.

Stan Sweet's expression was still pink, but the haunted look had gone from his eyes. He looked and sounded jubilant as he picked up the other envelope and read the address.

Raising his eyes his pushed it across the table to Mary. 'It's addressed to you.'

Mary half suspected she was being called up until she saw that the address on the envelope was hand-written.

Ruby winked at her. 'So you have got an admirer you've never told us about.'

'No I haven't.' She shrugged. 'I wasn't expecting a letter. I haven't a clue who it's from.' Then she saw the postmark. Scampton! He'd written. Michael had actually written her a letter at a time when she'd thought their friendship had ended.

'Of course you won't have a clue,' her father exclaimed jovially while giving her shoulder a good shake. 'Not until you open it. Then you'll know.'

Feeling both her father's and her sister's eyes studying her, Mary took a clean butter knife to slit the envelope along the top. The paper inside was blue and of good quality.

Aware of her sister's and father's eyes studying her, she unfolded the letter and read it.

Dear Mary,

I'm sorry we parted on bad terms. It wasn't what I'd intended. I am visiting my aunt at Christmas and would love to see you. Perhaps I might invite you and your family to dinner at Stratham House? Knowing that you may already have made arrangements for Christmas Day, perhaps we can expect your company the day after, on Boxing Day?

I do hope you can make it. I only have a few days to spare. Things are beginning to hot up. Who knows where we might be next year, next month, next week.

I shall come knocking at your door, and if you don't open it I shall know you are still angry with me, but I sincerely hope not.

Best wishes,

Michael Dangerfield.

PS. I meant what I said. I know my own mind and make it up quickly. Just to make sure you haven't forgotten what I was asking you, will you marry me? Let me know when you decide.

She looked down at the letter as she refolded it and was totally unable to stop a pink flush coming to her cheeks.

She felt Ruby's eyes studying her. 'So who is it from?' Mary sucked in her lips. 'It's from Michael Dangerfield. The man from the baking competition. He's asked me to marry him.'

18

It was a few days before Christmas and the air in the bakery was warm and dry in direct contrast to the deepening cold outside the stout stone walls.

Ruby was standing at the kitchen table trying hard to concentrate on what she was doing. Her hands seemed to be working without her mind being aware of their actions. Cream butter, add sugar, sieve flour... she didn't need to concentrate. Instead of thinking of the cake she was making, she thought instead of Mary and the proposal of marriage she'd received from Michael Dangerfield. She was doing her best not to be jealous but it just wasn't working.

'I thought he was joking,' Mary said on admitting that he'd asked her on the day of the baking competition.

Ruby fought to control her expression, not wanting her sister to know how surprised she was or, more importantly, how jealous. 'What are you going to do?'

'Do?' Mary shrugged. 'Nothing. I mean, he's...' She was going to say very nice, but the fact that he'd won a competition when he'd known the judge still grated upon her. 'He has some explaining to do before I even think about being friendly towards him.'

'So how about this invitation?'

'It's just an invitation. His aunt's very nice.'

'Very nice,' Ruby repeated in a sarcastic tone. 'Dad said we should go. I don't mind going. A day off our feet.'

Mary sighed. 'Wish Charlie was home in time though.'

They were all hoping that Charlie would be home in time for Christmas, though they were still a little unsure of exactly where he was.

'I'm going to carry on drying the beans. And the carrots. And the sprouts.'

The vegetables were piled on the other end of the kitchen table to Ruby's cake-making ingredients.

'Well, we're not going to run out of vegetables any time soon,' Ruby exclaimed.

They both agreed that their father was doing a sterling job in the garden.

Drying vegetables was hardly the most exciting job in the world, yet Mary was glad to be doing something simple while she thought about Michael. At certain times she found herself panicking that she'd forgotten something important about his features and immediately searched her memory, not wanting to forget a single thing about him.

Concentrate, she said to herself. Get on with what matters; keep yourself busy. After drying a few bowlfuls, she could no longer ignore her restlessness.

'I'm going for a walk. I need some fresh air.'

Ruby carried on unconcerned, singing along to the wireless, the ingredients for the Christmas cake laid out in front of her. It was a bit late to make a proper fruit cake base and the ingredients had not been easy to get hold of. In fact, most of them had sold out quickly. Fresh supplies were slow coming in, even on market days at Kingswood where the shops were bigger and most things were available – or had been before the war. The reason was that people were rushing to stock up before rationing was introduced.

In the absence of sultanas, candied peel and glacé cherries, she'd made the decision to improvise. Instead of a fruit cake she planned making a plain sponge with jam in the middle. Nobody would know the difference once it was covered in local fresh cream rather than royal icing. She even had a small tin soldier – rescued from Charlie's old toy box – and a tiny ballerina to use for decorations.

People were beginning to hoard sugar, which wasn't really surprising. As Charlie had told them before he'd left, although sugar beet was grown at home, sugar made from raw sugar cane was brought in from the West Indies, which entailed a long voyage across the Atlantic.

'We're going to be crossing the Atlantic in convoys, ships carrying just about everything coming together on the eastern shore of the United States. Mark my words, the enemy will target every food ship coming over. It won't be easy. Not at all.'

The sugar at the bottom of the blue paper bag made a rustling noise as she shook it. On peering in she saw there was only a handful left, just enough for tea and perhaps a few fancy cakes to sell in the shop.

Ruby sighed. Selling anything besides bread was getting harder to do, but she refused to give in. Merchant seamen had suffered terrible privations in order to deliver the food the country urgently needed. She felt it only right to put on a brave face and make the best of everything for this Christmas despite the war. All it takes is a little bit of ingenuity, she thought to herself. Like the cake. Anyway, most people preferred sponge to fruit cake – except for her father. But there, he'll have to adapt just like everyone else.

Frances, who was really looking forward to Christmas, especially now there was the chance of Charlie coming home, came into the kitchen and asked if she could scrape the leftovers from the bowl. Ruby said that she could. 'Can I watch?'

'Of course you can.'

As she chattered on about her time in the forest, Ada Perkins and her friends at school, Frances tilted her head to one side so she could better read the writing on the sugar bag.

'Tate and Lyle,' she said thoughtfully. The name rang a bell. She'd heard it before – no – she'd read it before! Her face suddenly lit up. 'That's the same words as on the sack I saw that man give Mr Stead. "Tate and Lyle". That's what it said. It cost him ten shillings.'

Ruby looked at her and frowned. 'What sack? What man?'

'I told you,' Frances exclaimed with exasperated intensity. 'The man who came to see Gareth Stead!'

Ruby pursed her lips. Gareth rarely crept into her thoughts nowadays, and when he did, she cringed with embarrassment. She studied her cousin's fresh young face. Frances was very imaginative and could be a cheeky little beggar, but on the whole she was no different or worse than any other child in the village. She was also very observant and honest.

For her part, Frances enjoyed receiving Ruby's attention. Mary's and Charlie's attention she'd always had. Ruby had always been a little more distant.

'This man. What did he look like?'

Frances smacked her lips, her gaze fixed on the eggs being dropped into the cake mixture, the measure of sherry being poured from the bottle, the gradual adding of the self-raising flour. Frances noticed the fancy cakes cooling on a tray.

'Well?'

'Can I have a cake?'

'Just one.'

Frances shrugged. 'I've just told you! A man in a cap gave him the sack and Mr Stead gave him ten bob. I heard him say it. Ten bob.'

'What did he look like?'

'Dirty. Dirty dark clothes. He wore a cap on his head and a scarf up around his face. Like this...'

Frances proceeded to wind the sleeves of her cardigan around her lower face in the manner of a muffler. She followed that by placing an empty Victoria sandwich tin on her head.

'Don't do that.' Ruby snatched the tin and placed it back on the table. 'Was he short or tall? Fat or thin?'

Frances shrugged. 'Ordinary.'

Ruby took it that she meant average. 'And you never saw the colour of his hair or anything else?'

Frances shook her head and crossed her eyes; she'd found crossing her eyes was the best thing to do when you were concentrating on sticking your tongue into the creamy centre of a fancy cake. Bit by bit she licked the lot out.

My cousin is inventive, Ruby thought to herself and couldn't help smiling, though her smile was replaced by a deepening frown.

'So he wasn't from the village.'

Frances shrugged. 'I ain't never seen him before.'

'Haven't. You haven't ever seen him before or you have never seen him before,' Ruby returned, emphasising the correct words. Their father had always encouraged them to speak properly, even though he slid easily into the local accent himself, dropping aitches and adding 'l's and 'r's all over the place, especially after a drink or two.

'That's right. I have not!'

Ruby's thoughts were jumping like a box of frogs. It came as no surprise that the man had been a stranger. She guessed Gareth was getting some supplies on the black market. Perhaps he had acquired a contact at Bristol or Avonmouth docks, a docker willing to make a bit extra on top of his wages no matter the consequences. She guessed that his contact had stolen a sack of sugar and Gareth had bought it. Give it a few months of rationing and he'd have everybody queuing at his door for sugar – at a vastly inflated price, no doubt.

Ruby gritted her teeth. 'Did you hear anything else they said?'

Frances shook her head. The scrapings of the bowl were not available yet and there wasn't much chance of getting a second fancy cake. Once she'd swallowed what she'd had in her mouth, she went on to explain about where the sugar had come from.

'The man said it hadn't fallen off the back of a lorry like it usually did, but had fallen off a ship, which is really quite stupid and must be a lie, because if something falls off a ship it must land up in the water. That was silly, don't you think?'

Ruby agreed that it was and even managed to smile at her cousin's joke.

'He said his name was Bob Green. The other man. That's what he said his name was.'

'Bob Green,' Ruby repeated thoughtfully.

Judging by the description of his clothes, he certainly sounded like one of the rough men who used bill hooks to grab hold of grain sacks or half sides of frozen beef from the hold of a ship.

Frances gobbled down the scrapings of the mixing bowl just before a sudden hammering on the back door heralded the arrival of her village friends. She rushed to open the door.

'Coming out?' asked Billy 'Snotty' Stephens, his name obviously earned by the way he wiped his nose on his coat sleeve.

Beefy Martin, Gloria Swaine and Connie Jerome, plus a few

other kids, were crowded around the door, their eyes bright, their faces dirty, some smeared with jam.

Frances beamed. 'Where you going?'

'The orchard.'

'There's no apples there.'

'Of course not. It's winter.'

'We can climb. Just climb,' suggested Beefy.

Frances shrugged nonchalantly. 'All right.' She looked at Ruby who smiled and told her to go ahead.

Once she was gone and Ruby was alone, she stood silently thinking about Gareth and getting her own back on him. A plan was slowly forming in her mind.

Under normal circumstances she would shop her ex-employer to the police as a racketeer, but that would be letting him off too easily. She still had an axe to grind with him, a rejoinder for the way he'd treated both her and her young cousin.

Sugar would soon be scarce and there was no guarantee the contraband would be circulated to those who really needed it. Besides, she felt that her family had a stake in that sugar. Her brother had been serving on a merchant ship that had been attacked and sunk by an enemy warship. If the battleship hadn't in turn been attacked and forced into a neutral port, Charlie would have been interned in a prisoner of war camp until the end of hostilities. It just wasn't fair that people like Gareth should make money based on the misfortune and gallant services of others.

To Ruby's mind that meant she had a right to some of that sugar, if not all of it. Her family might not approve, certainly not her father and she doubted Mary would either. It didn't matter because she wouldn't tell them. She'd made up her mind.

There was no sign of Mary back from her walk and the only sound was of her father painting Charlie's room prior to his coming home. He'd found a pot of distemper from two years back. Ruby went up to tell him where she was going.

'I thought I might see if Mrs Martin's hens are laying yet. She's got a new batch. She might even have a boiler going spare.'

'Roast chicken?' her father asked hopefully.

'No, Dad. It's an old boiler. Stew most likely.'

Once outside, the chill wind making her face tingle, she headed towards the Apple Tree pub. Gareth Stead was about to get a very big shock.

After eating lunch with her father, Mary went upstairs to change the beds. Once in her own room she couldn't resist reading once more the letter she'd received from Michael Dangerfield. Perhaps she had been mistaken and read it wrong. Perhaps he was only joking when he asked her to marry him.

The words she'd read sometimes came to her mind in the middle of the night. On the one hand she regarded his proposal with disbelief, but on the other hand she wanted it to be true.

Just after returning the letter to its hiding place, she heard the squeal of the rusty hinges on the side gate. A spider scurried for cover when she lifted the curtain back, just enough so she could see who it was. Her assumption was that Ruby had changed her mind about fetching eggs, or perhaps seen Mrs Martin or one of her brood and been told the new hens were not laying.

A figure wearing a knitted black hat and a faded black coat slid through the gate, cautiously looking from side to side like a hen seeking corn.

Mary recognised Miriam Powell. She was about to tap on the window with her fist but due to Miriam's furtive manner thought better of it. She was creeping along towards the outside lavatory, a solitary brick place now used to store gardening equipment thanks to the new one built closer to the house. Judging by the furtive ducking around of her head, she was loath to be discovered.

There was a flash of white as Miriam took something from her pocket and ducked behind the small brick building, popping out again just as quickly.

As a child Ruby and Mary had posted each other notes, slipping them into the gaps where the mortar had fallen out between the bricks. Unseen in the upstairs window, Mary smiled to herself. It was very likely that she'd left Charlie a note, just as they'd left notes for each other as children. She must have heard the news that Charlie was safe and that he would be home visiting soon.

Poor Miriam. She was a nice person and might even look quite attractive if her mother didn't insist on her wearing clothes suitable for a matron twice her age. Perhaps then Charlie might consider her as more than a friend, though she doubted it. The fact was that Charlie could have his pick. He'd always been popular with the girls.

Mary chewed at her bottom lip, her eyes narrowed as she tried to guess what Miriam might have written.

Overcome by curiosity, she waited until the coast was clear and the garden empty then ran down the stairs and out through the back door.

The frosty air took her breath away and she immediately regretted not having grabbed a coat on her way out. Wrapping her arms around her shivering body, she hurried to where she'd seen Miriam taking the white note from her pocket. Peering round the side of the old outhouse, she saw the tip of a piece of paper poking out between the bricks.

The paper was jammed quite securely although the mortar was long gone. She paused before prising it out. If Miriam had wanted

Charlie to find it, why hadn't she left more of it sticking out? Why was it folded so neatly and forced so tightly into the gap?

Using her finger and thumb like a set of tweezers, she gripped it tightly and pulled it out. Rather than taking it indoors to read, she decided to read it there and then.

Judging by its jagged edge, the piece of paper had been torn from a writing pad and folded into four. On unfolding it and reading what was written she was surprised to see not a love letter but a prayer, though not one she recognised.

Sweet Mother, hear my prayer. Grant Charlie Sweet safe passage home, and when he gets here show me the way. Show me where my path lies and show him too. Sweet Mother hear me.

Mary frowned and read it again. Miriam and her mother attended Baptist chapel, Methodist and St Anne's Church of England. They did not attend a Catholic church, but then, there was no Catholic church in the area. Yet the prayer appeared to be to the Virgin Mary.

Charlie Sweet was on his way home; they all knew that. It was just a matter of time.

A sudden thought came to her that there had been previous prayers to the Virgin Mary.

Holding the note in one hand, she prised between the brickwork with her fingers, her nails filling with dirt. Her fingertips touched another piece of paper. Carefully, so that it wouldn't tear, she pulled it out, unfolded it and read another prayer.

Sweet Mother, I pray for the life of Charlie Sweet. Spare him the cold clutches of death. If you do this I promise I will worship you forever.

Goodness! Was it possible that Miriam Powell was about to become Catholic? What would her mother say about that? Mrs Powell had as much say in her daughter's religion as she did in her clothes. Her word was law.

Mary refolded the two slips of paper. Whether there were more of them secreted in between the brickwork, she didn't know and wasn't about to seek them out. It was Miriam's business and nobody else's; she forced them back into their hiding place.

19

As she opened the pub door, Ruby was greeted by the familiar smell of stale beer and tobacco. No matter how scrupulously the place was scrubbed, the smell remained; years of nicotine and sour yeast had yellowed the roughly plastered walls, the low ceiling, the floor and the stained pine furniture.

There were no pictures hanging from the walls except for a brand-new war poster entreating everyone to dig for victory. The only other object was a dartboard hanging from a nail on the wall. The darts were kept behind the bar.

On the floor beneath the dartboard, a set of chipped skittles stood upright with a battered ball inside a wooden triangle specially made to keep them in place.

Ruby glanced up to where she'd hung a few old horse brasses on to the beams. They'd been brightly polished when she'd nailed them in place. Already victims to nicotine, they were lacklustre and totally neglected by Gareth and his cleaning lady.

Shame, she thought. The Apple Tree could look really nice in the right hands. It certainly had character, but to her mind it needed a woman to make it look its best. Not that she was volunteering for that job any longer; her romantic notions about Gareth Stead had long gone.

A log fire glowed red among mountains of white ash in the centre of the large inglenook; nobody bothered to rake it out because it was never allowed to burn low until spring. The ash merely piled up. The oak Bessemer above the fireplace was pock-marked with holes, made, so legend had it, by Cromwell's Round-heads thrusting a red hot poker into the wood, one for every cavalier they'd done to death in the battle fought for the seaport of Bristol. The city's castle had been destroyed in the battle.

The only other customers that bleak lunchtime were two old gentlemen sitting either side of the fireplace, their faces almost as red as the glowing embers, their hair ash white.

She recognised them as regulars, a travelling salesman who dealt in farm machinery and a knife grinder. The latter's grinding wheel was carried in a wooden box at the front of his bicycle. He ground knives by means of a drive belt connected to his bicycle pedals which turned the stone when he pedalled, the back wheel of the bike disconnected during the procedure. The old men, friends for all their lives, turned to see who had entered, recognised her and nodded acknowledgement. The salesman, who she knew in passing from when she'd served behind the bar, asked how she was and added: 'Miss your cheery face, me dear. Old Gar here is nowhere near as pretty!'

He always referred to Gareth as Gar and always chortled at his own jokes.

Rather than snapping a hasty 'never' she smiled and said that the war had intervened. It seemed to her mind that the war was a useful excuse for everything.

The knife grinder wished her good day. She'd heard his tooth-less smile had been acquired in his youth when he'd boxed in bare-knuckle bouts at fairgrounds.

Gareth was behind the bar pulling a pint of cider for the knife grinder. He looked up, his expression firstly one of surprise that was swiftly replaced by casual nonchalance.

She could tell by his already rosy cheeks that he'd started drinking early this morning and most likely cider, a pleasant enough drink in moderation, but ruinous over a long period. Most hardened cider drinkers downed at least eight pints a night. She wouldn't put it past Gareth that he was drinking more than that.

'Well!' he said, as cocky as you like. 'Welcome back. Took your time, didn't you? I suppose you want your old job back. You can have it, but I can't pay you what I did before. You're not that special.'

Ruby smouldered with anger, wanting to tell him exactly how disgusting he was, but restrained herself. She had to stay focused. She was here for a specific reason and that reason was her main priority.

She held herself stiffly. 'I need to talk to you. In private.' Her tone was sharp as a knife – not that he seemed to notice.

A smug expression came to his face. He raised his eyebrows and beamed as though he knew very well what she wanted to see him about.

He winked. 'Thought you'd come round,' he said, once he'd served the knife grinder his drink and pocketed the money. Her eyes followed the money to his pocket. If he went on drinking the profits and pocketing the rest he wouldn't be in business much longer. But then, there was business and there was business. If her instinct was correct and young Frances was telling the truth – a fact she didn't doubt – then it seemed Gareth was branching out.

Still wearing an insolent grin, he opened up a section of counter. 'Come on through.'

The heat of his body was close, too close, and his shirt sleeves were rolled up. She closed her eyes to the sprinkling of golden hair on his bare arms.

The heat and the stink of him repelled her. Why hadn't she noticed it before, or was it just that he was letting himself go, drinking himself into a stupor he might never come out of?

'I'll see to you in the back room,' he said, patting her bottom as she passed.

Ruby whirled round. 'Don't do that,' she hissed. 'Don't you ever do that again!'

In the past he'd told her it was just fun and she'd been gullible enough to accept it. Now she knew it for what it was: a sly excuse to fondle a female body. Any female body. She'd seen him do it to other women. Some of them had laughed and called him cheeky. Some of them had been furious. One had slapped his face. 'Just a bit of fun,' he'd said to Ruby, and she'd believed that was all it was, his true affection for her and her alone. But now she knew otherwise. It wasn't funny at all.

The living room behind the bar was unaltered and relatively clean and tidy thanks to Mrs Pugh, the cleaning lady. The only addition since she'd last seen this room was the brand-new radio, a smart affair in a walnut cabinet with Bakelite knobs.

'I'm doing well for myself,' he said on seeing she'd noticed it. 'Buying a motorbike soon too. Got a contact in the trade. Can get me a good deal. Take you for a ride if you like, you can sit pillion on the back.'

He was crowing. Well, she'd soon stop that.

She spun round to face him. 'Stolen goods usually are a good deal,' she said tartly. Inside she quaked. Outside she hoped she gave an impression of a confident woman no longer infatuated by an older and manipulative man.

The self-satisfied smile died on his lips. A wary look came to his eyes. 'Ruby! Daft girl! You don't know what you're talking about.'

He reached out to touch her. Ruby hit his hand away.

'I'm not daft and I do know what I'm talking about! You're involved in the black market. You've been seen.'

Gareth Stead, the man she had wanted to marry, blinked like a frightened rabbit, but such was the effect of the cider and his overblown confidence he still attempted to brush her accusation aside. 'What do you mean?'

'Exactly what I said! I dare say your contact will get you the petrol for your bike too.'

'Could do!' His tone had hardened noticeably, most likely because he now accepted by her manner that she wasn't here to make up with him.

'Is it the same one who sold you the sack of sugar?'

Something flickered in his eyes. She'd startled him. Very shortly she hoped to frighten him, but first he had something she wanted.

'I want that sugar.'

He laughed. 'What?'

'Sugar. You were seen receiving a sack of sugar from a man who works at Avonmouth Docks.'

She didn't know for sure whether the man worked in the Bristol Docks or Avonmouth Docks; she'd merely hazarded a guess.

'I see,' he said, nodding and sucking in his bottom lip. 'I see. You want a piece of the action, as old James Cagney would say. Well. Can't say I blame you. Tell you what, I'll do a special rate for you, for old times' sake.'

He grinned. God, but she wanted to wipe that grin off his face – and she would!

She shook her head, her smile tight and expression intent with purpose. 'I want it for free. You owe me wages anyway. I'm taking the sugar.'

'Huh!' he exclaimed, regarding her with disbelief. 'Are you bloody kidding?'

'No. I am not bloody kidding!'

She felt like adding that she'd grown up. She also felt like adding how angry he made her feel. Dirty scum like Gareth Stead were taking full advantage of the dire situation the country found itself in.

She levelled her most menacing look at him. 'If you don't give me that sugar, it'll be the worse for you. I'll tell the police all about you, Gareth Stead, which means that you'll lose your licence. I mean it.'

His smirk wavered at first then widened once he'd had chance to consider it. At the same time he caressed the top of his new wireless, looking eminently pleased with himself.

'Look, if it weren't me, it would be somebody else. People are going to want a few luxuries during this war. Everyone wants to indulge themselves in the things they like. Even you.' His sneer was derisive, but she still had the ace card to play.

'May I remind you that sugar is a basic food stuff. As for indulging oneself, well, you should know a bit about that, shouldn't you. You're quite a one for indulging your secret passions.'

The sneer froze on his face. 'What you on about?'

'I'm talking about you being attracted to young girls, and I don't mean me. My father would kill you if Frances should ever tell him what you tried to do. Or if I told him. I wouldn't want to be the doctor who tried to patch you up. I wouldn't know where to start.'

Even the red face of a hardened drinker can turn pale when faced with something truly frightening. Gareth's did just that.

Ruby plunged in. 'Now. About that sugar.'

It gave her great satisfaction to see a trickle of drool run from one corner of his downturned lips. It was even better when he mutely agreed to deliver the sack of sugar when the rest of the family were out.

On the walk here she'd planned everything out. Tomorrow her father, Mary and Frances were going into Kingswood to visit Aunt

Betty, her mother's sister. Someone had to stay to man the shop; Ruby had volunteered. She ordered him to bring it over the stile and along the back lane, leaving it by the back door. From there she would manhandle it down into the cellar, though not until the shop was empty of customers.

'Eleven o'clock sharp. And don't be late.'

His jaw moved in time with the grinding of his teeth. 'Don't look as though I've got much choice.'

'No. It doesn't.'

'We could go halves—'

'No. We cannot. Eleven o'clock. Sharp.'

If he keeps grinding his teeth, he'll lock his jaw she thought to herself and felt triumphant. She'd done it. She was taking her revenge.

'You're a blackmailer,' he growled.

Ruby smiled and felt quite proud. If a man deserved to be black-mailed it was this one. 'Yes,' she said. 'I suppose I am!'

* * *

News came through that Charlie was being brought home on a merchant ship carrying beef up from South America to Southampton and wasn't likely to be home until after Christmas.

Stan Sweet considered postponing their celebrations until he arrived. Frances burst into tears at the prospect. 'I came home for Christmas! I'd sooner have stayed with Ada if there isn't a Christmas!'

Stan Sweet wasn't a man given to changing his mind unless there was good reason. His niece's outburst was reason enough. 'Hmm,' he said, pipe in hand and clearing his throat. 'On the other hand it's the right time for a celebration. My boy is on his way home. There's no law says we can't celebrate Christmas twice. Now I'd better see to making some dough for proving.'

Mary and Ruby planned a trip into Bristol. 'At least we can look in the shop windows if nothing else,' said Mary. Their spirits had risen enormously since receiving the good news about Charlie.

Ruby was impatient. 'I don't want to just look. I want to buy something.'

'Let's hope there's something left,' returned Mary. 'You heard what it said on the wireless. People are determined to enjoy this Christmas, which means...'

'Nothing left for us.'

The news that people were panic-buying turned out to be more or less correct. What goods were available in the shops were swiftly snapped up. They did what they could, buying presents for each other. In their case they also had Charlie to think about so perhaps they bought a little more than they should have. The good news had cheered them up no end and energised their buying, that and the prospect of this being the last decent Christmas they'd have for a long time.

Mary bought her father a pipe rack shaped like a five-bar gate. Ruby bought him a book about making the most of an allotment; not that they had an allotment, but like most folk in the village, they did have a pretty big garden. Part of that garden was taken up with flowers, a riot of colour from spring all the way through until the first frosts. Stan Sweet had already stated his intention to turn the whole garden over to vegetables.

'Can't eat flowers,' he said to them. 'I'll bring one of the pigs over to snuffle up the roots. That should save me having to do too much digging. Might be as well to keep a few pigs close by. They'll be safe here. It doesn't do to keep them out of sight at present.'

Mary patted her father's shoulder. 'That's fine with us. It won't be so far to go with the pig bin.'

The pig bin received all the leftovers suitable for making pigswill. Stan Sweet took it over to his pigs on a regular basis. The fact that one had gone missing recently grieved him.

'Just wait till I gets me hands on him,' he growled. 'I'll give them pigs if I bloody well gets hold of them! Old Sam Fowler had one pinched a while back, and now the same's happened to me.'

The prospect of keeping a few pigs in the back garden wasn't to either Mary or Ruby's taste, but Frances was quite taken with the idea.

'I can give them names.'

Buying something for Charlie was more difficult. 'Nothing knitted,' Ruby warned. 'Everyone is knitting. Everyone is giving servicemen socks and gloves for Christmas. Charlie deserves something better than that.'

Mary had been thinking this through. They all wanted to get him something special, something that Charlie would appreciate.

'He loves our garden. Perhaps we should buy him something for that,' she suggested.

Ruby was scathing. 'Oh no. Not a spade or a shovel, surely!'

Mary bristled at her sister's habit of jumping to conclusions. 'Of course not! I was thinking of a plant for the garden. Something flowering among all those vegetables. I shall miss our summer flowers once Dad's dug them all up.'

Just for once, Ruby agreed. 'That would be nice. But what?'

As usual, Mary had thought about this in great depth.

'Mr Forbes at the nursery is keeping a rose bed among the tomatoes and cucumbers in his greenhouse. Young rose bushes mostly. He has one called Charles Stuart. What if we all clubbed together and bought one?'

Ruby's face considered it only briefly before nodding in agreement 'Charles Stuart. Charlie! He'd love it.'

So did Stan Sweet. 'A single rose bush among the cabbages is hardly wasting good growing space,' he said contemplating just how Charlie might plant it in to best advantage. 'And the fact that it's named after our Charlie...'

Mary exchanged a grin with her twin. 'I think Charlie Stuart was a king of England. I think the rose was named after him, Dad.'

Frances bought her uncle some cotton handkerchiefs with the money she'd had for helping out at the big house. Living in the forest had not given her much opportunity to spend her earnings from that day so she was happy to spend it on her family.

She'd also not come back from the Forest of Dean empty-handed: when Mary had fetched her home from Ada's place, she also found herself having to struggle back with a large sack containing a smoked salmon big enough to last them for three meals, including soup. There were also herbs and bags of nuts plus a much appreciated flagon of sloe gin. The eyes of Stan Sweet lit up at the sight of the latter.

'Lovely on a cold winter evening.'

'It's for Christmas and special occasions,' said Mary who attempted to snatch it back from him.

'It is a special occasion,' he said, hugging the flagon close to his chest. 'Our Charlie is safe and on his way home. Let's drink a small one to his health. No doubt we'll drink the rest in the New Year when he gets back.'

Ruby fetched four small tot glasses.

'I think our Frances is too young for sloe gin,' remarked Mary.

'No I'm not,' protested Frances. 'Please...!' she whined when it seemed she might not get any.

Her uncle regarded her with amusement. 'Can you give me one good reason why you should have a tot – a very tiny tot mark you,' he added.

'Because I helped Ada make it,' Frances declared with a thrusting out of her chin and a haughty toss of her head.

Stan relented, though he wasn't sure he agreed with Ada Perkins having a child help her brew alcohol. However, he knew Frances cared deeply for her cousin and was thankful the news he was safe had coincided with her coming home for Christmas.

Stan raised his glass and proposed the toast. 'Here's to our Charlie. Thank God he's on his way home. No matter if he don't get home for Christmas. It's enough to my mind that he's on his way.'

20

Christmas Day lunch consisted of a cockerel Stan Sweet had raised from a chick and kept in a shed alongside the pigs in the paddock bordering Hollybush Lane. The fluffy yellow chick had been pretty and cuddly; the cockerel it had grown into had been huge and aggressive. And as a family of bakers, no one needed a cockerel to wake them in the morning.

A large bunch of sage had been brought in from the garden and hung to dry over the gas rings on top of the stove weeks before. The onions used to make the sage and onion stuffing was all that were left of the last lot they'd bought from one of the French onion sellers. The next lot would be home grown.

Everyone enjoyed opening their presents; only Charlie's present remained partially covered, the root of the rose bush sitting in a bucket of water.

Frances had made paper party hats from newspaper. The old rooster smelled wonderful, its skin crisp and brown, the stuffing oozing on to a willow-patterned meat platter. Roast potatoes, carrots, sprouts and cabbage provided a plentiful garnish.

Everyone sang 'God Save the King', following which there was a rush for knives and forks and arguments over who was having the legs.

'Whoever breeds a chicken with four or more legs is going to make a fortune,' remarked Stan Sweet.

Mary had made a Christmas pudding from a mixture of breadcrumbs and flour, added suet, as much dried fruit as she could spare, plus a dash of apple brandy. Charlie and his cronies had made the latter before dashing off to war. They were all thankful so many apples grew in these parts, thanks to generations of cider makers who had planted vast apple orchards from Hereford all the way down to Taunton and beyond. They were also glad that a few had been left untouched hereabouts, including the one Frances and most of the village kids had played in all their lives. The big orchard up at Perrotts' Farm had been the first one to go. There could be more, but for now the one next to the Apple Tree pub had been left alone.

Ruby rounded off the day with the Christmas cake she had managed to make from what she had, with a little divergence from the traditional recipe.

As it turned out everyone stated that they approved of the cake being more like a sponge than a heavy fruit cake. She'd also used jam because marzipan was in short supply, though she had managed to ice the top with the very last icing sugar from a shelf in the village store.

'Thought I'd save it for you,' Miriam Powell had confided. 'I suppose you'll save a piece for Charlie?'

Ruby had noted the adoration in Miriam's eyes and assured her that she would indeed keep a piece for Charlie's return. She wondered how things were going for Miriam with the new Methodist minister; perhaps not so well seeing as her affection seemed to have reverted back to Charlie.

'In fact I might very well bake another cake,' said Ruby. 'Providing I can get at least some of the ingredients.'

'Don't you worry about that,' whispered Miriam, leaning close so that nobody else could hear her. 'You let me know what you want and I'll get it for you. Never you fear.'

Ruby reiterated her promise to Mary who remarked there would likely be a price to pay that had nothing to do with money. 'She's in love with our Charlie.'

Ruby shook her head. 'She's got no chance. Miriam wants a husband and Charlie's not the sort for settling down.'

Mary said nothing about the notes stuffed into the gaps between the bricks. Neither did she remark about the way she'd seen Charlie staring at the handsome woman at the village fete before he'd gone off to war. Mary hadn't seen her since, not up until a few days ago when she'd come into the shop, bought a loaf of bread and swiftly disappeared. Mary had been too discreet to ask personal questions and as far as she knew, the woman was married.

Stan Sweet was given the honour of cutting the cake. He was also given a tot of sloe gin to go with it.

Mary passed the plates of cake along the table. She'd bought Ruby a dark red scarf for Christmas. Ruby had bought her a dark blue one. That's the way it always was with them, they consistently thought alike and they'd both laughed at what they'd done.

Frances had been the lucky one because Stan had managed to get someone he knew at the aircraft factories in Filton to make a scooter in the engineering workshop. All three of them had clubbed together to meet the cost. Frances was over the moon.

In the middle of the afternoon, they put on their coats and went outside. Stan Sweet fetched his spade along with the rose named Charles Stuart. They were going to plant the bush in a space where it wouldn't impinge upon the vegetables and could still be seen from the kitchen window, ready for Charlie to see when he returned.

'See you soon, our Charlie,' Stan Sweet said once its roots were embedded in the dark rich earth. It was the signal for them all to go back inside, take their coats off and enjoy the rest of the day.

Comfortable and warm in the sitting room at the back of the bakery, Stan Sweet looked at Mary. She'd always acted in a more mature and responsible manner than her sister. He'd found it odd but also endearing. She reminded him a lot of his darling Sarah who'd had the same slim waist as her daughters, the same dauntless look in her dark blue eyes. Yes, he thought. The twins resembled her in looks, even Ruby who fussed so much over the mole on her face. Mary was the image of Sarah in her quiet air of efficient pragmatism. This evening she was quieter than usual, not really quite herself.

'Well,' he said, eyeing her soft dark hair, the concentrated way she was bent over the book he'd given her for Christmas. *Tales of Dickens*. He'd noticed she'd been on the same page for the last ten minutes.

She looked up. 'What?'

When her eyes met his, he felt a sudden jolt in his chest. The ghost of Sarah lurked in those eyes. 'You're too thoughtful. What is it you want to say? Speak up, girl.'

Mary put down her teacup. 'We've been invited to Stratham House for tea tomorrow. All of us. I did mention it to Ruby, but I wasn't sure...'

Stan Sweet wasn't one for going out and about as he called it. Once a week he went to the pub, usually the Three Horseshoes, where he'd sink two or three pints with some of his old chums, but on the whole he was a bit of a stay-at-home.

To Mary's surprise, on this occasion he sighed with relief. 'Is that all?'

'Yes.'

'Well, well. What a turn up. Mrs Hicks inviting us all over for tea! Very nice of her. Very nice indeed.'

Mary shook her head. 'Not Mrs Hicks. Her nephew, the son of the brother who went to Canada. His name's Michael Dangerfield.'

'He's the one who won the regional final down in Bristol,' her twin added in a tight-lipped manner. Mary guessed she'd never forgive him for taking half her glory at the local event and certainly not for actually winning in Bristol. 'Not that he deserved to—'

Mary interrupted her. 'His bread looked very good in fact, even if he did admit to knowing the judge.'

Ruby stopped pulling her hair over her left cheek and sat bolt upright. 'I knew there was something.'

Stan Sweet raised his hands. 'This is the first I've heard of this. You say it was at the Vic Rooms?'

'Yes,' said Mary. 'I came out to tell you all about it, but then we heard the news about our Charlie. After that it didn't seem important. I would have willingly let him win if it meant getting our Charlie back – and we did, so perhaps that was the price to pay.'

Ruby couldn't quite see the connection between Charlie coming home and her losing out to a man who knew people, rich influential people. 'We should still have reported him. It's not right.'

'It wasn't right that you lied to me about dropping my loaf at the village fete. Or that you entered my loaf under your name in the first place! '

'Girls!' Stan Sweet had had enough. 'It's Christmas. Can we have some peace and goodwill here?'

'Of course,' said Mary. She had no wish to argue. Despite Michael's behaviour, despite everything, she badly wanted to see him again, even if it was only to hear him apologise that he hadn't withdrawn from the competition.

'I have told Mrs Hicks we'll be coming. I hope you don't mind,' she said to her father.

Stan Sweet made an instant decision. 'There's enough conflict in this world at present without us bearing grudges over a bit of baking. Of course we'll go.' He paused. 'This nephew of hers. Did you say he's in the forces?'

Mary nodded. 'He's a bomber pilot.'

Ruby grabbed her chance to muddy the waters just a little. 'Go on, Mary. Tell Dad the rest. Tell him what you told me.'

'I don't think there's any need for me to say anything else,' said Mary wishing Ruby hadn't mentioned what Michael Dangerfield had asked her.

Ruby looked as though she were about to explode. 'All right! Then I'll tell him. Dad! He's proposed! Can you believe that? After two chance meetings and a couple of letters, he's actually asked her to marry him!'

Stan Sweet beamed with happiness for the second time in so many days. 'Then I look forward to meeting him.'

'Can I be a bridesmaid?' young Frances asked, her face aglow at the thought.

Mary flushed with pleasure. 'I haven't accepted his proposal – if indeed he was being serious.'

Stan looked surprised. 'Well, was he or wasn't he?'

Mary shrugged. 'I don't know whether he really meant it or whether he was only joking. Joking, I'm sure of it,' she said at last, laughing while nervously rubbing the nape of her neck.

Ruby scowled. 'Getting married is hardly a joke.'

'On this occasion I think it is. Now, I have to get on,' she said, getting up from her chair. 'I've got some plum tarts in the oven. We can hardly go empty-handed.'

Her father got up from his chair. 'Before you go...'

She stopped by the door. Her father spoke softly. 'You're right about being cautious. Young men off to fight in wars are very aware they might not come back. Death does that to a man, wanting a bit of happiness before he dies.'

The words, although logical, were also heartfelt. Mary felt a tightening in her chest. Michael might indeed have been clutching at straws, wanting to experience love and marriage while he could. And who could blame him?

21

Boxing Day dawned crisp and cold. Trees, lawns and the roofs of village houses were coated with what looked like a dusting of sugar.

Mary was dressed but looking in the wardrobe for a dress to wear at teatime. First she pulled out a beige one scattered with tiny flowers and a sweetheart neckline. She finally decided on a blue satin one with a keyhole neckline, puff sleeves and padded shoulders. They'd go very well with her best shoes, which had peep toes and platform soles. Never mind the cold weather. She wanted to look her best.

'Getting ready early, aren't you?'

Ruby had only just shrugged off her dressing gown and was currently sitting on the bed wearing only a peach-coloured brassiere, roll-on girdle and lace-trimmed knickers.

'We might get other visitors today, and if so, I might not have time later on to get ready. You know me. I like to plan things in advance.'

'A bit forward of him. Inviting us.'

'He's just trying to be friendly.'

Ruby sniffed as she rolled her stocking so she could get it on more easily without it snagging.

'I think he's got more than friendship in mind!'

Mary was stung. 'He's not like that.'

'All men are like that,' Ruby muttered, seemingly to herself. It was hard for Mary to tell.

Ruby concentrated on smoothing her stockings carefully up each leg as though it were the most important task in the world. In a way it was. At least momentarily. Stockings were getting difficult to get hold of and the alternatives were best suited to old women. She intended taking care of hers.

Mary glanced frequently at the kitchen clock, willing it to tick away the hours more quickly than it was doing. Teatime seemed such a long way away.

Ruby, who had agreed to bake something sweet to take to tea at Stratham House, noticed. 'You won't make time go any faster,' she said sullenly.

'What are you making?' she asked not wishing to answer.

'Plum pie.'

'Won't those plums be a bit sharp?'

'No!' she snapped somewhat abruptly. 'Quite sweet, in fact.'

Ruby made a big effort to sound nonchalant. Let everybody guess why her baking was that much sweeter than anyone else's. The sugar was well hidden behind a boxed crate in the cellar and inside a waterproof bin. A tray of mushrooms was growing in front of it in a box her father had made especially for them. As the mushrooms were picked the rest kept growing. Nobody disturbed them.

Everyone was surprised at the quality of Ruby's baking even though there hadn't been that much time to bake and sell bread and cakes before Christmas. Even so, she'd done very well.

Even Mary was impressed. 'I don't know how you do it,' she said, shaking her head.

Ruby remained flippant. 'Call it a secret ingredient.'

It gave her great pleasure to take sugar from her secret hiding place. If anyone had wondered at why her cakes, tarts and pies were so sweet, nobody had tumbled to the reason. Her secret was safe.

And let it remain so, she thought to herself.

Once alone in the bedroom, Mary reread the letter Michael had sent her. She did this quite frequently, reassuring herself that she hadn't dreamed what he'd asked her. He wouldn't know it, but his proposal had unsettled her and she had never been the sort to be unsettled or manipulated by a man; that was more like Ruby.

She smoothed the outfit she had selected, wondering if he'd notice how much care she'd taken getting ready. The dress material was soft and smelled of lavender. Would he like it, would he like her? Would he confirm that he really wasn't joking?

It was after she'd cleared away the breakfast things that somebody knocked at the shop door, a heavy hand that sent the glass quivering in its frame, the door rattling.

Startled, Mary almost dropped a breakfast plate.

'Whoops,' said Ruby and grinned when she saw the look on her sister's face. 'Not lover boy already, surely!'

Mary looked at the clock. It was only ten-thirty. 'He didn't say he'd be calling this morning.'

He hadn't said, yet she instinctively knew it was him, that he'd always intended to call on her before teatime.

Ruby made no move to answer the door, merely raising her eyebrows tellingly while quietly smoking a cigarette.

On opening the door, Mary found herself reassessing Michael Dangerfield's frame and face. He had dark blue eyes very similar to hers and brandy-brown hair streaked with sun-kissed yellow. He was wearing his Royal Air Force uniform, the colour matching his eyes. His cap was tucked under his arm. He looked handsome, cheerful and full of New World confidence.

'Hi. Nice to see you again.' He spoke in a deep drawl in a voice as warm as his smile.

Mary forced herself to be formal. 'Hello. I won't say your letter didn't surprise me.'

'I like surprises. I thought you might like surprises too.'

'I think I do.'

'Now how long's it been?'

'We last met at the baking competition. You won. We lost,' she said, smiling sweetly as she shook his hand.

Still he smiled. 'I didn't mean to.'

'You didn't mean to win?' She'd hoped for an apology, but hadn't expected one this quickly.

'Oh, I always go all out to win. What guy doesn't? But I didn't mean to ask you to marry me.'

'Oh. I see.'

Actually, she didn't see. Although she'd taken his proposal at the competition with a pinch of salt, with amusement rather than in serious regard, she had also been flattered. What girl wouldn't be? Now he was saying he hadn't meant to. And what about the letter?

The conversation came to an abrupt halt. They stood there, looking at each other and both searching for something nice to say.

'What I meant is that it was unfair of me. Springing it on you like that.'

Mary didn't know what to say or what to believe and the feeling of being flattered was less distinct.

She laughed as though she didn't care one way or another. 'Oh. I don't mind. I quite like surprises. And jokes. You know, like that one about the dog that has no nose, so how does he smell...'

The words tumbled out of her mouth and finally stumbled to a halt.

He must think me stupid, she thought, aware that he was staring, his eyes looking intently into hers.

'Sorry. That was silly,' she murmured.

'What was?'

'What I was saying – that stupid joke about the dog...'

'I don't know. I wasn't really listening.'

'You weren't?'

'No. I was thinking about your eyes. I don't recall them being so blue. Damn it, but they're lovely.'

'I don't recall... your nose!'

Mary swallowed. She could have said I don't recall you making my legs turn to jelly before, but knew beyond doubt that it wasn't true.

'My nose?'

She laughed too. 'Oh my. Now I really do sound stupid. Sorry. It just came out.'

'No need to apologise. I've never had anyone admire my nose before.'

He smiled, the soft tan of his complexion emphasising the whiteness of his teeth. She guessed that piloting an aeroplane involved being outdoors a lot. 'Quite frankly I wouldn't be without it,' he added.

Still laughing, Mary shook her head. 'Of course you wouldn't. How would you smell?'

He took his cap from beneath his arm and pointed it at her. 'Hey. I know that joke. I heard that one on the wireless. Or was it at the theatre?'

'I think it must have been the wireless. I've never been to the theatre.'

'Well, we'll have to do something about that.'

'We'll see,' she said more demurely than she felt. Aware that the smell of cigarette smoke had followed her out, she glanced over her shoulder. Ruby was standing in the doorway of the living room, leaning against the surround, watching her through a haze of smoke. She must have overheard everything.

'Look, I have to go,' Mary said hastily.

Michael's smile diminished into an amiable grin. 'No problem. Just came over to tell you that tea is at four. You okay with that?'

She nodded. 'Yes. I'm okay with that. We'll see you then. Oh, just one more question.'

He half turned, looking at her over his shoulder. 'Fire away.'

'Felix. Is he with you?'

She presumed not; Felix the dog was owned by another airman.

'Yep! He had nowhere else to go. The skipper drew the short straw. He's on ops all over the holiday season. I offered. Felix – and Guy – accepted. Don't worry,' he added reassuringly. 'He knows you now. I promise you he'll be wagging his tail at the sight of you.'

Mary smiled back. 'So no more new dresses.'

'Not unless you really need one.'

On closing the door, she avoided meeting her sister's eyes, turning into the kitchen rather than pushing past her into the living room.

Ruby followed. 'He seems keen,' she remarked.

'He's just friendly.'

'Asking you to marry him after a chance meeting isn't just being friendly, though I wouldn't put it past him that he's out to get what he can before dumping you.'

Angered by her sister's remark, Mary stopped wrapping up food they were taking to tea. 'Ruby, not everyone is like Gareth Stead. Some blokes are decent and I think that Michael is one of them.'

'I don't know how you can say that! He won the competition because he knew the judge.'

Mary shook her head. 'I fully admit that our entries didn't stand up well to the rest of them. But that's something I have to put down to misunderstanding. That's all.'

'It still doesn't excuse him winning with his foreign muck!'

Mary couldn't help rounding on her, eyes blazing. 'It is not foreign muck. In fact, it looked good and no doubt it tasted good.'

Ruby pulled a face while blowing out a spout of cigarette smoke. 'I still think he's just having you on, saying he wants to take you out and all that.'

Mary tossed her head. 'It doesn't really matter. I wasn't taking it seriously anyway.'

'You would have turned him down if he'd asked?' Ruby failed to avoid sounding surprised.

Mary laughed. 'What else do you expect me to do? As you pointed out yourself, I hardly know him.'

Ruby pursed her lips. It was hard not to feel jealous. How rare was it for a man to propose to a girl he'd only just met? It had never happened to her and she had not heard of it happening to anyone else. It was rare for the twins to fall out and even rarer for one to be jealous of the other, but on this occasion Ruby couldn't help herself. 'Are you sure you're not looking a gift horse in the mouth?'

Mary eyed her sister over her shoulder and frowned. One moment Ruby was more or less warning her off and the next she was hinting she should consider his proposal. 'What do you mean?'

'Well, what with the war and everything, who knows what tomorrow may bring? Strikes me that we have to grab the moment while we can. I mean, he could get killed...'

Mary froze, saucepan lid in one hand, wooden spoon in the other.

On seeing her sister's shoulders stiffening, Ruby regretted what she'd said. She bit her bottom lip quite hard before saying, 'Sod it! I shouldn't have said that.'

'No,' said Mary coldly. 'You should not.'

Keeping busy helped the time pass, but even so Mary couldn't concentrate on anything serious. Reading a book resulted in the words bouncing up and down before her eyes, the thread of the story lost, the favourite book abandoned.

A little mending helped for a time until she realised that she'd sewn the sock she was darning to her skirt.

It was hard not to look at the clock ticking away on the wall, its long pendulum swinging underneath measuring the hours, its chime measuring each quarter of an hour.

By four o'clock the whole family were dressed in their Sunday best, Mary paying particular attention to her hair, retouching it as though afraid the smallest tress had escaped from her shoulder-length style. She'd decided on the blue dress and found a pair of stockings without snags or ladders. She folded a blue scarf around her hair, tying the ends at the nape of her neck. The colour complimented her eyes.

Ruby wore a green dress sprigged with black leaves, the sweetheart neckline skimming the beginning of her cleavage without giving anything away.

Frances had to be forced to wash behind her ears and was dragged away from her Christmas presents.

Once a truculent Frances had stomped out of the bedroom and down the stairs, Ruby turned to her sister. 'You really like him.'

Mary smiled sweetly, refusing to be drawn. 'Has Gareth offered you your old job back?'

The question resulted in a look of shock on Ruby's face. 'Of course not!'

'I hope not. If Dad should ever find out...'

'He won't!'

'Thank goodness for that.'

'What makes you say that?'

'I saw you talking to him.'

Ruby stared. 'You couldn't have.'

'Yes I did.'

Mary was speaking the truth. She'd been taking the loaves they hadn't sold that day over to Mrs Nixon, a widow with four children. She'd seen her sister and Gareth on the other side of the stile at the end of Paradise Lane where Mrs Nixon lived. They'd appeared to be talking avidly, heads forward, necks stiff. Ruby was the one who seemed to have the final say, stalking off with her head in the air leaving Gareth looking beaten.

'Believe me,' said Ruby. 'There's nothing in it.'

* * *

Although the exterior of Stratham House was imposing, the interior was quite small, the rooms cosy rather than grand.

Mrs Bettina Hicks was a tall woman with kind eyes, a crinkly mouth and hair a pale shade of grey that might once have been blond. It was teased into a cottage loaf style and in a certain light almost matched the pale violet-coloured clothes she was fond of wearing.

'I'm so glad you could all come,' she said on opening the sturdy oak door of her stone-built house.

Mary noticed she was leaning on a walking stick with her left hand, opening the door with her right.

'Mr Sweet. Pleased to meet you.'

They shook hands politely.

Stan Sweet eyed her quizzically. 'Didn't you used to be Betty Allen?'

Her smile widened. 'And you are Stan Sweet. We were at school together. Strange that we haven't kept in touch, but I spent so much time away from here when my husband was alive and of course, you live at one end of the village and me at the other. Now please don't tell me that I haven't changed a bit,' she said, her smile as coquettish as a woman half her age.

'It's true!' Stan Sweet took off his hat.

'How very chivalrous. I do like a man who is chivalrous.' Like most people in the village, Mrs Hicks kept chickens, but the hen coop was silent now, the cockerels gone for slaughter and the hens newly acquired to replace those that had stopped laying eggs.

Her voice was refined; her warm smile echoed in her eyes. 'I've got quite a houseful at the moment. Everyone is here except for my dear nephew who Felix nagged into taking him for a walk. He'll be back soon. Come in, come in why don't you. This is Gilda, the daughter of a friend of mine. She'll take your coats.'

A figure hovering in the background came forward. Gilda greeted them warmly as she took their coats, her pink lips widening in a bright smile, her dark eyes smoky with welcome. Mary recognised her as the one who had rushed into the shop and rushed out again, the one her brother had taken an interest in at the village fete. She was certainly striking with her velvet-brown eyes and chocolate-brown hair. Her skin was heavily powdered, her face oval-shaped, her eyes widely spaced either side of an aquiline nose.

Mrs Hicks explained that Gilda was the daughter of an old friend and that she and her children had been living in London up until now.

With a beatific smile that seemed to brighten the room, she explained the situation.

'I insisted that she and the children would be safer here. If anywhere is going to be bombed it's most certainly going to be London. It's a bit of a squeeze there being only two bedrooms, but Michael volunteered to go up in the attic. There's an old camp bed up there and he's managed to make himself comfortable.'

Two children, their eyes and hair as dark as their mother's, gazed shyly at the new arrivals; finally at their mother's urging, they shook hands politely, the boy bowing, the girl nodding her head respectfully.

Frances stood mutely, her eyes locked with the boy Isaac and his sister Marianne until nudged into reciprocating.

Stan Sweet presented Mrs Hicks with two loaves of bread. 'Looks as though you could use them,' he said, nodding at her guests.

Mrs Hicks thanked him and Gilda took the loaves.

Mrs Hicks sighed. 'To tell you the truth, I'm rather glad Gilda is here. I don't know how I managed without her.' She smiled. 'I have a little trouble with my hip, you see. Old age. That's all. Now let me see, this twin is Mary,' she said pointing correctly to Mary. 'And this twin with the beauty spot is Ruby. Michael described you both perfectly.'

Ruby's jaw dropped. The cold air had whipped her hair back from her face exposing the hated mole and now here was Mrs Hicks referring to it as a beauty spot. Nobody had ever called it that before.

'Well,' said Mary. 'He certainly doesn't miss much.'

'You're quite right,' said Mrs Hicks, the sparkle in her eyes undiminished. 'And he's kind. Hence looking after the dog for his friend. A pity the wretched creature damaged your dress, my dear.'

'I managed to buy something, though it isn't easy now. There's not much left in the shops,' exclaimed Mary.

'What a shame! I really feel that a young girl should have nice dresses. In fact, I insist on giving you some dress fabric I bought some time ago. I never got round to doing anything with it and I'm not likely to now. You girls can have it if it's of any use to you – that's if the moths haven't got at it! Now! I'm sure Michael won't mind if we begin our tea. He'll soon catch up once he gets back.'

The table was already laid with sandwiches, a fruit cake and mince pies all laid out on pink and white crockery on a pretty lace tablecloth.

Mrs Hicks waved her hand at the cakes and pies. 'Michael brought them down for me from Fortnum and Masons. They look very good, though of course you don't get many for the price,' she added with a smile.

Ruby surveyed the expensive mince pies with dismay. For a moment she was loath to add her own donation until it came to her that her pastry had a far superior look to the bought versions.

Plucking up courage, she brought the pies out of her basket.

They were on a plate and covered with a clean tea towel.

'I made mince pies too. The mince is to my own recipe and quite sweet – seasoned fruit mixed with suet.'

She didn't mention that she'd added a tablespoon of sugar from her secret supply hidden in the cellar. It was a secret she was keeping to herself, the magic ingredient that she would still have when everyone else was running low.

Mrs Hicks beamed at Ruby's offering. 'Oh, my dear, they look quite delicious! In fact I would say they look better than those my nephew brought with him. Now there's a thing, and just as well. There were only six mince pies and now there are twenty-four. I bought some cream from Mrs Martin. She delivered it specially.' A mischievous grin lit up her face. 'She brought her daughter Lily with her. I think she was hoping my nephew might be interested. He wasn't, of course.'

Mary checked her smile. Sweet as Lily Martin was, she loved her food too much, a great shame seeing as she had a pretty face and would be even more attractive if she wasn't so fat. With a sudden pang of jealousy, Mary realised she didn't want Lily to lose weight, not if it meant her new slenderness attracting Michael Dangerfield.

Everyone agreed that Ruby's mince pies were better than the ones from London. 'Don't tell Michael,' Mrs Hicks whispered.

They were eating mince pies and sipping sweet sherry when Michael and the dog returned. The dog wagged its tail seemingly confident that these people – especially the children – were not intruders because they were already in the house on his return. Mary was put at ease.

Michael's eyes lit up on seeing her. 'Well, isn't this just fine and dandy! Merry Christmas one and all.'

Having also greeted everybody, the dog chose his space in front of the fire, lying full stretch on what looked like a Persian rug, though worn with age. Steam rose from his damp coat.

The rug was in keeping with the rest of the furniture and furnishings – very good quality and well looked after, but showing its age.

Over tea and mince pies, the talk turned to the war and where they might be this time next year. Stan asked Michael about his career with the RAF and where he might be posted. 'Unless it's all hush-hush,' he added.

To Mary's relief he didn't mention anything about Michael's marriage proposal. She'd asked him not to and he'd kept his word even though the idea appealed to him; a married daughter wouldn't be one of the first to be called up – if at all.

Michael shrugged in answer to Stan's question. 'Not at all. So far it's been training and more training. The fighters have been out and about, but so far nothing much happening at Bomber Command. We're not dropping anything yet, well, not high explosives anyway. Just leaflets. Can't wait to get going on the real thing.'

Mary couldn't help noticing the gleam in his eyes. Her father noticed it too and was obliged to comment. 'Young men have no patience, though I suppose that's understandable. The old men in government seem to have given up talking and don't seem to know quite what to do next. Ran out of words. Shame but true.'

Michael stood in front of the dog and the fireplace, legs slightly parted like a knight of old about to mount up and head for war. 'Now it's the turn of the young men,' he added tellingly, both his voice and his presence seeming to fill the room.

Mary shivered.

Stan Sweet smiled a sad, knowing smile. 'All young men want to have their turn.'

'Aren't you frightened?' Mary asked him and felt she melted when he looked at her, a hint of a smile on his lips, the light of excitement in his eyes.

'In a way. That's why I'm looking forward to doing something I've been trained for. I've got a good crew. We've been trained to fight for this country and freedom, and fight we will – eventually.'

Stan Sweet looked thoughtfully down at the floor while unconsciously groping for his pipe. Suddenly he remembered he was in someone else's house and slid it back into his pocket.

Bettina Hicks saw the action. 'It's all right, Stan. You can smoke.'

He looked up and saw the sudden brightness in her eyes.

'My late husband Alf used to smoke a pipe. I quite miss having the smell of pipe smoke in the house.' Her voice was tinged with a hint of sadness.

Stan thanked her and lit up. 'Smoking calms me down and helps me think,' he said.

'You served in the Great War if I remember rightly,' said Bettina.

He nodded. 'I did, and listening to your nephew, I realised that nothing much has changed. Young men still want to be warriors, not that I disrespect them for that.'

'A terrible blight has infected Europe,' said Bettina Hicks, her eyes briefly landing on Gilda, who visibly paled despite the heavy

make-up. Bettina had already told them she was a refugee from
Austria.

'I realise that,' said Stan, 'though that wasn't really what I was
thinking of. I was thinking back and realising there is nothing more
exciting than at the moment you have to fight for your life. You do
things you would never do in peacetime.' His gaze dropped to his
pipe.

The pale eyes of Mrs Hicks flickered as they alighted on Gilda
who suddenly looked very troubled. Mary too saw the disquiet on
Gilda's face before she disappeared into the kitchen. She got up to
go after her, but Mrs Hicks signalled for her not to. 'She's had a
terrible time,' she said. 'There are moments when she has to be
alone.'

Stan Sweet didn't ask what the problem was with Gilda and
neither did anyone else. Her husband wasn't with her; that in itself
was telling enough. This war was going to be worse than the last, he
thought, and we're going to have a fight on our hands.

He got up, went over to where Michael was standing and shook
his hand. 'I wish you all the best, young man. Take care of yourself.'

'Thank you sir.'

Stan knew that winning was going to depend on the bravery of
young men like Michael Dangerfield and Charlie, his only son.
He'd almost lost his son in this war already, but Charlie would go
back to sea. From the very first he'd wanted to go and do his bit.
This young Italian-Canadian had the same attitude, one that could
get him killed, though Stan fervently hoped it wouldn't come to
that. He'd already decided he liked young Dangerfield. He'd also
noticed that Mary liked him too though she was doing her best not
to show it.

Gilda came back from the kitchen with red-rimmed eyes which
they all pretended not to notice.

Somehow the talk got round to gardening and how best to get as much fresh produce as possible from even the smallest patch of garden.

Mrs Hicks was all ears as Stan outlined his plans to plant those things he thought would be in shortest supply. 'I know it's cold outside,' she said suddenly, 'but perhaps we could take a walk around my poor vegetable patch. It's a little run down thanks to my hip, but I would appreciate your advice – if you would like to accompany me that is.'

Stan said that he would. 'Might even be able to give you a bit of a hand,' he added, much to the twins' surprise.

'Good,' said Bettina, leaning on the stick and rising unsteadily to her feet. 'We can leave the younger generation to their own devices – and the dishes,' she added with more than a glimmer of humour.

Ruby washed and Mary wiped. Frances was absorbed in playing snakes and ladders with Isaac and Marianne, the game spread out on the floor, the three children lying on their stomachs around it.

'Did you get it for Christmas?' Frances was asking them.

'Sort of. We don't celebrate Christmas. Not really,' said Marianne.

Frances looked astounded. 'How awful! Why is that?'

Isaac brushed his dark curls behind his ears, his attention fixed on the game spread out in front of them. 'Oh. It's because we're Jewish,' he said, matter of factly.

Gilda, who was putting away the pretty lace tablecloth and generally tidying the room, winced at her son's comment, as though she didn't want it mentioned.

'I need to make the beds,' she said, excusing herself from the room.

'I know where everything goes,' said Michael while taking the dried dishes from Mary. 'Or at least, I think I do.'

His grin was infectious. It came to Mary that one day she

would look back on this event, this passing of dishes from her hands to his, and know it was truly the moment when they'd fallen in love.

She gave a little gasp, hardly able to believe the unbidden thought. Where had it come from?

'Whoops!'

Luckily Michael had a firm grip of the plate she'd been in the process of passing to him. She still had hold of it; that was when she noticed that their fingertips were touching.

Ruby came wandering out from the living room just as they were putting the last of the dishes away.

Mary went to use the bathroom, not really because she needed to, but just to give Michael the opportunity to be alone with her sister. She wanted them to be friends, but Ruby was still hostile, smarting because Michael's baking had beaten hers.

'Those mince pies were good,' said Michael cheerfully as though he really hadn't noticed Ruby's sullen glare. 'I was hoping there would be enough to take back to the boys, but nope! Seems we've ate the lot. Best I've ever tasted.'

Ruby had been aching for a fight, but Michael's flattery had totally disarmed her. 'Really? So you can't make them better than I can?'

Michael continued as though he hadn't noticed her tone. 'Never said I could.'

'I suppose you've already spent your prize money on drink and wild women,' Ruby said accusingly.

'No. I gave it to a deserving cause.'

'Your wife?'

'I haven't got a wife, but I think you already know that. I gave it to Gilda. She came here penniless. She needs it.'

'She's very attractive. I suppose you and she—'

'Are friends. Just friends.'

Despite him cutting her short, Ruby was unrelenting. 'Hasn't she got a husband to provide for her?'

Glancing over his shoulder, he saw that the children were still playing with their game. He closed the door between the kitchen and the front room so their conversation could not be overheard.

'Gilda's husband is in some kind of labour camp in Germany. He was arrested for anti-Aryan propaganda. That means he dared to say something that the local Nazi party didn't like. Being a Jew is also something they don't like. More and more are disappearing into these camps. We're not quite sure what happened to him. Gilda was advised to get out of the country. It was quite a traumatic experience. That's all I can say.'

Ruby was inclined to press for more details, but sensed none would be forthcoming.

Suddenly the door behind them opened and Isaac was there, his hair awry, his cheeks rosy red. He was holding on to the dog's collar.

'Felix wants to go out. He won't stop clawing the door and he keeps growling.'

Michael shook his head and looked at the dog. 'Felix, you've only just come in.'

The dog's ears were erect, his eyes unblinking and his head was turned back into the front room where the door led into the hall where the front door opened into the garden. Sharp canine teeth showed when he growled, eyes fixed on the door, his head twisted at an awkward angle.

Michael's amiable expression disappeared. 'Okay, Felix. I get it. There's somebody outside.'

Leaving Ruby behind him, he went into the living room craning his neck in an effort to see out of the window to a frosted world cloaked in mist and the dying light of a winter's afternoon.

Michael instructed Isaac to shut the dog in the kitchen. Stan

Sweet had come in from the garden and was now sitting comfortably with a brandy clasped in his hand.

Michael explained the problem. 'The dog's upset. There's somebody outside. Leave it to me.'

The sound of knocking at the door set the dog barking even more furiously than before. Once he was sure Felix was under control, Michael opened the hallway door and then the front door.

The girls stayed with their father and Mrs Hicks. It had not escaped their notice that their dad and the widow got on very well indeed. Up until the interruption from outside, they had been discussing the planting of spring beans, though judging by the look in their eyes, there was something more interesting than beans going on.

'I expect that's the vicar's wife,' said Bettina reassuringly. She seemed totally casual that she might have an intruder. 'She collected for the poor before Christmas. Now she'll shake her begging bowl and tell me it's to help people make a new start away from whatever sins they're guilty of. Either that or the reform of some obscure cannibals they're inclined to turn vegetarian.'

It was hard not to smile at her comments, though all eyes stayed fixed on the front door. The sound of men's voices preceded its reopening. A blast of cold air came in before Michael Dangerfield, followed by another figure in dark navy blue.

Michael was grinning broadly. 'I've got a surprise, folks. Looks as though Santa Claus is a day late!'

Behind Michael, his face half hidden by his navy blue hat, was the freckled face and cheeky grin of Charlie Sweet.

He was home!

22

Stan Sweet sat next to his son, his eyes shining with a mixture of pride, relief and unshed tears. His hand had settled on his son's shoulder the minute he'd sat down and there it had remained. It was as though he were afraid his son would disappear if he removed it. It would take more than a few minutes, a few hours or even a few days for him to believe that this was not an illusion and that the flesh-and-blood Charlie really was home.

At the sight of him, Ruby had dashed to retrieve the cake she'd made for this special day. She rushed over to the bakery, grabbing the old toffee tin in which she'd been keeping it. She also grabbed a cake stand – not the best one they owned, but the one nearest to hand. She was sure Charlie wouldn't mind, after all, they hadn't really expected him this quickly.

Her hostility to Michael Dangerfield now forgotten, she ran back to Mrs Hicks's and placed the cake on the stand in the centre of the table. Once everyone had remarked how wonderful it looked, she cut the first slice which went, of course, to Charlie.

'Merry Christmas, Charlie,' she said as she passed him the plate.

Everyone else wished him the same.

'And a Happy New Year,' added Frances who was sitting on the floor, one arm clasped around his knee.

'Let's hope so,' he said, tousling her hair as he always used to do before he'd gone away.

While everyone remarked how nice the cake tasted, Stan noted that his son had gained a maturity he hadn't possessed before. He had the look of a man who had seen things he would never have seen stuck in a village all his life. Stan could guess how terrible some of those sights might have been. He'd seen enough himself in the last war.

The voice of Bettina Hicks interrupted his thoughts. 'You must have a secret supply of sugar,' she said to Ruby who almost choked on a mouthful of cake, but quickly collected herself.

She had told nobody of her secret cache and she wasn't about to do so now.

'I happened to have some honey from last year,' she lied.

She saw Mary frown. 'I thought we'd used it all.'

'Not quite all,' she said cheerfully.

'I can taste the sherry in this cream,' her father remarked. 'Or is it brandy?'

'Both,' said Bettina Hicks who had supplied the cream for the mince pies and winked at him. 'Alf also liked a tot of sherry or brandy when the occasion deserved it. His supply of liquor has remained intact since his death. He would approve of it being drunk on such an occasion as this.'

Charlie was a bit thinner than when he'd left, but his face had a healthy tan, the kind that comes from facing a variety of weather and wind.

Michael was keen to hear of his exploits. 'So how was it?'

Charlie sighed before draining the last of the tea from his cup. 'No picnic,' Charlie said, looking up at him with a hint of pride.

Despite the smart uniform, it was him, Charlie, who had been in the thick of it. As yet the war hadn't come home to roost like it had in the South Atlantic. 'And it's not going to be. The enemy is well armed and determined. We've got one hell of a battle if we mean to win it.'

'We have to win it. Those people are monsters.'

The speaker was Gilda who had been quietly moving around refilling cups and passing out plates of cake and mince pies.

Charlie looked up at her, remembered the dark-eyed girl he'd noticed at the village fete and blinked. 'I've seen you somewhere before.'

She shook her head. 'I don't think so. I haven't long arrived from London.'

'You must have come for a short visit. I'm sure I saw you at the village fete?'

She nodded. 'Ah, yes. I was here on a visit before I decided to move down.'

Because English was not her first language, she spoke very precisely in order that she might be better understood.

Charlie couldn't take his eyes off her. 'I thought so.'

Stan Sweet gave his son's shoulder a quick squeeze. 'You can't imagine how it feels to see you home, my boy.'

Charlie's smile lit up his face. 'You can't imagine how good it feels to be home.'

'Would you like another cup of tea?' asked Gilda. The look in her eyes closely resembled that in Charlie's. Despite the make-up it seemed she was blushing.

Charlie would have preferred something stronger, but couldn't say no to this beautiful woman. 'Yes. Yes, please.'

Mary noticed her brother's eyes following the dark-eyed beauty before he glanced at the children and took another sip of his tea.

Ruby tried to force another slice of cake on him. 'Come on, Charlie. You need filling up.'

Charlie grinned. 'You're trying to make me fat.' Everyone laughed.

Charlie looked at his family and the others gathered. Only Michael and his own father could possibly know how he was feeling at this moment in time. Something momentous had happened to him. He'd experienced a situation that somehow set him apart from them all. Nothing would ever be the same again. 'Son,' said Stan. 'Son.' He couldn't stop saying the word. 'When we heard about the sinking of your ship, well, I don't mind saying, I damned that battleship *Graf Spee* and damned the captain and all of his men too. Especially the captain, the black-hearted—'

'He wasn't black-hearted, Dad,' Charlie interrupted. 'He was only doing his job, just like we were doing ours.'

Stan was visibly affronted. To his ears it had sounded as though his son was defending an enemy captain.

'He was out to kill you!' Frances piped up. She had snuggled herself up close to her cousin, gazing up at him fondly and hanging on his every word.

Stan Sweet looked at his son in amazement. He'd come close to death and he'd despaired at ever seeing him again. Yet he was standing up for the enemy.

Charlie put his arm around Frances's shoulders and hugged her. 'No. He was out to sink the food cargoes coming up from South America; beef from the Argentine and grain from Brazil. His orders were to sink our food ships so our people would be starved and we would have to surrender.'

'Britain won't surrender – will it?'

He looked up to respond to Gilda's question. She was standing with the hot teapot hugged tightly to her chest. Her dark eyes were like liquid pools.

For a moment Charlie's eyes fixed on her, flashing as though taking in her details and saving them to memory. Regardless of her marital status, he couldn't help the sudden attraction.

'Not as long as we don't starve, and as long as me and my pals are willing to go out there and get those supplies, we'll stand firm. I'm sure of it.'

Stan Sweet was only half listening, still mulling on what his son had said regarding the German captain. Had he heard right? Was his son defending the man?

'As for the captain merely wanting to kill us,' said Charlie, Frances smiling as he tapped her on the nose, 'Captain Lansdorff wasn't that kind of man. He was a decent man, obeying orders he didn't necessarily approve of.'

'You sound impressed,' said Michael Dangerfield, his eyes narrowed and for once fixed on Charlie rather than on his sister, Mary.

'He was a decent man,' Charlie reiterated. 'I would probably have taken the same view as you if there hadn't been a mix-up when the boat went down. All the ordinary seamen were put into boats by the Germans and told to row towards the African coast. It was only the officers who were taken prisoner.

'I was out cold and the medical officer was looking after me, so I ended up with the officers by mistake. No. I can't say he was a bad man,' said Charlie shaking his head. 'It's just the war. Just the bloody war!'

Mary started to protest about the deaths by drowning when the ship went down. Her father raised his hand from Charlie's shoulder, a signal for her to be quiet.

'Let Charlie have his say,' he said steadily, his eyes on his son. 'Go on, my son. Tell us all about it.'

Charlie nodded. Everyone stayed silent as he began his tale, recounting how his ship had been sunk by the *Graf Spee* off the Cape of Good Hope. He'd been one of the lucky ones, picked up by one of the *Graf Spee's* support ships, eventually transferred on to the battleship herself.

Despite being well treated, Charlie and his pals had not liked the thought of being interned for the rest of the war.

The big turning point came on the 15th of December when the battleship was attacked by the Royal Navy. Having sustained damage, the *Graf Spee* steamed her way from the mouth of the River Plate where the battle had taken place and into Montevideo, Uruguay.

Charlie's face lit up at the memory. 'A neutral port. Under international law the captain had no option but to release us.'

'I bet he hated doing that,' spat Ruby who was sat next to the cake she had baked, her fingers clenched around the carving knife.

'I'm not so sure,' Charlie responded. 'Not if what happened next is anything to go by. You see, he scuttled his ship rather than face the Royal Navy. All the prisoners were taken off and released, and all the crew except for a skeleton crew in charge of destroying the ship. I like to think he didn't want more men to die – his or ours!'

Before calling an end to Boxing Day, the three men went out into the garden, two with cigarettes and one with his pipe. They stood contemplatively, blowing smoke into the darkness and exchanging opinions about the likely progress of the war, whether the Yanks would get involved, whether the force sent into France would be strong enough to repel the enemy army.

'No trenches this time,' remarked Stan Sweet. 'Certainly not on the Germans' part anyway, judging by the way they invaded Poland and the like.'

Charlie remarked that he was glad he'd chosen to go to sea. 'Despite losing my first ship.'

With a loud guffaw of laughter his father pointed out that it was the captain's responsibility if a ship was lost.

'Here's hoping it won't happen again,' said Charlie.

Michael listened quietly, but said nothing as he thoughtfully sucked the smoke into his mouth before expelling it into the frosty night where it mingled with the steam of his breath.

He was thinking of Mary. He'd been stunned that morning. Seeing her again had only reaffirmed how he felt about her. He wanted to throw his arms around her; he wanted to kiss her, and much, much more. On the one hand it was early days in their relationship, but on the other these were desperate times. It was downright crazy asking her to marry him, but the idea had struck him without warning, and now it had struck, he couldn't let it go. How crazy was that?

Suddenly he realised that Charlie was addressing him. 'Fancy going to the pictures tomorrow – you know – the cinema? They're reopened them and the girls might like the break.'

'What? Oh, yeah. Sure.'

'It's only a bus ride. The Regent in Kingswood. We could get the late bus back. Might even find a fish and chip shop open if we're lucky, though it's a bit soon after Christmas.'

'Yeah. That would be great,' said Michael, thinking that his one Christmas wish might yet come true. It was an opportunity to be with Mary. It was also an opportunity to make amends for his cloddish behaviour at the Victoria Rooms and perhaps to get more intimate with her – if intimate was the right word. I'm not thinking getting fresh with her, he thought to himself, not with her brother and sister in tow.

'Great,' said Charlie sounding dead pleased that he'd thought of the idea. 'I'll pop back inside and see if Gilda would like to come, too. Seems to me she needs some cheering up.'

After he'd gone, Stan Sweet stood there silently, noticing

everything but saying nothing. He had no doubt that Gilda would leap at the chance of a night out. He was also certain that Bettina would offer to look after the children and possibly also invite him over for another taste of her late husband's liquor stock. He would not refuse. For the first time in years he was actually enjoying the company of a woman. They were both getting on. Two people who'd lived a long time and loved just once in their life.

Eyes narrowed, he sucked his pipe with great satisfaction. His children were still uninjured by war and Mary and Charlie at least were seeking happiness with another human being. He'd seen the way Mary looked at Michael and the way Charlie had looked at Gilda. Shame about all that make-up, though. The girl was good-looking without all that stuff. He wondered about her experiences in Europe and the exact situation with her husband. Somehow he couldn't help thinking the worst.

'Sir,' said Michael Dangerfield, suddenly interrupting his thoughts. 'Do you mind if I court your daughter. Sir?'

Stan eyed the good-looking Canadian with a mix of admiration and sadness. He'd liked him on first sight and was convinced that his daughter liked him too, though very possibly it was much more than that, given the letter he had written. He was happy for her of course, but also saddened. It would soon be time for all his little birds to flee the nest.

Clenching the stem of his pipe in the corner of his mouth, Stan told Michael that as his daughter wasn't far off twenty-one, he wouldn't stand in her way.

'Not that she'd take that much notice if I did,' he said with a chuckle. 'She's like her mother in that regard: pleases herself no matter what I say.'

Content with each other's company, they turned their gaze to the clear night sky, the full moon and the stars.

'Lovely night. Cold but lovely,' said Stan while thinking to himself that it would do his parsnips the world of good.

'Yeah,' said Michael, sounding more subdued. They called it a bomber's moon; the crew could see the ground and the enemy, but the enemy could also see them. He hoped he wouldn't have too many of them.

23

The film was *Goodbye Mr Chips* starring Robert Donat and Greer Garson.

Ruby declared at the very last minute that she wouldn't be coming.

'Why not?' asked Mary.

'Do I look like a gooseberry?' Ruby was adamant. 'Look, I can see you and the Canadian cook are getting lovey dovey with each other.'

'We are not,' Mary responded hotly, her face turning pink.

'Then you should be,' said Ruby. 'But don't say I didn't warn you.'

'Will you be all right?'

Ruby pouted. 'Of course I will. Anyway, I'm in training.'

'For what?'

'To be a spinster. I've decided it will suit me very well.'

Mary tossed her head and sighed, thinking how exasperating her sister could be at times.

'She's staying behind for a reason,' whispered Charlie, giving Mary a sharp nudge in the ribs while winking at their sister. 'I can see it all now,' he said, his voice spooky like some actor they'd seen in a ghost story at the Regent back in the summer. 'Once we're out of the way, she's going to change into something lacy, ready to meet the tall handsome man that's gonna come knocking the minute we're out of the house.'

'Get on with you,' snapped Ruby, giving him a playful slap. 'Anyway, Dad's here, so the tall handsome man will have to make it another night. Now go on. Enjoy yourselves. I'll be fine.'

Frances came hurtling down the stairs. 'Wait for me!' Charlie had tried to dissuade their cousin from coming, and Ruby had a good notion why. He hadn't been able to take his eyes off Gilda and it worried her. Gilda was married and had two children. She told herself he was just being kind, but somehow she wasn't convinced. Still, at least having Frances tagging along would keep things in check for both Charlie and her sister and her Canadian beau.

The living accommodation above the bakery took on a strange echo once everyone had gone. The silence was interrupted by her father coming out of his bedroom. She noticed he'd changed into a clean shirt and pullover.

She did consider asking him where he was going or telling him he looked nice, but didn't.

Purposefully he picked up a bundle of leeks wrapped in newspaper from the table. Normally they would still be muddy from the garden, but she'd noticed him washing them off beneath the cold tap in the kitchen.

He paused before leaving. 'I'm just taking over this bunch of leeks for Mrs Hicks. Won't be long.'

Ruby smiled to herself. She couldn't blame him for seeking company of his own age; he'd been alone a long time, dedicating his life to bringing up his children.

The door closed behind him and once again she was aware of

the echoing silence and the warmth of the ovens captured in the floor and walls.

She listened until she was quite sure she was entirely alone.

Laying aside her note book where she scribbled down recipes, she headed for the cellar.

Her breath steamed into the cellar air, easily seen in the light of the torch she was forced to use, the cellar having no electricity supply.

Although chilly, the cellar was dry. First she moved the box of mushrooms, though only after checking that a new crop had come through following her cropping them two or three days ago.

Moving the box of mushrooms exposed the airtight bin. So far it had served to prevent the sugar from becoming damp.

Ruby had brought a two-pound sugar bag down with her plus a large teaspoon. Setting the lamp to one side, she prepared to fill the sugar bag.

After opening the bin she dipped in the teaspoon and gradually spooned the sugar into the bag until it was about three-quarters full. So far Mary hadn't questioned the fact that they'd hardly taken any sugar for household purposes from the firm that supplied the bakery.

Back in the bakery she rolled out pastry then took out the jar of chutney she'd made from apples and sultanas. Before doing anything else with it, she spooned it into a bowl, added extra sugar, tasted it and decided another spoonful wouldn't go amiss. One more taste. Lovely. It was just right.

With the swift skill of somebody who's done it a hundred times before, she took a palette knife and spread the pastry with the sweet chutney, rolled the pastry over and over until it resembled a Swiss roll – which it was – though her own special recipe.

Once that was done, she covered it with greaseproof paper and set it beside the bread oven for baking, though not until the last batch of bread had been baked.

There were still some people who bought ready-baked pastries, though only when the price was right. She decided that at a penny a slice, anyone could afford a piece and make their own custard to pour over it.

* * *

Stan Sweet was surprised at himself. He'd never realised he'd been lonely and had never wanted to alter his situation until he'd become more neighbourly with Bettina Hicks.

They had a lot in common of course, both having lost their respective partners and both getting on in years. Mrs Hicks's brother lived in Canada and her daughter lived in South Africa.

'They couldn't be more far-flung if they tried,' she'd said ruefully to him while leaning on her stick to pour him a second glass of brandy.

Stan felt the brandy burning the back of his throat. 'They only belong to you temporary,' he said to her. 'Kids that is. You sacrifice the years to take care of them, but at the end of it they fly away. I hadn't really faced up to that until now, though I don't mind telling you I am a bit afraid of what might happen to them. I lost a brother during the last war and another once it was over. I remember my mother and my father crying for nights on end. My father tried to pretend he didn't cry, but he did. Still...'

He heaved a big sigh between drinking brandy and puffing on his pipe. He'd expected to feel a trifle guilty to spend time with Mrs Hicks, as though he were being unfaithful to Sarah – which he couldn't be. Sarah was dead. Had been for years.

'They're gone,' she said suddenly. 'I don't mean the children have gone, I meant your Sarah and my Alf. They're gone and all we can do is make the best of it.'

Stan looked at her, noticing the warm smile, the blue eyes twinkling like stars behind her glasses. Luckily he rarely resorted to glasses except for reading. He was one of the lucky ones, but who was to say that in time he wouldn't need to wear glasses for his day-to-day activities.

'Tempus fugit,' she said suddenly. 'Time flies.'

He nodded. No matter his promise to his wife, the time had come to begin anew even though it seemed a bit late in the day.

'Funny we didn't keep company earlier,' Stan said to her.

Bettina nodded in agreement. 'There's always a right time. It comes along eventually.'

She lifted her glass to him in a toast. He returned it, thinking how warm he felt in her company, how lucky he was that his family was grown and he had a few years left for himself.

* * *

There was a queue for the stalls so both Michael and Charlie coughed up the extra and they all went up in the circle. There were only a few seats left and they couldn't all sit together. Mary, Michael and Frances were seated on one side of the aisle, Charlie and Gilda on the other.

Frances had brought a bag of caramels with her that she'd been given for Christmas. Everyone dipped into the bag until Frances decided that she'd shared enough and the rest were for her.

She fell asleep halfway through the film, her head resting on Mary's shoulder. In response to the weight, Mary shifted slightly so she could put her arm around her cousin's shoulders.

On sensing her movements and glancing round her to see the sleeping Frances, Michael put his arm around Mary's shoulders.

She turned to look at him and the inevitable happened. He kissed her. His lips were warm yet the touch of his cheek against hers was cool.

She didn't close her eyes but noticed he closed his. When he opened them again she felt tongue tied.

'That was a great kiss. So how about we get married?'

She covered her mouth so the sound of her laughter wouldn't upset those engrossed in the film, or wake her sleeping cousin. The kiss, she decided, was her undoing. How could she concentrate on the past life of an ageing schoolmaster following a kiss like that?

Her emotions were in turmoil and if she'd been made of chocolate she would have formed a puddle on the floor.

Mary couldn't see what Charlie and Gilda were up to on the other side of the aisle, but Michael could. They were cuddled up together, staring at each other rather than at the film.

Michael turned his eyes back to the screen. He knew Gilda was married. He also knew the circumstances of why her husband had been placed in a concentration camp and why she was here, but he'd been sworn to secrecy. He would say nothing until Gilda gave him leave to do so.

* * *

A few days later, Frances was despatched back to the Forest of Dean and the house of Ada Perkins. She seemed surprisingly happy to go back, chatting about the friends she'd made and what might be going on in the forest.

'I'll catch you a salmon,' she said, 'and post it to you.'

'No you will not,' said Mary. 'That's poaching and poaching is stealing. Besides with the post these days, by the time it arrived it wouldn't be fit for anything!'

Frances didn't seem quite able to comprehend that poaching

salmon and tickling trout had anything to do with stealing. Her new friends didn't regard it that way.

Two weeks after Frances left, Charlie was scheduled to leave on the train into Temple Meads Station in Bristol, changing there for the train to Blandford Forum where he would change once again for one that would take him to his new ship in Southampton.

'If I don't get lost seeing as they've removed all the station names,' he quipped jovially. 'There's no way of knowing where you are unless you know already or ask somebody.'

'It's to confuse the enemy,' Mary said to him.

He grinned. 'I don't know about that, but it certainly confuses me'

He said his goodbyes to his family and also to Gilda who had accompanied them to the station. Nobody was surprised at her presence, having noticed that something more than friendship had developed between their brother and the foreign woman with the velvet brown eyes. Something had also changed in Gilda herself. There was a brittle happiness about her now and less sadness. It was also noticeable that she no longer plastered her face with make-up, using just enough to enhance. After seeing Charlie off, Gilda hurried away, saying she had to pick up her children from school.

'It was a bit too much,' Ruby remarked while running her own bright red lipstick over her mouth. 'I mean, it's not as though she needs it.'

Mary had to agree with her. Gilda was a good-looking woman, though they had to remind themselves that she was married.

'It was like a mask,' she said without really thinking. 'As if she was trying to hide behind it.'

The twins exchanged one of their knowing looks. Ruby had obviously been thinking the same thing.

'I wonder what happened back there in Austria.'

Bettina Hicks had told them that Gilda and her family had been living in Vienna when the *Anschluss* occurred, the absorption of Austria by Germany. Hitler's army marched in to ensure all went smoothly.

'I asked Charlie. He said it was her business. Basically he was telling me not to be nosy.'

'But he knows,' said Mary, linking arms with her father and her sister as they made their way home.

'A man likes to keep some things to himself,' their father stated. 'We all need to keep a few secrets to ourselves.'

Mary wasn't sure about that, but Ruby agreed with him, though her secret regarded not a man but a bag of sugar.

24

Gareth Stead washed, shaved and put on the cleanest of his dirty shirts. Mrs Pugh used to take his washing home with her once a week, but since her daughter had given birth to her fifth child, her hands were full coping with the other four.

On sniffing at each armpit, he decided it wouldn't do and anyway he had a whole box of new shirts courtesy of his friend who'd carried out a midnight raid on a department store in the city of Bath, just a few miles down the road.

Once the shirt and detached collar were all in place, cuffs fastened with mother-of-pearl cuff links, he plastered Brylcreem on his hair combing it flat until it looked as though it were painted on to his head.

'Gareth, she'll be all over you,' he said to his reflection.

He looked down at the shiny packets lying on the table in his living room behind the bar at the Apple Tree.

Especially when she claps eyes on them, he thought to himself.

He'd picked up the six packets of stockings a friend of his had nicked from that big store at the bottom of Park Street in Bristol.

Nylon stockings were guaranteed to earn you the favours of any girl you fancied and he had a few favours he wanted from Ruby Sweet.

Keen to get on with the job and work his wicked charm, he tucked all six packets into the inside of his jacket before thinking better of it. Why give her six pairs of stockings when two might do the trick? He took out four, leaving two in his pocket.

It was getting close to midday when he was finally standing across the road from the bakery waiting for the last customer of the day to come out. He could see the woman's hat bobbing about and guessed she was talking nineteen to the dozen, relating all that was or was not happening in the village. Every village had one, a nosy parker whose life revolved around what everyone else was doing. Better than a newspaper they were. Knew everything.

'Come on out, you old bat,' he muttered to himself. He gave the bulge in his jacket a reassuring pat. He was pretty sure that it was Ruby's day serving in the shop, but even if it was Mary, he could handle it. He might even give her a pair of stockings by way of a peace offering. On second thoughts he could keep the stockings to give to a more amenable girl and buy a loaf of bread. Mary didn't like him and he didn't like girls who could see right through him.

The incidents with the kid hadn't helped. The truth was he hadn't realised it was the younger girl, after all she was tall for her age and looked a lot like her twin cousins. On top of that, he had been drunk both times. He couldn't help himself. He'd thought it was her. Ruby should know better. He loved her. Surely she knew that? Yes, that was the right word to use. Love. Not lust, and he certainly had plenty of that for her, though no more nor less than for any woman he'd ever known.

He took another glance at his wristwatch, acquired from the same acquaintance who'd lifted the stockings. If that old biddy didn't clear off, he thought, I'll go over there and drag her out.

Suddenly he heard the bell above the shop door jangle as the woman finally shuffled out, a single shopping bag dangling from one hand.

'Cheerio, Ruby me love,' he heard her say.

Ruby! He was in luck. It was Ruby's day to serve.

He watched the old woman totter away. 'Bugger off, you fat old cow,' he muttered under his breath, not wanting to make a move until she was out of sight.

Once the old woman was at a safe distance and making sure nobody else was around, he darted across the road.

He had already made sure that Stan Sweet's bread van wasn't around, knowing this was the one day when he used up his petrol rations to deliver bread to other villages hereabouts. He took it that Mary had caught the bus to Kingswood and the weekly market and he knew the kid was back with Miriam Powell's grandmother in the Forest of Dean.

He pushed the door open just in time to catch Ruby on her way to lock up and pull down the blind. 'All right then, Rube?'

Ruby stopped dead, her surprised expression replaced by one of contempt. 'Don't call me Rube. My name's Ruby and I'll thank you to call me that.'

She didn't like the fact that he was here. What was he doing? And what was that she could smell? Brylcreem? Cologne? A mix of both, yet still she detected something rancid and greasy about him, if not his body then definitely in his manner.

His smile was as oily as his hair. 'Sorry, Rube... Ruby... I didn't meant to call you a blackmailer the other week either. But there you are. Slip of the tongue. I've got no axe to grind.'

She eyed him steadily, one foot tapping her impatience. 'Have you been drinking?'

He shook his head vehemently. 'Whatever makes you think that?'

'You're rambling. You always ramble when you've been drinking.'

'Well, I haven't. So there.'

He had, but assured himself that she wouldn't know any different.

'Must be a red-letter day.'

'No. Nothing to do with letters. I wanted to see you.'

'The feeling is not mutual.'

'Oh, come on, Rube... Ruby...'

'What is this about?'

'Us.'

She shook her head and laughed before her expression hardened, her soft lips set in a straight line. 'There is no us.'

'I'm sorry you see it that way. As for me, well I reckon it was just a little misunderstanding, and look, I've got you a present, well, two presents, actually.'

Gingerly he reached inside his coat for the stockings he'd brought her. He'd been so sure they would work, but her attitude had come as a bit of a surprise. Ruby Sweet had changed a lot in the past few months. However, he didn't consider that he had. On the contrary he was rather smug and pleased with himself, his confidence acquired from increased drinking with the new friends who came out to see him from the city docks. He reckoned he now knew the right people and that this war would make him his fortune.

'Well,' he said, his arm outstretched, the cellophane packets of nylons dangling from his hand. 'Take them. They're for you. A peace offering to say I'm sorry.'

Ruby eyed them stiffly but did not touch them. She folded her arms, her fingers tapping against her elbow in time with her foot.

'I take it they're stolen,' she said accusingly.

Gareth shrugged, not quite comprehending that anything was wrong about doing deals with men who were out-and-out thieves.

'Take them!' He jerked them forward so they were only inches from her face.

Ruby drew her chin back and looked daggers. 'I don't want them.'

'Take them and I'll forget you stole my sugar.'

'I didn't steal it,' Ruby responded hotly. 'You gave it to me as a direct consequence of your bad behaviour – your very bad behaviour!'

He dropped his hand slowly, his bright expression totally gone. 'I didn't mean to do it. I was drunk.'

'You're always drunk.'

'It was a mistake.'

'Giving me the sugar was a mistake?'

'I meant about the other.'

Ruby stiffened. 'You behaved badly towards my eleven-year-old cousin. If things had gone any further, you would now be in prison. Do you realise how stupid you've been? Do you?'

'I am not a pervert,' he growled, clenching his jaw so hard that his teeth hurt. 'I was drunk both times. I thought she was you – in my head, that is. She looks like you, and she's tall and I was missing you so much—'

'Get out!'

'You and me had something special. You're throwing it away.'

'Get out,' repeated Ruby, though louder this time. 'I won't tell you again. Once more and I'll call the police.'

Gareth stuffed the stockings inside his jacket, his expression as black as thunder.

'I always thought you was a sweet girl, a real bit of all right. Sweet by name, sweet by nature. But you ain't sweet. You're a right fucking bitch!'

Ruby had got used to his bad language when she'd worked for him, and had once thought it funny to see how it shocked people.

She didn't think so now. He'd needed to shock people, needed them to think he was something different and not to be messed with. On the last count she wished she hadn't messed with him – in any sense of the word.

'And you are a disgusting excuse for a man,' Ruby responded. 'And you smell. It's bad enough that you stink as though you have not washed for a week, but what with the boozy breath... no plastering yourself with Brylcreem or drenching yourself in cologne will ever hide that!'

Burning with anger, he levelled a finger at her. 'It works both ways, Ruby Sweet. You're just as guilty as I am and just as likely to get in trouble. You're stockpiling a basic ration. Be careful I don't report *you* to the authorities. Then we'll see who gets in the most trouble.'

Ruby grabbed the door, the brown blind rattling on its track as she jerked it open. 'For the last time, get out of this shop. Now!'

'I'm going, but mark me well Ruby Sweet. No matter your threats, if the chance comes I'll shop you. You just see if I don't!'

With that he wrenched the door from Ruby's grasp. It slammed shut behind him, the old doorbell jangling crazily, the glass rattling in its frame.

For a moment she leaned against the closed door in order to catch her breath. Her heart was still racing though not with fear. She had held her ground and hadn't flinched.

No matter what Gareth had offered her, she was beyond him now. Even if he'd asked her then and there to marry him, she would have refused. His behaviour towards Frances had been bad enough and he deserved her anger. However, she had also enjoyed seeing him look surprised that she refused to be intimidated by his threats or bribed by his stolen gifts.

Her only concern was that he might exact his own revenge and spin a tale to the authorities about her hoarding and dealing in black-market sugar. She wouldn't put it past him and it did worry her. The sugar was carefully hidden and sparingly used. Even her family didn't know about it and she wouldn't tell them. It was her little stockpile, her precious something to make her cakes eatable and her pies tasty.

All she hoped was that Gareth would sober up and keep his mouth shut.

25

FEBRUARY, 1940

Rationing had come in. Everyone had known it was coming and nobody had been looking forward to it.

As a bakery producing bread for general consumption, Sweets Bakery was an integral part of the war effort and answerable to the Ministry of Food.

The twins were sitting on either side of the kitchen table looking through the various leaflets they'd been flooded with.

Ruby had given up smoking in order that she could send her ration to Charlie. He was issued with cigarettes anyway as part of a serviceman's right, but she had no doubt he would appreciate having her ration as well. Mary also sent hers, no loss seeing as she didn't smoke anyway.

Mary sighed at the piles of leaflets, handy hint cards and booklets with advice on everything from how to be economical with cooking times: using water in which meat had been boiled to make soup, cooking potatoes in their skins in order to preserve their nutritional value. It was also pointed out that less fuel was consumed and cooking hastened when saucepans were fitted with lids.

'As if we didn't already know that,' grumbled Ruby.

The ration books and how to use them demanded their attention more so than anything else.

Mary read it out. 'Four ounces of bacon and ham, meat to the value of one shilling and sixpence with the exception of sausages and offal unless stated otherwise. Two ounces of butter, two ounces of cheese...'

Ruby, a great lover of cheese, sighed. 'Hardly enough to keep a mouse.'

Mary carried on reading the rest of the list of rationed items. 'Four ounces of margarine. Four ounces of cooking fat. Three pints of milk. Eight ounces of sugar. One pound of preserves every month, two ounces of tea, one shell egg a week...'

Ruby interrupted. 'Unless Mrs Hicks's hens are laying well.'

Mary continued. 'Twelve ounces of sweets.'

Ruby sat holding her head in her hands trying to take it all in. 'And this is for one person?'

'One person, per week. Not a lot is it?'

Ruby shook her head. No, it wasn't a lot, though the fact that they lived between city and countryside was going to help, at least as far as local game and farm produce was concerned. And Frances seemed to be faring better in her temporary home. Deciding she was now fully informed, Mary opened the ration book and studied exactly what they'd done so far and how the whole system would work.

'Right. We've registered for meat at Masters in the High Street, greengrocery at Mary Tiley's on the corner of Court Road and general grocery at Powells'. Bread doesn't apply to us, even though it's not rationed. I dare say we're going to get a run on it though, people stocking up on it to use as a filler with other food. An alternative to pastry. Did you like my Brown Betty last night?'

'Yes I did.'

Mary read out the details from their little blue book in which they were accustomed to record the dishes they contrived.

'*Slice apples as you would for an apple pie, place in dish, add a little water. Topping: stale breadcrumbs mixed with a dessertspoon of sugar or honey, sprinkle on top, place in oven for half an hour. Serve with custard or cream.*'

'Or pour over the juice from the apples. Not everyone is going to be able to get cream and even custard powder might be in short supply.' Ruby shrugged. 'We can't be sure yet, can we?'

Mary shook her head. 'No. We can't be sure of anything.'

Her thoughts naturally turned to Michael. He'd kissed her so passionately when he left she'd been in danger of fainting from lack of air. That's what she'd told him.

'We've got no married quarters at Scampton,' he'd said. 'I think you should know that.'

She laughed. 'Just as well we're not married then, isn't it.'

He'd grinned. 'Give it time.' Then he'd kissed her again.

He was still at Scampton but she hadn't heard from him for days and the news coming in from France and the Netherlands wasn't good. She had a suspicion he might be flying over there, bombing the enemy positions, though of course she couldn't know for sure.

'No news is good news,' Ruby said to her as though reading her thoughts.

Mary sighed. 'Perhaps I should have taken him at his word and married him before he went back. I know it's crazy, but who knows what time any of us have got left?'

Ruby refilled their teacups adding milk but no sugar. Only their father refused to go without, though had cut down from two teaspoons to one as a gesture of support for his son and all those bringing much needed supplies home.

They were interrupted by somebody knocking at the shop door.

Ruby snorted. 'Ignore it. We're closed. Give it a minute and they'll remember we close at midday.'

The knocking continued.

'Obviously they're not remembering,' said Mary getting to her feet.

Unwilling to let her cup of tea go cold or to give up the precious little time she had to herself, Ruby continued to pore over the leaflets, scrutinising the advice on how to deal with various forms of gas attack and details of where to get emergency rations should an invasion occur, and amused by warnings not to use gas mask cases as handbags.

'I'm sorry. We're closed,' she heard Mary shouting out in the shop.

Whoever was at the door said something Ruby couldn't quite catch, except that it was definitely a man's voice. Next thing she heard was the rattle of the bolts and the shaking of the fragile glass in the top half of the door. Whoever it was, Mary was letting them in.

More muffled voices, though this time one particular phrase stood out.

'I represent the Ministry of Food.'

Ruby's blood turned cold. Gareth! He'd done it! He'd shopped her to the authorities just as he'd threatened he would.

She leapt to her feet, her first thought to dash down to the cellar, take the sack from the airtight bin she'd hidden it in and bury it among the coal – or anywhere it wasn't likely to be found.

There wasn't time.

Mary entered the kitchen followed by a tall, fair man with a ruddy complexion and glasses. It occurred to her that she'd seen him before, but she couldn't remember exactly where. 'Ah,' said the man on seeing the official pamphlets and ration cards spread all over the table. 'I see you're in the process of familiarising yourself

with the rationing system. I'm sure you'll soon get the hang of it –
all things considered.'

Mary took a deep breath. 'This is Mr Sinclair, Ruby. Mr Sinclair,
this is my sister, Ruby. Ruby, Mr Sinclair is from the Ministry of
Food.'

Mr Sinclair doffed his hat. Ruby felt her knees give way but
managed a muted hello. Her thoughts were still with the sack of
sugar in the cellar. Perhaps he'd be lenient if she owned up.

Mary asked him if he would like a cup of tea.

Ruby gulped. Why was her sister being so inviting to this man?
She reminded herself that Mary knew nothing about the sugar.

'We don't have much sugar,' Ruby blurted.

Mary looked at her as though she'd gone mad. 'I'm sure we can
spare Mr Sinclair a teaspoon for his tea, Ruby.'

With a sinking heart, Ruby pulled out a chair and sat down.

Mary invited Mr Sinclair to sit down which he did, taking off his
hat and setting it on the table next to his teacup.

Mary asked him if he'd like a biscuit. Ruby shot her sister an
accusing look. She'd made those biscuits in an ad hoc manner
using oatmeal, honey and a handful of unrefined flour that Spillers
had sent them by mistake. Neither Mary nor herself had tasted
them yet. Besides that she considered them hers and not to be given
out generously without her say so. What with that and the worry
about his reason for being here, she was not best pleased.

She wondered what prison she might end up in; hopefully one
near her home. At least then she'd get visitors. Damn Gareth Stead!
Damn him to hell!

Mr Sinclair smiled beatifically and said he would love a biscuit.

Mary obliged, laying two on a tea plate which she placed
between his tea cup and his hat.

Before Mary had a chance to sit down, Ruby shot her sister a
questioning look. *What is he doing here?*

Mary told her. 'Mr Sinclair was at the Victoria Rooms. He wants to talk to us about our recipes.'

'Oh!'

Mr Sinclair took a bite of biscuit then beamed. 'Scrumptious! I take it you made these yourself?'

'Yes. I made them,' said Ruby feeling a sudden surge of satisfaction.

Mr Sinclair shut his eyes. 'I taste honey and the crunchiness is due to oatmeal flour. Unrefined. Am I right?'

His eyes blinked open. Even though he wore spectacles, Ruby could see they were very blue.

Her mouth hung open in surprise. How could he possibly know that?

Mr Sinclair noticed her surprise and smiled in an oddly secretive way. 'I have an acute sense of taste. The sensitivity of my taste buds was the reason my first job was with the Tea Council tasting various brands and blends of tea from all over the world. I could tell instantly whether the leaves had been grown on the southern slopes of the hills in Assam or on the terraces of Darjeeling. Of course I could be much more specific than that and say which plantation they had been grown on and which slope, terrace or field on that plantation. It was quite a demanding job, but I much prefer the variety of tastes I get to savour since I joined the Ministry of Food.'

His eyes twinkled with pride.

Mary was impressed and also intrigued.

Ruby wanted to laugh at his pronouncement, but thinking he might resent her laughing at what he obviously considered a skilled profession, merely smiled and said, 'How interesting.'

'I think you mean unusual,' he said, his eyes twinkling, 'unless you've met a tea taster before. But never mind. Let me get to the point of why I am here.'

Clearing his throat and readjusting his spectacles, he reached for his briefcase which he had placed on the floor at his feet, unclipped it and brought out a buff-coloured folder. Before continuing he polished off a second biscuit and drained his tea cup. He declined a second cup.

The eyes of both Mary and Ruby went to the folder. When he opened it they recognised the recipes they had entered for the competition.

Mary craned her neck, her eyes following Mr Sinclair's hands as he read quickly through a piece of paper fastened with a paperclip to the inside of the folder.

'Ah,' he said after reading the note. 'You didn't win the actual baking competition.'

'No,' snapped Ruby feeling disagreeable at being reminded that she hadn't. 'We were too downmarket for her ladyship. She certainly doesn't favour ordinary cooking on a budget, which most people round here have to do all the time. I wonder where she'll get her caviar and sirloin of beef now there's a war on and rations coming in.'

It was hard to read the look Mr Sinclair shot at her. 'What a pity.'

Mary shot her sister a warning glance. Her voice was getting loud and she wasn't caring too much about what she was saying.

Mr Sinclair appeared unruffled. 'However, you must have noticed that no prizes were given for the recipes submitted, but then, that wasn't the point of myself and my colleague Mr Potter being there. You left suddenly and I sent him out to find you. Did you not notice us at all?'

'Yes,' said Mary sensing that they were about to hear something very interesting. 'You didn't seem to belong there and I noticed all the recipe envelopes were passed to you.'

He nodded. 'That's right.' He took off his glasses and laid them on top of the paperwork. Resting his elbows on the table, he clasped his hands beneath his chin. 'The Ministry of Food have it in mind to generate a healthy food culture – waste not, want not, if you like. You may already have noticed some of this advice among the things you have here,' he said, waving his hand at the array of printed matter they'd been perusing. 'This war is not likely to be over in a matter of months, much as we would like it to be, and the fact is that we import a lot of our food, a factor likely to be interrupted by enemy action.'

'We know. Our brother is in the merchant navy,' Ruby explained. 'His ship got sunk, but he's gone to sea again on another.'

'I hope he stays safe,' Mr Sinclair said kindly. 'We were very impressed by your recipes because they were simply made from simple ingredients, including the use of leftovers from one meal to the next. Not wasting a thing is going to be very important to the war effort. We intend using your recipes in our information leaflets and on the wireless, in newspapers and also on the silver screen.'

Ruby gasped. 'Fancy that! Our bacon and bubble and squeak fry-ups on the screen at the Regent in Kingswood!'

Mary sagged back in her chair, utterly amazed. 'So you've come here to ask our permission?'

Mr Sinclair shook his head. 'Not really. The fact is that we are on a war footing and therefore have the right to requisition items we feel likely to be beneficial to the public interest. I trust you don't mind?'

Ruby folded her arms defiantly. 'I'm not so sure about that! Sounds like a bloody cheek to me!'

'So they're no longer ours,' said Mary, wondering why she felt there was something else going on here, that he wasn't here just to tell them that their recipes were being requisitioned.

'They remain yours, but the use of them is in the public interest,' said Mr Sinclair. 'But that is not the sole reason for my visit.'

'You need our continuing assistance,' said Mary, pulling up a chair and sensing something special was about to happen.

'Ah,' he said, putting his glasses back on before continuing. 'Very perceptive, Miss Sweet. I am indeed here on a very specific mission. The fact is that you were the only entrants who based their recipes on a single weekly shop for an ordinary working-class family. You actually planned the meals for the week around a Sunday roast, that is, roast on Sunday, cold on Monday, mince on Tuesday, etc., fresh vegetables and other more perishable items being added throughout the week.' He turned to Ruby. 'We were also impressed that you acknowledged that people need to be cheered up now and again with a little luxury, a sweet dessert to lift the spirits, and again, done on a very tight budget with very basic ingredients.'

Ruby positively preened. 'Well, war does seem to be a gloomy business and after seeing what our rations are going to be, it's only likely to get gloomier.'

'So why are you really here?' asked Mary. 'It's not just to ask us to invent more recipes, is it?'

Off came the glasses again. 'Quite right. I'll get straight to the point of what I am here to ask you. We need women with good cooking skills and the right attitude to give talks and demonstrations to women's groups such as WVS members, women shopping in high streets and at local markets, village halls, etc., at the same time distributing Ministry of Food leaflets.'

Mary could hardly believe what she was hearing. 'I'm not sure we can do that. We already get up early to help our father in the bakery and take turns serving in the shop until noon.'

'I take your point,' said Mr Sinclair. 'The fact is that most of these demonstrations occur in the afternoon or on an evening. Surely you can help the war effort – and those out there risking their lives on the sea to bring us much-needed supplies, might I add. We'll even provide you with extra petrol coupons, perhaps even a vehicle and a driver at some point – unless either of you can drive?'

Mary shook her head.

Ruby nodded. 'I can. A bit.' She had begged her dad to give her lessons in the van.

'Perhaps you could share the work between you. We will also pay you, which in turn means that you could pay somebody to take your place serving in the shop, It's your cooking skills we need. Might I remark that those skills are wasted behind a shop counter?'

Ruby sat silently, her thoughts reeling. Mr Sinclair's suggestion was extremely appealing.

'I don't know that we can...' Mary began.

'I'll do it. Gilda can help in the shop,' Ruby said forthrightly.

Mary was taken by surprise.

'You accept?' asked Mr Sinclair.

Ruby nodded enthusiastically. 'Oh yes. Yes indeed. I would love to do it.'

Suddenly the door leading out into the garden opened. 'Do what? Do what?'

Nobody could fail to recognise their father's booming voice and nobody had heard him come in from the garden, his face pinched with cold and the smell of earth clinging to his clothes.

'This is Mr Sinclair,' exclaimed Mary, springing to her feet. She made a point of standing between the two men, just in case her father decided he knew best what was going on here.

'Ministry of Food,' said Mr Sinclair as he rose to his feet and offered his hand for shaking. 'We've taken the liberty of requisitioning your daughters' recipes for some of our information publications. I'm sorry. I presumed your daughters were over twenty-one and could make their own minds up. I apologise again. I should have asked your permission first.'

Mr Sinclair showed no sign of being intimidated. On the contrary, he spoke clearly and with an air of authority. Stan Sweet couldn't help but be impressed.

If they could have read his mind on entering and hearing the tail end of their conversation, they would have known he feared Sinclair had come on a mission to hire single women for war work or, worse still, to join one of the women's branches of the armed forces; a few in the village had already left. His relief must have shown on his face and also in the manner he grabbed Sinclair's hand, shaking it enthusiastically as he told him how pleased he was that his daughters' efforts had been officially recognised.

Recognising a protective parent, Sinclair praised them to the rafters. 'Your daughters' interpretation as to what is required on the home front are invaluable. The recipes in themselves are absolutely wonderful, and the fact that one of your daughters has agreed to give demonstrations and advice to women's groups in the area is invaluable. You must be very proud of them.'

Stan Sweet looked unsure. 'What do you mean demonstrations? Where and when will these demonstrations take place?'

'Around the area.'

'She won't be leaving home, mark you. I'm confirming here and now that my girls are not yet twenty-one so can't leave home without my say so,' he said, stabbing the table with a dirt-encrusted fingernail.

'No, of course not,' said a smiling Mr Sinclair without a hint of being ruffled by their verbal exchange or by the size of Stan Sweet's fists. 'Afternoons and evenings, perhaps some weekends, and we will be paying her a salary for her services. You may of course use some of that salary to help towards hiring part-time help running your establishment – if it's needed, that is.'

'Gilda!' Ruby exclaimed before her father had time to object or ask awkward and possibly trivial questions. 'Gilda has a few mornings to spare and she's desperate to help with the war effort, especially since she met Charlie.'

Stan Sweet knew when he was beaten.

Ruby accepted the job, though advised Sinclair that she would share it with her sister. 'To keep our dad happy,' she added.

That Sunday morning Stan Sweet stood over Sarah's grave telling her all about it. The only sounds were the cawing of rooks and the soft footfall of people coming to church. The bells that usually summoned them to church had been silenced for the duration of the war.

'At least it's not the armed forces for Ruby or leaving home on a permanent basis. Hopefully that means Mary working with me will be regarded as a reserved occupation. That Mr Sinclair suggested they share the job between them, but I have to admit that our Ruby is keener than our Mary. I suppose it has to be and I should be thankful. While I had two of them at home, one of them was likely to be regarded as reserved occupation and the other likely to be called on to do something else.' He sighed. 'It looks as though we've been lucky. Anyway, don't worry about us overworking ourselves. Gilda Jacobson, who's vaguely related to Mrs Hicks and is staying with her, is willing to help out in the shop. I've already told you about her. She's from Austria but was born in Holland so has a Dutch passport, which is why she hasn't been interned with all the other alien refugees – poor buggers. They travelled here to get away from Hitler's prisons and concentration camps and ended up getting imprisoned here instead. Rough justice if you ask me. Anyway...' He paused as he contemplated telling her the rest of it. He decided that he would, after all, he'd never been able to keep his deepest secrets from Sarah when she was alive. Even now she was dead he could still hear her in his mind, urging him to spit it out, as she used to say.

'I know, I know,' he said as though responding to something she was saying to him. 'Our Charlie and her, this Gilda, are closer than they should be. It was love at first sight and before you remark, remember it was like that for us. One day and I knew, we both knew... and somehow...' He sighed and tried again to collect his thoughts. 'The thing is I can't condemn them even though she is married with two kids. I'm not sure I know all the story as yet. She's Jewish, you see; fled from the Nazis in Austria. Her husband didn't get out and I'm not sure whether he's alive or dead. All I can say is that she brightened up the minute she met our Charlie and well, there seems to be some kind of secret surrounding her husband. No, I don't know what it is though I get the impression our Charlie does. No doubt we'll hear all about it in time, but for now it's a case of letting sleeping dogs lie. Oh, and before I forget something funny, before returning to base, Felix the dog chased Melvyn Chance from the front door of Stratham House to the gate. I've got a sneaking suspicion Mrs Hicks let the dog out on purpose. Nobody much liked Melvyn Chance when he was a black shirt. They dislike him more now that he's a turncoat!'

He was about to turn away when a thought tugged him back. He hadn't been going to tell her about his friendship with Bettina Hicks, but there, he'd never been good at keeping secrets from Sarah.

'She's the first female friend I've had since you passed over. It's just a friendship. You do understand that, don't you?'

A soft breeze stirred the top of the trees, yet the rooks did not fly away. It caressed his face like soft fingers. It felt like his late wife's touch.

26

It was Ralph who caught the rabbit and Deacon's idea to light a fire down in the old quarry.

Everyone brought along what they could to the proposed feast except for those who were members of big families where meal-times were a scramble for whatever they could get. Frances brought half a loaf of bread and some potted jam.

There were many old quarries, small rocky inserts into the land made by men with pickaxes centuries ago. Their digging had left rocky crags jutting out below the roots of trees and half hidden by vegetation.

The roots of the trees had barely enough soil to cling on to, their branches overhanging to form something of a roof over their heads.

Ralph had a lot of brothers and sisters and perhaps because of that was the best at snaring rabbits, tickling trout and stealing spawning salmon from under the river gilly's nose. It was the gilly who looked after the fish in the river, especially the salmon and trout.

Ralph was more at home in the forest than anywhere else. To a great extent he fended for himself leaving whatever was placed on the table at home to the rest of his family.

By the time Frances had got there with her bread and jam, the rabbit had been skinned, skewered on to a stick and was presently roasting over a smoky fire that nonetheless was cooking it nicely. The smell was fantastic as was the sound of sizzling as globules of fat fell into the fire.

Dusk was turning to darkness as stomachs began growling with hunger. Frances and her friends sat around the fire, their eyes fixed firmly on the rabbit as though willing it to cook through. Pink tongues licked hungry lips.

Deacon had also added a wood pigeon to the twig that was acting as a skewer.

'Enough now for everyone,' Deacon exclaimed, his dark-blond hair cut in a pudding-basin style that most of the kids around the forest – the boys at least – seemed to favour.

Up until the point he'd killed the pigeon, there had been suggestions that girls – that is Deacon's sister, Gertie, and Frances's new best friend, Merlyn – should not be included because they weren't members of Deacon's gang.

Frances was regarded as an honorary gang member because she could climb trees better than any boy – and she'd brought the jar of jam and half a loaf of bread.

Every bit of food they'd brought with them was consumed during the vigil of waiting for the meat to cook with the exception of the four spuds Evan Evans had brought with him. These were first stabbed with each boy's pocket knife before being buried in the ashes at the perimeter of the fire.

There was a period of patting full bellies and licking of lips before attention went back to the spit-roasted meat.

'How 'bout we play hide and seek while we be waiting,' suggested Ralph.

Deacon's sister sucked in her breath. 'It's gettin' dark.'

'Scaredy cat. Chicken!' He accompanied his accusation with flapping arms and strutting around like a farmyard cockerel.

'There might be ghosts out there or monsters,' said Gertie in a quivering voice. Round eyed, her gaze flickered towards the blackness beyond the bright ring of firelight.

In response, Evan made howling noises and lifted his arms in an apelike fashion so that his hands drooped at the sides of his ears. He had big ears, like that Dumbo the elephant, thought Frances.

'Stop it,' shouted Gertie.

'Aw, come on. I like playing hide and seek with girls,' whined Ralph which he followed with a toothless grin.

'No kissing,' said Frances, pointing her finger in warning.

Ralph grinned, which yet again exposed the fact that his two front teeth were missing. Apparently his father had come home drunk one night and hit them out.

Frances had experienced one of his kisses before Christmas. He'd come at her with a bunch of mistletoe and pinned her against the back wall of the girls' toilets at school. Her bottom lip had been sucked into the gap in his teeth and she'd had trouble extricating herself, for one horrendous moment thinking she'd be stuck to him forever. She hadn't been keen on the prospect. And as first kisses went, it hadn't whetted her appetite for another.

'Come on, then,' said Merlyn who if rumour was correct had a schoolgirl crush on Deacon. 'But I don't want to be "it". I want to hide.'

Nobody could agree, though Frances would have liked to. However, she didn't want to appear too keen. Accordingly Deacon broke a handful of twigs into different lengths and handed them round.

'Shortest is "it",' he proclaimed with an air of authority. Deacon, it had to be said, had leadership skills.

Frances clasped her stick tightly hoping it was the shortest. If she had to hide it would be in the opposite direction to Ralph Tate. If she was 'it', the one who counted to fifty while everyone else hid, she wouldn't get kissed, at least not by Ralph.

Each of them in turn took a stick clenching it tightly until there were none left. The reckoning had come.

Deacon gave the order, 'Go!' Everyone showed their sticks.

Frances's heart leapt with joy when she saw hers was the shortest. 'I'm "it"!'

She couldn't have been more pleased as she headed for a thick tree trunk, resting her forehead against her folded arm and closing her eyes.

'One, two...'

'Count to thirty,' she heard Evan say. 'No. Fifty,' said Deacon.

Deacon was the gang leader so Frances began counting to fifty.

She smiled at the sound of her friends scurrying away, crashing through the undergrowth, looking for any small crevice in the rock face where ivy and tangled lengths of sloe intermingled to soften the harsh outlines left by the long-ago quarrying.

She knew how some kids dithered over the best place to hide so wasn't surprised to hear what she thought were returning footsteps, somebody undecided of where to go.

'You'd better hurry up,' she shouted. 'I'm on thirty-three, thirty-four, thirty-five...'

Whoever it was seemed to pause and take notice before yet again there came to her the sound of someone or something disturbing the fallen leaves.

'Fifty,' she shouted at last. 'Coming, ready or not.'

She left the tree and dashed back down the slope towards the fire.

On seeing the fire she gasped, her feet coming to an immediate halt.

The fire was still burning. The cooked rabbit and the pigeon were gone.

27

By April 1940, the enemy had taken both Norway and Denmark and rationing was beginning to bite. There was also bad news from the North Atlantic: convoys containing vital food supplies were under continuous attack by enemy submarines.

In late May, Ruby reported to the Ministry of Food in London to be briefed on her duties and how to go about them. The train journey had been long, the carriages packed with people, most of them wearing a uniform.

Despite the war, London was still colourful in a busy, booming kind of way. Sandbags were piled around important buildings so they looked like the entrance to Egyptian pyramids or temples. The proliferation of gas masks, military uniforms and shop windows covered in tape, to prevent injury from flying glass should a bomb fall close by, gave every indication that the war had turned a corner into a very serious phase.

'We think you can do this,' said Mr Sinclair from the other side of his wooden desk in Whitehall. 'The prime minister is very keen that everyone should be properly nourished and not a scrap of food wasted,' he said to her.

'Has he seen how little we're supposed to survive on?' Ruby asked.

His smile was somewhat sheepish. 'Um. Yes. He has now. When he first took a look at it he remarked that it looked very substantial for one day's rations. It was pointed out to him that it was for one week not one day.'

'And what did he say to that,' Ruby asked.

Mr Sinclair recognised that Ruby was not the sort to be intimidated by anyone, including the prime minister, Winston Churchill. 'He said, my people, my poor people.'

Ruby and Mary immediately understood why they'd been selected. It was all very well for middle-class women to devise recipes based on their own standard of living previous to the war. It was quite something else for those on low incomes whose main meals had never stretched to prime cuts of meat such as chops, steak and succulent lamb cutlets.

Ruby had seen the British canteen price lists with such items on as liver and bacon for sixpence. What the upper classes didn't grasp was that a lot of housewives only spent about one shilling and sixpence on a meal to stretch among six people. Whole families were living on offal, mince, pigs' tails and such like before war was declared; the rationing would now bite into those humble items too.

Ruby also pointed out to him that not everybody was proficient at reading and writing so wouldn't be able to read the leaflets and newspaper items the Ministry was so keen on. 'Then we'll have to get you on the wireless,' he announced with great aplomb.

Ruby gasped. 'Wireless? Me?'

'Why not?'

'I'm not... I mean, I don't speak posh. Perhaps Mary could...'

She stopped. Sinclair had agreed that they could divide their duties at home and their duties to the country at large. Mary had always been better dealing with upper-class people, even to imitating their plummy accents.

Sinclair asked her whether she'd drawn up any precise plan.

She said that she had. 'I think it would be a good start to give our first demonstration at the bakery. We could advertise in the shop window and there's plenty of room for demonstrations inside. Plenty of room for leaflets too.'

He smiled and congratulated her on her resourcefulness and forward planning – whatever that was supposed to mean.

'A good start. Going out and about and wireless broadcasts after that. Oh, and I think we can provide you with a vehicle and a driver. We'll be in touch with the details.'

* * *

Mary read the letter she'd received from Michael for the third time.

> *Darling Mary,*
>
> *Just a line to let you know that I am still alive, still flying and still wanting to marry you. This war is no longer phoney. It's for real. I am no longer dropping leaflets. I am dropping bombs – can't tell you where of course but no doubt you're keeping track of the news.*
>
> *Still the same base so if you want to write, you know the address. We have a padre on the base and lovely church down the road a shade, so with all that to hand it stands to reason I am going to ask you that question again. 'Will you marry me?'*
>
> *Love Michael.*
>
> *PS I am a persistent kind of chap who won't take no for an answer, in other words, I'll keep asking until I get the answer I want.*

Please take care of Auntie Betty for me.
Love Michael. (Again)

Smiling and feeling warm from the tip of her nose to her toes, Mary folded the letter and put it away with the others she'd received from him. This was her twelfth and all written in a very short time, the last four arriving within days of each other.

'He's keen,' Ruby had remarked. Just for once she didn't sound peevish about her sister's beau. Her moodiness had almost vanished since becoming one of the Ministry of Food's kitchen economists.

'I suppose he is,' Mary replied, though didn't mention he'd asked her to marry him in every single letter.

She'd asked herself why she didn't say yes and came up with various excuses. Number one, she had known him for so little time. Number two, there was a war on. Number three, she had Dad to think about. There were a whole list of other more trivial reasons, though basically it was all back to it being too soon after meeting him.

'I noticed that the last four letters came hot on the heels of each other,' remarked Ruby.

Mary sensed her sister was digging for details, but didn't bite.

'Almost as though time was running out,' Ruby added. 'I only meant...' she began, suddenly aware she'd been a little thoughtless. 'Oh, Mary, I'm so sorry. I didn't mean...'

Mary had been in the process of laying out fresh leaflets on the shop counter for the women expected to attend this afternoon's event. On hearing Ruby's statement her fingers seemed to freeze in the process of sorting them out. The fact was that Ruby was right. The same thought had occurred to her. Why the sudden deluge of letters unless he was being posted somewhere? Hopefully it would be somewhere safe and in this country, but there was no telling.

Ruby apologised immediately. 'Don't mind me. You know how I am, don't think before I speak, half the time.'

Mary was her usual stoic self. 'He's a pilot. Who can say?' She went back to sorting the leaflets. Not another word passed between them after that and Ruby could see there was no point in prodding her to be jolly or anything else. Mary had turned in upon herself, alone with her own thoughts, throwing herself into getting the demonstration and talk ready.

Unlike a few demonstrations they'd attended at the insistence of the ministry, theirs would not be centred on cooking meals from fresh ingredients. Not all the ingredients used in such meals were available in country districts or indeed to the poorer sections of the community. What they did have was access to local game and fish, fresh field mushrooms, wild garlic, nettles and all different kinds of fruit.

They'd also devised a Country Kitchen Cookbook, though it was far from being a book, just a number of useful recipes handed down and adapted to wartime conditions. Mary preferred to call the recipes 'meal plans', as the whole week's meals were planned from one shop with perhaps a few top-ups of fresh items during the week.

Central to the idea was the Sunday joint. They'd been lucky enough to be given extra meat rations for use on the job. The result was a very big piece of beef brisket, a cheap cut most of the village women would be familiar with.

Their father and Gilda Jacobson helped set out the chairs ready for the audience. They'd collected them from all over the house and some belonged to Bettina Hicks. Bettina had contacted a number of her friends, some of whom used to employ cooks rather than cater for themselves. However, things had changed and they too had been affected by rationing and shortage of domestic labour. They needed to know how to cook for themselves.

Ruby nervously surveyed her father and Gilda's handiwork and pronounced that fifteen chairs might be a little optimistic. She just couldn't believe that somebody would want to come along and hear someone of her age lecture on meal planning and food frugality. The thought of it was making her nervous. 'I reckon you're wrong there. I reckon you'll have a full house,' stated her father, before adding that he'd also acquired a couple of wooden forms from the village school. 'They're not needing so many what with kids being evacuated.' The clock struck two.

'Time for the kick-off,' stated Stan Sweet as he strode towards the bakery door.

The blinds at both the windows and the door were still down. On pulling up the blind covering the door, he found himself faced with a queue of inquisitive-looking women, all chattering away like magpies.

He turned and looked at his daughters. 'Have you seen this bloody lot? Must be half the women in the village outside my door. Quick. Set that bench out now and get the other one in from the back. Lucky I got two.'

Gilda jumped to do his bidding with Mary to help.

Bettina Hicks chuckled. 'Stand back, Stan, and let them in or you'll be trampled in the rush.'

Ruby would have laughed if she hadn't suddenly got cold feet. She began taking backward steps. 'I can't do this,' she said shaking her head. 'I can't do this! The ministry really should have chosen older women. You know what village women are like, they all make the best jam, and their recipe for chutney has been handed down and there's nothing to touch it. They're also used to feeding a huge family on next to nothing. They'll say it's like trying to teach a grandmother to suck eggs and we were making jam and dishing up roast dinners before you were born.'

Her father laid his hand on her shoulder and gave her an affectionate squeeze. 'Then you have to speak to them from a more personal angle, one they can sympathise with but have no experience of.'

'Such as?'

Her father smiled. 'You'll think of something.'

'I can't.'

'Yes you can.'

Mary pushed her forward so she was jammed up against the counter.

Stan Sweet deftly slid back the bolts top and bottom, undid the door and stood well back.

'Jesus,' he muttered as the women stampeded through like a herd of cows heading for the best grass in the meadow, though in this case it was the front-row chairs. Chair legs scraped and some chairs creaked under the weight of the wide bottoms sitting on them. Some women were asked to remove their hats, and smaller women asked to change places with the meatier females who'd bagged the front row. There were a few snorts of protest, but on the whole the mood was amiable and everyone wanted to see what was going on.

Once everyone was seated and facing forward, Mary gave her sister a nudge.

'Go on,' she whispered. Ruby got to her feet.

'Ladies,' she shouted, her heart pounding in her chest. 'Welcome to you all and thank you for coming.'

Even to her own ears she sounded incredibly confident, just like that toffee-nosed woman who'd judged the baking at the Victoria Rooms – though not such a cut-glass voice of course. So here she was, standing in front of women older than she was and trying not to be tongue-tied. The nerve of it! She was going to tell this lot how to cook economically and nutritionally in a time of war.

A personal perspective... food... war...

Suddenly it came to her.

'Some of you may be questioning why someone of my age has the right to stand up here in front of you, handing out advice like a mother to her children. On reflection I feel I have earned that right, in fact, I have a vested interest in ensuring that all of us do our utmost to take the pressure off the brave men of our merchant ships whose job it is to supply this country with everything we need to win this war and that includes food.

'Some of you may be aware that at the end of last year my brother Charlie was taken prisoner by the Germans after having his ship shot from under him, a ship containing a very large amount of food destined for these shores. At first we were told he was missing and of course in anybody's books, that means he might possibly have been dead. We were lucky. Charlie was lucky. He was released and is already serving on another merchant ship. We are here to support men like him.'

There followed murmurs of approval and a nodding of heads. The women were hanging on to her every word. Ruby was thrilled and it gave the rest of her talk fresh impetus.

'I think we all agree that we women left to fight on the kitchen front must do our bit. That is why the Ministry of Food recruited me. I hope my advice and ideas will be of use to you. If any of you have some helpful hints yourselves, both I and the Ministry of Food will be very grateful to hear of them. So will your country. After all, as I have already said, we're all in this together. Every scrap we can save will help my brother Charlie do his job. Thank you and God Save the King.'

The women erupted in an echoing chorus of 'God Save the King' accompanied by enthusiastic clapping.

'You couldn't have put it better,' whispered Mary who was sitting in the chair at her side, clapping along with the rest of them.

Her father, Stan Sweet, gave her the thumbs-up sign. Mrs Hicks smiled benignly before whispering something into Stan's ear.

Ruby glowed at the praise, returning to her subject feeling far more confident than she had before.

'We shall begin with advice on fuel saving. Please take one of the small leaflets with you on the way out. It covers all sorts of fuel sources that many of you may use in your cooking; electric, gas and coal-fired ranges – I know a lot of you have the latter.

'Note the advice in the leaflet regarding saucepans. A clean unpolished bottom absorbs heat more effectively so food is cooked more quickly. Also note the advice about always using a saucepan lid for exactly the same reason. If you don't have a lid, use a plate. And if you can steam a pudding or something on top your vegetables, do so. Steamers are very fuel efficient.'

A hand shot up. Ruby recognised Mrs Martin, the farmer's wife, whose joints of beef were celebrated and usually too big to put in a normal oven.

'I don't have a steamer.'

'Then use a colander,' answered Ruby. 'Just place it on top of the saucepan with whatever you want to put in it. The steam from the cooking vegetables beneath it will do the rest. Oh, and never put a small saucepan on a large gas ring; that too is a waste of heat.'

The crowd murmured approvingly. Ruby allowed her shoulders to relax. The first hurdle had been crossed. Now it was time for a demonstration and discussion centred around the Sunday joint.

The brisket, meat nicely cooked and fat glistening, was still in its roasting tin, an island in the middle of congealed fat.

Ruby went on to discuss getting a decent-size joint, enough to meet everyone's ration.

'Roast meat for Sunday with vegetables. Scrape the fat off from around the joint before making gravy and place in a bowl. The fat will be used for cooking other things. You may need it in future to make pastry, seeing as the usual fats are in short supply. Use some of the dripping jelly left for the gravy, the rest for supper that night scraped on to bread and sprinkled with salt.'

'Lovely,' somebody shouted. 'I do love a bit of beef dripping.'

'Once that's done, add water to what's left in the roasting tin, mix well and empty into a saucepan. It'll make a good stock for soup. Oh, but one word of warning: don't add vegetables to the stock pot as they tend to go sour if you leave your soup or stew for a week. And if you can, let your gravy cool before adding it to shepherd's pie and other dishes. It thickens and goes further that way.'

They went on to discuss other options for both the dripping jelly and the fat left in the bowl, but making meals from the meat was the task they focused on.

'Cold on Monday with bubble and squeak – in other words any leftover vegetables you have to hand. Tuesday, minced to make cottage pie, topped with potatoes, Wednesday, if you've still got some left, cut into pieces to make Cornish pasties or a stew. If there are any bones, remember to remove these before cooking; after all, we don't want to waste heat cooking bones. Not that we're discarding those bones. Like the juices from the tin, they'll make a good stock base for a soup. Oh, and if you want to "fill out" any of these dishes, add oatmeal. It's cheap and relatively plentiful.'

'So what about Thursday, Friday and Saturday?' Mrs Martin again.

Ruby grinned. 'Well, those meals depend on whether Joe Long has bagged a few rabbits.'

A great hoot of laughter went up from some, and a more muted response from others. Sam Pickard could be relied upon to shoot fresh game when it was available. Only time would tell if there was enough to go round.

Everyone agreed that the event went well. There was a rush at the end to grab leaflets but also to ask about recipes, plus advice from those who knew all about managing on a budget. 'We'd beat that bloke Hitler hands down if it was all down to us making a meal from a turnip and a rabbit's leg,' chortled a farm labourer's wife. 'Been living like that for bleedin' years!'

One of Mrs Hicks's friends was Mrs Darwin-Kemp, the woman whose husband had connections in London. She came up to Ruby, smiling in a very smug manner.

'Congratulations, my dear,' she said, her smile smothered behind the stiff net veil at the front of her hat. 'I knew you could do it.'

Mary overheard and knew immediately that Mrs Darwin-Kemp had had a hand in their appointment. 'Might I ask how you knew?'

'Your young cousin who came over with the sliced bread insisted you were excellent cooks.'

So. It was down to young Frances.

'You're both very skilful,' she said, her gaze alighting on one twin then the other. 'If you should ever be in need of a domestic appointment, I would be willing to employ you. I so appreciate a good cook.'

'Thank you but I don't think so,' said Ruby, her smile barely hiding a grimace.

'We have family,' added Mary.

If she did hear, she ignored the remark turning her attention instead to Mrs Hicks. 'You're lucky to have them so close by, Bettina. I dare say you won't starve.'

'Of course I won't,' Bettina snapped. 'I can cook! Not like you, Agatha. Waited on hand, foot and finger all your life.'

Mrs Darwin-Kemp laughed as though Mrs Hicks had cracked a particularly silly joke. Mary concluded that she didn't really know what Mrs Hicks was getting at, or if she did, didn't really care.

Bettina's attention was interrupted by Isaac who came to tell her that a telegram had arrived for Mrs Hicks. After reading it, she looked across at Mary.

'It's from Michael's commanding officer. I'm afraid there's a problem.'

28

Frances wrote to her cousins about Ada Perkins, her friends and what she was up to. She also wrote about the apple orchard she had found which also had pears, plums and cherries in it.

'Not so big as my orchard,' she wrote loftily, as though the orchard next door to the pub was hers and hers alone.

She thought about mentioning the feast that had disappeared that night in the forest, but decided not to. All the other kids had their own suspicions as to where it had gone, and for a while she'd been chief suspect, after all she was the one who'd been left to count to fifty and could easily have eaten it while the others were hiding.

On returning from hiding and told their feast had vanished, this had not gone down well with her friends. Deacon demanded proof that she hadn't ate it.

'Cross my heart and hope to die,' said Frances, crossing her heart and closing her eyes to show she really meant it.

'That's not proof. Anybody can say that,' declared Ralph, and of course he was right.

Deacon leered right into her face. 'Open your mouth.'

'What?'

'Open your mouth!'

The others held her while Deacon prised her jaw open and peered in. He shook his head. 'Nothing.'

'She might already have swallowed it,' said Evan.

Deacon frowned. 'There's only one thing left to do. If she's ate it she'll taste of it. There'll be grease and everythin' around her mouth.'

The others sucked in their breath, awestruck by Deacon's deduction and knowing beyond doubt there was only one sure way to tell if she had ate it; Deacon had to taste her.

His mouth sucked on hers so hard that her lips were drawn into his mouth.

'Yak!' he exclaimed when he finally withdrew, wiping his mouth with the back of his hand. 'Nothing. Just jam.'

'P'raps it was a dog,' offered Ralph while wiping his nose with his coat sleeve.

'Or a wolf!' Gertie exclaimed, her round eyes looking this way and that just in case the creature was still around and still hungry.

Merlyn merely looked up at the treetops, as though the answer might be floating around up there somewhere.

Frances shook off the hands that had held her. 'Don't be so stupid. There are no wolves in this forest – are there?'

She looked round for confirmation because she didn't herself know for sure.

Evan, Deacon and the rest of her school friends all exchanged shrugs and dumb looks. Nobody knew, though she could tell by the look in their eyes that the prospect excited them.

She decided that her new friends weren't nearly so knowledgeable as her friends back in Oldland Common. It seemed it was time for her to take charge of matters.

'Are there any tracks?'

'What do you mean, tracks?' It was Deacon who asked. 'Like in cowboy and Indian films. They track the bandits by following their footprints. Are there any footprints?'

Wary eyes studied the area around the fire where the crime had taken place. And it was a crime. Whoever had stolen their supper was a thief and deserved to be punished.

The ground around the fire was soft and there was no foliage to hide the footprints.

'That is not wolves' paw prints,' stated Frances. The gleam of triumph shining in her eyes, she pointed at what could only be the impressions of a pair of hob-nailed boots. 'Wolves don't wear boots!'

Everyone looked down at the footprints then at their own feet. Evan was wearing a pair of scuffed brown boots, hand-me-downs from his brother and still too big for him. His boots were the biggest but still no match for the footprints.

Everyone scrutinised everyone else's boots, Frances, still their chief suspect, most of all. She was wearing wellington boots over a pair of hand-knitted socks. Like everyone else her feet were too small to have made the footprints.

Satisfied that none of them were the culprits, Deacon took charge again and suggested they followed the footprints.

'Just like the Indians,' he added in an attempt to make it sound as though the suggestion had been his in the first place.

Frances was happy to let him.

Twenty yards later the foliage hid the soft earth from view. The search party, keen to hunt down the real thief came to a dead end, feeling quite disappointed.

Deacon flicked his hand over the tops of the bushes so that they whipped backwards and forwards. Everyone could see he was exasperated, though none dare challenge him and say so. He was gang leader after all.

Even though most of them were not yet in full bloom, the bushes carried enough leaves to hide the ground.

'Damn his eyes,' snarled Deacon the words reflecting the fact that he was very keen on anything to do with pirates and had picked up a few of their phrases.

'He's got away. The bastard's got away,' added Ralph. He'd picked up his damning phrases from his father mainly on his return from the pub and filled to the gills with cider.

Frances frowned as she regarded the bushes. There were so many directions the thief could have gone in.

'I'm hungry,' whined Gertie, who was digging her knuckles into her tired eyes and yawning.

Merlyn was humming softly to herself while stuffing a piece of paper into a hole in an oak tree.

'It's a prayer to the earth mother,' she said.

Frances jerked her chin as though she knew that, when actually she didn't. Anyway, it was what would happen next that she was interested in.

'So what do we do? Call the police?' Deacon asked wryly.

Frances shook her head. 'Of course not. They wouldn't do anything. We're just kids and they'd tell us to shove off home to our parents. What we have to do is to set a trap.'

'What sort of trap?' asked Evan.

'Something tasty. Another rabbit perhaps or a pigeon. Anything that sizzles over a hot fire. Anything we can get hold of. When the thief smells it and shows himself we'll jump on him. Right?'

Everyone agreed except Deacon. 'How do we know he's still around here? Whoever it was might already have gone home.'

They all thought about it.

'Well, if nobody takes it this time, we can eat it all ourselves,' suggested Evan.

It was agreed. Frances felt proud of herself. Not only had she integrated well with her new friends in the Forest of Dean, she'd also proved she could lead them when they were unsure what to do next. She liked that.

Two nights later, after eating their tea and promising to be home before dark, they gathered at 'their place', the gang's forest headquarters where the trees drooped over the narrow gorge and the wind swooped overhead; a nice sheltered spot.

Deacon had already got the fire going by the time everyone else arrived.

Ralph arrived with his offering for the feast, a fresh trout plus what looked like a pot full of wriggly worms.

Frances took one look and gagged. 'Yuk! He won't come out and steal a pan of worms!'

Ralph sniggered and everyone else joined in. Frances felt like an outsider again because her friends knew something she didn't.

'Elvers,' said Ralph. 'Baby eels. Only get them this time of year. What you do is boil 'em up, then fry 'em off in a bit of butter or dripping. Me mam didn't 'ave any butter, so I nicked some dripping.'

He held up a brown paper bag, the top screwed round and round so the dripping wouldn't leak out.

Evan had brought a dead and rather squashed pheasant.

He grinned broadly. 'Me dad ran over it in the tractor. I scooped it up before he noticed.'

'It ain't bin hung. It'll be too tough to eat,' remarked Deacon.

'Might not be seeing as it bin squashed,' said Evan. 'It'll still smell all right,' Frances added.

The fish was skewered on to the stick and the handle of the pan containing the elvers was slid along too.

The pheasant had to be plucked and drawn, the job being willed to Ralph who didn't seem to notice the smell of the bird's innards as he pulled it out like so much slimy string.

He also seemed oblivious to the plucked feathers left clinging to his sticky hands, fluttering upwards and settling in his hair.

It took a while but eventually the aroma of food cooking in the great outdoors was rising upwards. So was the steam from the elvers.

Frances heard her stomach rumbling. Nothing, she decided, smelled as good as food cooking out in the fresh air.

They all began smacking their lips.

'Might as well eat the elvers ourselves,' suggested Ralph. The others agreed. Soon he was scooping them into a rusty old frying pan he'd also stolen from home.

'It won't be missed. Me mam only uses it for cooking up potato rinds and mash for the chickens,' he declared.

Gertie screwed up her face at the rust, but didn't seem worried that poultry food had been cooked in it.

The moment the dripping was sizzling, the elvers were dropped into the pan. They weren't long cooking and Frances had to admit, even if only to herself, they did smell good.

Everyone ate a handful with relish. Frances looked on. No matter how good they smelled and no matter how much the others encouraged her to try some, she couldn't bring herself to do it.

'Only when I'm starving,' she said to them.

'All the more for us,' laughed Ralph. Even Merlyn was tucking in.

'I can't help it,' said Frances, wrinkling her nose. 'They still look like wriggly worms.'

The time came when the stars were beginning to appear and the food was almost perfectly cooked.

'Time for hide and seek,' said Deacon.

Nobody was in any doubt what he meant. The time had come to leave the trap they had set, but this time, instead of hiding from each other, they were going to hide in the bushes around the fire and wait for whoever it was – wolf or man – to come for the feast.

One by one, they hid themselves, arms wrapped around their knees, eyes fixed on the food. The silence and the waiting became unbearable, not least because the smell of the food was making them hungry, despite having eaten the elvers.

Gertie fell asleep. Merlyn looked up at the sky. Evan sneezed and Ralphie sucked his fingers, relishing the residue of taste left by the baby eels.

Frances prided herself on not moving. Only Deacon, strong, alert Deacon, sat as still as she did, eyes narrowed and focused on the trap they'd set.

It was Deacon Frances wanted to be like. She admired him greatly, not just because all the other kids looked up to him, but because she liked his smile and the freckles scattered over his nose. In fact she wished that she was a boy, though only if she was exactly like him. She even liked the way he'd kissed her even though he'd really been tasting her, not really kissing; she felt a thrill every time she thought of it.

'Shh,' Deacon said suddenly when Evan stretched his legs setting a small avalanche of stones and earth sliding out through the bushes they were hiding in.

'Sorry,' said Evan.

Darkness was falling fast, the familiar sights of the forest glade black beyond the glow of the fire.

All of them had promised to be home before dark, the reason Evan was fidgeting. His dad was likely to clout him around both ears for being late home and making Gertie late home too.

Frances had also promised to be home but had decided that while Deacon remained, she would remain. She would not give in. Let Evan give in and take Gertie home with him. She would most certainly not.

An hour passed. Even Deacon began to lose his patience, grinding his teeth and making low growling noises. 'It's no good. I have to go,' he said suddenly.

Frances was taken completely by surprise at him giving in before everybody else – that was before she heard the tinkling of water as Deacon relieved himself against the trunk of a tree. 'I'm off home,' Deacon said, having finished relieving himself.

Frances was dismayed that the boy she looked up to was giving in. Everyone else recognised the fact too. Gertie was nudged awake, sleepy and yawning.

'Might as well call it a night. Everybody home.' Deacon issued what constituted an order though his tone was casual.

Something inside made Frances want to see this through. Everyone was giving up, including Deacon. Well, she would not. Clenching her jaw she hunched her knees further into her body, wound her arms around them and fixed her gaze on the dying embers of the fire.

The knot of figures faded into the shadows, the bushes rustling as they headed along the narrow path that would take them back to the main track.

In the darkness, barely able to see each other, they didn't notice that she wasn't with them.

Stomachs full of elvers, they'd left the trout and the squashed pheasant to sizzle and blacken on the fire. The smell was still appetising if a little burnt.

To Frances, teatime seemed a long time ago. Normally at this time she'd be given two digestive biscuits and a cup of Horlicks on her way to bed.

She'd be in trouble when she got back, but she couldn't bear to leave – not just yet. On the other hand she was very hungry and good food shouldn't be left to go to waste – everyone was saying that at the moment, what with a war on.

Carefully so as not to slip down the slope and disturb the small stones and loose earth, she was within yards of the fire when she saw him, a ragged figure, black from head to toe.

The figure kicked at the fire, covering it with earth until the flames were extinguished. All the while he was doing this, he cussed and swore, using words Frances knew but wasn't supposed to utter.

Afraid of being discovered, she slunk back into the shadows.

Just as the man reached for the food she lost her footing.

With an anguished cry she fell on to her backside and went hurtling down the slope like a toboggan on snow, finally coming to a halt on the other side of the embers from the man in black.

Flat on her back, she managed to raise her head and met a pair of pale green eyes staring from out of a dirt-encrusted face.

He had already bitten into their feast, bits of scorched trout skin hanging from his mouth. One hand held the stick on which it had been grilled and still held the pheasant, its flesh a little blackened, but edible.

The fire was still warm and she was lying next to it. There was also a lantern, a funny old-fashioned sort made of iron and holding a flickering flame.

Like a pirate's lantern, she thought, and wished that Deacon was still there.

Suddenly he spoke. 'You not s'posed to leave fires alight in the forest. Cause a fire. People get angry if you make fires. Hear me?'

His words were halting and heavily accented; it didn't help that he spat out bits of bone as he spoke.

Curiosity replaced the fear of monsters she'd been feeling. She was still frightened, but not so much as she had been.

Anyway, what right did he have to lecture her about fires when he was standing there calmly eating trout and pheasant that didn't belong to him and had been cooked on the fire that he so disapproved of.

'That's our food,' she shouted from her supine position. 'You stole our food the other night and you've stolen it again.' He slid his teeth along the flesh of the trout so that half of it disappeared into his mouth. To her amazement the whole skeleton was all that remained which he flung aside.

'No. I took. It was left for somebody who was hungry. I was hungry.'

Frances watched him fascinated because he had begun eating the pheasant in a similar fashion to the trout, flesh stripped and skeleton left intact.

'Where do you live?' she asked him.

He chewed and tore as he eyed her. 'There and there.'

'There and there? What's that supposed to mean?'

'Like I say. There and there.'

Frances looked all about her, suddenly aware that night had fallen and she wasn't sure of her way home.

'I need to go home.'

'Nobody stopping you.'

'I think I hurt my head when I fell. It aches.' She touched her hand tellingly to her head. It was aching, but she didn't want to find her way home alone. The forest was so dark.

Two green eyes looked at her from over the fleshless carcass of the pheasant. 'You not from here?'

'No. I'm not. I'm staying with Ada Perkins. I don't know the forest that well.'

It was hard to see his expression in the darkness, but his silence conveyed that he was considering his options.

'You not stay out here.' He sighed. 'Come.'

Something scrabbled for the bones he threw into the undergrowth as he strode away, pushing at bushes as he went. Frances followed him, a black figure in black surroundings.

She wondered how long he'd been living in the forest. Did he really know the way or was he going to eat her too?

The prospect was worrying so she decided that once she recognised her surroundings, she would run away and leave him behind.

Suddenly she saw a light ahead and smelled the tasty odour of things being smoked. Home was up ahead. She began to run, screaming out Ada's name and shouting for help.

The door of the shack opened and Ada's amiable figure came into view. 'What's all that noise, and where the devil have you been?'

'There was a man,' shouted Frances, running so fast her face ended up colliding with Ada's bosom. 'He had green eyes. He ate our feast. Everything down to the bones.'

When she looked round she saw other figures. Men were shouting. 'It's him! It's the Italian.'

Frances looked up at Ada. 'The man brought me home.'

Ada sighed. 'He might well 'ave done, but anyone who's foreign is suspect. When you didn't come home I sent out a search party and called the bobby. They've been looking for Mario for a while.'

'Mario?'

Ada shrugged. 'He's lived wild for years; bit of a hermit you might say. The problem is that he's Italian and they count him as an enemy alien. Enemy aliens have to be interned. Stupid when it comes to Mario. I've known 'im for some time. But there you are. That's war for you.'

29

It was hard to concentrate on what had to be done once they'd received the message from Michael's commanding officer telling them that he'd had to bail out over the North Sea.

'His colleagues insisted that they saw his parachute open. We are doing our best to locate him.'

Every day Mary visited Mrs Hicks hoping for news. It had been five days now and still nothing.

Ruby lifted the brown glazed mixing bowl, tilting it so Mary could see what was in it. 'Look what I've made.'

Mary peered into the bowl and tried to sound enthusiastic. 'It looks good. What is it?'

'I mixed some of that dried egg with some preserved gooseberries from last year. I added an ounce of sugar and whisked the whole lot together. It's a kind of gooseberry fool. I thought I'd crumble ginger biscuits into the bottom of each ramekin and pile the mixture on top. Do you think it works?'

Mary had to agree that it did. 'Have you written down the recipe?'

Ruby winced. Devising dishes was one thing, writing down

measures of ingredients was something she kept forgetting to do – even though the ministry required it.

Mary shook her head in mock disapproval. 'Ruby! Mr Sinclair will not be amused!'

'I'm nervous,' she added. 'I mean, this is the first real demonstration I've had to do, and not just one, three of them.'

Mary reminded her that the one here in the bakery had been very successful.

'A lot of them were people we know, and Mrs Hicks has told a lot of her friends. This time I'm going to be standing up in front of a hall full of strangers.'

'I can go if you like?' offered Mary. 'Nobody will know the difference.'

Ruby shook her head. 'I got myself into this. It's my responsibility to do a good job. Anyway, if our Charlie is brave enough to serve on a ship bringing in the food I should be brave enough to stand up in front of a farmers' wives group and show them how to put it to best use, should I not?'

Mary agreed that she should. She looked up at the big old black clock above the kitchen mantelpiece. 'What time is your driver coming?'

'Half past nine.' She took a deep breath. 'I'm not looking forward to the company I must say. He's probably an old codger who served in the last war and won't be taking kindly to driving a silly girl around.'

'Our dad's an old codger – if you care to look at it that way.'

Ruby laughed. 'I supposed you're right. Anyway, it's only until Mr Sinclair thinks I'm capable of driving myself around.'

'It had better be soon if they really are considering giving you a mobile kitchen to drag along behind you.'

Mary helped Ruby place everything she needed into the large wicker picnic hamper they used to use on those pre-war days when the fields were yellow and the sky was deep blue. Sometimes they'd taken it along to the vicarage when he was holding one of his garden party events for the village school.

Henceforward it would be used to cart ingredients, recipe cards and leaflets giving advice on everything from how best to conserve fuel to how to turn a blanket into a brand-new coat. She also had a small leather case in which she placed leaflets and recipes, some of which were those devised by herself and Mary; it still gave both of them a feeling of pride to see their creations actually in print.

Besides the leaflets she placed her own precious blue book, plus a small bag containing her hairbrush, lipstick and a small phial of Evening in Paris. Mrs Hicks had given her the bag and the perfume. 'Standing up in front of all those people, you have to look your best.'

She breathed a deep sigh at the same time as patting her stomach, not that it did much to keep the collywobbles at bay!

'All set?'

Her eyes met those of her sister. She nodded. 'Yes.'

The bell above the shop door jangled as the clock struck the half-past. Ruby almost jumped out of her skin. Mary got up to answer it.

'It's him. Well here goes,' said Ruby.

When Mary opened the door, the young soldier with the clean-shaven face eyed her impersonally and stated his business.

'Corporal Smith. I'm here to collect a Miss Ruby Sweet.'

His tone was clipped and he didn't look at her as a young man usually did.

Mary called over her shoulder. Ruby came out carrying both the wicker basket and the brown case.

'Oh. I was expecting somebody... else,' said Ruby. It didn't seem right to say to him that she'd been expecting somebody older.

'Sorry to disappoint, but I was all they had.' His tone was surly and he didn't offer to carry anything.

His attitude was infuriating and Ruby had no intention of letting it pass. 'I could do with some help. You do have some muscles, do you not,' said Ruby in what she called her wireless style, the one she'd use if she did get to broadcast with the BBC.

'Certainly, miss,' he said, his hostile expression leaving her in no doubt that he resented her as much as she resented him. He took hold of the hamper, opening the car door and placing it on the back seat. He then made as if to take the case from her too, but Ruby jerked it away from him.

'Up to you,' he said, leaving her to slide into the back seat while he opened the driver's door.

The twins exchanged a muted grin through the car window. They both mouthed goodbye, Mary fingering her mouth as she smiled and pulled a face in the driver's direction.

Folding her gloved hands in her lap, Ruby settled back, determined to enjoy the ride and the day out despite the morose attitude of Corporal Smith. She also studied the back of his head. He had a thick neck sprinkled with golden hairs that the army barber had failed to razor away. They were only discernible in a certain light, perhaps the reason the barber hadn't trimmed them off.

Ruby amused herself picking specks of dust off her new gloves. They were of grey leather and again offered on loan by Mrs Hicks. 'We all want you to be a great success, my dear.'

Ruby guessed she was doing her best to keep herself occupied while Michael was missing. Mary too was keeping herself busy, buzzing around the shop and the house, even helping their father out in the garden.

Ruby got out her powder compact and touched up her nose. Then she took out her lipstick, plastering on another coat of red, sucking in her lips to ensure it was evenly spread.

She sensed Corporal Smith glancing at her via the car's rear-view mirror, but didn't manage to catch him at it. He faced straight ahead unmoving. as though he were carved from wood.

The fields and village cottages were left behind as the road wound up through Hanham and into St George, a suburb of Bristol. Soon the semi-detached houses gave way to a shop-lined street.

'Are we nearly there?'

'Yes, miss.'

'It's very different here,' she said, meaning it was different from the more rural aspect of her home village and the suburbs they had so far passed through.

'This is where ordinary people live, miss; them that work hard for a living.'

Unsure that she'd heard right, Ruby frowned. 'I get up at five to begin making bread. Me or my sister.'

He grunted something unintelligible. Ruby sat back again.

The demonstration was to take place at a Methodist church hall somewhere around here. The closer they got, the more nervous she became, though the collywobbles weren't as rife as they had been, a fact she was very glad about. However, if she didn't concentrate on something other than giving the talk and demonstration, they could easily return. Despite Corporal Smith's previous statement, she decided to attempt pleasant conversation.

She poked the corporal on the shoulder, partly to gain his attention and partly by way of reprimand.

'Have you done this before, corporal?'

'Yes, miss. I've driven a car many times. It's what I do in the army.' His tone was unaltered, in fact he spoke in a dull monotone as though he had no wish for the conversation to continue, as though he made himself be uninteresting so she wouldn't bother him.

Ruby wasn't giving up that easily. 'I meant, have you driven a

Kitchen Front Economist around before?' That's what Andrew Sinclair had declared was her title: *Kitchen Front* Economist.

Corporal Smith was slow in replying. In fact she fancied he was chewing, either that or grinding his teeth. Anyway she perceived that his jaw was moving. 'No. I drove a colonel around.'

'Oh. I expect that was far more interesting than driving me around.'

He said nothing.

'Well? Was it more interesting driving the colonel around?'

She sensed the grinding of teeth again, the flexing of his jaw. 'No, miss. It was more dangerous. Right. Here we are.'

There was no more time to ask him more questions. They'd arrived at a red-brick church hall, the window panes carefully taped as required.

The only question she did ask him was if he could help her get her picnic hamper and case down the front of the hall to a table prepared for her on a raised platform at the far end of the room. Once that was done, he turned to go.

'Excuse me, corporal. I'd like you to stay.'

'Why?' He looked at her grimly as though fully intending to refuse.

'I think my audience may need reminding of exactly why I am here this evening. It's because of you, corporal. I need to remind them why I am here. We have to support our armed forces and one way of doing this is to ensure that the ships coming into these shores are used primarily to bring arms to help us win. That's why we have to get the most nutrition we can from food. And before you begin talking that tripe about people who work for a living, I work for a living and my brother is presently serving as a merchant seaman. He's already been sunk once and survived. It sounds as though you too survived, you and your colonel.'

At first she didn't think she'd got through to him, but suddenly, the surly countenance softened.

'You're right. And you're wrong. I survived. My colonel snuffed it.'

Ruby was lost for words. She guessed he was one of those not long back from Norway.

'I came back before Norway fell,' he told her as though reading her mind. 'Orders. Unfortunately we were attacked by a low-flying fighter. Couldn't be helped. It's war. Isn't it.'

His tone was chilling. There was no point in sympathetically stating how awful it must have been. She could see that from the look in his eyes.

'Will you stay?' she asked him. 'The sight of a uniform does tend to remind people of why I'm doing this.'

He nodded curtly.

A hum of conversation ran through the audience, mostly of women, though Ruby was surprised to see there were also a few men sprinkled among them. Some wore uniform; some did not.

On this occasion there was nobody else to bang on the table for silence or to hand out leaflets. Everything was down to Ruby. She looked around her and told herself they could hardly hang her for speaking. Once on her feet she used her knuckle to bang on the table and shouted at the top of her voice.

'Ladies! And gentlemen!'

The response was muted, a gaggle of irrepressible chatter continuing to warble among the hardened few, mostly from the older ladies who thought that as they'd been cooking all their lives there was nothing a whippersnapper like her could hope to teach them.

Beside her, Corporal Smith sprang to his feet. 'Fall in! Eyes front!'

His voice rang out and immediately brought everyone to silence.

Corporal Smith sat back down, folded his arms and crossed one army-booted foot over the other. He looked totally uninterested in what was going on, his attention firmly fixed on his boots.

Having already laid out her demonstration items on the table, Ruby faced her audience. 'Unfortunately there is no cooking range or gas stove here, so I'm afraid I have to talk to you quite a lot. I have, however, brought some samples of items I have made from the most frugal ingredients. This war may last a short or a long time, but while it lasts nothing in our kitchen goes to waste. Our boys in the merchant navy will appreciate our efforts. Every bit we save helps them survive. Believe me I know this. My own brother serves with the merchant navy. With our help victory will be achieved!'

When a huge cheer went up, Ruby breathed a sigh of relief. She'd learned stirring up patriotic fervour was the way forward. She went on to discuss meal planning, the leftovers of one meal being reused in the next one, bulking out with oats, bread and vegetables.

'You've all heard of the Woolton Pie, of course, contrived by the chef at the Savoy Hotel in order to preserve meat rations and named after Lord Woolton, the man in charge at the Ministry of Food. Well, the recipe for one pie isn't the answer. Recipes to my mind are a day-to-day thing in these troubled times. We can plan, but we must also be flexible.'

She went on to outline a weekly recipe plan based on the Sunday joint, but rolling over ingredients from one day to the next.

'Our slogan must be, waste not, want not, or use up, don't throw out.'

After the basic talk, she touched on the subject of desserts. 'Something special to cheer us all up. We all need a little luxury at some point in our lives, something to look forward to and indulge in.'

The recipes for Brown Betty and a crumble using stale bread-crumbs instead of flour and fat, and a custard tart using dried eggs had been printed by the ministry; Andrew Sinclair had very much approved, telling her that his mother had got their cook to make it.

Afterwards she invited the audience to sample the food she'd brought with her.

'A good nosh-up. That's all they've bloody come here for,' grumbled Corporal Smith.

Ruby told him to be quiet. 'I'll save some for you.' He gave no sign that her generosity was appreciated.

She found herself studying him. His features were quite gaunt, very similar in fact to how her brother had looked when he'd come back home for Christmas. His manner was unerringly grouchy, not that she could hold it against him.

Once the audience had filtered out of the church hall, still chat-tering away and chewing the samples they'd been given, Ruby was left with just Corporal Smith and the caretaker.

'Something to take home with you,' she said to the caretaker, carefully wrapping up a large slice of apple pie. 'It's got sultanas in it.'

The caretaker was most appreciative and brought both of them a cup of tea.

Ruby turned to the corporal. 'I don't know about you, but I'm starving. I'll wash these spoons and we can finish one of the puddings.'

His only response was to shrug his shoulders. 'If you like.'

'It's not poisoned. I promise.'

Her attempt at humour made no difference at all. He shrugged himself into the wide shoulders of his khaki jacket and sipped at his tea.

After she'd washed them, she handed him a spoon. 'I've brought a little cream. Do you like cream?'

She didn't wait for him to answer but spooned the cream out on to the pudding.

He ate in silence; she watched him, wanting to see him smile or at least say one word to her that wasn't monosyllabic or openly hostile.

'Here's a loaf of bread,' she said when they'd finally eaten their fill. 'I made it myself this morning. It's a fruit loaf. It's got dried blackcurrants in it. I used to make one before the war with bananas in it. I can't do that now because I can't get bananas, but last year's blackcurrants seem to do the trick. Smell,' she said, thrusting the loaf close to his face.

He eyed her warily over the sweet-smelling bread. She wasn't entirely sure whether he'd sniffed it or not.

'It's yours,' she said, placing it on the table in front of him. 'If you don't want it, leave it. I'm sure the caretaker will make good use of it.'

She began putting everything left over back into her picnic hamper. The food was gone and so were half of the leaflets so she refused the corporal's offer to carry it for her.

'I'm not helpless. I mix vast bowls of dough when the electric mixer breaks down and I heave trays of bread around probably long before you're even out of bed.'

He looked stung at first then accepting. 'Please yourself.'

'By the way. You don't have to drive me around forever. It's only until I get used to driving myself.'

Again one of those curt nods, yet this time she perceived a pensive look in his eyes.

The atmosphere in the car on the ride home differed from the outward journey. To Ruby it felt as though her driver was considering his options.

Just before arriving back at Sweet's Bakery, Ruby consulted her diary for the following day. First a demonstration at a factory making nuts and bolts in Bristol, then one to a group of ladies at Mrs Darwen-Kemp's house; quite frankly the latter unnerved her far more than the former. Ladies who had benefitted from domestic staff were usually more pernickety than women who cooked on a daily basis because they had no idea about preparation. She sighed. Another day with Cheerful Charlie Smith, her less-than-friendly driver. Oh well, both feet first!

'Corporal Smith. We must endure each other's company again tomorrow and for some time in the foreseeable future – unless you ask for a transfer. In order to make it as pleasant as possible, perhaps you could tell me your name – your first name.'

She saw him look at her via the rear-view mirror. 'John. Johnnie.'

'And I'm Ruby. Ruby Sweet.'

30

Andrew Sinclair, their contact at the Ministry of Food, had acquired the habit of dropping in unannounced.

Mary opened the door to him. 'What a surprise! You do know Ruby's out giving a demonstration?'

He smiled and accepted her offer of cake and a cup of tea.

'It was you I wanted to see. I've arranged with the BBC for one of you to broadcast on a programme entitled *Women at War*. It doesn't matter which one of you does it, though of course your sister is very busy on the demonstration front and I know you were speaking of dividing duties between you.'

'Well,' said Mary, who had just finished mixing dough before setting it aside for the final evening prove, 'it's quite a privilege.'

He smiled. 'I'm glad you think so. No need to worry about transport. I myself will take you there. The ministry has provided me with a car and an almost inexhaustible supply of petrol coupons. I do hope you can come.'

His smile was warm, his look intense. From the very first he'd been able to tell the two of them apart having seen the mole on Ruby's face – no more than a beauty spot and quite attractive – but it was Mary he was interested in. She had such a serene look in her eyes that it calmed the day-to-day stress of his job. He couldn't help being attracted to her.

Mary hoped the film of flour on her cheeks – she always acquired some – would help soften the blush she felt rushing there. Was she interpreting his words correctly? 'Well I'm not sure...'

'I thought we might go to the theatre afterwards. I hear there's a good show on at the Hippodrome. It's only just down the hill from the BBC place in Whiteladies Road. I suppose you know the BBC have made it their headquarters for the duration – London's too dangerous.'

Mary nodded and said that she did know. She was now very much aware that Andrew was interested in more than her culinary skills. He seemed nice enough, but Michael was missing. She couldn't get interested in anyone else until she knew how he was.

He suggested the following evening, but Mary declined. 'My brother's coming home on leave. Only a few days, but I would like to be here for him. Can we leave it until he's gone back to his ship?'

Andrew looked disappointed but agreed.

The following day Charlie arrived home. On this occasion Frances stayed with Ada: coming home meant she would have missed school and seeing as she'd settled in well, Stan decided it was best that she stayed there.

As it turned out they saw little of Charlie, nights out were declined in favour of him being with Gilda. Even his old cider-drinking friends up at the farm were surprised that he only popped in to say hello.

'Lovesick, that's what 'e is,' said one of the Martin boys.

Mary and Ruby were inclined to agree. They saw little of him during that leave including one night when he didn't come home at all.

'Mrs Hicks is away. I'm staying overnight to keep Gilda company.' He saw the looks on his sisters' faces. 'I'll be sleeping on the settee.'

The twins knew their brother well enough not to believe him and voiced their concern to their father.

'It's none of your business,' their father said to them. 'He's a grown man.'

Even so, it was easy to see that Stan Sweet was troubled.

His concerns were aired only to Sarah.

'I can't tell him what to do,' he said over her grave. 'He's a grown man. I'm not too sure of Gilda's circumstances. She's got two kids, but it's difficult to make out whether her husband is alive or dead. Troubled times, Sarah. Troubled times.'

So he said nothing.

Gilda had been helping out in the bakery – mostly in the shop – ever since Ruby had taken on the position of *Kitchen Front* Economist.

They'd got to know her better, though she was hardly a chatterbox, but polite to customers and a hard worker. The only time she came truly alive was when Charlie was home. The moment Charlie came into the room, her face became more alive and her eyes sparkled. Charlie reacted in pretty much the same way.

Gossip was rife in the village.

People came into the shop just to look at her. One or two commented behind her back that it was disgusting; her being a married woman leading on a nice young man like Charlie.

'That's their business,' Mary said to those who dared comment.

'I'll only buy my bread when you're serving,' Mrs Powell declared to Mary. 'Or Ruby. I don't approve of such carryings-on.'

Stan Sweet declined to dismiss Gilda from the shop. 'I won't be intimidated by sanctimonious busy bodies!'

The twins decided it was down to them to have a word with her, to tell her about the gossips. 'Though tactfully,' warned Mary. 'Personally I can't stand gossips, but she has to be made aware of what's being said.'

Ruby agreed. 'And Charlie?'

Mary pulled a rueful face. 'Charlie doesn't give a damn about gossip.'

It was true. He aired the view that it was his business and nobody else's.

'Then I'll have a quiet word with her,' stated Ruby. Charlie looked her in the eye and raised a warning finger.

'Don't. You might not like what you hear.'

'What did he mean by that,' Ruby said to her sister once Charlie was out of the room.

Mary frowned. 'I don't know. Perhaps we shouldn't mention it.'

'Oh, I think we should,' said a more headstrong Ruby. 'A woman-to-woman talk. Where's the harm in that?'

Mary was in two minds, but ultimately decided that it was a good thing if it prevented hearts being broken.

It was after midday closing when they decided the time was ripe to warn Gilda about the gossip going on behind her back. Charlie had left earlier that day to re-join his ship. Gilda had helped out that morning and Ruby came back early from handing out leaflets in Hanham High Street. Mary had made tea and cut up two of Ruby's meatless pasties that she'd made the night before.

So it was that once the shop was closed and the three of them, Mary, Ruby and Gilda, were sitting around the table, the subject was finally tackled.

Mary took a deep breath and dived in first. 'Gilda, there's something we want to speak to you about. Something very important.'

Gilda's complexion turned pale and her eyes were filled with alarm. 'Can I still work here? If anything is wrong...'

'Nothing is wrong, Gilda,' exclaimed Ruby. 'Not as far as the bakery is concerned anyway. It's about you and our Charlie.'

Mary covered her eyes and shook her head. Her sister had the habit of charging forward without uttering a few reassuring words first. Mary tended to be more tactful.

'Gilda,' Mary interjected before Ruby did her bull-in-a-china-shop routine. 'This is a small village. Charlie is a single man and you are a married woman with two children. Besides that you're foreign, and believe me, even coming from Bath or Bristol means you're foreign in these parts. What I'm saying is the facts have not gone unnoticed—'

Suddenly Gilda burst into tears.

'Gilda! We're not going to sack you...' Ruby began.

Gilda's tears went on unchecked, then retreated into sobs leaving her shoulders heaving.

'I am no longer married...'

She reached into the pocket of her apron. They knew Gilda received letters from relatives in London, but the one she drew out of the pocket of her apron was rumpled and looked as though she had had it for some time. She handed it to Mary.

Mary felt her throat constrict as she read it. Once she had, she gave it to her sister.

Ruby reacted in much the same way as her sister. They both now understood why Gilda was crying.

'Have another one,' said Mary and poured her a second cup of tea. What other consolation was possible in the circumstances? Gilda's husband was dead.

'It's my fault,' Gilda stammered, her words shrouded by sobs.

'Oh, Gilda,' murmured Mary, giving the woman's shoulder a squeeze. 'That's foolishness. How can it be your fault?'

Gilda wouldn't be comforted, her tears running down her face and into her mouth. 'It is,' she said still sobbing and stammering her words. 'It is. It is all my fault.'

Ruby slid along on to the chair next to Gilda. Like Mary she squeezed Gilda's shoulder. 'Do you want to tell us about it?'

'You don't have to, but it might help,' Mary suggested.

Gilda blew her nose. For a moment she seemed to think about it, though couldn't say a word until her sobbing was under control, and even then the odd one escaped, her shoulders convulsing each time. Slowly her sobs came under control, though her shoulders still quaked.

'He has been dead some time.'

Mary exchanged a quick look with Ruby. They'd both read that he'd been dead sometime in the letter which had come via the Red Cross. Death by hanging, it said.

'They promised he would only go to a concentration camp. They broke their promise. I should have known,' said Gilda, shaking her head sadly. 'I should have known.' Gilda continued pulling the same lock of hair, twirling it around and around her finger one way then back in the opposite direction.

As she spoke her eyes stayed fixed on the message, the scrap of paper looking so insignificant, even trivial despite the Red Cross letters written boldly at the top, yet it held the most severe message a wife could possibly receive. Her husband was dead.

'It's my fault,' she whispered softly so that both twins had to listen carefully in order to catch what she was saying. 'I had to make a choice. I was forced to make a choice.'

Mary frowned. 'Go on,' she said calmly.

Gilda continued to twirl the strand of hair, all the while staring at the piece of paper.

'I am Dutch. Frederich was Austrian, a professor at the University of Vienna. We were happy enough even after Hitler came to power in Germany, after all, why wouldn't we be? It was nothing to do with Austria. Naively we chose to ignore that the two nations spoke the same language and regarded themselves as all part of one big Aryan family. Austria was an older country than Germany, which had consisted of many principalities in the previous century until Bismarck had united them. As Jews we thought we were safe, but as time went on, things began to change. Eventually Germany annexed Austria. There was much jubilation, though we were not joyful. Suddenly we feared what might happen next. We had heard what was happening to Jews in Germany. Suddenly it began happening in Austria.

'Frederich lost his post at the university, replaced by a jealous underling of less aptitude but of Aryan blood.

'My husband didn't take it lying down. He protested and got involved in a small resistance movement. There was a scuffle one night during a protest and a policeman was killed. Although Frederich hadn't been present, he was arrested and so was I. Our children were placed in an orphanage.

'At my interrogation I protested my innocence. I also pointed out that I was a Dutch national, a citizen of the Netherlands, born in Amsterdam.'

Gilda paused, her eyes downcast. She swallowed deeply as though her mouth was dry. Mary poured milk into her cup which she drank in one gulp.

The twins waited silently, their apprehension mounting.

Gilda continued. 'My husband had told them he was at home that night, as indeed he was. My interrogators told me they wished me to tell the truth and that he was not home, that he had lied.

'I told them he was telling the truth.

'They hit me then, slapping my face about six or seven times. After that they took me back to my cell then brought me out again the following day. It was then, after I had suffered the privations of being slapped and kept in a cold cell, that they told me what they wanted me to do. They needed me to say it was a lie. They wanted to pass the death sentence. My evidence would help them achieve that.

'I said I would not, but these people...'

Gilda took another deep breath as though her heart was breaking – which it was. It was obvious to the twins that explaining what had happened was taking its toll. She'd already said she hadn't told many people; they guessed that Charlie, and perhaps Michael, was one of the chosen few.

'They said that if I did not testify as they wanted, my husband and children would be sent to a concentration camp.

'"At least we shall all be together," I said to them, defiant despite my sore face and my fear.

'I remember the way he smiled, that man, the one who was obviously more German than the others. Gestapo.

'"No. Not you, Frau Jacobson. As a foreign national you will be deported back to the Netherlands, your husband in a camp for men, your children, being Austrian born, in a separate camp. Many children die there without parents to take care of them."

'"You let children die?" I said to them. Only Jewish children, they told me. We only let Jewish children die.' She shook her head in disbelief. 'I shall never forget the evil look on the man's face. He went on to say that if I complied with their request I could leave with my children and return to Holland.'

It seemed to Mary as though the oxygen had suddenly been sucked from the room and she was close to fainting. She didn't look at her sister but sensed she was feeling much the same. Her gaze remained focused on Gilda.

'They made me choose between my husband and my children. I knew my children would never survive a camp alone without me, but that Frederich might. They promised he would not be executed as long as I confessed. They gave me hope but their promises were hollow.' Gilda shook her head. 'I betrayed my husband. Now he is dead. I had no choice.'

She went on to explain that she'd wanted to hide from the world after that. The make-up helped but it was only a mask.

'I felt I had no right to happiness ever again. Then Charlie came along and everything changed. So now you know.'

Mary felt tears in her own eyes; Ruby patted Gilda's hand. 'You did what you had to do, Gilda. I would have done the same in your position. I'm glad you've found happiness again.' Mary tossed and turned all that night, fighting to shake off nightmares of prison camps full of men in uniform, all wearing RAF uniforms. Michael Dangerfield was one of them.

31

Frances Sweet was home for the weekend and snuggled under the bedclothes.

At the other end of the village the sound of machines and men shouting were enough to wake anyone who wasn't already up.

Frances couldn't help thinking about Mario, the man who lived in the forest. It was totally unfair that he should be carted off and interned as an enemy alien. She hadn't known Italians were enemy aliens. In fact, she hadn't even realised that Mario was Italian.

'He can't be an enemy,' she'd shouted at Mary on her arrival back home. 'He helped me find my way back to Ada's.'

Mary had looked undecided. Even when Frances had pointed out that he'd carried her all the way to Ada's house, she maintained an undecided expression.

By ten o'clock Frances was washed, dressed and eating toast with plum jam. One bite and she screwed her face up at the taste of it. 'This butter tastes funny.'

Mary turned round from turning the handle of the mincer. Cottage pie was on the menu tonight and some of the beef from Sunday's roast was the main ingredient.

'It isn't butter. It's margarine.'

'Yuk!'

'It's no good complaining, Frances. We all have to make sacrifices, even you, and anyway, you can't really taste it with all that jam piled on top.'

Frances eyed the jam she'd spread lavishly on top of the margarine. Suddenly alarmed that Mary might suggest scraping some of it off and returning it to the jar she finished off her toast and drank her tea in record-quick time, grabbed her coat and headed for her friend Elspeth's house.

As it turned out she didn't need to walk that far. Elspeth and a few other old friends were halfway along the High Street right outside the doctor's surgery.

They were walking quickly in the direction of the Apple Tree pub and the orchard.

'Quick,' shouted Edgar, the youngest of the Martin boys. 'They're digging up our orchard.'

Frances gasped. 'Our orchard?'

Elspeth nodded solemnly. 'For the war effort.'

Frances couldn't begin to guess what part an old neglected orchard might have in the war against the Germans, but she didn't want it dug up like the one up at Perrotts' Farm.

Like a flock of homing pigeons, they ran as one, determined to get to their destination, though no plan was in place of what they would do once they got there. They'd played in that orchard from the time they were big enough to climb over the gate or the ruined wall, so when they were finally there, seeing what was going on, all eyes were filled with dismay.

'They're burning them,' young Edgar exclaimed with disbelief.

Frances took a deep breath and tasted apples, fallout from the bonfire. The orchard was ruined. Trunks were being loaded on to a lorry; bigger branches were being sawn into manageable logs before being distributed to those villagers already gathered. As the word spread about free firewood, more joined them and arguments were breaking out.

A bonfire of twigs, roots and dried leaves crackled and spat in the heart of the orchard.

Even the long grass where voles and rabbits and other small creatures lived was being cut down and there were gaping holes where the trees had been ripped from the ground.

Frances stared. 'They can't do this!'

'Oh yes they can.' Miriam Powell was pushing an old perambulator piled high with logs. 'They have to, Frances. It's an order from the very top. We need more land to plant vegetables and wheat. We have to be able to feed ourselves and anyway, we've got enough apple trees, certainly around here. Never mind though, eh. You'll find somewhere else to play with your friends.'

Her smile was sickly sweet, almost as sickly sweet as the smell of burning apple twigs coming from the heart of the orchard.

Frances was just about to say there was nowhere quite like the orchard when she caught sight of Gareth Stead standing in the middle of the pub yard watching the proceedings with an odd look on his face.

At first she thought he was looking at her, but it wasn't so. He was looking beyond her to where two men were pondering the contents of a sack.

'Governor,' one of them shouted. 'We've found a bag of bones.'

A big man with powerful arms and a black moustache strode over to them.

'Just bones?' He sounded as though he wasn't too pleased at being disturbed.

'And a dress,' one of the men said. 'There's a dress in here as well.'

The man speaking pulled out what looked at a distance like a bundle of material. Frances looked to where Gareth Stead had been watching. He wasn't there.

Scared, she decided. Gareth is scared and she thought she knew why.

'Mister,' she said, running over to the man the others had addressed as Governor. 'Mister. I know who buried those bones.'

'You do?' The man looked at her kindly. 'And how's that then, me 'andsome?'

'I saw him bury them. It was him,' she said, pointing towards the Apple Tree pub. 'It was him. I saw him, but he didn't see me.'

The man's expression turned in a flash from friendly to serious. He touched the dress and peered into the sack. 'It's bones all right. Could be bones of anything, though.'

'Only women wear dresses, Governor,' the man who had brought the sack over pointed out.

The man with the black moustache conceded that the other man was right and shook his head. 'I don't like this. I don't like this at all.'

Frances saw her chance to get her own back on a man she disliked intensely. It was probably his fault that her orchard was being ripped up, though everyone said it was because of the war.

'I expect it's his wife,' she piped up to the man with the black moustache. 'Nobody's seen her for years.'

32

Stan Sweet and Sam Pickard were mighty pleased to hear that the person responsible for stealing one of their pigs had been caught. Everything to do with pigs and livestock, slaughtering in particular, had to be accounted for to the Ministry of Food, slaughtering in particular.

Paddy Casey, the village bobby, who hailed from Dublin and had married into the village in his youth, wiped at his forehead with a large handkerchief as he related the story, his comments interspersed with loud guffaws of laughter.

'At first we thought it was his wife. Thought he'd done away with her. Can you believe that.' His face reddened when he laughed. 'He'd wrapped the bones up in an old frock. More fool him, and then young Frances...' Again, laughter. 'She told them it was probably his missus who ain't been seen fer years.'

Paddy laughed. Stan laughed. Everybody laughed. Paddy's laughter was that infectious.

'If the silly sod hadn't wrapped the bones up in that old frock, and if young Frances hadn't said as were probably 'is missus...but you should 'ave seen 'is face – Mr Stead's, that is. Went white as a sheet.'

'So where is his wife?' asked Stan once he'd stopped laughing.

Paddy mopped his forehead, his face, his nose and his chin as he spoke. 'Nowhere to be found, but that don't mean she's dead, only that she don't want to be found. Can't say I blame 'er. Stead ain't one of my favourite characters.'

Stan got to what really concerned him. 'I take it you're charging him with regard to my pig?'

Paddy shook his head. 'No real evidence.'

'But my cousin saw him burying that sack,' Mary pointed out.

Paddy shook his head again. By now he was mopping the sweat at the nape of his neck. 'She's only a child, and anyway, she did suggest it might be his wife. Kids tell stories. We all know that.'

Paddy's green-flecked eyes flickered in Stan's direction.

Stan was sitting quietly, his eyes downcast.

Paddy paused by his chair on the way out. 'Stan. Don't you be taking the law into your own hands. Hear me?'

Stan got to his feet. 'Thanks for letting us know what's happening, Paddy. It's much appreciated.'

It wasn't lost on Mary and Ruby that he'd not acknowledged Paddy's request.

A few days later news spread around the village that Gareth Stead had left very quickly and nobody knew where he'd gone. Nobody threw aspersions in Stan Sweet's direction, though everyone knew about the stolen pig. Also the rumours of Gareth dealing on the black market were rife. That was also the day when Mary discovered the sack of sugar.

'Will you say anything?' Ruby asked her.

Mary shook her head. 'It's not worth worrying about, though you could have told me.'

'Will you tell Dad?'

Again Mary told her she would not. 'I've got other things on my mind. More important things.'

Ruby knew she was referring to Michael Dangerfield. 'He'll be fine,' she said, giving her sister a reassuring hug. 'No news is good news.'

33

Ruby was pleased with herself. This afternoon's demonstration to factory workers in Bedminster, South Bristol, had gone well. The women were making pins of some description. The pins that came to Ruby's mind were hat pins, safety pins and sewing pins. It turned out that the pins these women were making were for munitions.

Corporal Johnnie Smith commented that she was looking pleased with herself.

'They were the hardest audience I've had, but they understood what I was talking about. I bet most of them have made a meal from a penny all their lives.'

She fancied she saw him smile, but couldn't be sure. He was a hard nut to crack and never failed to take her down if he could. It occurred to her that he considered her too young and too classy to know what she was talking about. From what he'd said so far, she guessed he came from a pretty tough background, London, if his accent was anything to go by.

'Just don't do that again,' he growled, his mood already back to normal.

She looked down at her hands so he couldn't see her amusement. She'd actually got him to come up on stage and assist her with the cooking demonstration. He'd been reluctant but both herself and the women in the audience had cheered him on.

'After all, an army marches on its stomach and you should ensure that yours is always well filled. I'll make a cook of you yet,' she'd added in a low whisper.

'I don't need to do cooking. I get it done for me.' He paused. 'The army supplies everything I need.'

'I will ask you to do the same again. It's your duty and if you don't, I shall have you replaced.'

'Oh yes!' he exclaimed angrily. 'That is so bloody typical of your sort. Miss Bloody High and Mighty. Looking down your nose at the rest of us!'

Ruby lost patience. 'How dare you! I do not look down my nose! It's you with the problem, you with the chip on both shoulders!'

Silence reigned all the way home.

On arrival Corporal Smith helped her around the back with the picnic hamper and the suitcase. The back door was unlocked, the kitchen empty. There was no sign of Mary or her father; Frances had returned to Ada's place in the forest and Gilda, who usually lingered to sip tea and sample Mary's latest recipes, wasn't around either.

'Thank you,' Ruby said to Johnnie Smith as he set her baggage on the table. 'See you tomorrow.'

He grunted his usual agreement before sidling off; that in itself was different. Usually he strode off as though marching across a parade ground. Today he was slower.

After taking off her hat and gloves, Ruby considered putting on the kettle, but instead decided to walk along to Stratham House. Perhaps everyone was there taking tea and biscuits with Mrs Hicks. It occurred to her that Michael might have returned, or perhaps there was news of his whereabouts.

It now being June, the air was pleasant and warm, the smell of summer in the air. Nobody would think there was a war on, she thought to herself, yet terrible things were happening in France.

The old gate grated on its hinges when she pushed it open. Because of the weather she'd expected everyone to be sitting outside in Mrs Hicks's secluded garden listening to the buzzing of bees, the air heavy with the scent of lavender and lilac.

A wrought-iron table and four chairs sat unoccupied in the middle of the lawn.

Ruby felt the first pang of unease. Her father wouldn't go far with the back door left open.

The sound of the creaking gate had been heard. The front door opened and Mrs Hicks appeared.

Ruby was about to make a remark about everyone hiding from her but stopped herself. The corners of Mrs Hicks's mouth were downturned and so, it seemed, were the corners of her eyes. Her whole demeanour was one of extreme sadness.

Ruby was overcome with a sudden feeling of weakness, as though her legs refused to walk, her heart refused to pump blood around her body. Something terrible had happened.

Michael! It had to be Michael! 'Is it Michael?' she whispered.

Mrs Hicks shook her head. 'It's Charlie. Your father came straight over to tell me and Gilda. Mary is here with him. You'd better come in.'

The news was hard to believe. Charlie had survived one sinking but not a second one. This time his ship had been torpedoed by a submarine. Some members of the crew had survived; Charlie had not.

The rest of the day passed in a blur. Charlie had drowned. There would be no body to inter, no walnut coffin or bright array of summer flowers.

It took days for it to sink in. The fine summer weather did

nothing to lift anyone's spirits. People came in to pay their respects. Miriam Powell kept shaking her head and muttering that she'd done everything possible to help him survive. Mary thought about the note – a prayer to the Virgin Mary. She hadn't mentioned it to anyone and wouldn't mention it now. There was no point. However, she didn't want her father to find it.

He visited the churchyard more frequently now, a lonely figure walking across the dewy grass in the early morning, bare-headed, his trilby clenched in both hands.

He looked down at Sarah's grave and began to tell her what had happened. His words stuck in his throat. He fell down on his knees, bent his head and sobbed until he could sob no more.

I know. Remember you've still got two children to care about...

It wasn't until he had dragged himself to the lych gate that he understood more clearly those words that had entered his mind. Whether they had come from her for sure, or from his own wish that it was her speaking to him, he'd never been clear. What did strike him was that of course she would know. Charlie was with her and in a strange way it gave him great comfort to know that.

The church was filled with old school friends, the family and those in the village to whom Charlie used to deliver bread on his bicycle.

The vicar opened the memorial service by thanking God for heroes like Charlie, whose final resting place was known only to God.

'He lives on with God and also in our hearts. May I repeat those famous words, at the going down of the sun and in the morning, we shall remember them. We shall remember all those who paid the final price. We pray that Charles Henry Sweet will rest in peace.'

The vicar's moving words were followed by muffled sobs until drowned out by the sound of a packed church rising to its feet.

The words of the seamen's hymn soared to the rafters.

Eternal Father, strong to save,
Whose arm doth bind the restless wave,
Who bidst the mighty ocean deep,
Its own appointed limits keep.
Oh hear us when we cry to thee,
For those in peril on the sea.

The words of the hymn were blurred by the tears in Ruby's eyes. She held the hymn book with one hand, her other arm hugging the sobbing Frances who didn't even bother to try and sing, her shoulders were shaking that badly.

Frances had loved Charlie dearly and he in turn had been like an older brother to her. Ruby was convinced that when Frances was a woman, every man she met would have to measure up to her cousin Charlie.

At the end of the pew, on the other side of their father, Mary was sitting straight-backed and staring straight ahead singing the words from memory and thinking of Charlie as a child, clinging to a homemade raft he'd proudly launched on to the Avon, only to have it sink beneath him. Cussing and swearing and spitting out water, he'd clambered to the bank. He'd always been one for seeking adventure and had always loved the water. Even back then he'd wanted to float away and had done once, his home-made craft getting as far as Hanham Abbots.

She lifted her head and smiled at the thought of him and chanced to glimpse Gilda Jacobson, her glossy black hair tucked into a black snood, the brim of her hat tilted so that it hid her eyes but not her tear-stained cheekbones. Every so often she bowed her head, wiping her face with a lace-edged handkerchief.

Lace-edged! How luxurious. A lot of people were down to tearing up old pillowcases and sheets to make handkerchiefs. Or even underwear. So how come...?

Mary stopped singing and almost stopped breathing. She had to admit to herself that she was becoming too serious, too engrossed in war work. Almost as though the war will be lost if I don't goad women into being frugal, she thought to herself. Poor Gilda. She really had loved Charlie and Mary was quite certain he had loved her back. What did it matter if Gilda had been married before and had two children? Each day was there to be lived. Clearly she was devastated and must be feeling terribly alone. She wasn't family. Neither was she from the village. Mary made herself a promise to speak to her after this was over, a sisterly talk assuring her that she had a place in the family, just as Charlie had had a place in her heart.

Ruby was thinking of Johnnie Smith. He was miles away yet she could hear his voice ringing in her ears, telling her not to be so bloody uptight, so bloody superior! He had been luckier than Charlie. He had survived, though never spoke of his time in Norway or the colonel he used to drive for. It was as if the whole episode was a closely guarded secret, one he had no intention of ever betraying.

Mary slid her arm through that of her father. She felt him tremble. She pressed his arm with her free hand – a small gesture of reassurance, to tell him she would miss her brother as much as he would, though instinctively she knew it couldn't possibly be the same. It was a terrible thing to lose a child.

She looked up into her father's sad face, hugged his arm and tried to smile bravely. His look was unreadable and there was no smile. He turned back to face the front.

Her gaze returned to Gilda. It struck her then that these were the two people, her father and Gilda, who had loved Charlie the most. Her eyes met those of her sister who stood on the other side of her father. On the other side of Ruby, Frances sobbed and clung on to her arm.

In her heart, Mary added other words to the prayers for Charlie. 'Please God, bring Michael home.'

The congregation rose for one more hymn: 'I Vow to Three My Country'. The vicar gave the blessing and then it was over. 'Come on, Dad,' whispered Mary, clinging steadfastly to her father's arm as she glided sideways out of the pew. 'Let's get home. Don't want that food going to waste. Not after all the effort put in by our...' She'd been about to say, our boys in the merchant navy.

Charlie had been one of those boys whom the merchant navy had so depended on.

At first she didn't think her father had noticed. His head was bowed, his shoulders stooped. It was as though he'd aged ten years in a matter of days.

They emerged from the subdued light of the church into a sombre day. The sky was marbled with clouds and the smell of rain was in the air.

The vicar, a tall gaunt man with a bald head and wire-rimmed glasses, shook Stan's hand. 'I'm terribly sorry, Mr Sweet. A great loss. A great loss indeed.'

He spoke softly and although the sentiments were no doubt sincere, they seemed rehearsed and probably were. The village had experienced many deaths over the years; even though Charlie had been young and a beloved son, what was one more?

'No doubt there'll be lots more before this war is over,' her father murmured. 'Just like the last. Just as bloody. Just as much a waste of bloody time!'

The vicar winced at his use of language. 'I do hope not. I do hope there is a deeply moral purpose for all this carnage.'

'Behopes,' muttered her father, not sounding for a moment as though he believed it was so.

Mary eyed him warily, noting the rigid set of his jaw, the down-turned corners of his mouth. On the outside his manner portrayed a reserved, polite individual brought up to accept his lot in life and put up with almost everything. Inside she knew his heart was breaking.

She slid her arm through his again. Ruby did the same on the other side. Frances clung to Ruby.

They walked back along the path. Stan shook his head. 'You never expect to outlive your children,' he said to her once they were out of earshot of the vicar. 'Worse still is not having the remains to grieve over, just a line or two added to his mother's headstone.'

'Mr Sweet.' Gilda Jacobson called from behind them, her heels clattering on the flagstone path.

Stan turned. The girls turned with him.

Gilda had a haughty tilt to her chin, which Mary interpreted as being an effort not to break down and howl at God for not looking after the man she'd loved, understandable seeing as he hadn't looked after her first husband either.

'I want to say something to you, Mr Sweet. I want to apologise, but also to make you understand...'

She sounded nervous and her tone was brittle. Ruby surmised it wouldn't take much for her to break down and cry.

Stan Sweet frowned. 'Apologise? What do you have to apologise about?'

Ruby eyed Gilda not without some hostility. Her brother had been a sucker for a pretty face. Regardless of her sad experiences, Ruby couldn't get over the fact that Gilda was older than him and had children.

Gilda's eyes fluttered, dark lashes brushing her pale cheeks. 'You may not think so, but there has been gossip. Some people might think me flighty – I think that is what they say. Flighty, in that I chased Charlie, a man younger than myself. But it was not like that. My husband died because he printed pamphlets opposing a brutal regime. I fled with my children, coming a long way to escape prejudice. I never thought I would ever be happy again. I never thought I would love again.' A pink haze appeared on Gilda's high cheekbones. Stan stood silently between his daughters waiting for her to go on. 'Charlie understood that,' she said. 'He made me laugh again. It had been a long time since I laughed.'

Stan Sweet stood like a rock in front of her. He cleared his throat, looked down at the ground then directly at her. 'Young woman. Allow me. Before my son went away we had a little heart to heart about a lot of things... things fathers and sons don't talk about too often. Loving somebody was one of them. I loved my wife Sarah. We were married for just a few years and then she was taken from me. I've missed her every day since. That's what me and my boy were talking about. Love for a woman. As I said, men don't often talk about that kind of stuff in case our mates thinks we're all softies. I'm glad he was happy before... well... I'm glad he was looking forward to something and someone.'

To Mary's surprise he placed an affectionate hand on Gilda's shoulder. 'I know what you went through, my girl. Charlie told me – about your husband being imprisoned and what you had to do in order to protect your children. I wish Charlie was still here to make you happy. I wish I could have seen him settled down and giving me grandchildren. But it didn't happen and I'm sorry for that. In the meantime, all I can do is to share my grief with you. You're welcome to call on me whenever you want to.'

Mrs Hicks had prepared the food at her house and had also attended the memorial service. The children had been left with Mrs Gates who had plenty of her own children for the two of them to play with.

Bettina was waiting there when they came back from the church. Mary sought her out.

As she took off her hat and coat, she asked if there had been any news from Michael, Bettina's nephew.

'Nothing, but the way telephones and telegrams are at the moment...'

She had been going to say that communications were overwhelmed what with the dire way the war was going – so many things going wrong, so many young men being killed, but she stopped herself. She didn't want Mary fearing the worst.

'Michael always was a good swimmer,' she said cheerfully. 'If he has gone down in the sea he'll likely swim all the way home!'

'I expect you're right.' Although Mary wasn't fooled she pretended that she was. There was the distinct possibility that Michael's plane had gone down on land, in which case it might have blown up on impact. If it had managed to land safely, he might very well have been captured and therefore likely to spend the rest of the war in a prisoner of war camp.

She picked up a plateful of sandwiches and one of her homemade Madeleines.

'Shall I take these in?'

'If you could please,' Bettina replied. 'Ooo! Madeleines! Michael's favourite. He'll be disappointed he's missed these!' Mary wasn't sure that they were Michael's favourite cakes, but she smiled anyway and said that he should have made sure he got here in time to eat them.

The sandwiches and cakes were well received. Mary's jaw ached repeating the same responses to the oft-repeated condolences. Inside she wanted to scream that she'd prefer silence rather than platitudes, but it was unfair to call them that. People felt awkward. Not knowing what to say they stuck to the tried and tested.

'Those look good.'

The speaker was Andrew Sinclair from the Ministry of Food. She'd had to stand him up on a BBC broadcast but on learning of the reason, he'd sworn then and there that he would be at the memorial service. She thought it sweet of him, though realised he wasn't attending purely out of sympathy. He hadn't known Charlie, but he did want to know her better. As she circulated around the room with more sandwiches and other cakes, she felt his eyes on her and couldn't help blushing. Unlike Ruby she had never invited male attention, in fact, she'd always felt awkward when a man had shown interest in her, like a gauche adolescent rather than a grown woman.

She saw Ruby talking to Fred Mortimer, an old friend of her father's. Of her father she could see no sign.

After acknowledging Fred, she asked Ruby where their father had got to. Ruby looked around the room, didn't see him and shook her head.

'He wasn't feeling very sociable. Perhaps he's gone home. I think somebody should go and see where he's got to.'

It was obvious to Mary that Ruby was as worried as she was.

'Never mind,' she said before Ruby could put down the plate of fruit cake she was passing round. 'I'll go.'

Court Road seemed desolate, West Street even more so. A light drizzle began to fall which did nothing to brighten the day. A cloud of steam rose over the hump-backed bridge that crossed the railway line. The train to Gloucester was pulling out, no doubt packed with people wanting to change for London or other places where there were army barracks and other places where they had to go.

The hinges on the back gate were in need of oiling. Usually her father attended to the hinges on a regular basis, but hadn't done since before Charlie had been posted as missing, presumed dead. On lifting the latch and pushing the gate open, the hinges groaned as though in pain.

She was passing the old brick privy, its mossy stones mostly devoid of mortar, when she spotted flashes of white. Miriam's notes were still embedded in the gaps between the bricks. She pulled both of them out, unfolded them and read them again. One of them fluttered from her grasp. Just before she was about to pick it up she heard the creak of the back gate.

'Mary! I've been looking for you. What's that?'

Quick on her feet, Frances picked up one of the notes before Mary did, unfolding it before reading it through.

'It's a prayer,' she said hesitantly.

'Yes,' said Mary. 'It is.'

'"To Mother Earth, the goddess of the forest." One of the kids in the forest did that, wrote a prayer for the Earth Mother.' Mary, who had thought the prayer was to the Virgin Mary, was taken aback.

'The Earth Mother?'

'Yes,' said Frances. 'You write a little note – a prayer for her help – then stick it into a hole in the tree. Or between rocks.'

'Or bricks,' murmured Mary. 'Were you looking for me?'

Frances shook her head. 'No. I went to the orchard.'

'In your Sunday best?'

Frances shrugged. 'Sorry.'

Mary sighed. 'Never mind.' She quickly looked at the dark-coloured dress Frances wore. 'No damage done by the looks of it.'

'There was nobody else in the orchard. Only me,' Frances said solemnly, her eyes downcast. 'Nobody to talk to, except Mrs Jacobson. She couldn't stop though. She said she had a train to catch.'

The steam! The train to London.

Mary groaned. She'd so wanted to talk to Gilda in order to help ease her pain. Now she was gone.

'Did she say where she was going?' Mary asked her.

'I've told you. London.'

'That's not good enough. London is a very big place!'

Frances pouted and looked as though she might burst into tears. 'It's not my fault!'

'Oh, no.' Mary raised a hand to her forehead and closed her eyes. If only she'd said something earlier. She hadn't foreseen Gilda leaving so abruptly.

If Frances hadn't mentioned Gilda leaving, Mary might have dwelled on Miriam's prayer to Mother Earth not working, for Charlie was dead. As it was, Gilda's leaving affected her more deeply.

She looked up at the home she'd known forever without really seeing it. She was suddenly aware of movement in the window of the room that had once been her brother's.

'Go back to Mrs Hicks's and tell Ruby that I've found our father.'

Frances looked for a moment as though she was going to refuse, but seeing the look on Mary's face set off without saying a word.

Her father was sitting on Charlie's bed. At his feet was the old tin box in which Charlie had kept his childhood toys. For years he'd been urged to get rid of them, that some youngster in the village would appreciate the train set, the number one Meccano set and the tin crane with a handle that worked by clockwork. Charlie had just smiled and told them he might want them for his own son one day.

'Dad?' Mary sat down beside him on the bed.

He was holding a clockwork toy car, a bright yellow one with black wheels and brass headlights. 'He wouldn't get rid of any of this, would he? Said he would pass it on to his son.' Suddenly he began to sob.

'Dad!' Mary covered his hand with hers. 'Dad...'

She swallowed. There was nothing she could say, nothing that really mattered, except...'

'Dad. There might one day be a grandson to pass Charlie's toys on to. As you already know, Michael's asked me to marry him.'

He nodded and smiled through his tears. She knew he was happy for her, though perhaps her giving him a grandson wasn't quite the same.

It was hard to prevent tears running from her eyes, but she persevered. Somebody had to be strong.

'Are you coming back to Bettina's with me?'

He shook his head. 'No. You go on. Make your excuses for me, will you? I'll stay here. I'd like some time alone.'

Mary bit her lip, wanting to tell him about Gilda leaving but not sure that she should. Eventually she decided it might as well be now; he'd find out about it anyway in time. He sighed when she told him, his arms seeming to hang heavily from his shoulders as his back slumped in despair.

'You can't blame her,' he said softly. 'There's nothing left for her here now. And besides, you know what the village gossips are like. She'd be crucified especially if she latches on to somebody else. They'd call her flighty then all right.'

'But she didn't say... not at the church...'

'Of course not. She just wanted to set the record straight, though she didn't really need to. We could all see what it was like between them, couldn't we?'

Mary nodded. 'Are you going to be all right here by yourself?'

He kept his head down when he nodded. 'You go on.'

* * *

Ruby looked shocked when she told her about Gilda. 'Gone? But why? Where's she gone?'

'London. As to why, well, I suppose there was nothing left for her here.' Mary frowned. 'Dad's in a bad way. I've left him in Charlie's old room looking through the toy box. He told me to apologise for his absence.' She wrapped her arms around herself in a tight hug. She felt so cold. So lost, in fact.

'He's going to be a long time getting over this,' said Ruby mirroring Mary's own thoughts. 'Does Mrs Hicks know about Gilda leaving?'

Mary slapped her forehead then shook her head. 'I don't know. I didn't think...but she must. Surely.'

Ruby put down the tray of dirty plates she was holding. 'You look as though you could do with some fresh air and a minute to yourself. You go on. I'll tell Mrs Hicks.'

She'd wanted to add that Mrs Hicks had just received a telegram and had gone up into her bedroom to read it. Whatever the news was, it wouldn't hurt for Mary to have some time to compose herself. She'd find out soon enough what it said.

'Go on,' she said, lightly touching her sister's arm in an act of reassurance. 'Get some time to yourself. Go and tell Mother all about it, just like Dad does.'

'I might very well do that.'

Mary walked in a daze down the hill, over the little stone bridge that crossed the stream and up the other side.

The churchyard was empty, the stone angels and carved head-stones her only company.

The rain that had threatened all day arrived, though only in the form of a light drizzle, droplets of water spangling her hair.

Grasping the cast iron ring of one half of the oak door, she swung it open. The smell that only churches have, of dust, incense and old hymn books came out to greet her.

Her footsteps echoed in the stillness between the ancient stones as she made her way up the aisle. The last rays of a setting sun shone through the arched window immediately to the right of the altar, the coloured glass throwing a mote-filled rainbow across the silver cross and candlesticks. She vaguely recalled them having been bequeathed to St Anne's by some long dead benefactor.

She stood there looking up at the altar and the cross hanging behind it for some time. Her thoughts naturally turned to Charlie and then to her father. Today he had voiced his sadness that there would be no grandson – well not from Charlie anyway. But what about her? What about Michael?

Perhaps I won't have children either, she thought to herself.

If Michael never comes back...

She looked around her at the church, the windows, the altar, thinking that she'd quite like getting married here.

Turning her head she imagined him standing there next to her, tall and handsome in his RAF uniform, smiling down at her, completely unscathed from his ordeal – she hoped for that most of all.

Love matters very much during wartime, she decided. Inside she held the vision of Gilda fleeing a monstrous regime that had killed her husband, falling in love again only to have that same regime take his life too. Neither Gilda nor Mary and her family would ever get over it.

Michael was right. There was only the moment and not necessarily any tomorrow. War was cruel and also unfair. It had seemed headstrong and foolish to marry after such a short acquaintance, but now she realised just how right it would have been. At this moment, she wished she had accepted his proposal.

Closing her eyes she imagined a church full of flowers and relatives, the organ playing, the singing of a choir, she and Michael standing before the altar. She imagined him there beside her.

Something clunked behind her, but she gave it no attention. Churches and old buildings famously contracted and made noises towards evening.

'I do,' she said softly, and in the quiet of the church she imagined him repeating the same and the vicar pronouncing them husband and wife.

'I do? I sure hope you mean what I think you mean.'

Her eyes snapped open. It wasn't a dream! It wasn't a vision. It was Michael. He was looking a little careworn, but alive and well.

'Michael!' She threw herself against his chest, breathing in the damp moistness of a jacket soaked with rain.

'I'm wet,' he said to her and sounded amused.

'I don't care. I don't care! You're here!'

He tangled his fingers in her hair when she looked up at him, her face flushed and eyes shining. His kiss was long and furious, strong enough to take her breath away.

'You're here,' she whispered again, her voice racked by sobs which might have been sobs of happiness, but were also of relief. 'When...?'

'I tried to get a message to you, but apparently the lines are down between here and London and the east of England. I couldn't get through... Ruby told me you might be here.'

The church seemed to spin around them as he kissed her again, neither of them letting go until they just had to take a breath.

'I was so scared. I thought you were dead. There was no word...'

He laughed as he stroked her face, not once averting his eyes from hers as though if he did she might vanish in a puff of smoke.

'I got shot down but was picked up by a Danish fishing boat. They helped me get home.'

'You're here! You're here!' She couldn't stop saying it. Even to her own ears she sounded totally surprised and not entirely believing.

'I'm here.'

'Can I pinch you?'

'If you like.'

She pinched the back of his hand. His flesh was firm and warm. 'You're real.'

'I hope I am. Let me check.' He smiled the way she remembered him smile as he pinched the back of his hand just as she had. 'Yep. That hurts. I'm real.'

'I didn't hear you come in.'

'I know. But I heard you. In fact, I believe I heard you say "I do". You marrying somebody by any chance?'

'Yes,' she said, her eyes moist with tears and her mouth smiling with happiness. 'Yes. He keeps asking me. I can't hold him off any longer. I don't want to hold him off any longer.'

'Then don't,' he said and kissed her.

On the way back to Stratham House, she told him about Gilda taking the children and leaving for London.

'I can't quite believe it. I so wanted to speak to her about Charlie, to make her feel, well, as though she were part of the family. I don't think your aunt knew she was going, but I haven't asked her yet. Ruby might have told her by now.'

After thinking about it, Michael shook his head in a sombre manner. 'Poor kid. She's been through a lot. It takes some guts to go through what she's been through, but everyone has a breaking point.'

'And losing Charlie was the last straw.'

Mary tried to imagine how she would have coped with everything Gilda had coped with; first having her husband arrested, then being forced to testify against him or put herself and her children in dreadful danger.

'I don't know how I would have coped with all that she coped with. It makes me shudder.'

She found herself clutching his hand more tightly.

Michael thought about how he'd been rescued and the rumours he'd heard about the horror that went on in the camps. Poor Gilda had been in the thick of it all. Mary wasn't the only one shuddering at the prospect of being invaded by such a ruthless regime.

Michael was in tune with her thoughts. 'Let's hope the enemy never gets here and subjects you folk to the same treatment.'

'Let's hope,' whispered Mary.

Ruby and Bettina Hicks were standing at the end of the lane when they got back up the hill. Both were smiling and looked purposeful.

'You found her,' Ruby exclaimed.

Michael's arm snaked around Mary's shoulder. Holding her close, he looked down into her face. 'She was exactly where you said she would be.'

'I'd only just read the telegram,' exclaimed Bettina, while passing a wicker shopping basket to Ruby. 'I nearly fainted when I saw him in the living room as large as life.'

Michael looked from his aunt to Ruby. 'Are we going somewhere?'

'Yes,' said Ruby. 'We're taking these cakes to Dad. He's feeling pretty low and needs something to cheer him up – and I don't mean Madeleines,' she said, winking at Mary. 'It's been a sad day, but now we have some good news to share. Michael's home. I think he'll be very glad about that.'

HISTORICAL NOTE

There really were Home Front Economists and Kitchen Economists who went round demonstrating how to conserve both food rations and fuel. When it comes to recycling and preserving what we have, never has it been done so efficiently and effectively as it was during the Second World War.

The recipes below are similar to those the Sweet sisters entered in the competition. At that time the ingredients would have been relatively plentiful, though stockpiling had begun. It wouldn't be long before they were rationed and things were very different. Oh, and it really is true that the first vegetable to become scarce was the humble onion.

NB: All the measurements are imperial, unaltered from when they were first devised.

Blackberry Loaf

- 7 oz preserved blackberries
- 2 oz margarine
- 7 oz self-raising flour

- Half a teaspoon of bicarbonate of soda
- 1 fl oz of boiling water
- 1 tablespoon of golden syrup or 2 tablespoons of sugar
- 1 egg
- Pinch of salt

Grease and flour a cake tin. Mix the blackberries with the golden syrup or sugar, melted margarine and boiling water. Leave to cool, then add the beaten egg. Sift flour, salt and bicarbonate of soda together. Stir into the blackberry mixture and mix well. Put into prepared tin for 50 minutes in a moderate oven (gas mark 4 in modern parlance).

Trench Cake

- 6 oz margarine
- 6 oz brown sugar
- 4 oz mixed dried fruit
- 12 oz flour
- One and a half teaspoons of bicarbonate of soda
- 10 fl oz milk

Cream the margarine and sugar. Warm the milk and pour on to the bicarbonate of soda. Add the prepared fruit, the milk and the flour to the margarine mixture. Mix well. Bake in a seven-inch cake tin in a moderate oven for about two hours.

Syrup Loaf

- 4 oz flour combined with two teaspoons of baking powder
- Half a teaspoon of bicarbonate of soda

- A pinch of salt
- 2 tablespoons of warm golden syrup
- A quarter pint of milk

Sift flour and baking powder and salt. Heat the syrup and milk, pour over the flour and mix well. Pour into a greased one pound loaf tin. Place in a moderately hot oven for thirty minutes or until firm.

NB: Whenever a joint was cooked, the dripping was skimmed off to use as fat for baking, cooking fats being in short supply. Oats were used as a filler and thickening agent. The glaze from cooked meat (jelly) was used as a base for the stock pot or spread on bread then sprinkled with salt for supper. Nothing was wasted and the Sunday joint itself provided the basis of many recipes that would hopefully last until Friday, Wednesday at least.

Oldland Common was only a village at the outbreak of war. It grew into a suburb of new houses and schools during the sixties and seventies when I lived there.

The characters are all fictitious although my grandmother's family were called Sweet.

Real characters at the time of war are mentioned, including the owner of the dog that I have named Felix in this book although his real name would be regarded as non-pc at present. His owner, Guy, is the famous leader of the Dambuster raid, the squadron based at Scampton in Lincolnshire.

For further reading on Wing Commander Guy Gibson VC OSO and Bar, DFC and Bar, I recommend the book *Enemy Coast Ahead*. He died at just twenty-five years of age, one of the most celebrated and decorated pilots of World War II.

MORE FROM LIZZIE LANE

We hope you enjoyed reading *Wartime Sweethearts*. If you did, please leave a review.

If you'd like to gift a copy, this book is also available as an ebook.

Sign up to Lizzie Lane's mailing list for news, competitions and updates on future books:

http://bit.ly/LizzieLaneNewsletter

Why not explore *The Tobacco Girls* series, starting with *The Tobacco Girls*.

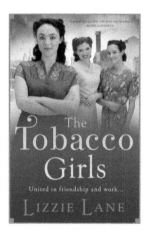

ABOUT THE AUTHOR

Lizzie Lane is the author of over 50 books, a number of which have been bestsellers. She was born and bred in Bristol where many of her family worked in the cigarette and cigar factories. This has inspired her new saga series for Boldwood *The Tobacco Girls*.

Follow Lizzie on social media:

facebook.com/jean.goodhind

twitter.com/baywriterallat1

instagram.com/baywriterallatsea

bookbub.com/authors/lizzie-lane

ABOUT BOLDWOOD BOOKS

Boldwood Books is a fiction publishing company seeking out the best stories from around the world.

Find out more at www.boldwoodbooks.com

Sign up to the Book and Tonic newsletter for news, offers and competitions from Boldwood Books!

http://www.bit.ly/bookandtonic

We'd love to hear from you, follow us on social media:

facebook.com/BookandTonic

twitter.com/BoldwoodBooks

instagram.com/BookandTonic